MULDOON

ALSO BY DON BREDES

Hard Feelings

Muldoon.

DON BREDES.

HOLT, RINEHART AND WINSTON
New York

Library of Congress Cataloging in Publication Data
Bredes, Don.
Muldoon.
I. Title.
PS3552.R363M8   813'.54   81-20316   AACR2
ISBN: 0-03-058281-4

First Edition
Designer: Amy Hill
Printed in the United States of America
1   3   5   7   9   10   8   6   4   2

Grateful acknowledgment is made for use of
portions of the following:
"Dance with a Dolly," by Terry Shand, Jimmy Eaton, and
Mickey Leader, copyright © 1940, 1944 renewed by
Shapiro, Bernstein, & Co., Inc. All rights reserved.
Used by permission.
"Can't Take My Eyes off of You," by Bob Crewe and Bob
Gaudio, copyright © 1967 Saturday Music, Inc. and Seasons
Four Music Corp. All rights reserved.
Used by permission.
"Hello, I Love You," words by The Doors,
copyright © 1968 Doors Music Co. Used by permission of
author and publisher.

ISBN 0-03-058281-4

ACKNOWLEDGMENTS

For their counsel and generous support during the long writing of this book, I want to thank Don Congdon, Herman Gollob, Elmer Griffin, Dean Lloyd, Alice Marble, Humphrey Morris, Howard Mosher, Szilvia Szmuk, Fred Weymuller, and St. John's University (New York), Stanford University, the Vermont Council on the Arts, and the National Endowment for the Arts.

PROLOGUE

Now I guess I'll never write my mother's autobiography. This is the book I cranked out instead, and it's nothing like the epic Lou envisioned when she talked me into it. More than just a chronicle of her juicy life, what she wanted was a modern history of the game, a popular all-purpose classic, with herself at the heart of it as narrator.

"And jammed with photos and facts," she said then. "You know, like with diagrams and stats and records and lists of champions, and old engravings, and with philosophy mixed in here and there. And humor and all that."

"But still basically about you," I said.

"Well, sure. You start with me, and you end with me. Like say it begins, 'I, Louise Fraser Muldoon, was a tennis great, a star, a name. . . .' That's no good, but somehow you set the tone of my authority, and then maybe you go on and put in how I met your father at Germantown, how we got married at sea after my first Wimbledon, how you came into the picture, and how I had the accident. Then you can leave it hanging and digress about the origins of the sport or something, see?"

"Sort of," I said.

She sighed. "All right, so that sounds tricky, but it's research is all it is. The facts are available. And where they aren't you just take some liberties, how's that? Look, Will, you can do it. You have all my clippings and crap, and I'll be only a phone call away, so whatever help you need—letters, connections—you know my number. How about it? Would you give it a shot?"

The reasons I said yes are part of what this book is about. It's also about Lou and my crazy father, and there is some tennis history thrown in as it pertains to them, but mostly the book's about fate, love, hope, doom, greed, passion, madness, and salvation as they pertain to me. In fact, *I* am truly what the book's about—though I did take some liberties, as you will see, along the way.

Fate comes first. If not for mine, I'd be hitting tennis balls right now instead of typewriter keys. That's absurd, I know. Fate wouldn't be fate if it allowed alternatives. What I mean is before the day my fate declared itself, my life's path seemed about as tenuous as a freeway. I was so sure of where I was going that I never thought about it. Then in that one day everything changed.

It was early fall 1963, in Balboa, California. I was a high school junior suddenly wide-awake to cars, beer, and girls, and yet that Friday afternoon I was at the club, faithfully putting in my hour serving out a shopping cart full of balls, aiming at cans in the corners, when Lou materialized ten feet behind me.

"What in the name of God is *that*?" she yelled. She was standing up to the fence in the shade of the eucalyptus trees.

"Mom! Jesus! Where did you come from?"

"Mongolia, where do you think? Would you just tell me please what you're trying to do with that circus-act motion?"

I glared at her. My mother had never crept up on me that way through the woods. She had on a sleeveless blouse and pedal pushers, her traveling clothes. I said, "What motion?"

"*What* motion? What do you think, I'm blind? What motion. Yeah, that's a good question. That dipsy-doodle stuff makes you look like a hooked tuna. Where did you pick that up?"

"I invented it."

"My fanny, you invented it. Twenty years ago when it *was* invented, it looked like a shot you're so far away from it isn't funny."

As it happened, I was trying to perfect an American twist, a delivery Lou had forbidden. She believed a twist belonged only in doubles (if anywhere), where its kick would sometimes open

2

up an angle. But since hitting it right required such contortions, she was sure it produced more injuries than points.

"By invent I mean I copied it," I said. "Nobody taught me is what I mean."

"You don't say," said Lou. "Well, don't tell me nobody taught you about keeping that kind of junk out of your game." She laced her fingers through the fencing and tugged at it. "C'mon, Will, it's just flash, believe me. It's too fine. You can't groove it for any percentage. Half the time the thing drops short and you dish up the old caterpillar ball, and the guy steps on it—*squash*, right? Is this old news, or what?"

"Mom, I'm just building a repertoire. It's a shot, OK? I want all the shots. That's fair."

"Hey, you know, I wish you'd just concentrate on learning how to hit the shots you got without wasting your short hours on junk fireworks you drag out on the Fourth of July."

"I just started it this week, Mom. In a month I'll be getting enough on it so you'll split your shorts to reach it."

"Sure, and you'll crack your backbone to hit it. Listen, you want to know what I'm doing here? You could probably make a good guess."

I looked at my feet. For four years since she left the tour and moved my father and me south from San Francisco, Lou had spent her work week in Berkeley. The hills were her home, where she'd grown up, and she had big lesson contracts at the Berkeley Tennis Club. Her usual flight left Oakland Saturday morning. She would fly back from Orange County each Monday. Today was Friday. Though it wasn't strange for Lou to break her routine for almost any reason, this time I figured her accusing presence could mean only that I'd dropped out of West Coast Top Ten, Eighteen and Under. I was expecting it, and Lou always got word of the rankings before I did. But I said nothing.

"Yeah, that's right," she said, "the numbers are out. And you, Will Muldoon, are falling out of sight."

"Where am I?"

"That's what I'd like to know, Will. Lord, you know, all the time when I phone you down here now your father says, 'No, he's out surfing.' 'Sorry, he's gone to a party.' 'He's at the mov-

3

ies. He's got a date.' Or else usually he doesn't know where the hell you are, you're just gone. Where *are* you at night when you got a home to be home at?"

I shrugged and shook my head.

"Hunh? Hey, I'd be very interested."

"Nowhere. The beach. Driving around."

"Nowhere. That sounds about right. OK, I'll tell you where you are: seventeen. Cool? Is that cool, baby? And at thirteen, you'll be overjoyed to hear, is one Alan Silverman."

"So?"

"So that's nifty with you? That's the taste that satisfies? Letting that goofy-looking Jew-boy loop-the-loop artist jump past you in the numbers? Come *on*. That shoe pinches just a little, doesn't it?"

"Oh, Mom, ease off. I'll come back." Lately I'd played some bad tournaments, but every athlete had slumps. I'd been taking tennis seriously for too long to be very anxious about my special place in it. The days when I'd have to compete for scholarship slots at UCLA or Stanford seemed a long way off, and I was still holding my own then with other California comers like Bobby Lutz and Stan Smith. Sure I'd come back.

She said, "Oh, yeah? Not from nowhere you won't. I'm beginning to suspect you got nowhere as your goal in life. Hey, and if you can sympathize a second, how do you think it looks for me when my own boy wonder doesn't make Top Ten?"

I said, "So get another boy wonder." She's a bitch, that's all I remember thinking. I can't really explain it. For a moment I felt her eyes hard on me, like drills, and then it cracked, the shell around what I knew I was, and something vital leaked out fast and left me dizzy. I was watching my racket twirl around in my hand like a baton, but all at once my fingers forgot how to make it go, and the racket flew away and bounced on the court.

Lou told me to wait right there while she changed; we had an hour of good light coming. I heard her rustle out through the dry leaves. When she got back I was sitting down on the baseline facing the fence.

From the net she said jovially, "Finally got you John Bromwich."

4

His autograph, she meant. Until high school I had a collection, but then I got bored with it. Lou was away too much to realize that, teaching up north, or coaching Wightman Cup, or something. I didn't move.

"C'mon, Will, off your butt. Cross-court and down-the-line. You start across. C'mon, *up*."

I got up. Where I'd sat there was a dark spot on the asphalt in the shape of a heart.

My father, W. R. Muldoon, the sportswriter, was climbing far back into the half-empty gallery of the Germantown Cricket Club in Philadelphia in the summer of 1946 when he first saw my mother. (But they did not meet there, and they would not meet for weeks. Lou misremembers.) He was trying to bring his head around to the task of covering the Davis Cup tie with France that had been scheduled for later that day. On the sun-browned grass below him, instead of maybe some soothing stroke practice, to his irritation a furious match was under way. He rubbed his eyeballs with his fingertips. The flash of competition made his head ache. Yet he could not quite ignore the rhythm of the exchanges and the spontaneous reactions of the small crowd at courtside. He squeezed his eyes shut, then opened them and squinted down at the contest. They were girls, a heavyset brunette and a tall, grim-looking blonde in a visor. They seemed young, how young he couldn't tell from his high perch. In court presence they both seemed mature, untroubled by the parched surface, familiar with ball boys and linesmen, contained and deliberate between points. In tactics, though, one was stubborn and the other timid. Given their skills, these flaws probably meant they were quite young, say fifteen. Gusts of applause floated up to him. He groaned, wondering what grand victory these two gleaming children were battling to win.

After his own tennis career had collapsed in 1929, my father found work on a Connecticut daily, later graduating to a solid reporter's post on *The New York Times*. When the army sent him into the Pacific in 1942, he luckily landed a job with the *Stars and Stripes* writing bright features, keeping up fighting morale. On Guam in 1945, on a dusty court under the palms, he happened to witness a fine army-navy doubles match between Don Budge and Frankie Parker and Bobby Riggs and Wayne Sabin. For my father, that was a pivotal occasion. He realized he missed the game. If coming back to it again was by then a hopeless fantasy, still he could write about it. He could reenter tennis as a journalist, and on his return to New York a tennis journalist is what he became.

A year later, in Germantown, my father was already a jaded fan. What he truly loved was the ideal of the game, not its shortfalling practitioners. He loved its geometry, its sweet triviality, and its peace, which were at odds forever with the quirky personalities that gave it life. For three years on troop transports and jungle islands all that had mattered to him was his own life and how to keep it. Now he was back safe in the pristine, wonderful, free land he had kept himself alive to come back to, but it did not seem pristine or wonderful the way it had while he was at war. It was just free. The people, giddy and ignorant Americans, ruined it. For most of them the war could have ended ten years ago instead of one. Cretins is what they were, numb to all great cause and consequence.

The war dead haunted him. The dead, all the healthy and forgotten dead, thousands upon thousands of dead, meat for fish, grit for sand, dead so he was free to smoke his Luckies, drink his Canadian whiskey, cruise in his Buick, broil T-bones in his kitchenette, have his little toothaches and piles, and dead so these beauties could spend their innocent days wearing the wool off of white balls, running, panting, sweating into ironed cotton, year in, year out . . . Christ. He leaned back on one elbow and tugged the brim of his hat down over his brow.

That those girls could spend their days this way, some would say, was an expression of the wonderful pristine thing my father had helped preserve, but he would not believe it. The price had been too high. And now it was as if all that happened overseas didn't matter anymore. Before long the Japs and the Germans would be out again under the same sun, stroking balls again, too, sweating and running their hearts out, and again sending over their Cup teams to play and be friends.

Down below my father in the still heat of noon, my mother,

the blonde in the visor, battered her way through the first set against a dogged retriever, and then with more confidence ran out the second at love. She was seventeen years old, and she had become the National Junior Women's Singles Champion of 1946. The newspapers took thorough notice because she was strong, beautiful, and personable. She was a good story. She had never lost a match in tournament tennis, and she liked to chatter with reporters. By the time she did lose, in the semis at Forest Hills later that summer, she was a featured face on the ladies' tour. Her life was tennis—trains and steamships, magazines and massages, showers and calluses, sacks of laundry, chaperones, coaches, new friends, bad food, fame and a silver future, and maybe her own fortune along the way. With luck.

A lot of forlorn hopes lie entombed in the past—Lou's, my father's, mine, everyone's. Once you lay them to rest you can move on. That's why we came to Balboa in the first place, to move on, to move away from the past, to provide our languishing little family with the sort of seaside peace that might stir its recuperation.

During my mother's touring years the old man and I stayed at home in our duplex in San Francisco's Sunset district, a few minutes from Golden Gate Park. I progressed through grade school, and he wrote local sports pieces for the *Chronicle* and spent his mornings researching and outlining a huge book he was calling "The Golden Age of Sports." It was about the twenties, the years of Big Bill Tilden, Bobby Jones, Babe Ruth, Jack Dempsey, and Red Grange. It was to be his grand opus, a cornerstone of the literature. (Eventually it shrank to a disconnected series that was bought by the Hearst Syndicate.) The two of us played a lot of tennis in the afternoons. I was building a foundation of ground strokes, flat and deep, the only part of my game I'd ever have real confidence in. I did well in a few kids' tournaments and got some notice. I was, after all, Louise Fraser Muldoon's strapping boy. I knew I would become a champion.

When Lou came home, as she did for a week at a time, arriving in a rush with a heap of scuffed leather suitcases and often a tennis companion or two, I was struck with an unusual shyness and amazement. Here was my mother, this flashing, boisterous, swanky, slam-bang celebrity. And here were my father and I, disrupted and bedazzled, trying to make a show of warm welcome. It was not for us. When Lou was around, our house was full of noise and smoke, the telephone rang and rang, and we ate peculiar foods, and my father drank in the mornings as well as at night, and no one paid attention to me except as a courtesy.

Then, when I was twelve, Lou was worn down enough to announce her retirement from steady competition. She was turning coach, she said, and she pronounced me the prime beneficiary of her savvy. Her folks had sold her their architect's showplace in Berkeley after they moved to Phoenix for her mother's emphysema, but my father refused to live there. In fact, he was even then on the verge of refusing not only to live anywhere in California but also to allow anything Californian to hold sway over his remaining days on earth, including Louise. He wanted to go to Idaho or Wyoming and build a cabin and the hell with her. The hell with me, too, I guess, though I never really took his ranting to heart. And rant he did, fueled by booze and naturally fermenting bile, but he did not head for the hills, not then. Lou found a way to reconcile him to us and to civilization, a condition of humanity whose value he held in increasing suspicion. She talked him into writing her autobiography. It would be called "Between the Lines," and it would be much bigger than Louise. It would be a magnificent sports epic, a cornerstone of the literature. He knocked off about half of it, too, in four years. By the time he quit that for good, my mother was depressed enough about the course of her dull tennis life and about the sad state of the modern game in general that she didn't care then whether the book got written or not. She never asked for a look at the work-in-progress, a look my father would not offer anyone, so the typescript lay untouched, locked away in my father's overseas steamer trunk until the night, years later, when he stole it from me. Once, before then, I discovered the trunk key inside the wood Haig & Haig box my father used as a sewing kit and so was able to desanctify that huge black presence in our attic, but the book, among all the other artifacts crammed inside—uniforms, trophies, mildewed shoes, shaving brushes, shirt studs and collar stays, a mushy infielder's glove without webbing, bundled letters, sepia photographs of long-gone tennis greats and picnics and city streets, and a .45 automatic wrapped in oilskin—was not what impressed me. I only glanced through it. It seemed unreadable; the typing was full of x-outs, and the margins were festooned with pencil scribbles.

So anyway, we went south for that, too, for the quiet my father would need to create, and for me, for my tennis future, and for the absurdly enticing promise of change.

Balboa is a little beach town of shops, amusements, restaurants, bungalows, and palms spread over a spit of sand four miles long and a half-mile wide. The spit, Balboa Peninsula, reaches out into the ocean from Newport Beach and curls back parallel to shore to form Newport Harbor. Along the ocean side of the peninsula is the best swimming beach on the Coast and some of the costliest real estate on earth. Along the harbor side, overlooking the anchorage of yachts that never take to sea, there was then an arcade for lovers of pinball, bumper cars, and chocolate-covered frozen bananas. Balboa was peaceful enough in the off-season, and at the tip of the peninsula, where Lou found us a spacious home, it was private and serene all year round. Our house was all glass and tile and plaster with its own dock on the harbor channel, three blocks from the Wedge. At twelve, however, with friends and a familiar neighborhood and my whole life's memories up in the city, I was dead against the move. But the beach was a sugar-coating. For one thing, I knew the Wedge to be a famous spot for board surf, and Lou bribed me with a promise to buy me a board (a purple one) and a wet suit the day we moved in. Also, the Balboa Racket Club would be just a mile from our new home. Most of the ranking Coast players then were from the sun country, I knew, though I myself had managed to rise to the fifth spot in California Twelve and Under. I was playing and practicing every day, even in the rain, fog, and wind of the north. Some days I worked so long that just to reach across the table at supper for a bowl of beets felt like punching a volley. Now, waiting in Balboa, besides the board, the beach, and the house, I was promised no bad weather, daily coaching, and top competition close by in LA.

Still, that first Southland summer proved harder on us than we'd expected. For me, the Wedge turned out to be only a legend, its big surf long since ruined by a rock jetty built to protect the harbor entry. Of course, there was plenty of surf around, but I fixed on the missing Wedge as the focus of my disappointments, and I refused to try out my new board. "You promised this place would be perfect," I yelled at Lou, "and it isn't. It *stinks*."

Lou thought so too. The ocean bored her, and most of the local tennis folk were fawning and stupid. So she got Lenny Spielman, her childhood mentor at the Berkeley club, to arrange lesson contracts for her. The weekly commute was never a real strain on her; she had always loved to fly.

The key to our failing family life was my father, who was getting weird. Just after we settled in the Channel Road house, his enthusiasm for the new book began to pale. He declined into stints of musing about doom. He began reading about earthquakes. Doom in any form had long been his swelling obsession—he entertained himself with it. And he taught me to find pleasure in contemplating all the means at doom's disposal for our disposal. I remember spending many afternoons straddling the purple Fiberglas and foam, bobbing on the waves just beyond the break, climbing the back of each surge, just rising, falling, rising, watching the snaggled row of beachfront properties appear and disappear behind the berm—disappear as they would that hour the earth twitched its hide and let the sea rush under the peninsula so every million-dollar box on it would go down whole, like the end of the Monopoly game when you fold up the board.

As an obsession, doom for my father was mostly more joyful than fretful, though he was always serious about it. He preached doom, and he practiced on me. Any moment through our early years in the city, say while he knelt whipping new laces into my sneakers or sat on his breakfast stool spooning in oatmeal, or while he drove or shaved, he was apt to burst out

10

with some assurance of cataclysm, as if to dispel any hopes for deliverance that may have been sneaking up on me. "No water," he might pronounce, giving me a steely look. "That's all it will take. This is not speculation, now, Will, this is Science. You think it can't happen here? Hah! *Wait*, that's all, that's all I ask. This is a desert, Will, don't forget it. The water cannot last forever. One day it will run out. And when the last drop is gone . . . what will happen? Think of it. Filth, fires—and *plague*. Yes, you heard me. The virus is right here. Bubos. Fleas have bubos. Rats have fleas. And we have rats, my buckaroo, up the derriere. So? *Plague*," he would breathe at me, letting the black certainty of it seep into my brain. "You mark my words. No water. That's all it will take."

In the summer of 1960 the old man's doom-sense attached itself most faithfully to the quake. He plunged into research. He scoured library books by the dozens and papered his study walls with geological surveys. Bolstered with figures and esoteric words, his disquisitions became really shocking, but his delivery was unbearable. I believed in him, but I was sure no one else could. He sounded like a madman.

The trouble was he corrupted his science with evangelism by laying The End to greed and guilt and just deserts. Who wants to hear he's so riddled with badness that the very planet won't suffer it? Even if it won't. Because undeniably, a jolt *is* due— sometime. Sometime; but beyond that vague, unthinkable certainty, no one takes the threat to heart. No one expects to die under tons of rubble and sand. Everyone has a solid house, a career, a family. You don't throw all that over and head back to Indiana just for some dim fear. "So you all deserve what you get," my father would tell them. "You're a race of goddamn ostriches. *Ostriches*, waving your fat bums in the breeze." Maybe then he would roll into his number on the Long Beach Fault, the fissure in the network veining the coastal bedrock that runs under the peninsula. "This is a liquefaction area—do you know what that means? You don't want to think about that, do you? It means nothing under your dishwasher, nothing under your canopy bed, your grape arbor, your stucco three-car garage, or your own two shoes but the blue Pacific. Whoooosh—

all gone! Yes, we have our own fault. It's *our own fault*—think about that. One sunny day . . . one lovely day it will slip and jerk . . . *catastrophe unparalleled*! Think about it!"

"*You* think about it," Lou would reply, arriving on the slate patio in the nick of time with a tray of cheeses. "You love to think about it. You're a catastrophe yourself. You're bats. Go hoard some canned goods, or something." The harangued guests would chuckle in relief. Always a sarcastic person, Lou bit off her words and usually followed whatever hard thing she said with a mollifying laugh that rasped in her throat, heavy a smoker as she was then. Before the Balboa days, when the old man's gloomy presentiments had a more general focus, she would laugh him off. Nothing ever worried her. "You take what comes," she used to say, "and what comes, comes."

But there on the channel when he took up his earthquake study instead of drumming out her autobiography, her tolerance evaporated, and her disdain condensed into venom, which for a while she contained. Quake talk had always made her impatient anyway. Newcomers to the Coast have a way of quizzing the natives about where their courage comes from, or their capacity for denial. Lou would say, "Look, when I get uncomfortable with things here, I'll move, all right?" If the china should begin to chatter in the cupboard, her advice was to stand in a doorway.

So, my father wrote hardly anything. The cartons of Lou's jumbled photos and memorabilia sat untouched in the upstairs hallway, where the movers had stacked them the day we moved in. Yet some mornings you could hear him up there pecking away, making hesitant progress, then subsiding into long thought, then bursting into exposition again, and if you stood right outside the door, you might catch him giving voice to new phrases as they hit the page. In the afternoons all he dutifully did was drink. He drank and went fishing, or he drank and read books, or usually he drank and watched television. We had an RCA tube big as a freezer that functioned constantly (like a freezer) in a corner of the dark kitchen, glowing and flashing, with the sound off. My father watched only the serial dramas, which he hated. He would mutter and bellow at the actors, looking on from the edge of his chair, so angry at them and full of mocking remarks that you'd expect him to reach out and flick them into blackness any minute. He was in that state enough so I was embarrassed to invite my friends in out of the sun for Cokes.

I turned into a kid who fended for himself. I cooked my meals, changed my bedsheets, bought myself new socks and toothbrushes, and remembered my vitamins. I surfed and grew red knots on my shins and feet. Evenings I ran through drills Lou had set up for me with Skip, the crew-cut pro at the Balboa Club, and every Saturday I had my three-hour lesson with the star, my mother.

That is, I did until that fateful Friday she blew up and everything ended. Of course, as I am trying to show, that day of endings was a long time in the making. The blade did not just come hissing out of the blue, as I felt it had at the time, nor was Lou alone the hatchet man.

My last lesson with Lou went nowhere. But she wouldn't bag it the way she usually did when one of us was lost to some kind of funk. She worked me steadily up-and-back and side-to-side until the horizon behind her gave up any hint of glow, and finally she said, "OK, Will, last ball." I tried to bash it into the harbor. In the wind it might even have carried.

Then came our last family dinner, pork chops, coleslaw, corn muffins, and apple sauce. A multidish, sit-down meal like that was rare for the old man and me, but Lou was too wound up to let us enjoy it. My father said, "We're not arguing now, Louise. We're eating. We can argue later."

She carried on, though. She was in a ferocious mood. I took my plate and glass of milk out to the patio. There at least I did not have to watch. Lou could turn mealtime into an inquisition just by not taking her chair, but by pacing behind it instead, making her case against the sorry chumps in the dock. My father, who loved food, would not be drawn into combat. He would retreat into bovine calm, sighing and munching. That night, however, there was a keener edge to all of us. When Lou in her summation declared that my father was "wasting her money just to set a putrid example of so-called manhood" for his son, he advised her to keep her contaminated mind out of our home life. "You have no true interest and no true place in it anyway," he said. She was silent for a moment. "OK, Flaubert," she shouted, "that does it. I want you to turn over everything you got up there in those boxes to me right now—so I can give it to a *real* writer. You hear me? Now!"

He said she could blow it out her ass.

She poured pork chop grease on his head and stalked outside.

He climbed the stairs to his study and slid some furniture against the door.

I went inside for the phone. I had a school friend whose older brother was a surf god named Steamer Lane. Steamer had half-promised the two of us a ride to San Onofre the next afternoon so we could camp on the beach and surf all weekend with the real hotshots. I'd just dialed a few digits when Lou pounded into the hall, slammed her fingers into the cradle, and wrenched the phone from the wall. The receiver clunked away and I jumped back, shocked.

"Get the ball machine!" she yelled. "Go on, get it! And wheel it out to the mailbox."

"It's *dark*," I said.

"Go on, goddamn it, *do* it!"

On the way to the garage I tried to figure out what else she'd found out about me to send her into such a complicated rage. But she wanted the ball machine to lay siege to my father's room. The night was warm and breezy. From the street my mother shot balls over the balcony and through the glass panes of the French doors off the study. I stood on the pavement watching. She yelled, "Hand over the goddamn manuscript or get out of the goddamn house! One or the other—or *both*. Right *now*!" My father did not respond. Over the hedge behind the house I could see the lit-up masts of sailboats gliding by below in the channel. My mother had on a white tennis dress. Her hair was frost-blonde and stiff, like a helmet. She was yelling, "Hey, drunk, I'm gonna have you committed. How about that? Hey, got that, Mr. Wacko? Committed!"

After a few minutes he opened the broken doors, stepped out in his bathrobe, and heaved the cartons of clippings and programs and photos one by one off the balcony into the dichondra courtyard below. My mother switched off the cannon and sat on the curb, her face pressed down against her wide knees. She wasn't crying. I darted around snatching up the pieces of paper I could see before they blew out into the channel.

The real grand finale didn't get up steam until after I'd gone to bed. Lou waited for my father to come out of a long shower. She had subdued herself. She wanted to talk it out, come to terms, settle the immediate issues in advance of some overall solution. "Obviously we can't fix everything at once," she said. "I mean especially with me up north and you down here just exercising your elbow all day. So, for what it's worth, I'm asking you to stiffen up, OK? This time you have *got* to make some changes. Is that too much to ask?"

Lou, I guessed, was pacing. I eased open my door to hear better. My father, from his recliner probably, said no, that was very reasonable. What changes?—as if he were ready to agree to any plan she proposed.

"A little discipline," she said. "A little sign that somebody around here cares how he spends his time."

"Ah-hah! A whiff of criticism taints the air."

She snorted. "More than a whiff. There's something rotten in the state of Denmark, pal, and you're it. You're the rot in his life, you know that? *You're* the contamination. If he'd leave, I'd fly the kid north tomorrow. The worst decision we ever made was to plant ourselves on this screwy beach. But now . . . oh, Christ, that's done, that's over. What I'm saying is take another last chance, would you? Take a *last* last chance. I mean—and I *mean* this now—you have got to shape up *now* for the kid's sake, and the sake of his future."

"I didn't know it was in jeopardy," said my father.

"He's going nowhere. Can't you see that? He needs some *guidance*."

"Guidance? Just a bare minute ago it was discipline."

"*Right!*" she yelled. "Discipline you can give him. You used to. You can't give guidance to your own dink."

"Oh-oh, we're getting nasty, Louise. Below the belt, and all that."

"I wouldn't give a rat's fart for what's below your belt."

He laughed. "You probably have one to give, too."

"Listen, you, we have nothing, you and me, but the kid—
nothing. And he needs us both, God save him. Less than two
years now, that's all, two years, and he's gone. That's all the
time we have left to get him ready. We've come this far, Lord
knows how, and we can't chuck the whole production now. You
have just got to keep your pickled head above water a little
while longer. Hey, I'm asking you. Please. Just cooperate, OK?
Keep him home nights. Feed him right. Be happy and interested. I mean, see if you can recollect one or two ways how to be
a dad, OK?"

"Maybe you could give me a for instance."

"For instance, *be* here, you know what I mean? Be awake, be
sober, and just talk to him. How's that? About anything besides
the goddamn end of the world. Just do your half of the simple
job we signed up for, will you? Christ knows the poor kid deserves it."

"The hell with what Christ knows," said my father. "Ask *me*,
I'll tell you what the kid deserves." He stood up. I heard the
recliner thump shut. "He deserves his own life. Let him *be*,
Louise. Quit treating him like a lump of clay. He's a person. Let
him be himself."

"Him*self*? What's that? What self has he got? Let him be
himself—*crap*! That's your way of selling out on the poor kid.
You listen now, you and I made a commitment once over a
bottle of wine to that boy's tennis future, and we—hey, buster,
don't you walk out on me while I got something to say to
you. . . . Hey—"

From somewhere far off in the house, my father shouted,
"You're wasting your breath, Louise!" He laughed loud.
"You're a pitiful beast. You're like the rhino—all snout and no
vision. If only you could douse your blazing illusions and let the
smoke blow off, maybe you'd catch a glimpse of the truth.
Which is, the kid *has* no tennis future. Open your sun-baked
eyes, Louise. It's not there! Sure, ten years ago we could dream.
Why not? He was six years old, and he could pound the hair off
the ball. Remember? By God, back then he must have been the

16

best six-year-old in the history of the Christ-bitten game. But that was *it*! If that kid came into the world with a tennis future, he lived the whole thing by the time he was twelve. It's *gone*, Louise. His tennis future's in the past, just like yours. It's history. And for his sake, for *his* sake, that's a bitter fact you have got to swallow."

"For his sake, you should have a coronary, you cynical sack of fat. OK, so I'll do it myself! I want you out of the house, and out of the kid's way by tomorrow night. You got that? I want you out!"

"Hah!" he said. "I'm in the kid's way, am I? Well, let me say this: you can't know who's in the kid's way until you know where he's going. And you don't. Wise up, is my advice. I'm only—"

"No advice!" yelled Lou. "We've had it, hear me? We've *had* it! Get out!"

"I'm good as gone, Louise. I'm only sorry for the time he still has left to suffer your ignorance. Good-bye, Will!" he shouted.

In a minute his Chevrolet roared to life and backed into the roadway, sending bits of car-light across my walls. I lay awake for a while in my bed waiting for my mother to slip into my room with some words of comfort, but she didn't. All I heard was the pulse of low music on my grandmother's toad of a radio, a mahogany floor console my mother had once long ago painted white with a spray can and masking tape. She did a careful job. But when my father saw it, he grabbed up the fire poker and rammed it through the coffee table. "That's an improvement!" he shouted. "See how nice it looks now? Nicer than nice." That time was the only time I saw my mother cry, and now here I was crying myself, crying the same way she had then, in silence, letting the tears run where they would, like mice.

My mother, Louise Fraser Muldoon, was a tennis great, a star, a name, Louise Fraser until she was eighteen, the Muldoon added then by her coach and chronicler, my father, when he made her an honest woman in 1947. He was more than twice her age. They were married at sea on the S. S. *America*, steaming home from Lou's first Wimbledon, my first Wimbledon, too, as it happened. In fact it was my tumefying self that kept her out of the quarterfinals. I sickened and depressed her. She struggled to the round of sixteen, where she tanked a dull match with Doris Hart. Oddly, the nausea that did her in left her aboard the ship, and in a flush of relief and romance, she wed the dashing writer, W. R. Muldoon, right then rather than wait for the planned nuptials in Berkeley.

All the same, Lou could not play much more that summer. In September she had to pass up the Nationals at Forest Hills, where the year before as a glowing blonde of seventeen she'd reached the semis. She reached the brink of fame, too, thanks to my father, who was writing her up for *The New York Times*. "The next Alice Marble," he called her. That's when they met and fell in love, at an interview in the lobby of the Forest Hills Inn.

When she finally popped me that December, Lou expected her swollen miseries to pop, too. Instead they got worse. The day before Christmas she ran her car through an intersection and got clobbered by a bread truck. Lou was a sensible driver, but she was so color-blind she couldn't see ripe apples on a tree. Traffic lights she interpreted by position, and that once she screwed up. Her ankles were broken, and some ribs, and her lungs were seared by the fire. It was two years before she could really run again, and five before she was back on her game enough to make any kind of showing in competition. She never did recover her wind.

Through the years, as historians of the game have overlapped one another, my mother's come to be called "the greatest player who never won a major championship." By that distinction singles is implied, since Lou won big doubles titles all over the globe with four partners. In singles, though, whenever the weightiest chunks of silver were at stake, Lou was not up to the likes of Hart, Brough, Gibson, Fry, Hard, Osborne, or Connolly. "Weak in the bellows," my father was treasonously the first to write—not that anyone was hard put to find that out. So Lou's hopes for greater glory were deferred early on to me, the green apple of her undiscerning eye. Those hopes were half the burden of my young life. The other half, at least partly, was blame, which I shared with the old man.

My early years were the years of my mother's recuperation. We were a close family then, the three of us, joined toward one end: to make Louise the fleet, cool, world-class competitor she had been before I was born. It was my father who took charge of Lou's climb back to the heights. Moved by love and by guilt in some measure, he took a leave from his sportswriting to turn full-time coach. Lenny Spielman, her teacher in Berkeley, was furious. He tried to get my grandfather, Big Jack, to intercede on his behalf, but Big Jack got nowhere. Lou wasn't willing to put her broken game before all the once awed eyes across the Bay until she was sure she could mend it. She wanted private attentions and discipline, and that was all.

Snapshots in albums show she began with barbells and jump rope once the casts were off, but my earliest memories of my parents are of them lazily playing the game, loping along opposite baselines, yet close in touch, communicating with each other with balls instead of words. No pair of movie screen dancers could have looked more romantic.

I must have got out there too at age three or so with a sawed-off racket, but I don't remember. I don't remember my sunny bedroom, my red tricycle, our pet terrier, or our Buick sedan. Even the evidence of hundreds of old snapshots stirs no true memory in me of anything apart from them, the colossi, my parents. It is as if, before the age of five, I couldn't see anything but them, in their white clothes, with their smiling wavy blond-red look-alike heads.

After I turned five and began developing a game of my own, tensions rose up in our daily play. "A tennis court is your garden," is how my father's analogy went. "All cleanly met balls hit to prechosen spots are the fruit of your labors and cooperating Nature. Mistakes, I'm afraid, are inevitable as weeds." The time came when Lou believed her garden would produce well enough despite the parasites she was too impatient to root out. She wanted to compete again. She was restless. She wanted to travel. My father would not allow it. Instead, during that spring of 1953, he alone competed with her, playfully at first, then more fiercely as she kept beating him. They began wrangling off the court as well. Underneath, their fights then were usually about one thing: whether Lou was ready. The old man drank plenty, and so did Lou. That June, when Bill Tilden, my father's boyhood hero and the only god he ever allowed into his life, died penniless in a little Hollywood apartment, my father lapsed into spells of mute brooding that could last days. By July, in the face of my father's loud doubts and warnings, my mother had left us. She went home to her parents in Berkeley, to a regimen of training matches with a bunch of odd-lot talents that Lenny brought to the club for her. There, everyone was crazy about Lou. They all egged her on to go east and intercept that tyke from San Diego, Maureen Connolly, at Forest Hills. The bobby-soxer, at seventeen, was already twice American champion.

The old man and I meanwhile ate out of cans and worked on my tennis garden, chucking the rocks out of it mostly. I was big for my age and very serious, so I made headway. We went on playing every day, though we missed Lou's inspiring drive. Now as we practiced we had only my future to anticipate, and it was too far off to give us any heat. We were depressed. Lou did not come home often, and my father and I never crossed the Bay because he and Big Jack hated each other.

That August, Lou finally went east to Southampton to tune up for the Nationals. In September, I entered first grade. In October, Lou came back to us, tired and unhappy and the first to admit her foray into the highest echelons of tennis had been premature. When she did meet Mo Connolly in the second round of the Nationals, Lou scratched out only three games. At the peak of her own abbreviated career, Maureen had gone on to win her third and last national title, without dropping a set.

Our family spent a peaceful winter together again in the foggy flats of west San Francisco. My father typed. Louise exercised. Afternoons we took to the courts. We had quiet suppers in our cream-tiled kitchen. We watched Kate Smith and Roy Rogers on our new television. For Christmas I got two six-guns and chaps with fringe and silver studs along the seams. It did seem like a good time to me. I can't recall sensing Lou's undiminished restlessness or the old man's vague frustrations. His "Golden Age of Sports" book was resisting his efforts to shape it with theories. Her game, she knew, needed pressure-testing that no endless hours of stroking could provide.

In the spring Lou made a friend of Eileen Pierce Becker, a lanky, raven-haired top-ten player who hit nothing but forehands. She was ambidextrous. Lou called her "the Freak." When anyone new was within earshot of them together, she would sing out, "Oh, Eileen, you know I'd give my right arm to be ambidextrous." Except for that, they had much in common. They were the same age, they were both from monied California families, they had married older men, and they had taken time away from tennis to have babies. Eileen was then on her way back after two years off the tour. They drove south in March to the La Jolla Club Invitationals, where they won the doubles, and where Lou found her strength and defeated Little Mo Connolly, the only time the Champion lost a match anywhere in the world during her three years as queen of the game. Lou broke into headlines up and down the Coast. Louise Fraser was back, they said.

Years ago I used to wish my mother had lost then in La Jolla, as she should have. I used to imagine how different my growing up might have been if the capricious angel that possessed her for a while that afternoon had passed her by. Lou's triumph signaled the end of what brief family life we had. For the next six years she cruised the globe lured on by the memory of that fleeting magic she had once and lost.

Still in all, she fashioned a glittering career, no question, and she was a personality besides. Beneath her tennis skirts brazen Lou was one of the first to reveal shocking panties frilled in pastel lace that drew gasps in chorus at the All-England Club. Everyone on the tour liked Lou. In her harsh way she was vivacious. She basked in the attention of fans and reporters, who respected her in turn for her knowledge of tennis and her courage on and off the court. She kept herself beautiful to look at, tan and trim, and she was always easy to talk to. Among all the characteristics common to public figures, like her outspoken-ness, was a rare one: she could listen. Maybe this trait, more than her beauty or her gamesmanship, insured her place at the center of the diffuse, tennis-loving world.

Indeed, her life story would make a splendid book. That much Lou was right about. But she was wrong to think the old man could successfully assume the task for her—unless his as-suming the task was all she wanted. I mean, without the project for an anchor, the old man might have cast himself adrift much sooner than he did, leaving Lou marooned with a helpless stranger, her son.

Anyway, not long after the grand finale (my tears were still cool in my ears when I woke to the sound of shoes scraping overhead in the attic), my father returned to lock away what he had of the manuscript in his steamer trunk. In her dejection Lou had not commandeered it, nor had she even thanked me for gathering up the papers he'd dumped off the balcony. I listened to the trunk creak open and thump closed and to his stealthy descent of the stairs. He paused at my open door, then sidled in.

"Will?"

"What?"

"Get dressed. I'm taking you out for breakfast."

"I'm sleeping."

He sighed, running a hand through his hair, and slowly lowered himself to a corner of the bed. "Oooff, phooey. Sorry, Will. I'm kind of frazzled myself. But, see, it's just that. . . . Oh, balls. Say—the captain's booted me off the squad, hasn't she. Thunder of that battle reached you up here, eh?"

"Yeah."

"Yeah. Well, hell, so then there are some matters to make clear in your impressionable mind before I sashay into the sun-rise. OK? How's about *huevos rancheros*?" He gave my foot a shake through the sheet.

Never before that night (it still felt like night, though dawn was graying in the windows as I dressed) had it occurred to me that my father's demands on my future were separate from my mother's. She wanted me to become a tennis champion, pure and simple. He wanted me to survive, which wasn't simple at all.

"That's right, I said *survive*," he said, glaring at me across the width of his cream and plum 1958 Chevrolet Bel Air. He was directing our course to Tijuana with the purpose of pitching me into some larger awareness of what I had and what I was up against. More than breakfast, he wanted to give me a new view of human life. "Because mere living is not surviving, Will. It doesn't come close. Any sorry package of bones and blood can push along sucking in air and dropping out turds—like a worm. The world is riddled with worms. Gutless worms. Sometimes I think you got a worm for a mother, I'm sad to say. So ask me, what's surviving? OK, surviving is understanding what you want—what's *worth* wanting—from your life. Can you tell me now, Will, what you want?"

"What do you mean, what I *want*?"

"How old are you?" he said.

"C'mon, Dad. I'm almost sixteen."

"Right, sixteen. Well, hell, you're old enough. Think of something."

"I don't know. God. How about happiness?"

"OK. Good. Except, you can't have it. Listen, Will, the first step in understanding what you want is understanding what you can have. Happiness is out. Wanting happiness is like wanting to ride an endless wave—it does not exist. Not as a goal anyway. Try me another."

I sat forward. I lifted the backs of my bare thighs off the hot vinyl and put my sneaker heels on the seat. I loved rolling, traveling, the landscape unfurling. I loved being in pursuit of the future. "Well, to be honest, I want just what we're doing," I said to please him. "You know, I want to have adventures." I looked over at him. His knuckles stood on the steering wheel like a range of mountains.

"Adventures?" said my father. "You do? Then you want danger and fear and pain? Do you? Don't stop being honest."

"Well, not pain."

"But fear, you want fear?"

"I'm not afraid of anything," I said.

"Sure you are," he said. "You're afraid of pain. I got news for you: adventures come with fear and pain. You still want adventures?"

"Sure."

"Good, that's fine, but that's because you're young. You're a kid. All kids want adventures. Then they grow up and they want a Cadillac dealership and a glass box in Laguna. Then they can drive back and forth between them every day with air-conditioning and their radios tuned to the weather." He groaned. "Listen, Will, OK, so it's very tough to know what you want. That's nothing new. Maybe a way to crack that one is to figure out first what you *need*, right? But don't be fooled. It's just as tough to understand what you need. Consequently, not many survive, Will. Look around. Bunch of zeros going in circles, sniffing up each other's asshole like mill-wheel donkeys. They don't understand what they need. And they think what they want is money. What about you, Will? What would satisfy you? Money? Fame?"

"Fame," I said. I knew I was being strung along.

"The fame of the World-Beater?" he asked. It was Lou's expression. She liked to call me the World-Beater-to-Be. "The fame of the greatest ever? Or just the greatest since Kramer? Since Budge? Since Vines?"

"Ever," I said.

"The greatest ever," he said. "OK, that's reasonable. Why not the greatest ever? Right now, however, I don't have to tell you we already got a 'greatest ever.' Do I?"

I shook my head. It was Tilden.

"Right. And in forty years nobody's come up who could touch him out there, Will, *nobody*. I don't have to tell you that either. But hell, forty years is a long time. Some shit-lick could come along tomorrow and make us all forget him. Why not you? I could write you a book, too—'Fame Was My Destiny.' Why not? I'll tell you. Because it's worthless. Listen, Bill had it all. The talent, the grace, the money, the fame. . . . Then he got old. And it all dropped away like the hairs out of his head. When he died he was just a broken-hearted old dickie-diddler. No friends, no bucks, no respect, nothing but a few trunks full of tea trays and punch bowls, the ones he didn't pawn.''

"But he was a fairy, Dad, wasn't he? He was different.''

"That's what I just said. Sure he was different. Everybody's different, Will, that's the point. Everybody's a lot bigger than tennis. A lot smaller, too, if you know what I mean. I mean, you make tennis your life, and you know what happens? You got no life. *Tennis*, phooey. It grabs you and rams you around the world like a billiard ball on a table, and then one day you drop out of the light, and who notices? Nobody. Because that's what's supposed to happen. And what have you got left? Bursitis and photo albums. Maybe a job teaching at some little club, hosing pine needles off the courts, and making the men's and ladies' ladders out of tongue depressors. Tennis is a sick game, Will, believe me when I say it. What other noble game gives away points when you falter, when your talent fails? Take basketball: when you do it right, when you drop that pumpkin through the hoop, you get your two points. Baseball: swing a smooth bat and you park the horsehide. Golf. Bowling. Football. You name it. You do it right, you get your reward. But tennis? Sorry, pal. The margin in tennis—by miles—is mistakes, simple mistakes. In tennis, the only reason you try to do it right is so you don't do it wrong. The perfect tennis player doesn't win points—the other guy *loses* them. It's backwards and sick. Fill your life with it and it makes you sick. That's not what you want, Will. Because you won't survive the madness. You'll succumb. And surviving is all that matters. There is nothing else.''

On we went down the desert coast toward Baja with nothing in our ears for some minutes but the hum of the road, until the logical question came to me. "OK, but what about you, Dad,'' I said. "How will you survive the madness?''

He shot a smile out over the hood of the Chevy and said nothing. I watched his profile against the blur for a sign of reply, for a clue to something, and what I saw was his bushy eyebrows, how they curled around and down from his brow to meet his eyelashes, like the tubes of breaking waves that a surfer-flea could glide through. He raised those eyebrows, and kept smiling, but that was all.

We left the land of plenty. We crossed the magic line where golden America just stops as if somebody kicked out the plug, and we cruised Tijuana's outskirts to scrutinize poor Mexicans in their fruit-crate hovels all heaped together on the dry hills. Then we ate our Mexican breakfast and made our way home.

So the damage was done. I quit, pow, just like that.

The old man disappeared (off to Wyoming at last, I wondered, or would he choose just to melt into the South Seas, or the Yukon?), and my mother stayed home doing her best to coax a racket into my fist. I was intractable. The worst of it was I wanted to play. I loved tennis—there was nothing else I knew how to do better. But I killed it. I carved the game out of my days and tried to fill the hole it left with waves, movies, and platter-size chiliburgers. Someday, I'd drift back onto the courts again—I *knew* that—but like any teenager with no sense of his limits, I really believed I'd always have the eye and the edge it had taken me my whole life to sharpen.

My mother cajoled me and fought with me to the point of seeing it was no use, which took her a week, and then she gave up. After I absolutely refused to return with her to Berkeley (a rejection that was probably more a relief to her than not), she established a budget and a bank fund for me, hired a cleaning lady, apprised our neighbors of the setup, and left me on my own.

A cab came for her. She shook my hand good-bye. Then she dipped toward me like a tree in a gust of wind and brushed her face against my cheek, and she said, walking backward over the flagstones, her eyes glistening, "I'm always ready when you are, Will, now. You remember that, OK? You know my number." That's how we parted.

My father's orbit was unpredictable. He did begin to show up now and then in Balboa, though never without phoning first to ascertain Lou's whereabouts. At first I was happy to see him, but his inwardness and blowhard speeches were harder to take in sporadic doses. We could not connect. Usually he would stay a day or two. He would take a bath and wash his shirts and underwear. Then while cooking up a chuck roast, he would lecture me on such topics as health and hygiene, or the overlooked importance of frequent oil changes, and I would pay no attention. He had little interest in my immediate life or in what I could tell him about it, and he resisted telling me about what I wanted to hear most; that is, himself. "I roam," is how he might finally respond to my prodding. "That says it all, Will, believe me. You can picture it. Town to town, valley to valley, gas pump to gas pump. I've grabbed off some freedom, sure, but it's not the kind most people would suffer. Pretty lonely. Pretty hard on a man, all told. Roaming's not really a way to live—it's a search for a way to live. So actually I'm looking to stop, see? I will when my money's gone, but I'm hoping for a better reason, don't ask me what."

I was in worse shape with Lou. She would get me on the phone once in a while to try to have conversations, but I responded like a stone. Even when I felt things in me I wanted to say I wouldn't talk to her. In fact I didn't know I had any affection at all left for my mother until she flew down for my graduation from Newport Beach High School almost two years later, in June 1965. She was abrupt then with me, angry at my plan to go east for college. Not only was that ridiculous when you ticked off all the good West Coast schools I was passing up, but she was sure the plan was part of my father's plot to put some final distance between me and her. Through a connection he'd gotten me a scholarship to the Syracuse University journalism school, and actually I was excited about the change, the chance to see some new terrain, to travel and roam. "You're a jerk," my mother couldn't resist telling me. "You know, don't you, that all you had to do was swing a racket for two more years and now you could be going to Cal or Stanford, for Christ's sake, for free?"

A wave of queasy regret washed over me then, not for tennis but for Lou. I realized she wanted me, that was it. She wanted me close to her. She always had, in her way. But just as I had squandered my chances, she had squandered hers. She must have felt the same thing I did at that moment, on the torch-lit high school lawn after the awards banquet, the happy families milling around us. It was our small love we felt. That, and how we had to waste it in the satisfaction of our tyrannical destinies, our fates.

I told her California sucked—I'd hardly left California my whole life.

Beside the point, she said. Travel was one thing, and school was another.

But I'd never been farther east than *Reno*, I said. (Neither of us knew then that Balboa is farther east than Reno.)

"OK, forget it," she said finally. "God knows I can't stop you. If you have to go, go. You'll have to find out for yourself whether they got what you want in crappy upstate New York. You can always transfer. But just . . . just don't forget my standing offer, OK? OK, Will?"

I said I wouldn't.

"I'm ready when you are," she said. "Just call me. Call, that's all you have to do."

When I finally did call, it was about exactly four years later, and I was drunk. I hadn't hit once since my last lesson with Lou when I was sixteen. Now I was twenty-one. I'd grown a heavy mane of hair that was red like my father's, threaded with gold like my mother's, and tennis balls had turned green. I don't know what made me decide to play again. It didn't make much sense at the time. That alone is probably what appealed to me at first, in a perverse way. A lot of senselessness and perversity were going around then, like diseases.

It was still the sixties, it was May 1969. It was wartime, and all my years of schooling were finished. My new degree was worthless in the face of the draft. My life was up for grabs. Besides the wild plans for escape, no plans mattered. The army would foreclose on any ambition. So I decided to become a tennis star. I would go home, dig in, and just do it. Why not?

I was as crazy going back to the game as I'd been when I quit. I could go anywhere, and I decided to aim for home. But being crazy wasn't the reason. It wasn't my young girlfriend waiting

28

for me there, beautiful Cici, nor was it the dependable sun, the soft ocean, the empty house on the channel, or my own retreat from true challenge. It wasn't Lou, either—not some debt to her I was settling. I figured I could get my $50,000 trust fund from Grampa Jack whether I came home or not, so it wasn't that. And Bad Barry was only a part of it, because when I first saw them together, on television, I didn't consciously react to him. He was just another tennis jock.

I was sitting in some dorm basement, still in my graduation gown, which I'd worn all day, though I didn't attend the ceremony, watching a sports spectacular with a few friends, and out of nowhere came a tape of the US Clay Court Indoor finals, I think, from Chicago. There on the sidelines was my mother in a big hat, brown and trim as ever, operating as some kind of coach for Barry Glines, the thunderous new California talent. The camera found her once as she leaned up in the front row to give him a word on the change-over. Amazing, my own mother. She used to do that for me. She would say, "Stop pressing. Lay back." Or, "Mix it up, mix it up." But it wasn't the memories roiled up by my seeing her that brought me around. It wasn't even the pure tennis. That did nothing for me—I might have been watching a pair of bowlers. I don't know. It was something inside me, that's all, like longing or love, something that popped its cocoon and crawled into the light blinking and flexing, not thinking, not knowing anything had changed.

Drunk as I was that day, my purpose was plain to me. My resolve was exhilarating. It made my heartbeats quicken and my back muscles shiver. I got a little drunker, and late that night I sat down, breathed deep a few times, and spun Lou's number out over the long wires. It rang a long while. But the rough voice I finally managed to summon was not Lou's. It belonged to Bad Barry Glines.

"Hello?" he growls.

I listen for a moment to the hollow sound of long-distance.

"*Hello?*" he shouts.

"Hello, is this the right number? Is this— What is it . . . is this Lou Muldoon's Berkeley residence?"

"Who the hell is this?"

"I'm her son, Will."

"Who?"

"Her son, the one and only Will Muldoon the Second."

"Oh, yeah. She has a son, that goes to college. So, what do you want to do—leave her a message?"

"You mean she's not there?"

"Yeah, she's over in Australia. I think Sydney."

"Oh. Well, who is this I'm speaking with, may I inquire?"

There is a long pause.

"Anybody home?" I say.

"Who the fuck *is* this?" he says.

"Hey, asshole, I told you who it is. Who the fuck are *you*?"

He hangs up.

It doesn't matter. Lou is in Australia. With the Federation Cup team probably. So I call Patti Autrey's house in Santa Barbara. Patti is my age, an old tennis friend, and a perennial Cup team member. Her father says he's glad to hear from me. Yes, he says, they're all down around Sydney, some at a hotel, some at the homes of the Australian players. He doesn't know where

Lou is, but call the hotel if it's urgent, he tells me, and they'll get her a message.

It's urgent, so I call the hotel. She's there, locked into a game of bridge with a few other tennis greats of a bygone era.

"Well, what do you know," she says when she finally shakes free to take the call, "if it isn't the prodigal son. *Qué pasa*, prodigal son?"

"Not too much, Mom. How's your bridge?"

"Hey—ha ha. Pretty shrewd, I must admit. What's that noise? You hear that noise in there?"

"Maybe some mackerel's nibbling at the cable."

"Yeah, maybe." She laughs. "So, you in jail, or what?"

"No, I just graduated. I'm a bachelor of the arts."

"That's great. You have my heartfelt sympathies. Seriously, Will, this isn't some cat's-ass-trophy, is it?"

"By no means. It's an announcement."

"Fire away."

"I want to play tennis, Mom. I'm ready." I wait, but she doesn't reply. "I'm ready," I say again. "You said call when you're ready, and this is it, I'm ready."

She sighs. "Well, jeepers creepers. Break out the smelling salts and we'll have a toast. Christ. So, tell me, when did you begin noticing these symptoms?"

"I mean it, Mom. I'm coming home this week, and I swear I'm going to *do* it. With you or without you."

"You sound half in the bag, you know that? You all right?"

"It's just a little beer. It doesn't affect how I feel about this. I made a decision, and it's forged in iron. I wanted to tell you right away. I should have waited, maybe, but I couldn't."

"*Waited!* That's good. That's real good, Will. You know how long you waited already? How many *years*? How many? Christ. You're a psychedelic hippie now, aren't you? A hippie and a peace marcher? I'd be surprised if you knew a fake poach from an incense burner."

"Mom, if you want to fling shit at me, I'll hang up and you can call me back. What's gone is gone, OK, Mom? I'm twenty-one. I made a decision about my life that I thought you would appreciate hearing. If you don't care, well—"

31

"Hold it. Listen, you just pull your head out of the clouds for a minute and take a look around. Welcome to nineteen-ought-sixty-nine, kiddo. Amateur tennis has hit the big time. What do you think, you can work with me for two, three months now after you been jerking off for five years and I'm going to make you into a power and a threat just like that? Like presto-change-o, with a wave of my old Max-ply? Think again. Do you have any slim idea what just the drone-level competition these days looks like? Christ, an old bag like me could give you thirty tomorrow and drop you oh-and-oh. I don't know, maybe—hey, maybe if you can qualify for the Nationals by next year, I can be an astronaut. What do you think?"

She goes on and on, and I don't stop her. Maybe I deserve it. I should have expected it from her anyway, even though she knows she isn't telling me anything new. Of course, the odds against me are terrible, but at any of your life's crossroads when you fasten your eye on some incandescent vision of your future, you'll find its brilliance blinds you to any odds. You'd expect Lou to know that better than most, too. If she does, she sees no way to restore me to a sane person's sense of the truth by pummeling me over the phone. So, without offering her blessing or even some small encouragement, which is all I wanted, she ends the call. "Well, I'm not sure when I'll be getting down there, so don't press me on that. I got obligations. You can sit tight for a while. Try getting yourself in shape, and we'll take it from there, OK? I'm giving you the big benefit of the big doubt, Will, which is gonna have to satisfy for now. Fair enough?"

"I suppose."

"Swell. Stay off the beer, Will. There's a start. And I'll see you when. 'Bye."

"Remember, Tilden was twenty-five!" I get in before she breaks the connection. No hurry, no worry, my father used to tell me years ago to soothe me after a bad tournament. I had plenty of time to build a tennis career was what he meant. And it was stout determination that would see me through, regardless of how long it took. "Let Big Bill inspire you," he would say. "Remember, he was just another club bozo until his early twenties. Relax—and look at it this way: you got the jump on the king of the game."

I still do, though Lou wouldn't see that. She was back at the card table, leaving me with nothing, no glad-you-called, no happy-graduation, not even a good-luck-Will-you-dope-you'll-need-it, nothing, which is about right. Except, goddamn it, this was long-distance, it was *long* long-distance, and we heard the fish chewing on the cable. Well, the hell with her. I don't need her really. Everything I really need I have already. Everything but time, maybe, which could loom as the major question: Will I have time enough on the courts before the army mails me a ticket to the paddies? If I get good enough fast enough I can get at least a pro's job anyplace I have to go to skip the war, like Vancouver. That's what I am hoping, I realize, in the back of my mind.

In high school a friend or two and I sometimes could put together the right lies and circumstances to cut classes and bomb up to LA International, where we'd lie in the high grass outside the fences and shiver in the wash of the jets screaming in to land. They took out the sky like an aluminum overcast, and it seemed if you sat up they'd smash off your head.

We bank a bit, and I squint down, but I can't see me or anyone flattened against the brown ground below. I keep watching as the plane sinks to the tarmac, its shadow rushing toward us raggedly across the overgrown city. But nobody is waiting out there under the sun. It's too hot, I discover, when we put down. Everyone I know or don't know must be indoors or at the beach.

In the terminal I look on while my fellow passengers get hugged and squealed at, and all at once I feel grown up, alone, in very shaky command of my vast existence stretching away from this moment. Here I am, though, home. My mother by now is in Berkeley, I think. And who can guess where my father is hanging out? Not long after I started college he married one Vivian Rolfe of Sparks, Nevada, according to the announcement, and I haven't had a glimpse of him since. So I have a stepmother—an illegal one: my parents are not divorced.

33

For a while I fired off occasional reports of events on campus to his Sparks address. The only response they drew was a few postcards. The last one I got came months ago. It said, in wispy pencil, "I can breathe! I have a mission! Just imagine opposing waste with worth, madness with nobility, human clutter with pure nature, doing unarguable GOOD! No more selling turquoise jewelry and parking space and clowning around here with deadbeats and weirdos! I'm on the road again! Keep in touch." I tried. I sent him clips of features I was turning out for the college daily, and later just empty envelopes and once a shoe box full of milkweed seed. He sent me nothing until last week, when a telegram appeared in my postbox. He wanted to come to my graduation ceremony. "TIME HAS COME," said the telegram. "BIG CONGRATS. MUST SEE YOU TAKE DEGREE. CONFIRM DESIRE AND DATE. DAD." I tore it up and mailed him the pieces with this note: "Dear Dad, When will you come clean with me? My sheepskin doesn't mean shit to you, Nixon, or Ho Chi Minh. If you really want to see me, see me in Balboa. I'm coming home to play tennis and nothing else. I'm going to make it. No hurry, no worry—age is on my side, right? —W. II"

With the promise of a beer, I coax the limo driver into going the length of the peninsula, right to the door of the old house, because he has the time, and I have five suitcases. I don't know what made me expect there would be beer in the house, but I never doubted my key would fit the locks, as always. Each door, I soon learn, has been fitted with shiny new brasswork. The dormer over the stairway landing behind the house is unlockable, but I don't feel like fooling with the ladder in the heat—if I could find the ladder. The limo driver, who is skinny and has long clean gray hair, is unimpressed when I break a louvered patio window with a rock.

The draperies are all drawn shut. The place smells like paint and baking wood. Everything is dusty. The dark and dust are comforting, though. They mean the house is mine. Last summer, like the summers before, the house felt more like the Latino cleaning lady's. She had a cot in the laundry room and came and went as she pleased. Dorotea was strangely reticent yet audacious, like a cat that does whatever it wants when nobody's looking. She wasn't there for my comfort. Lou had her around to keep the place spruced up in case she got the urge to fly some friends down for a weekend on the beach. Now these signs of neglect imply that Lou has left Balboa out of her plans for the season. That would explain the new locks, too. In the open refrigerator there is a jar of bolts and an extension cord, nothing else. I take them out, plug it in, and close the door. Its chrome lettering says Hotpoint.

No stray six of Coors turns up in the pantry, so I go back to apologize to the limo driver. He doesn't care. I tip him well, and we lug my bags into the hallway.

It's suppertime. I open a few windows and smell barbecues. In my room in the closet I find the photographs Cici and I took last August. We were here in this room after a shower, naked, our blond hair wet and dark. For some we posed ourselves together. I shot them from a tripod with a timer. We were both astoundingly brown, clear-faced and wide-eyed. Cici's creamy breasts stood out like gibbous moons. One was of just Cici in relief, lying full-length across my bed and backlit by the sun so that the tuft of bright hair at her middle rose up like a butte on a prairie. All year at school, whenever I thought of Cici I would curse myself for leaving these pictures at home. I'd hidden them from Dorotea in a box of baseball cards.

I pad down the hot, still corridor to my mother's room, to the phone, to call Cici, but the phone is dead. I masturbate stretched out on the old lady's huge, rumpled four-poster.

I change my clothes and go outside. I'm feeling a lot of things, but the foremost is hunger. I decide to drive to Ray's Market and buy some beer and food. On the side steps between the rose trellises I stop first and sit to roll a number, out of old summer habit, and light up. I am home again. Home filters through everything else like taste coming back after a long cold. Boats putting in the channel, traffic rolling steady down the avenue, sea gulls creaking, helicopters tangling the air, and behind it all the thump of the Pacific, clock of eons. My knees crack nicely when I stand up.

In the garage I find my old gray Porsche coated with the yellow dust that the Santa Ana winds brought from the hills. The paw-prints of a cat are all over the windshield and hood. Hopefully, I unbox the six-volt, wire it in place, and flip the key, but she doesn't even wheeze. I push her into the street and flag down a Chrysler full of surfers. The Porsche jumps easily. I present the guy behind the wheel of the Chrysler a thick joint out of my pocket, and he says, "Very righteous of you."

"Likewise," I say, and I grin at him. California has a welcome ring to it.

The Porsche feels fabulous, even better than I remember. It's a '58 cabriolet with probably close to half a million miles on it, loose about the kingpins and spongy of suspension, but a lively marvel of German engineering just the same. I drive slow by the club courts, but I can't make out anybody familiar through the hedges. Well, tomorrow it begins. String up a few rackets and then hit with the machine for a couple of hours, run a little in the sand, swim some, and hit again all afternoon, ironing out the kinks, getting up some timing. Then (sure, why not?), I'll phone Lou—not to press her at all, just to let her know I have begun all by myself to shore up the rickety promise of my greatness.

By the register in Ray's I line up some beer, bread, cheese, eggs, butter, hot dogs, lettuce, and apples, and wait at the magazine rack for Ray to come punch up the prices. Above the magazines a sign says If You Can't Buy, Don't Read—If You Can't Read, Don't Buy. I look around. Other things have changed, too. The toy corner is gone. The windows have new, clear amber shades. I pick up a *Playboy* and flip through the spreads of skin—just the low-life habit Ray must now be out to quash.

A woman's high voice behind me demands, "Hey, see that sign?"

"Yeah," I say, looking at it again.

"So?"

"So where's Ray?"

She comes around from behind the counter, a wattle-necked woman in lime green. "Stroke," she says. "He sold out."

I keep gazing down at the colorful nudes. They drift by like fall leaves. I'm so exhausted my eyes feel grainy. Now the sun is setting, squatting low, a tomato in the smog. It rose for me this morning in Syracuse the same way, blood-red, which I took as a bad omen. I was up early to finish packing, and I ended up just throwing things away, my sheets, old letters and paperbacks, coffee cups and hot plate, my desk lamp, my tall begonia, even four Frisbees. Sailed them out the window. Now the sun is a good omen, and I feel pangs of regret. Why did I cast away all those loyal, useful things?

The woman bends herself toward me. She really has a disgusting neck. "Our policy," she says, "is buy it or beat it. Just so you know."

Another customer walks in, jingling the bell. I put back the magazine, and she hurriedly bags my groceries.

"I guess I'll just beat it," I tell her. I walk out to the hot sidewalk with nothing. The sun is gone, and my Porsche is dead again at the curb. I forgot to leave the motor running.

Cici has exams coming up. Her mother says she's at a friend's that night, studying. The word I leave is, *Surprise*, I am back, and she should come by the house if it isn't too late. Don't count on her, the mother tells me ominously. I stand in the booth a while wondering who else to call. My best high school friend, Foster Ketchum, was killed in a troopship accident last spring in the Philippines. Other friends are all gone to the gook-shoot or moved away. I leaf through the fat phone book, running a finger down the column of names, page after page, resisting the impulse to look up my own, which is my father's.

I buy pork chops and other supplies at El Rancho, but I can't cook the meat because the gas is off. I wait up for Cici in the dark, drinking cans of beer. She doesn't show. Finally I fall asleep, curled up in the wicker loveseat in the hall.

"Tennis? *Nuts!*" my father shouts. Wherever he's calling from, he is looped. He's been trying the line for days, he says. Now he has become my first call since Pacific Bell patched me back into the system this morning. I was sure he was Cici. "*Tennis?*" he shouts again, louder. "Ohhh, no. You're not holing up back there for *tennis*. It's a great excuse, though, I'll grant you that. You're back there because you're still a *kid*. You're a *kid*, and you have no place else to go. No backbone. No spirit. No job either, right? And no idea how to get one, right? *Right?*"

"I got more ideas than you got empty booze bottles," I say.

He says, "Christ, I bet you do at that. Except they're delusions, not ideas. If you had one sane cell in your brain, you'd be anywhere right now but where you are."

"I know. Maybe *that's* why I came home. You can be crazy here and nobody notices."

He snorts. "You went home for *money*. Admit it, money's the magnet back there, all that squeeze-'em-out and fuck-'em-over California land-grab money, that's what it is. Clock's struck twenty-one, and Grampa Jack shells it out, am I right?"

He is right. Partly. That's his whole problem. He is always right partly. Right, I have come of age, and I am due for a handout, and I want it before I have to blow the country to escape the army or else I'll never get it. Sure the money is part of it, but it's promised to me whether I come to Balboa or not, in a dribbling sort of outlay that I want to renegotiate. I need it all at once, now, as a hedge against the unforeseeable. "Money's money," I say to him. "Beyond that there's nothing wrong with it."

"That's the ticket, be frank with your old man. I know there's no dollar that doesn't stink. You might as well live with the smell, is that it?"

"Come on, Dad. How've I been living the past twenty-one years?"

"Eureka! That's the *point*! You been sucking Jack's eggs your entire life. Now you got the chance to get off the payroll. Be your own man. That's what you'll be when you can do that—a man."

"Gee, thanks, Dad. Funny, I don't remember Grampa's money doing you too much damage."

"Don't wise off to me, Will. You and your college degree, you're too smart now to take the counsel of your father's experience. So that's nothing new. But it's goddamn frustrating for someone that cares." He groans then, and says softly, "Ahhh, I don't know. I'm dying, Will, all right? My guts are rotting out of me. I'm a sick man."

I listen to him breathing.

"Now, Will, tell me, you all set up there now for the summer? The road to stardom's a long one, right? I mean, you're not hopping a jet for London today, I hope. Louise hasn't given you the green light to glory, has she?"

"Not yet," I say.

"Good. When's she coming down?"

"I don't know. I don't know where she is."

"You don't, hunh? How unusual."

"She doesn't answer her phone."

"Another old story. I bet I know where she is, Will. Probably sitting under a sunbonnet this very minute in some box at Roland Garros."

"Paris?" Of course, I realize. The French Open. Twice in three days I've switched off reports from the big tournament on my car radio before any names were mentioned. I know all the names, and I don't want to hear who beat whom, who played brilliantly, who played badly. For now, I want my tennis to be just lines and strokes, an abstraction, without personalities, without history.

"Yessir," says my father. "Gay Paree. Seems like you're outa touch. I'd keep up with the sports news around LA if I were in your sneakers."

"Why, she still making headlines down here?"

He laughs a big laugh. "Headlines? How's 'Bad Barry Glines Linked with Tennis Queen'?"

"What?"

"Listen, if it was me plowing into the black unknown with every last sail rigged, I'd at least keep me a weather eye, I'll tell you that."

"You mean Mom and Barry Glines . . . ?"

"I mean watch your tender ass, Will. You know, grow up, think straight, that kind of thing—that's all I mean. And also, *wait* on the damn money, for Christ's sake. Wait till I get there."

Oh, shit. "No, don't bother, Dad. Really, I'm doing fine by my lonesome. How are you doing anyway? Where are you?"

"Me? I'm out here on the fruited plains. Wandering in circles toward the void. I'm saved, too—that's the irony. I'm—ah, Jesus, never mind. Don't ask me any questions—you don't want to hear the answers. Here's one last word of warning: they don't call that big fool *Bad* Barry for nothing. Remember that, and take care."

" 'Bye, Dad."

"Drink your milk," he says.

The operator hooks me for the overtime. I swear at the phone, and I laugh, and then tears spring onto my sunburned cheeks and roll off my chin. I am miserable. I am lonely. I am living on beer and ice cream and stew and hash out of cans.

Now, after three days home, my tennis is a horrible joke. First day out I loped around for hours against the machine, relaxed and grinning to myself, exulting in the simple motion and in the rush of good memories. The next day the grins were gone. My dormant bad habits—the once-containable flaws of my young game—woke and seized me like a curse. I was hitting with Skip, the pro, a genuine tennis player and a face from my past, for the first time in five years. I had nothing. No eye, no timing, no wind, no rhythm, no basic dependable understanding of the ball—nothing. I was sweating hard. I was seeing spots sometimes, an awful new sensation. Two or three times a ball in flight would just vanish from my sight's fix on it, for no reason, like someone jarring the telescope. Every part of me was sore. The third day my hand had so much tape on it that I couldn't feel the racket. "Rest a week," said Skippy. "Do some sprints on the beach. Swim, get some sleep. And get a haircut, will ya? Or else I think I got a line of cute dresses in the shop you might be innarested in. Hunh? Seriously, you're offa campus, now, bub, and I can't work with guys that look more like drug addicts than tennis players, no matter who their mom is. Do us both a favor. See you back here in a week or so, after you take care of all that, OK? No rush. Call me."

Skippy can stick his dresses past his hemorrhoids. I am not cutting my hair an inch, not until Cici sees it at least. It's twice

40

as long now as it was last summer. She made me promise to grow it for her. But something's wrong at her house, *bad* wrong, as she'd say. Four times in a row her mother's told me she's asleep, or in the city, or after school for the yearbook, or walking the dog—what dog? She is getting my messages, her mother assures me, she certainly is. Well, her folks are a weird pair, weird enough so I have kept my distance, except when a trip to her place was unavoidable. Her dad is a heavyweight in the air force and spends almost all his time at a huge base out near Riverside. Her mother is a lounger, a primper, and a nibbler of chips. Cici is just eighteen, now in her last week of high school. She and her mom live in residential Costa Mesa in a long low house that has no windows on the street side so it looks like the wall of a bunker. Nothing breaks its blank façade but gigantic twin paneled doors. The right one opens, and the left is a dummy. The whole front yard is just a blanket of green-and-white crushed stone. Her mother doesn't allow anyone in the living room. It's huge, decorated in eggshell and lemon, and has a gas fireplace and plaster statues. Years ago Cici used to go into the living room twice a week for cello lessons, until she bailed out of the school orchestra. The one day she took me to the threshold of that room Cici said it was a room to look into, just as we were doing. It wasn't a room to walk around in. She said, "My idea is Daddy should make like a movie of this room, you know, a long movie, with some famous-composer music playing in the background, and then we could put like a swimming pool in here, and then in the back you could have chairs and a screen where you could watch the movie of the living room and swim in the pool." Cici has a suite—actually a wing of the house—to herself. It is three rooms, all done in lavender wallpaper figured with lambs, calves, colts, and piglets. Her bathroom is pink. She loves her rooms, though, and her whole house, even though it's often lonely there, she's said. She has a younger sister, Gwen, who is in a home for mongoloids.

Last summer I had a lifeguard job, and Cici had a turquoise V-dub that she drove out to the peninsula to her job at Brighter Day Foods. Every afternoon when my shift ended, I would saunter in there for a peach yogurt and another look at her. She is a wavy deep-blonde, far too calmly beautiful for as young as she turned out to be. She is slender and fine-featured, alert and graceful as a deer. She is my height exactly, and she has never shaved. Her brown legs are silky with fine platinum hair. It is gold under her arms. Her skin is smooth and smells like herself, or like granola baking.

There was no way at all to resist her. No one could. I moved right in with wide smiles and daily jokes for her. Her high school boyfriend, a jealous, petulant, and handsome king-of-the-prom type, made trouble at first. She loved Brian, and maybe if he'd given her a little slack, he could've held on. Instead he gave her the fatal ultimatum—*him or me*—and he ended up the casualty. But not before ramming a two-by-four through the windshield of my car and then a bit hysterically duking it out with me in the Purple Onion parking lot—all of which helped my cause, I guess, though it was no fun while it was happening. I have to admit, besides, that my conduct through the prolonged seduction was ruthless. I snowed her under with casual flattery (a weapon young Brian had not discovered) and with late-night monologues about her freedom, her woman's future, and her right to make new friends and have new experiences. Cici listens constantly to the radio and is much affected by certain songs. I found an old 45 of a tough-sounding girl singing "You Don't Own Me," which I played for her those first evenings we spent alone at my house. Too late, after she was irretrievably mine, Brian counterattacked by mailing her LP's with every cut scratched out except for one sentimental song that he expected her to listen to in wretched remorse.

All this intrigue and turmoil precipitated a lot of passion, naturally. Still, I went slow with her. Virginity was a ghost she gave up at last in August, not long before I had to fly back east. It was splendid. She did a lot of moaning, writhing, and crying, and so did I. In the sun of my room we excitedly discussed our bodies—how we felt about our sweat and breath, our earlobes and toes. And I began writing to her about hers from college, giving her lyrical rundowns of my devotion to its every part. (She is perfect, except for her nipples, which are wonderful.

They are mismatched, one rosier and more swollen than the other until they pucker tight in sex to look almost alike.)

She isn't good with words. Her letters were disappointing. Her literary attempts at eroticism were painful. But we connected by phone once a month, which seemed to keep our love alive for a while. We told each other we were in love. We *were* in love, but the distances were too great, and Cici is too beautiful, I knew that. Our correspondence, a torrent in the fall, dried up to nothing when she stopped writing in April. I was down then about my threatful future, doing a lot of bad drugs—acid, speed, Romilar cough syrup—and I had a couple of college girlfriends, pliant and pretty, but not like Cici. Even so, I was sure my radiant presence would set things right again at home. But it hasn't, and with her mother standing me off again and again in her sugary, cold voice, I have been at a loss for action.

Until this morning. It's Thursday. Cici is in school. I had just convinced myself to drive to the high school, snatch her out of calculus, and make her give me what bad news there may be— right there in the locker-lined hallway. I had shaved and dashed on some of the Canoe she'd sent me for Christmas and was on my way out the door when the phone rang. It was Cici, I knew. But it wasn't, it was the old man. Now that he's through with me, I'm feeling too glum to be seen in the light of day, so I sit on the floor for a long time watching the canned goods in the open cupboard like a television tuning pattern. I unfasten one of the two emergency joints I have clipped into my ponytail with bobby pins, and I smoke it. Sunbeams move slowly across the drainboard, slanting and thinning until they're gone. I fish out the other joint and smoke that. At last I get up, scrub out a frying pan, set it on the gas, and scramble up six eggs with a can of chilies. As I dump them on a platter the phone rings again. I stand frozen, clutching the iron pan, too fucked up to answer. When the ringing stops, I hurl the pan at the oven and crease the broiler door.

After eating, I drink coffee, three cups, to restore my reason. That does no good, so I switch to beer and wander out to the patio. My three shiny new rackets, Kramers, lie on a redwood bench, toasting in the sun. I pick one up and swing it at some dead geraniums sticking out of pots like fingers. At the end of the follow-through I let go. It flies off into the ice plant. My blisters really are bad. Then, fuck it, I say to myself. Aloud I declare, "I'm *making* it! I'm getting in shape! I am doing it! You watch me! *I am doing it!*"

I leap into a run, a sprint to the Wedge. Over the jade hedge, into the drive, pounding down the road past cars cruising and cyclists ankling along, pouring it on like a madman toward the sand. I dig in my heels at the frothy border of the soup and flop down, blowing like a workhorse. Since last summer a few hours of semiserious Frisbee in the cemetery on the edge of campus amount to the only exercise I've had. My temples pulse. I'm dizzy. Out on the seam of the familiar planes of blue rests Catalina, dreamy as ever, as if to remind me of possibilities, and impossibilities. I used to think I would swim to it someday. I told friends I would, in a shark cage, Newport to Avalon, through thirty-odd miles of indifferent sea. Crazy. I have never much enjoyed swimming. Too much goes on in all that water that you can't know or see or prepare for.

I do thirty sit-ups and thirty push-ups and then trot down the hard sand to the Balboa pier. I buy some vitamins and raw wheat germ at Brighter Day Foods. The girl filling the grain bins says Cici doesn't work there anymore, she got fired.

"How come?" I ask.

"Got me," says the girl. "One day it's cozy around here, and then bingo, the next day he cuts her loose."

"Yeah? And you don't know what for?"

"Really. See, she was weekend help, that's all, and she had boyfriends in here pretty much playing feelies with her in the stockroom, but that wasn't it, I don't think."

I look at the floor. "What boyfriends?"

She drops her scoop into the sack and sneezes. "Whew." She sneezes again. "*Dust*. Wow." She wipes her eyes. "No, like, see I didn't know Cici real good. She was weekends, that's all. She had lots of boyfriends. Why, you one of 'em?"

"Not really."

"Well, I didn't talk to her. Dig it, I didn't want to. Like, she's the kind of girl that makes other girls just fade into the background, you know? And just *give up*, because, forget it, no matter what you do, what you buy, you're never gonna look like her. She's the flower on the bush and everybody else is just the leaves and stickers."

Outside in the heat again I set my parcel on the sidewalk and drop down for another set of push-ups. The concrete hurts my sore hand.

Mr. Busch jumps out of Busch Hardware across the street and calls over to me, "Will?"

I get up and gently brush off my palm.

"I thought that was you," he calls out. "Step inside a minute, Will. I want to talk to you."

I want to say "Go fuck yourself." I feel terrible. I want to say "Go fuck yourself" to everybody. But I don't say anything. I'm not in good command of my faculties.

All through my last two years of high school, after my tennis was shot out from under me like a cowboy's horse, I did nothing seriously but surf. I'd get up at five to surf before school. After school I surfed until nightfall. It was a religion and a drug. I surfed a lot then with the son of Mr. Busch, Andy Busch, who was the kind of friend I guess I needed at the time. He hardly talked. His fat father used to tell him how much of a bad influence I was, a no-good bum of a kid, how nobody gave a hoot what I did, and how if he went on acting like me he'd flunk school and have to join the navy. The high school deigned to give both of us diplomas, however, and Andy stayed home and commuted to Fullerton State College. Back east I didn't get one letter from him in answer to mine, but our communications had been always companionate and wordless anyway. We lost touch. That first winter Andy broke his leg skiing at Mammoth, quit riding waves, sold his board, and ended up slaving summers away in the hardware store. Once or twice I tried to get him out in the real good stuff again, to no avail. Andy disappeared, the Andy I knew. I never thought about what changed him.

Mr. Busch's Andy disappeared, too, I learn in the flickering bulb-lit interior of the store. He left home right after Easter. For points unknown. Mr. B. wants to know if I've heard from him

45

or if I can suggest a way to locate him without hiring a detective. All they've had from their only son is a brief note of apology that he sent from Seattle the week he skipped out, zero since.

"Why do you want to locate him?" I ask.

"Why? Will, he's my son, my *only* son. I love him. I want to just know that he's all right. Help him if he's in any more trouble. I know he needs us. He needs *some*body. He's been tripping over his own shoelaces since he was three years old."

"He's all right. You'd hear if he wasn't, I would think." Mr. Busch is a sad sight, pale as a plucked chicken with flab hanging off his jaws and arms. People can get old fast. He makes me worry about my own father, who was lanky and handsome years ago, before the whiskey went to work on him. What will he look like now?

"*Maybe*," says Mr. Busch. "But why would a child do this to his parents? His mother is sick, sick with worry. We protected him, gave him all he needed, and more. By Jesus, parties, allowance, everything. Now he does *this* to us. If it makes sense, I'm sorry, I don't see it."

"Well, when he took off, did he give a reason? What did his note say?"

"What reason could he give? There was no reason." He spread his arms wide. "This is his home. This is his family. You tell me the reason."

Those are the reasons, I'm thinking. And Mr. Busch probably knows they are without realizing he knows. I feel sorry for him. But I don't care a damn where Andy is, so long as he's safe, which I do not doubt. I gaze down at the worn wood floor and give a shrug. "You won't like this, Mr. Busch," I say, "but my advice is relax. I know Andy. He's OK. He'll make contact when he thinks the time's right, but you shouldn't try flushing him out, because that will only—"

"Nobody wants to flush him out! How can I relax when I know there's a problem? A big problem. He left because this problem exists, whatever it is, whoever's to blame, and if I could find out the problem, if *we* could find out, we could lock horns over it and work it out. You don't hide from these things,

46

Will. You face 'em, and you lick 'em, or else they lick you!" He lowered his voice. "You say Andy's OK. Maybe you've heard from him—but never mind, I know you wouldn't tell me. If you *can* connect with him, Will, I'm only saying please express what I said just now to him, that's my message. You see? I'm not flushing him out. Where he is doesn't matter. *How* he is does."

I shake my head. "Whatever way you get through to him, no matter why, you'll be flushing him out. So I still say relax is the best you can do."

"What in holy hell is wrong with you kids?" says Mr. Busch. "Tell me why we deserve this treatment, and I'll be fascinated. *Tell* me! This rebellion of yours, what is it against? Goodness? Tradition? By God, look at the hair on your head. What's that supposed to mean, that you want to actually look like that? Tell me. You do it, so you must have the answers. But I never get answers. I get nothing."

"I like my hair, Mr. Busch," I say.

"Of *course* you like it. *Why* do you like it? I like my dust mop, but I don't wear it down my neck. This is civilization we're talking about, what is normal, what is accepted, what is good for the sake of peace, *social* peace. You're all saying *peace, peace*, well, why don't you do something to *make* peace? You think peace doesn't have to be made and bought and paid for like everything else? Maybe we gave you too much, is that it? Did we love you too much, so now you expect to get it all free forever? Free peace? Free love? Is that the problem? Because if it *is* the problem, well, I can't help but say to you you're the ones on the dark side of it, not us. Civilization, that's what this is all about, nothing less. We've been years putting it together and making it tick and protecting it, and now you want to scrap it and start over? With what? Subsistence farming and Zen beads and LSD? 'Andy's OK.' I have to laugh at that one, I'm sorry. And if it's your thought that it's normal and *OK* to do what that poor kid did, then I have to laugh at you, too. Before I cry. You understand? Am I getting through to you? Can you see a particle of sense in the truth here, or are you part of the lost cause?"

"I think you just lost me, Mr. Busch," I say.

A pair of customers who've drifted in during this soliloquy are idling over by the key duplication machine, listening without choice, and making me feel all at once like an exposed shoplifter. Long ago, in a phase, I filched many items from Busch Hardware—tape measures, castors, a wrench set, batteries, BBs, and curtain rods (to make into arrows). Now gusts of guilt and resentment are buffeting me. Drugged, I am not weathering them very well. My body feels like the ocean in a bad chop, and my brain is a moon in the fog. Mr. B. does not let up either.

"We've lost *you*?" he says, closing his eyes in exasperation. "Oh, no, Will. No, you have lost *us*. We have not lost *you*. Civilization is an old old road. It's a well-trodden road by the footsteps of our forefathers, yours and mine, and it's just not that hard a road to follow. And if you don't, you're stumbling through the trees and the underbrush, can you see that? Am I being too symbolical for you?"

"No, I see what you mean. You're on the road, and we're off the road. You're making progress, and we're fooling around in the weeds."

He smiles harshly at me. "Oh, yes, I forgot. You do have spunk, don't you. That's a good quality, spunk—if you keep a leash on it." He sighs, "Ohhh, boy," and he holds up a raised finger toward his customers. "Well. You back in town for the whole summer, Will?"

I shrug.

"Find him for us, Will," he says. "I'm going to beg you. Find him—no more—just locate him and express what we're suffering, his mother and me, everybody that loves him, and try to make him know that whatever his high-blown case, or his problem, whatever it is, we want to help, OK? Please."

I am shaking my head, but before I can say forget it, he pleads, "*Try*, try, that's all I ask. Believe me, I don't want you to rat on him in any way. Just . . . OK," he says, "here." He hurries his bulk over to the cash register and clangs it open. "Here's twenty bucks. You find him, and you'll get a hundred more—on your word, Will, no more. Can you do it?"

I take the twenty. "Yeah," I say dully, "I can do it. I can try.

48

I'll ask around. But no promises, Mr. Busch. I got a very busy schedule."

"Well, for Andy, your buddy, I know it's not too much to ask. You just come to me here if there's anything I can do to help. I appreciate this, Will, in a big way."

I lightly shake the hand he stretches out to me, pocket my money, and leave.

The tree-lined street is electric in the sun, and across the way the varnished wood Brighter Day Foods sign sends a pain through my chest. *Cici, you're the one I have to find, talk to, bring to reason.* Finding her won't be hard. She's in school. But if she's avoiding me, those impersonal brick hallways are no place to confront her. Especially with some new football Lothario there palming her buns. Call, then. Call, you idiot. Don't wait.

It takes fifteen minutes to run home. On the way I decide the best thing to do about Andy is nothing. Maybe I'll return Mr. B.'s twenty in the mail, or maybe not. "Ask around"—shit. Who's there to ask? And why me? Why anybody? Even if Andy is chained to a cactus in Baja by crazed Indian dopers with ants in his nose and his tongue like burnt liver, I don't care. *Me, I'm* the one I care about, the only one, the main one, at least. And that's cool, isn't it? Sure. I have to spend my badly taxed resources on me, on my own search for harmony. Which for the moment can come only in the miraculous shape of Cici Marla Bamberger.

"This is Colonel Edmund Bamberger," I announce to the school secretary. "I have a matter of importance that I must talk over with my daughter, Cici Bamberger."

"Oh," says the secretary. "Well, if you will hold, Mr. . . . *Colonel* Bamberger, for a few minutes, I'll see about getting Cici to the phone. Or can she call you right back?"

"I'll hold," I say. I'm sitting naked on the dusty hallway bench, prepared to shower if Cici will meet me and to jerk off in despair if she won't. That's as far ahead as I've been able to plan for three days. Maybe I'm getting better. Anyway, I feel a little better—or else it's just the chocolate milk and No-Doz I had for lunch. My vitamins couldn't be working yet.

49

"Hello, Daddy?" says Cici.

"*Cici!*"

"Hello?"

"Cici, it's *me*, the light of your life."

"*Will!* Holy cow, I can't talk to you."

"What do you mean? You're talking to me now. Don't hang up."

"I mean I *can't*. I just—"

"Why *not*?"

"Because—be quiet—because, oh, God, I don't know, this is the guidance office. I can't talk in the guidance office."

"Then move your sweet self out to a phone where you *can* talk, and call me back in five minutes."

After a pause she says, "I, I don't think there is one. And anyway—"

"*Cici!* What the hell is wrong? Out in the trophy lobby there's a booth, and you know it. Why won't you talk to me? What's going on with you? You *have* to talk to me, or I'll do something crazy, Cici. I'll come after you. Come on. Just explain the trouble, all right? Don't I deserve that much?"

Silence.

"Don't I? Cici?"

"How should I know?" she says quaveringly.

My heart is thudding. I want to set the receiver down softly on the bench, slip out, and roar off to the school to find her, shake her and hold her, but she'd be gone like a rabbit before I had my pants on, I know. No, my voice is all I've got. "I love you, Cici," I whisper, going for broke before I lose that, too.

She lets out a long breath. "My mother found your letters."

"What? What do you mean she *found* them? She *read* them?"

"What do you think, she made them into paper dolls?"

"Jesus fucking Christ."

"I know, and now I can't see you, and I can't talk to you."

"That's illegal. Cici, that's your personal private correspondence. She can't *touch* it."

"And she showed them to Daddy."

"Oh, no. No, no, no."

"Yes, and Daddy said he'll see you spitting teeth before you ever come near me again."

"Wow," I say. "Well, the old fart-sack'll have to catch me first—and he's got a ton of scrap metal pinned to his chest. Cici, is that really what's wrong? That's nothing, a few love letters. We can get around that. We're bigger than that."

"God, Will, come off it. Those letters, *God*. One of them was a whole long essay with perverted metaphors and things all about my *vagina*. God, Daddy blew up like an A-bomb. He ripped up your pictures and everything. And I never even got to open your last two letters. Daddy burned them in the sink."

"The prick bastard! That's a fucking federal offense. He could be court-martialed. You know that? He *should* be shot."

"You know, Daddy downed five MIGs in Korea."

I grit my molars. "Christ Almighty. Cici, Cici, don't let them do this to us. I need you."

"I have to go."

"Wait. Where can I meet you? Where can I see you? You won't get away from me, Cici—not over chickenshit like this."

"Nowhere!" she says. "I can't. I—" Her voice breaks.

"I'll be outside the band room at three."

She swallows and sighs. "Go ahead. But I get out early again for the doctor's."

"OK, what doctor? What for?"

Now the tears are in her voice. "I don't have to tell you anything. Would you please leave me alone, Will? It's all changed. You don't know. It's not the same anymore. You can't—I mean, oh, you can't fix it, Will. Not now. Good-bye."

"You *love* me," I say, not sure whether it gets through. The white phone *brrrrs* on in my ear, like the sound of my headache. I press the button with my toe to clear the line and dial out her old number, 522-4117, a pattern of numerals always charmed by her "Hello" at the end of it. This time, though, it's her treacherous mother.

"Mrs. Bamberger, this is the doctor's office," I say. "Is Cici certain to make her appointment this afternoon?"

"The doctor's?" she says.

"Yes indeed," I say.

"Dr. Fuller?" she says doubtfully.

"No, Fuller's associate, Dr. Busch," I say.

"Oh, yes. Well . . . yes, she has a note for two o'clock. It's not two o'clock yet, is it?"

"No, no, just calling to confirm. And to ask how she's been in your view since we saw her last."

"It's still the same," the mother says slowly. "Except . . . except, more food-balls."

Food-balls? "Food-balls. Yes?"

"In the same places, but now under her bed, too, Doctor. As if she does it, and then forgets. How can she *forget*?"

"How indeed," I say. "Food-balls same as always?"

"Well, mostly. They . . . they're . . . it's like they're chewed bread, like dough, and now there's the chewed vegetables—raw carrots and whatnot, we're getting that."

Though the name of the doctor—Fuller—is all I'm after, my ruse is such an exhilarating success that I get carried away, and stupidly, I ask, "Mrs. Bamberger, could you describe for me how Cici is bearing up under her father's anger?"

"His anger?"

"Yes. She's spoken of a display of anger—paternal anger, within the past month or two. Were you a witness to the anger?"

"Well, now, Doctor—uh . . ."

"Busch."

"I can't see how this—whatever you're referring to—is part of her diet problem, and I would have to talk this over with her father before saying . . . any comments. Also, we—"

"Mrs. Bamberger, the diet problem may be a very deep-seated problem."

"Are you a *psychiatrist*?" she demands.

"Psychologist."

"You know, we specifically asked Dr. Fuller to hold off on this mental kind of tinkering until we thought it over long and hard. Now—what are you again?"

"Dr. Andrew Busch, PhD in psychology and advanced psychology, Harvard University, 1959."

"Yes. Well, all right, Doctor. I'll bring it up with Colonel Bamberger on Friday when he's home. But ask Fuller—*Doctor* Fuller. He'll remember what her father said about any mental involvements."

"We understand Colonel Bamberger quite well, Mrs. Bamberger," I say. "And we will do no mental exploring at all without his approval—on our word as physicians."

"I know, but I'll tell him what you said anyway. I'm sure he'll get back to you."

"Fine. Well, if there's nothing else, Mrs. Bamberger, we appreciate your help. Good day."

I groan and slump from the bench to the cool floor tiles. Christ. *Diet* problem. Poor Cici. Nobody's more careful about what she puts into her unearthly form than Cici—tofu, bulgur, fresh fish, sunflower seeds, whole-grain everything, snacks of kohlrabi and ricotta cheese—she *knows* how to eat, and her lunkhead of a mother always gives her no end of shit about it, since every other night they have T-bones and eye rounds that Cici wouldn't touch with a ten-foot chopstick. Now they've sicced the medics on her, the fools.

I feel like I could use a medic myself. Or at least a massage. My shoulders throb from the morning's push-ups, and my feet are cramping from the strain of running in sand. Once I was swathed in elastic, reliable fitness like a wet suit. I could run the length of the peninsula and swim back in the same day without later feeling any residue of bodily protest. Now look at me. Twitching and aching like an old— But wait, what the fuck—I am only twenty-one years old! Come *on*! This is prime-time city! There's nothing in my way but work, hard work. Yes, that and maybe my own overanxious ambition. I have to take it easy. I'll do it. I can do it all.

I get up, brushing the sand from my cold ass. A faint-feeling passes behind my eyes like steam.

The dark downstairs bathroom, where the indoor shower is, smells of mildew and medicine. It has no window. The light comes from dim bulbs in sconces flanking the mirror. One shelf in the towel cabinet holds over a hundred prescription-drug bottles and vials with snap-lids, and drops, sprays, and ointments;

53

about half are Lou's and half the old man's. The metal walls of the shower stall are somehow nourishing a gray profusion of tiny life, in patterns, like ferns or frost. I shower fast. Even in the sun my hair will take two hours to dry, and I figure I'll need every fine advantage face-to-face with Cici. In the mirror my eyes look a little pink, but not bad. They'll clear by three. I bound upstairs to my room for another anointment of Canoe. It's awful stuff. Probably Cici has never smelled it. She doesn't know colognes, or sports, or cars, or books, or nature. Cici. She was so treasurably young last summer, wrapped up in wrangles with her difficult mother, in her first real job, in plans for college, in health food and yoga and drugs. And in the subtle wonders of passion. Thanks to God, and me. I take out her photos again. They're a treasure themselves.

The Yellow Pages reveal Jas. M. Fuller (MD, Practice Limited to Internal Medicine) to have two offices, one at Hope Memorial Hospital on the Coast Highway and another, by the address, a half-mile from the first on Harbor Boulevard in Costa Mesa. No trouble. I'll try the hospital first.

Decked out in red surfer trunks, sandals, and a black muscle shirt, I wait in the rippling air of the hospital parking lot until two forty-five, then stroll in through the busy lobby to the wall directory. Masters, Fuller, Gottlieb, and Thorgalsen share 201. On the door a gold sign says WALK IN.

The waiting room is empty. A hatless nurse in blue sits at a counter behind glass, like a bank teller. She looks up at me smiling. "You're not Shaw, are you?"

"No, sorry. I'm here to pick up Cici Bamberger, when she's finished with Dr. Fuller."

"You too, eh?"

I affect a puzzled expression. "You mean somebody else has already got her?"

"No," says the nurse. "Cici missed her appointment today—without cancellation. You're the second young lug in ten minutes who's come by to whisk her away. That shouldn't surprise me, I guess, knowing Cici."

"So you're saying she didn't show?"

"That's what I'm saying," she says.

I thank her and head back on the run to the parking lot, sandals slapping. I left the motor idling and the roof down, and I have twelve Coors on ice in a cooler on the backseat. It's very hot. I pour down half a can before I drop my hand to push for third gear. My head is blank as the sky. *Find her*, that's all I'm thinking.

I speed north as fast as the thickening boulevard traffic will allow but get bogged down a good mile from my turn west on Adams. *Shit*, it's the wrong way to come this time of day. I sit breathing exhaust in a sea of frustrated machinery that's churning and crawling along like lava. Two more beers of this is enough. I jerk around in my seat and motion for room to the woman behind me. She backs up a foot. I back and bull the Porsche out of my slot in the left lane, jump two wheels onto the traffic island, and scream down the side of the jam in first.

It's an accident at the intersection, three GM behemoths and a crushed Fiat askew on the glittering pavement, eight or ten citizens dazed in the heat, some standing, some kneeling, two on their backs in blood. A corner of Hell. No cops yet, but their ice-blue flashes are advancing out of the distance.

The winter before, twisted on cherry brandy and one or two other stimulants probably, a college friend and I were nabbed by a policeman for dumping oatmeal off the balcony of a movie theater. You had warm oatmeal in a plastic bag, and at the right moment you leaned out over the rail, yelled "Blaaaaah," and dumped the bag. It was Norton's idea. He hadn't done it since high school. Like the morons we were, we stuck around to see the movie's finish and were fingered by an usher for a cop waiting under the marquee. He sat us in his prowler and lectured and threatened us for twenty minutes before sending us back inside to get mops. Beside me on the car seat was his cop hat, from which I had the temerity to remove his badge. It unscrewed like a shirt stud.

Since then I've had the badge fastened into my black leather billfold ready for use in just the sort of emergency that I now find my selfish self, at the rush-hour wreck on Harbor Boulevard three thousand miles from Onondaga County, which is what it says on my chromium badge.

Only one of the cars, a station wagon hunkered down in a lake of engine coolant, blocks me from an open run down Adams. The injured look to be lying enough out of the way for me to slip by into the clear.

I jump out of my car and trot up to a knot of involved parties holding out my open billfold like a paperboy hawking Extras. I say, "Accident Investigation, Accident Investigation."

"We need an *ambulance*," says somebody. "Where's the darn ambulance?"

"It's coming," I say. I hope it is. I can't even glance down at the woman near my feet. I catch just her bare legs stretched out over the tar and sand.

Nobody says anything. There is some weeping going on.

"Whose vehicle is that? The wagon," I say, pointing to it. "That vehicle must be moved for the ambulance."

An older man in Bermudas goes over to the wagon and tries to fire it up, but it won't catch. Sirens are coming from all directions by the sound of them. The flashing police cars are closing in through the congestion ahead.

"Help push!" I call out. "Let's move this tank."

The older man hops out of the wagon, and with four others we shove it back six feet into a light pole. I run to my car, ease it around the white-legged victim and through the stricken throng, and move off at moderate speed down Adams toward Brookhurst, the road I should have taken to start with. I have to pull to the shoulder to let a white ambulance going *wheep-wheep* zoom past toward the accident. In my rearview the cop-lights now ricochet around the scene, cauterizing it, trimming its ragged edges. I reach behind me for a beer and shiver and shake my head to loosen the gruesome images inside. Those accident people were so . . . agog, that's it. Agog. And I looked no one in the eye. Well, anyway, it's a good thing we moved that smashed wagon. Really, I insist to myself, that was a good thing to do.

I can't chance a swing down Cici's curving street, windowless though her house is on that side—my Porsche is too familiar a machine by sound as well as sight, and the street is a cul-de-sac. Spewing gravel, I swerve into the access lane to a monstrous power-line tower in a compound set off by chain-link fencing, and I sit there as my dust overtakes me, dulling the glass of my gauges, twinkling down onto the seats, and over my wet skin. Shit: I've switched off the key.

Once—and not long ago—this was a sprawling orchard flat as a griddle. Now shaved of trees, it has sprouted fire hydrants, dark shrubbery, and lots of painted lumber. It's still flat. I'll never get the car chugging again without another person to push. Far off on one dry lawn two kids are fighting over something that has the smaller one wailing. They are the only animals in sight.

I fling away the beer can and open another before getting out of the car. I have no plan and no expectations. I want to see Cici, no more. My instinct can take it from there. But what to do now? Creep in the daylight through these plots of private dwellings to some possible angle of view toward the Bamberger estate? Yes. But how? And what then? Again, questions awaiting the reply of instinct. Seeing Cici is all that matters.

Looped from tower to tower, the high power lines cut an unimpeded swath through the neighborhood, marching on as far as I can see toward the buff mountains, where they seem to undulate in the heat-weary air. The next tower enclosure, I know, is at a corner of the Bamberger backyard, where it interferes with their television reception, according to Cici. That spot, which can be approached most easily in a roundabout way from another street a mile or two away, offers the only somewhat neutral ground within eyeshot of Cici's wing of the house. The quickest route to the tower, however, lies straight ahead, across just a few parcels of landscaped terrain. From my trunk I withdraw my yellow hard hat, an item I lifted one night last summer from a building site (Cici took one, too), to wear in disguise, and set out determinedly in the direction of the next tower. As I walk along through the first two yards, peering with a concerned expression into the pale sky, no one stops me, but when I hop the rail boundary of the third to pick my way (barefoot now) among a lot of well-mulched rose bushes, a woman's voice calls out: "Excuse me! Excuse me!"

"Excuse *me*," I say, turning toward the house. I see no one.

"Just what seems to be the problem?" comes the irritated voice.

"That's what we're trying to find out, ma'am," I say. I still can see no one, no face in the windows.

Then she appears around one side of the house, rolling along a ramp in a gleaming wheelchair. "This is private property, I'll have you know," she says breathlessly.

"Certainly," I say. "But the air corridor belongs to the company. Just a quick inspection, ma'am. Sorry to disturb you."

"Inspection of what?" she says.

"Deterioration. Hawk damage. The company should have telephoned you about all this," I say, moving on calmly as I can. The next tower is between the next plot and Cici's house. She'll forget me, I hope, once I'm out of sight.

"Well, then, I'll telephone *them*," she says. "Where's your identification? Who's your supervisor?"

"Please do. Call Mr. Busch," I say, and I give her my Balboa phone number. "But nobody's there to answer at this hour."

"We'll see," she snaps and wheels around up the ramp and behind the house.

Trouble. But not very serious trouble, and I've come too far for retreat. I march unnoticed across the next bedraggled yard to the giant tower's barbed-wire-topped fence. A big sign there says DANGER—NO TRESPASSING—HIGH VOLTAGE—DANGER. I slink around the outside of the enclosure into the Bambergers' thick bamboo hedgebreak, which has been planted to block out the ugly chain-link fencing from their cozy domain. I'm safe in the bamboo, but I can't see much. I take off my hard hat. What I need is a periscope. I have one, too, but it's home in my closet. Well, you can't think of everything. Worse, sometimes you can't think of anything. Now my poor thoughts are still not adding up, and my instincts are not coming to the rescue. It is *hot*. I am sore to the bone—legs, feet, shoulders, stomach—all that frenzied exercising. I have to empty a full bag of beer, which, on my knees, I do, making a patch of froth on the ground. Climbing the tower was my first mad notion, but even if I could top the barbed wire—in bare feet—the view its height might afford would expose me to the risk of being spotted myself and to the risk of being electrocuted. Besides, what could I do from there after I saw her, *if* I saw her? I have no idea. But seeing Cici, her hair, her skin, just her lithe self in motion, at any distance, is still the prime imperative among all my otherwise whimsical needs.

I crouch in the bamboo, stinking richly of Canoe, trying to come up with some plan of further attack. I come up with zero. I crab along to the boundary of the little thicket, conscious of my fire-red trunks and my lemon-yellow hard hat, which I have in hand. Most of their yard is in sight, close-cropped grass, a spindly citrus secured by wire and stakes, their placid pool nearby, and a lot of pool junk around it. The house windows are curtained against the sun. Nothing moves. There is no breeze, no noise above the drone of distant planes and trucks. I shut my eyes, hoping for inspiration. After a minute they spring open at the sound of a screen door wheezing against its piston. I duck low to the ground. It's—shit, it's Cici's awful mother mincing toward the pool, her hair in a black lacquered heap, like licorice cotton candy. And God, look how she's dressed! In red-hot pants and a black sleeveless blouse—like me! Strange. Carrying a tinkling drink and a magazine, she settles herself in a plastic lounge chair just ten yards away. I hear her sigh. Then from the Bamberger kitchen, it seems, comes the ringing of a phone. The mother does not stir. She knows Cici will get it! Cici is home! Christ, if I can sneak by her mother and into the house I'll have Cici to myself for a few moments, maybe longer. And I can leave by the front door. Simple! Wait—the front door—that's *it!* I will creep silently back through the bamboo to the vacant yard of her neighbor, run to the street, and go *in* the front door. No sneaking called for. But the phone keeps ringing, yet the mother makes no dash for it. Maybe Cici is in the shower—the thought gives me goosebumps. The phone stops. All *right*, a *plan*.

As I ease backward into the denser growth of bamboo, the dry shucks crackle, and I freeze. Mrs. Bamberger pays no attention. I peer among the stalks at her profile. She isn't reading or sipping. She is lounging, letting her time pass. She hates me. Some part of her is probably hating me this minute. And why? Because I have kissed and adored her perfect daughter? No, because I have kissed and adored the shell-pink lips of her daughter's cunt. And she knows. She has read my florid words. But—well, Jesus, you sad old bitch, *look* at her! That's all it should take. One perceiving look and you'd know, you'd *know* if I am the first, I am not the last. Starting now, for twenty years at least, your California princess will stop the heart of every man she meets. And every man will dream of doing for her all the things I've done—and all the things I may never get around to doing. What would you protect her from? Love? Pleasure? Knowledge? Change? Forget it. She's gone. You're finished. You gave her what you could. Now it's my turn.

Hunching down like a cartoon Comanche, I pad swiftly over the neighbor's scorched lawn to the corner of the house next door to Cici's. Its draperies are drawn. Music wafts to me from across the way, a tune by the Monkees. A boy on a skateboard clacks by down the empty street. I stand still, panting. OK. In two seconds I'll scamper across the expanse of crushed stone spread before the Bamberger home, hop the steps, part the huge, paneled double doors, and slip inside like a wraith. I will tiptoe to Cici's suite, where she will be toweling her darkened mass of apricot hair, naked, and I will—

A white police cruiser comes whispering around the curve. I press myself to the searing wall. The wheelchair woman must have blown the whistle—unless this is his routine beat. But he's going too slow for that. *Shit.* He should be back at the accident. I dart behind the house. I am out of breath and drenched with sweat. The tops of my dirty feet glisten. My hair clings to my back. I glance around me at the zigzag horizon of roofs and wires, waiting for him to pass. He has three or four houses to prowl before the turning circle at the road's dead end. There's time to make the sprint safely if he doesn't pick out my red trunks in his mirror. And if Cici's front door is unbarred. I tuck my hard hat under my arm. The cruiser oozes by, brake lights glowing. I wait, stooped low . . . then break for the blank façade of the Bamberger home.

"Yaaaaahhh," I let out in a breath when my bare feet hit the crushed stone. *Jesus.* With knees bent I prance across the vicious stuff fast as I can. The hot brass lever gives to my palm.

The portal swings in, loosing a flood of arctic air. With my heel, I nudge the heavy door shut against the jamb.

The foyer is chill and dark as a cave. I blink frantically to tune in my sun-blasted vision. It is quiet: no radio, a bad sign. My pupils adjust. Nothing seems to have changed since my last visit almost a year before. Plush, unusable furnishings pose like props along the wide hall. Straight ahead, I remember, are the sitting room, dining room, and kitchen; to the left the vast, forbidden living room, and to the right a second hall leading to the complex of bedrooms, the Colonel's study, and at the end, Cici's suite.

I don my hard hat to free both my hands and press on into the dim interior. I tiptoe. Once I turn the corner I know there will be no escape if the slit-eyed mother returns to the house. But that is the risk, and not a bad one, since she hates me already.

When I round the corner and bend my ear to the veiled trilling of her voice, I am sunk. Cici is singing! She is imitating Frankie Valli: ". . . You'd be like heaven to touch, I wanna *hold* you *so* much. . . ."

"Cici!" I barely speak it, but there is a reply, a toneless muttering somewhere behind me.

I stop. Faintly, Cici sings on, even as I hear a *clickety-clickety* sound, like beans spilled over the tiled floor. I turn. The sound increases . . . until—fucking *Jesus*, a huge canine horror swings the corner. It faces me, stock-still.

"Good dog," I whisper.

It crouches. "*rrrrRRRR . . .*"

"Easy, boy, *easy*."

"*RRRRAOWFF!*" It leaps.

I scream. Then I do all I can do. I whip off my hard hat and smash it like a pie into the dog's evil maw.

Its glancing bulk spins me sideways, its lunge carrying it against the wall. I spring into the nearest room as it scrabbles for footing on the tiles.

"Ruby!" yells Cici.

I slam the door into the beast's hurtling chest, hoping to crush a leg in the door frame. But the door shuts clean. A thumbbolt locks it.

"Mommy?" calls Cici over the dog's ferocious clamor.

My eyes fly about the Colonel's dim study, searching for a weapon, or a window.

"MOM?" Cici shouts. *"MOM!"*

I run to where the sun is paling a long wall of draperies and beat them back. I blink in the glare. No latches, no cranks, it's all fixed glass—a modern home.

Behind a black desk, big as a bed, stands a great vinyl chair too heavy to throw. I yank at the drawers. They're locked. I take a furious swipe at a pile of letters and scatter them over the carpet. Then in a corner I spot a wrought-iron floor lamp. Yanked from the socket, its cord snags in the landing gear of a sky-blue jet fighter. The plane flips off its pedestal and crashes into a stand of files. With the lamp I bash out the window. Heat swarms in. I knock away the jagged pieces, step back, and somersault out onto a brick pathway at the side of the house.

I have failed. In spades. Also I have sliced a flap of skin the size of a soup spoon from the heel of my foot. Also, when I limp around the bend toward my dead car, that pearl-white police cruiser is nosed up to it like a jackal, with its radio spitting and grunting.

My father was not far wrong. Lou was in Paris, all right, and she was in Paris with Bad Barry Glines. For the fortnight of the French Open they'd been lent a spectacular little studio in Montmartre on the Butte over an old restaurant with six tables called La Maison Rose. Some nights they could hear the services sung at the Sacré-Coeur. And mornings from their oak breakfast table through many small panes of wavy glass they could survey the whole russet and ivory city from the Marais to the Trocadéro. It was bliss.

And befitting bliss in its treasured rarity, it was brief. Lou believed an afternoon of pâtés and cheeses is what did her in, but the doctor, a silver-haired woman in an office crammed with gilt furniture, said it was certainly a virus, which was a lucky thing, Barry told the doctor, because otherwise he would have gas-bombed the café.

When Lou got sick, they'd been in Paris six days. Barry had demolished a little-known Czech in the first round. In the second he met a relaxed and cagey Frenchman, familiar with the pressed-sand surface at the Roland Garros Stadium, who blocked back everything until he was forced to hit and then hammered placements with surprising precision. From a seat at courtside Lou gave Barry advice by means of a code they'd worked out that had to do with all the ways she could wear or hold her wide-brimmed hat. Barry won in three long sets, but in the process damaged a tendon in his elbow when he reached back to volley a ball that was almost past him. He half-heard and half-felt the little snap. The pain didn't start until they were entering the restaurant, for the cheese and pâté lunch, as Barry was trying to discourage a group of autograph seekers by gesturing at them like a person slapping another person's face and saying, "*Rien, rien, rien*" (using a high percentage of his available French), a routine that Lou thought hilarious. It was then he knew he was really hurt.

While Lou made for a sunny table, Barry hung back, flexing and massaging his big hairy arm, his heavy brow gathering together like a thunderhead over the plains.

"What's the matter now, sweetie?" asked Lou, who loved tyrannical, moody men like Barry and like Big Jack, her father, and so in loving them relished their little rages. As a girl growing up, on those days of her father's most combustible tempers, she of all the household was the one who went on as usual, not tiptoeing or making sure radios didn't blare or plates clash. Of course, Louise was Daddy's honey-baby, the youngest and prettiest of three girls, and she understood from the first that this charmed her. When Jack's wrath at last would erupt and he stomped and bellowed and broke things, Lou found herself pleased not out of relief, but in wry appreciation of strength, of touching bone-headed masculinity. Barry was much like Jack, except he was a burly boy, and hers to have, too (as Jack never was), like a bear on a leash.

Barry didn't answer her and didn't take his chair either, but stood kneading his arm and glowering about the noisy glassed-in room as if looking for some sawed-off Frog to blame and then clobber. This was his first trip abroad—if you forgot Mexico, which was not a bad idea. Mexico was an eighteen-karat shithole. England had been all right, what little of it he'd seen passing through on the boat train to Paris. It looked grimy and decrepit like the East Coast, say Baltimore, though of course it was obviously foreign. Not near as foreign as France, though. The French were dark and runty like Mexicans, but not weaselly and greasy like Mexicans. They were jabbering, cocky, and proud-acting, and hard to figure. Like, proud of what? The age of the place? No question, it was a fucking *old* country. It was so old even the new things looked old, like the telephones and the cars. OK, so some of the oldness was history, but most of it—buildings, roads, stores, even things like elevators and toilets—was just old. Not poor—*old*. You'd think they'd junk it and get with Today, move into modern civilization. Like on the sidewalks they still had these scummy green booths where you go in and take a piss, not into any drain, but right on the fucking pavement. And this was Europe, not some crapola country in South America. Unbelievable. The women were jazzy-looking, not exactly cute, kind of weak and pale, but—*ooo-la-la*, right? The men—half of them came off like fags, and the rest like either low-level hoods or high-level snobs. Hardly anybody looked normal. The whole place was just bent.

Barry himself didn't look normal, even in California. He was a giant. The effect of his six-five height was intensified by his weight-lifter's breadth and tree-trunk legs and accented by the mass of ebony curls he wore on his already enormous noggin. He was used to stares, but not to clusters of tag-along gawkers who pegged him as some kind of American celebrity worth a good look. Barry loved these attentions, but they were so new and constant that he pretended he hated them. His growling and dodging only made the gawkers—and particularly the photographers—more persistent. Moreover, his liaison with the forty-year-old tennis queen had made him an especially good story for some markets, and Bad Barry stood confused between his enjoyment of his infamy and his resentment of its consequences.

Lou leaned up for a handful of his shirt and tugged him back behind the table. He sat.

"Come on now. Tell Mom what's the matter."

"My elbow's fucked," Barry said.

She frowned. "Where?"

"Right along in here," he said, tracing the pain with his fingers.

"Here?"

"Yeah, deep in."

"Nuts," said Lou. "You strained a tendon. You haven't *lived* until you've strained a tendon."

"No, I've done that. This is worse."

"You *strained* it worse, maybe, but that's what the hurt is, if that's where you feel it." She smoothed his forehead with her hand. "They heal up, honey. You can play with it."

"I don't know, Louise. I think this time it's fucked."

She studied him. "Well, hell. Maybe you popped it. Christ. But how could you do that, Barry? Did you feel anything go in there—all of a sudden?"

Barry told her he couldn't remember, and after two bottles of Pouilly Fuissé that afternoon he really couldn't, though the pain remained undiminished through the night. He rubbed Lou's neck with his left hand only while she threw up into their marble-topped sink.

The next day was hot, which Lou said was fortunate. "Warm up," she advised, "with fifteen minutes at least of nothing but forehands, and then take two or three aspirin with two cups of water, rest five minutes, and hit as usual for another fifteen." Barry took a cab out to Auteuil alone early that morning and bulled through the few waiting fans into the players' lounge. There was a jolly poker game going on, which he ignored, throwing himself into a plastic chair that overlooked the empty stadium court. No one among the three or four others in the room who knew Barry well enough to tell him hello did so, sullen as he seemed. Today he had reasons for seeming that way, but no one cared or wondered what they were.

With great success in his short months on the circuit, Barry had cultivated a terrible reputation. The role of tennis's anti-gentleman, of the outrageous villain, was one nobody realized was vacant until Barry filled it. He was a natural. He had genuine godlike contempt for almost everyone and an adversarial view of the world at large. During matches, first of all, he always wore a black shirt. Also, he spat, swore, farted, stalled, glared at everyone, made derisive comments about his opponents and clapped at their mistakes. So far, this unheard-of behavior had been tolerated by officials and tournament committees because of Barry's youth and talent, and because he guaranteed a big gate. Disgusted players and fans were urged to forgive his antics—his "style" was a way some put it—and to let him mature and learn for himself how he was bleeding his own tennis for the sake of a unique public image. Anyone who really knew Barry, as Lou did, saw he would never change much, not toward some hoped-for rectitude at least. He was special. His angers were entrenched. And a lot of his brutal attacking game was actually fired by the sparks of true ill-feeling he was able to provoke in people around him.

This said, it was a subdued Bad Barry Glines that faced fifth-seeded Tom Okker that morning on the new show court at Roland Garros. The slight, speedy Dutchman whipped off the first set at love, making sure on the change-overs to cross around the net away from Barry to keep their contacts at a minimum. But today the brooding Californian showed no spirit at all until the last point of the set, when instead of guiding his racket through a return of Okker's service, he raised it like a hammer above his head and splintered it into the ground. The gallery booed. Barry stalked off without a glance at the umpire, who did not default him as Barry expected, but disqualified him for bad sportsmanship and recommended that the French Tennis Federation hit him with an eye-opening fine.

The scathing press accounts that followed did acknowledge his anemic play, and some, noting the absence of Lou's big hat and brash cheers from the bleachers, dared hint of some rift between the highly visible lovers. Okker had never played Barry before and declared only that he was surprised, not offended. Fortunately, in the dressing room before the match, Barry had run into Dwight Saunders, once a trainer for the British Davis Cup team and an old friend of Lou's. Briefly, they had talked about Barry's injury. "Well, go knock a bit and see," was Dwight's advice. "It's no shame to default should it come to that. Just don't plug gamely on if it's knifing you." After the storm Dwight gathered up Barry's abandoned gear and then made an effort to rein in the gleefully rampaging reporters by giving them the scoop on the elbow. Later, as coach, Lou passed on through Dwight some corroborating messages about awful pain, needed rest, possible cortisone treatments, and the chance that Barry would have to bypass Wimbledon, where tennis watchers had been predicting a comeuppance awaited the rude American.

"My *dick*," said Barry, crumpling shut the *Tribune*. "I'll play Wimbledon. I better."

"*Maybe* was all I would say," said Lou. "Perhaps, I said. Anyhow, if you get no tune-up on the grass, there's no point showing your ugly mug over there, and you know it. I got a hot doctor lined up in New York. We see him, then we decide if we're coming back."

"But no needles," said Barry.

"Baby, if you need a needle, you get a needle, and that's that."

"Fuck that. Hey, Mama, I *do* Wimbledon, and I *don't* do any needles."

"I hope so, Barry, truly. Hell, at this point I'd take any kind of needle if it would bring *me* around."

Barry slapped her gently with the newspaper. "Hey, I got a needle for you. I got the joy-jabber, I got the tube-steak. . . ."

Lou laughed. "You're cute, but nuts. No, now—no, *stop. Stop!* Just keep packing, sweetie. We're not missing this flight. It was tough enough getting it."

Lou was curled up in a long red nightgown on a velvet sofa with one armrest. On the floor next to her was a clean white enamel pot. Barry was folding clothes on the bed and tossing them in no order into four open suitcases that almost filled the rest of the room. He was drinking beer out of a liter bottle.

"Half these things stink, they're so dirty," he said.

"Can't be helped," said Lou.

He went on folding, not noticing now the musical voices rising from the cobbled street through their casements, nor the astonishing view tucked into two such small windows. Lou and Barry had agreed if they could buy the place, as they wanted to try to do, they'd rip out the wall and put in a bow window with a wide shelf under it for a seat cushion. They'd pick up all the right furniture, all suede and chrome, stick in recessed lighting and hanging plants . . . it would be marvelous, you could shoot it for *Vogue*, Lou had said just a few days before.

"And we could move here. We could *live* here," said Barry. He gripped her bare shoulders, holding her away from him. They'd been walking through the Versailles gardens, hand in hand, nuzzling, kissing. Then, Barry had played only his first match, against the hapless Czech, yet he was already thinking beyond Okker to probably Newcombe in the quarters, Laver in the semis. . . . Jesus, it would be too righteous to *win* this big mother. Well, whatever happened they'd stay a few more days resting before England, and maybe they'd return for a week after Wimbledon. And maybe they *would* buy the little love nest in Montmartre. How would it be to live in Paris? Bitchen, for a while. The food really was far-out. He'd learn French, buy a Maserati.

Lou was looking up at him with a broad loving smile. "Well, we could just come here whenever we wanted."

"*Come* here? You wanna come—right *here*?" Barry slid his thumbs down over her breasts.

She shivered and pressed her face to his chest. "Honey, I could come just smelling you."

But that was days before, days like weeks in a summer gone by. How can bliss be so frail and fleeting? Now Lou lay groaning to herself, and Barry, bent to his packing, in gray shorts and a gray shirt that said TROJANS across the front, was stewing over his terrible luck.

Suddenly he shouted, "*You* know how good I am."

She sighed.

"*Louise?*"

"Damn right," she said.

"Then what's *wrong* with these cocksuckers? Why do they keep writing this shit?"

"It's a living. Anyhow, my dear, you are no help to the cause."

"Bull*shit*! I'm good, OK? I'm *great*! I'm better than Smith, Riessen, Richey, Ralston, all those guys. Like that is *it*, and that's what counts. What can I do? Who do I gotta blow before I get treated fair, that's all—fair, like any other scumbag on the tour?"

"Give it time, kiddo. You just came up. Who've you knocked

off so far? OK, a few big names, but not Ashe, not Laver, not Rosewall, not—"

"Rosewall! You *saw* that match. We went over it. That punky guy—"

"Listen to me! Not even old Gorgo Gonzales. He won't even *hit* with you when nobody's looking! And—oh, hell. Come *on*, Barry, sure your game is as good as anybody's. Maybe better. But your act is bush. And that is the story, in more ways than one."

"That's got fucking nothing to do with it—my *act*. What am I, an athlete or a movie star?"

Lou snorted. "Yeah," she said. "When you can answer that one you'll have a lot of answers."

Barry grabbed an Anjou pear from a basket at the bedside and side-armed it across the little room into the plaster wall over Lou's couch. She didn't flinch.

Barry said, "I think they're ripe."

"You eat 'em. I'm sick."

"No, I'll save 'em for when you get better." He dumped the six pears into the suitcase.

As much as anything else, Lou was homesick. She'd been out of the country just three weeks, but she wasn't traveling as well as she did ten years before, not recovering fast enough from time changes and bad sleep to stay even-tempered. She had always liked Australia, so that part, the first leg, working with the girls on the Cup team, had been OK. But then she'd left early and alone on the endless Sydney to LA haul, getting bollixed-up across the date line just to rendezvous with Barry and scarf down a cheeseburg dinner right there in the terminal in time to jet over the pole to Heathrow (thirty-six hours in transit, like a goddamn footlocker), all so they could get Barry out of the state before his father, Austin Glines, the director, returned from doing location in Panama.

After Sydney's winter, London's sudden summer was like a sauna. Since he'd missed the Italian Open, Lou set up some training matches for Barry on the clay, but she made no progress toward stamina herself. She got a bad enough headache just sitting in the heat watching him lunge and slide around making dust. Then, Paris. The first few days were glorious, perfect. At last, together in their own secret heaven, with time for each other, without friends phoning and dropping by, without home-life routines eating up the hours. . . . Well, that was finished now. Now Lou was happy to be heading home.

Poor Barry, though: his first Wimbledon, and plugged into the draw without having to slog through the qualifiers, either. Shoot, if he really could do it, if she believed he could, they'd skip back across the Channel today, check into the Gloucester and ring up Marion at Queens Club to reserve a practice court for days and days. But now—hell, now his arm ached when he brushed his teeth. They'd need luck and magic to bring it back for Forest Hills. That news would touch him off but good. She'd have to break it on the plane. Or better maybe wait, huddle with the Doc, and let *him* break it. Then what? Then home, she hoped, and some rest on the beach, and Barry's pop, too, the old fire-breathing bull, and, and also . . . (What now came rising through her swirling thoughts was I, Will, her son waiting half a world away. Pears made her think of me. I used to do a trick with fruit, usually pears because I could eat them core and all. I would juggle five or six, snatching bites as they came around until they were all gone. When she was home, Lou would keep pears around so she could trot me out before her cocktail guests like the queen's fool. Under her shrewd and condescending gaze, if I did feel in those days like a fool—a boy cankered with hopeless faults—she did not see me as one. I was just a child, lacking sense and immediate value, like all children. But *now*, now that I'd set myself the task of becoming a star in a summer's time, she wondered if I wasn't still a child, stoned on fantasies.) Or else he's just another college-certified good-for-nothing, gone half-buggy on drugs, she figured. Here he comes roaring out of school with a degree in news graphics or some crap—useless, right?—and the army after him, and so he really imagines he can whip his future into shape on a tennis court, like he's a kid again, like the world was waiting while he grew hippie hair and gave his heritage the heave-ho, like I should welcome his half-assed dedication as if it's the blooming of his

71

potential and zoom home to give him hugs and solid help, for God's sake, instead of . . . instead of telling the poor dumbbell . . . oh, hell.

How could Lou know what she'd tell me when she got to Balboa? She'd go, of course, and she'd give me a good look, too. She owed me that. She had a debt of motherhood she could never square, sorry to say, though damned if she'd feel guilt over it. Then was then, and now, thank God, is now. Spilled milk, right? Right, spilled milk. All she needed was time enough to show me I couldn't put it back in the pail.

In Balboa I'm not reading the papers, just sometimes the headlines through the window of the coinstand, and I'm keeping the tube shut off, but all the same, Barry's ascent to a pinnacle of notoriety is making Lou a personality hard to miss. The morning after my disastrous invasion of the Bamberger fortress and my escape from a bloody sacrifice to lust and madness *and* from the clutches of the Costa Mesa Police (that part was easy: the prowl car was unmanned, and even though I was tempted to remove the cop's clipboard pad from the front-seat console, where it hung next to his shotgun and black club, because my plate number was entered neatly on its top line, I left it, figuring I was clear until accused, and pushed my car back slowly into the street, keeping it rolling until somebody pulled over to lend a shoulder), I wait and wait for Cici's call. From my hard hat in her hallway, I know she will realize, with a thrill at my daring, that I have come *that* close to her, that I am committed to finding her, to having her, that I love her. She will shiver. She will grab up the hard hat and sequester it in her bedroom, maybe nestling it on top of her own hard hat, and she will slip out her hidden photos of me and study my warm face, her head wistfully inclined, her eyes moistening, and she will know beyond her resistance to know that we belong together. But in the confusion following my breakout, naturally she will have no chance to call. She will wait, protecting me from police inquiries, until she can use a booth in the high school lobby. The morning wears on, however, without any arousal of my phone's patient

72

bell. I stew until noon. I do sets of push-ups and sit-ups and jump rope a bit out on the patio. I drink a lot of coffee and twice rewrap my wounded heel in fresh gauze. Then, leaving the receiver off the hook, I flag down a push for the Porsche and drive to El Rancho for canned goods, fruit, and beer. In the check-out line, to ease my tensions and give my frantic eyes some occupation, I pluck a *Midnight* newspaper from beneath the candy rack and flip it open exactly to my mother's picture.

It is Barry's picture mostly, but Lou stands to the side, caught between expressions it seems, while Barry follows through with a shove to the chest of a large bald man whose back is to the camera. She looks blank almost, as if she is sleepwalking or lost in thought. She has a new hairstyle since I last saw her, a shade darker maybe, though I have to remind myself I haven't seen Lou in living color for nearly a year. The three of them take their poses in front of a baggage cart piled with suitcases and a sheaf of rackets on top.

The cutline reads, "Un-jolly giant Barry Glines gives free-lance photographer Eno Versalla a taste of his forehand smash at Orly Airport, Paris." For himself, Barry looks amazing, not enraged, not even violent, but calm and sure in his offense as Zeus. The short article describes him as the "surly and burly tennis-bum son of film director Austin Glines (*The Heart of Hugo Weed, Masters Fall, St. Petersburg*)" and says he'd been fined $1,000 for a temper tantrum at the French national tournament. It says he and "tennis immortal Louise Fraser Muldoon, his live-in coach, agent, and globe-trotting companion," are jetting to New York for the cortisone therapy of Stanley Kaiser, famous physician to the troubled arms of Whitey Ford and Sam Snead. It says Versalla has sprained his back, is filing assault charges in Paris, and is considering a lawsuit.

I study the photo—it's a fine chance shot—and feel the whole thing beginning to sink in: too *much*, my good old mom and that dickbrain of an athlete. *Doing* it. Rubbing their animal skins together and loving each other, in love and letting the scene play in the open, before the ravenous eyes of us cannibals and innocents in the body public. Well, shit, hooray for them. Hooray for their pride and hooray for the irrefutable justice of

73

love. I buy the *Midnight*. I want Cici to see the photo. Maybe it will teach her something. There is no shame! Look, Cici, we could wear sandwich boards if we wanted. We could tell the world, sure, sure we're doing it. We dig it! We really do! So all the sick lonely people can dose themselves with vicarious delight. Look! The forty-year-old tennis queen, all smooth sinew and silver-blonde heat and the twenty-year-old superbeast, all cinders and rock, a volcano on legs. Or us. Or us, Cici. How we fit! Remember? Like lion cubs, like two birches in a glade. Even our fingers are alike, our pearly teeth, our satin asses. Please see me, Cici. See the sense of us. Our love is our loveliness—and that's only a start.

I wheel my goods out into the hot lot of cars. The mist of the morning has reluctantly lifted, and now the sparkling ocean lies ready to soothe every stuttering heart drawn here by its greater beating. They are clustering and preening along the boardwalks and in the alleyways all down the peninsula as I motor slowly back to the channel. Couples declaring themselves by their entwined arms make me writhe in my seat. We are supposed to pair up! It is order, it is God's design and human purpose. Without another you are lost and alone—*alone*, and that's death in miniature.

The big house, lonely home of my lonely boyhood, is not making matters any easier. It has leeched me of some poisons by receiving my dirt and rough treatment, but it gives me nothing. For days, now, I've been going around singing in it room to room, and talking in volatile tones, sometimes yelling and kicking at door frames, but the house is so full of junk it can not even echo in answer.

I am getting no answers anywhere, but not only that, I am making no real contact either, not with anybody except Andy Busch's father, whose twenty bucks have at least bought me a week's worth of beer. After I fill the refrigerator, as I replace the phone in its cradle, I suddenly realize what it is that has brought me this far—the telephone. As an appendage to the senses it has no equal. Inspired, I call the high school secretary again as Colonel Bamberger and learn what I could have learned hours ago: Cici has not gone in for her exams. It is hoped, the secretary offers, that Cici will be well enough to take the scheduled make-ups, or else she will not graduate with her class. The Colonel naturally promises the secretary that all will be well on that score—I resist adding "or I'm not Colonel Bamberger." This is not like Cici, but yesterday I heard her clear voice in song, and from what little I know of her plight I can imagine no dangerous circumstances that might have imprisoned her, excepting her nefarious parents, who can be defeated, I'm sure. Still, I have not seen her, not yet.

My next call is to Manhattan Island, to the office of Stanley Kaiser. Lou has been there once and gone. No point in leaving any message, said the golden-toned woman's voice in New York, because Lou is on her way now to California—or would be by that evening.

"To San Francisco or LA? Any idea?" I ask.

She has me hold and asks the doctor, but he isn't letting on whether he knows or not, she says. "But you could call the Americana," she suggested. "They're in seven-oh-eight."

So I do. They've checked out. Anyway, the old lady is good as airborne and homing in on me like a missile. Time of impact undetermined. But soon. Well, any advance notice is a lucky break. I can make a stab at cleaning house, buy some cut flowers maybe, try to conjure up an encouraging ambience for my reunion with the queen mother.

Beginning with my bedroom, right away I find Cici's pictures on the bureau. Christ, she is blinding. And I am no unlikely match for Adonis myself, I consider, in the few shots of us together, the same sunlight on my clean young muscle and flaxen locks. Lord, if Cici could just lay eyes on these images of beauty, if she could only see how perfect. . . . I hop up and bound downstairs four at a time, an old boyhood trick that has loosened the banister like a worried tooth, grab the *Midnight* from the hall bench and a pair of kitchen shears from the utensils drawer, and fly back up the stairs. I want to mail Cici the newsphoto of Lou and Barry and just one heart-stopping portrait of us. So she may understand that what was still is, even if preserved now in flat dimensions, like the seed of a sunflower blackened in the freeze. And also that love has defiance in it, because it must face an army of challenges. It must defeat doubt and change and the vacuum between souls. It must make unkeepable promises and deny facts. It must join up with faith to battle all the unblinking shapes of death. Well, I know that's really too much to expect delicate Cici to see, but she'll get *some* message, and maybe its valuable essence will melt her heart. Worth a try anyway.

In the old man's writing room, now lined with bookless shelves, I find a manila envelope and address it to Cici in block letters. In the corner for a return I print "Armstrong, Guidance Department, Newport Beach High School." And underneath: "PERSONAL." Hot *damn*, she'll *get* this. I feel great. I run it down to the post office.

On the way home I lope into the club and surprise Skippy in the pro shop stringing rackets. Out of breath, I just stand and watch his fingers weaving nylon.

Skippy bobs up his head once to see who it is and only looks at me once more the whole time I'm in there.

"Got any court-time this afternoon?" I ask him finally.

"Not a minute," he says.

"Not a *minute*?"

"Not a minute."

"Skippy, I gotta hit with you. Lou's coming home. You gotta help me out of the ruins. *Please.* Just an hour to give me some timing, then I can go with the machine. Listen, I feel OK. I been running and working out. My hand's healing up OK."

He sighs. "Willie, what in hell's wrong with you? Are you going mental on us again? The other day I told you rest a week. Didn't that get through? Hunh? Here you come in here, on two days' workout—after five years off, and you feel *OK*? Horse manure, bub. You feel like you look—sick. You don't need timing, you need a long nap. Your mom would agree with me. And one more thing—"

I slam my hand onto the plywood counter. "I'll give you ten-to-one you can't take three straight sets from me," I say.

His fingers stop. He looks up. "Yeah? Today?"

"Any day."

"You're kiddin'. My hundred to your grand?"

"OK."

He turns back to the racket. "Well, since you put it that way, be down here at four o'clock. Oh—and you get yourself a haircut first, or it's off."

"Then it's off, Skippy. I need my hair."

"Cheezus," he whispers after a pause. "He needs it. He *needs* it, like a drug addict."

"Four o'clock?" I say.

"Yeah. Yeah, Willie, that's swell. Say, I'm gonna really enjoy giving you this lesson, Willie. Too bad I gotta charge you so much for it."

"Later," I say, and run home. It's two-thirty. I have an hour to clean up for Lou, just in case Balboa's her target, which looks likely. A few peaceful beach days are usually what she wants after a little crisis or a hard trip. And also she has me to deal with.

First I straighten Lou's Guatemalan bedspread, take some folded sheets and towels from the linen closet and carefully pile them on her bare pillows. Second, a fast tour with the old Electrolux through the neutral zones, halls, baths, kitchen, living room, giving the rugs the once-over; then with its stick attachment a satisfying thrust at the sills and corners, where the moths are hanging out. That takes a while. By the time I get to the tables and chairs with the dish-sponge, I am humming. I'm into it, making a pleasant improvement that Lou will certainly notice.

With the sponge all I'm managing is a streaky sort of mop job, so I quit that, pop a beer, and walk around arranging throw pillows, knickknacks, and occasional chairs, and getting the debris of my habitation out of sight. There I run into trouble. In a conch shell I turn up half a joint, which I spontaneously put to the match and begin puffing. It will calm me is my deceiving excuse.

I make a round of inspection as I smoke, smiling at my achievements, but also opening my eyes to many spots that could get the way they are only through the inattentions of a slob, the toilet bowl for one, the refrigerator for another. Well, there isn't time for everything. The refrigerator yields one more can of Coors. When it's half-down, I reach the place where I can begin to recognize the direction this high is taking me (opposite from the direction I'd witlessly hoped for)—toward worry about a tennis match, toward anxiety about impending combat so refined that it has no intrinsic meaning, just the haphazard meanings you slap on from the outside. But then this is a money match, no Ulysses S. Grant even-up contest either, but a thousand big ones to the bad if I don't pry loose Skippy's resolute game long enough to win one set. And I don't *have* a thousand big ones. I'm living off dividend checks and a Mobil credit card. On the other hand, after I turned fifteen and got rangy at net, Skippy never took a match from me. I had the eye and the quickness he, at forty-four, had forgotten how to even dream about. Now he's almost *fifty*. Shit, if I can't put six or seven games together before that relic can, I'll know I'm hopeless and I can load up the car and strike out for Vancouver.

A rattling noise in the kitchen, when I realize I'm hearing it, lets me know the morning's coffee that I lit gas under a while ago is boiling to beat the band. I rush to the rescue. There is plenty left. I pour a huge mugful, add a lot of raw sugar and milk, and meander out to the patio to fetch my rackets. One is missing, I think, until I recall throwing it into the ice plant. It's there, beaded all along the throat and grip with dew, great for the new gut. What a turd I am. How can I treat such useful beautiful things so carelessly? They come to you too easy, my father would say. Maybe, but does that explain it? No! I see value, I give respect, I feel gratitude. *What* then? Spite? Just crazy spite? Well, I must have many renegade angers turned inward, I decide—a bad state for my head to occupy. I can't aim my aggression at my own Self. I have to like my Self. My Self is all I have—in fact, it's all that *exists*. And I have to like existence, for Christ's sake, or I might as well hold my useless breath and die right now.

I bring my rackets inside and get a few ice cubes for my coffee. I have to drink it fast, I have ten minutes. My old cream cotton Fred Perry shorts are a little tight, but they look fine. Most of my old tennis shirts are too small, though, so I put on a blue T-shirt with a white, embossed peace symbol and a dove on it. Now Skippy'll have something to aim for.

At the last minute I hit on the perfect touch for Lou's arrival: a welcome note. I write it on typing paper. "Dear Mom, 'If I knew you were coming, I'd of baked a cake.' Alas, the news came late, so I could do no more than I did, and I'm no Dorotea. But there's plenty of cheese and beer and anchovies around. See you for supper. Glad to have you home. I'm at the club. Love, Will."

No greeting for Barry, true, but I don't know how to mention him in any brief discreet way. Anyway, I'm hoping she'll have sense enough to leave the stud in LA.

I slam the door and set off trotting down the walk, across the street between cars, doing deep breathing to relax. My heel doesn't really hurt—it's a bleeder more than anything, and I have lots of gauze and tape.

When I round the bend in the road, I see it coming, the airport limousine. I stop still and wait. It's a good way off in the line of slow cars, wavering through the glare.

She's *alone*, I think, when it gets close enough. The single silhouette inside leans up to ask the driver to pull over. He's the same driver I had a few days ago. I bend and peer in.

"Dad!"

"Still recognizable, am I? That's good news."

But barely. His hair is white and thin. His face is swollen. His quick handshake through the window is dry and hot. "No, I thought you were Mom. I was expecting Mom."

"I haven't had to be your mom for years now. So she's still en route, is she? More good news."

"I don't know if she's even coming."

"You talk to her lately?"

"No, nothing."

"Well, I have. She's coming, Will, if only to save you from my satanic claws. I had to wing in from Reno instead of drive, to cut her off at the pass."

"You talked to *Lou?"*

"Sure. Miracles do happen."

"What for?"

"Big question. You off to play?"

"I got a match with Skippy."

"Good old Skippy. So—no time now for your long lost daddy-o?"

"I would, Dad, but it's a money match. It's serious."

"Serious. That's nice. OK, I'll be down to spectate in twenty minutes."

"Shit, Dad, don't. Don't bother. It's no big deal."

"*That's* the attitude, Will. Racket back now, and . . . follow through." He flips his hand at the driver, and off goes the limo. It shrinks and melts like jelly into the sheen of the day.

Christ. Now what? What last-minute mission of fatherhood could have urged the old buffalo off the prairies and out to dreadful Balboa? No doubt I won't have long to wonder. I wish I'd kept my mouth shut about the match, though. There's no way his ghostly puss in the gallery will make victory easier to come by.

I get there late, of course, so I'm glad to see the teaching court still strewn with lesson balls. Skippy's probably off bullshitting in the clubhouse. I start collecting balls with the wire ball basket, ramming it down over them like a shorebird feeding after a storm. I take my time. All around the border of the court, where the fencing meets the asphalt, a chartreuse ribbon of ball-fuzz lies washed up by the tide of play. I'm thinking it must cause cancer. It looks carcinogenic as hell.

"Will! *There* you are."

I look up. It's Mason Thatcher, a long-time officer of the club, a restaurant owner who once got me my first job as a busboy after I quit tennis. "Here I am," I say, shrugging.

"You're late, Will. Skippy's waiting over on number one."

"Really? I thought we'd be hitting here, sort of out of everybody's way."

He shakes his head. He's grown fluffy white mutton chops since the summer before. "Damned if you're not still the same shy kid. No, Skip's been playing this one up all afternoon. There's a few interested parties on the terrace waiting to see you two dogs pitted."

"Fine with me," I say. I've always liked fans. Now the old man's face will have some others to blend in with.

We walk together through the clubhouse lounge, across the terrace, and down the steps to number one. Skippy is nowhere in sight. The gabby folks on the terrace include nobody I recognize. I feel their eyes following my passage. Mason says he's umpiring the match—just to arbitrate any disputes—and I say that's fine with me, too. He climbs into the chair. I do some stretches, and then for the hell of it I measure the net with the official yardstick.

Pfsssst. A can of balls comes open behind me. Skippy calls out, "Finally decide to take your medicine?"

I turn around. "Anytime, Doc."

He stops on the top step above the court. Out of his tennis bag he pulls a pair of long paper-shears. He holds them up and works them in the air. "I'm willing to play this match for an even hundred and a haircut, Willie. How about it?"

Some people laugh.

"How about just a shave?" I say and get another laugh.

He turns to me. "Or how about just my hundred against your hair? Save yourself a thousand, Willie. What say?"

"No, you may whip me, Skippy, but I'm keeping my flowing locks."

Somebody claps amid the laughter.

"Wait now—am I getting this right? That fairy hairdo is worth a thousand bucks? Is that what you're telling us, Willie?"

Before I can answer, my father's voice sings out, "Where's your ear trumpet, Gramps? He's speaking plain enough for me. Anyhow, you got no chance in Hades of collecting a whisker, and I got another thousand here that says so." He raises a black vinyl briefcase toward us and takes a seat.

"That's a *bet*, old man," shouts Skippy. "You note that, Mason. That is a goddamn bet!"

Mason hitches himself up in his chair and says to my father, "Your word on that, Will? A wager before witnesses?"

My father nods and gives an indulgent smile.

We warm up. I feel truly fine hitting, as I did the first day out. Nothing really gives me any pain I can't put out of my mind during rallies. I am eager. I am confident, happy with the length I'm getting on my ground strokes, which is all I need, I figure—

just enough dependable length so I can work my way in and knock him off from the net.

I feel relaxed until we start hitting serves. My toss has a kink in it. I can't feel the ball leave my hand, and it goes to a different spot overhead every time. The serves are going mostly in, but short and with shotgun placement. As I start fiddling with it, hunting for the problem, I feel the tension ˙spread down through my arms and neck, back and knees. Of course, my brain *is* addled, but I have nothing to gain by toting up excuses. I have to play hard and think easy. Winning play comes out of your head, sure, but if you root around in there after it, more likely you wind up driving it out of reach.

I spin the racket, win on his call, and choose to receive. Right away I start wondering, Am I being smart or am I outpsyching myself, relinquishing what ought to be my early advantage? *Ought* to be, but isn't. Or is it?—I haven't really served yet. See? Already you're thinking up a storm. Well, this way, though, you're smart either way. If you break, you have a double advantage; if he holds, what's the difference: that's expected, and you'll be even. . . . All this before Skip's first measuring bounces of the ball. I just cannot stop my brain from dragging me all over, like a girl with a rag doll.

He holds. Then he breaks, holds again, breaks again, and holds again. To love–five in twenty minutes. And yet I don't feel bad. I mean, my racket-work is solid, except where anxiety makes my reflexes brittle—no surprise there. I am simply going for my approaches too soon, trying to make my volleys too good, and getting passed or hitting out. I try slowing the pace. As if anticipating me, Skippy just walks in behind his chip returns and knocks off a couple lobs for the set. He is better than I remember, old Skippy, and I am a fuck of a lot worse. My long layoff has left me with the kind of game teaching pros have—all-day strength up the middle and nothing else, like a good freeway car with no back-roads acceleration and no city brakes. I drop the opener of the second set after some lengthy parabolic exchanges, all of which I lose on misses. Skippy stays back, wanting me to see I have no tactic to crack him.

On the change I look up at the terrace for the first time. In sunglasses now, my father gives no sign that he's paying attention or even awake. A sudden flood of memories staggers me— all the early tournaments I fought through up and down the Coast with the old man always a casual witness perched by choice far off in the seats, on the grass, or slouched in the car with the visor down, waiting there to console or congratulate me, to pinpoint my problems and praise my good works. It is now just like then, it is the same. My jitters, my hopes, my resolve, my doubts . . . all the same. I turn my back on him and the others, sit, and drink some water. Mason recites the game score. I sigh.

"Little the worse for wear, Will?" says Skippy.

I look at him through the legs and braces of the ump's chair. He is toweling his throat. "I feel OK," I say. "Like I told you, I feel good. They'll come in for me."

"We're all waitin'," he replies in the melodious tones he uses in kids' clinics. "But we're not holdin' our breath."

"Do me no favors," I say. I stroll to the baseline, juggling three balls and my racket, an old trick, to show my nonchalance and sense of humor.

When I glance his way again, my father has one fist to his lips in the pose of a cavalry bugler—his old signal for me to *charge*. The sight sends a surge of nostalgia and love through my chest: my father is back! He is home again, the man who made and raised me, who knows and loves me best among a whole world of men. Has he really risked a grand on the resurrection of my withered talent? That is doubtful—not for lack of daring but of that much loose cash to gamble. No, the resurrection my father is hoping to preside over is of that us-against-the-rest-of-'em partnership we forged long ago to meet the trials of our exile in Balboa while Lou toured the globe. Evenings alone we would take our own tours, walking up the beach and down the boulevard, and my father would urge me: "Look around you, Will, look close. Look into their eyes. They are the lazy, bent on pleasure. Not us, we work. They are the empty ones. Not us, we create, we grow. Their heads all spin too fast for them to catch a whiff of their own madness. But we are steady, and we enjoy the smell of ours." It seemed true to me. We were unique, my

83

father and I. We had difficult pasts, and we strove toward splendid destinies. Daily we put in long hours at our desks or on the courts, wrestling with our Muses and ambitions, while all around us, to borrow from the old man's mordant narration, "the Sybarites loll, and the cretins only work to play." Even later, when our ambitions wilted, and our destinies (as we recognized them) reformed themselves, our alliance held up. In spite of my efforts to dissolve it.

At sixteen, after I quit tennis and he quit the home, my love for my father began to take the shape of hate. When his wanderings would bring him unpredictably to my doorstep, he was always dirty and half-drunk, expecting food, commanding me to sit still for his speeches about anything on his horribly fertile mind. It made no difference to him if my friends were visiting. Sometimes he would step out to the banister on the landing opposite his study door and declaim to anyone below—or to no one—"like a sick comedian doing the Pope," a girlfriend said once. True, it was as if he had an act. He was a performer forever refining his image. I told my friends he was just nuts. Oddly, he didn't seem nuts to them. They liked him. He asked their names and remembered them, and was always willing to drive them home or lend them a few dollars for pizza. As for his act, I think my friends then found it compelling, if mostly obscure. My father was so apart from all their fathers that he was beyond criticism as a father. His dignity and wit encouraged them to accept him on his own terms. I, however, ended up rejecting him all the more firmly because of the chiding of my tolerant pals. "Shit, *your* dad's OK," Andy Busch once told me. "So he's a boozer, so what? Who isn't? At least he doesn't hide it, or get so plowed he can't drive or *talk* even. And look-it, he's hardly ever here, and when he is he lets you do whatever you want, stay out and all, and he gives you no shit about anything that's really serious, you know, like in your *life*, like some guys' dads. Like *my* dad. Shit, you're lucky. And he's very smart, too. If you asked him, he'd probably write your League of Nations essay." He would have, maybe, but I had trouble just asking him to take my phone messages. I wanted no obligations, no ties to him at all. But that was hopeless, and inside I knew that the lone person on earth I had always been closest to was my old man, William R. Muldoon the First.

Now here he is again, serenely downing Gibsons at courtside as if he'd never gone, and here I am performing for him—for us—in this game that we both know means nothing and stands for everything, pride and pluck, will and heart, as always. As always.

I deliver a neat slice into Skip's body, step in, and crush his return into the corner. Clapping. It gets better. My serve finds its depth, my volleys their range, and back it all comes, the old touch, reflexes, and strategy-without-thought. Adrenaline courses down my spine and flutters in my throat like the rush at the start of an acid trip. Fabulous. It's *here*. I have it! The balls fly to me lovingly as birds to Saint Francis. Suddenly Skippy seems to be playing not against me, but with me. We're a team, and this is a dance, not a contest. And it doesn't stop. I own every rally, even the ones he wins. Between points I prance and howl to myself. This is the *best*, there is no better feeling. Now and then Skippy cries out in frustration. He slows things up, changes rackets, opens new balls, presses fingertips to his temples to hex me between games. But my magic is a cataract, and nothing checks it.

The second set goes to me, six–one. The bet thus settled, Skip declines to play a third, wordlessly shakes my hand, and leaves by the far gate while the small applause still patters.

"Some fine doings out there, Will. Nicely done," says Mason Thatcher, resting his hand lightly on my sweated shoulder. "You've been wearing out just a *few* sets of gut back east, now haven't you? You can admit it, Will. I know a hustle when I see one."

"You do?" I say absently. I'm trying to catch sight of my father among the milling club-folk on the terrace. He's got up from his table. "Did he take off on me, the old codger?"

Mason chuckles. "Yes, you'd better try and collar him before he gives in again to that yearnin' to move a-yonder, if he hasn't already. Say, by the way, Will, any word from Louise? There's a rumor she'll be gracing us with a visit this summer."

"Well, you know, you never know, Mr. Thatcher."

"No, I guess not," he says, and he chuckles again.

I bound up to the terrace.

"Good shootin' there," says someone.

"Nice match," says someone else.

In my victory high I'm not seeing faces. They don't register. I acknowledge the compliments with smiles.

The old man's fresh drink and briefcase are at his table, so I sit down. I order a vodka collins. From the shimmering blur of the match in my mind I'm trying to pick out and savor the extra-fine shots—this lob, that half-volley. I can't remember many. I have a second collins in hand before he shows up.

He drops his weight into the web-work of his chair and expels a huge breath through rounded cheeks, like Aeolus. "Christ. The old plumbing ain't what it used to be, Will, I'll tell you."

"You got problems?"

"I got words to the wise: don't get old. Die young. That's good advice."

"Well, maybe you should see a doctor while you're here."

"Oh, balls. I see doctors in my sleep." He draws in a long sip of Gibson.

Jesus. After four years here he is again, my one and the same father, lined, jowled, plumped, and faded; fading, yet instantly reconstructing the old maze of bewildering tensions and deference and resentment that I've bumbled through for all my youth. I'm not out of it yet.

I say, "So, *have* you seen any doctors?"

"You know it. In winged flocks. Black crosses against the sky, circling and circling, with satchels in their beaks."

I have to laugh. "Well, damn, it's been a *long* time, Dad. I mean, that's obvious, but still you don't look all that healthy somehow."

"Appearances! How I look means nothing. It's how I *feel* that matters."

"OK, tell me the truth: how do you feel?"

"Terrible. And also terrific. They mean the same thing. How do *you* feel?"

I shake my head at him. "I feel great," I say. "I feel fabulous."

"Well, it's temporary. Thank your stars for that. Cigar?" He pushes a wrapped White Owl toward me across the tabletop.

"Nope. Never touch 'em." I push it back.

"*Whew*," he says. "My last one." He starts peeling the cellophane. "I bet you're some pothead now, though, aren't you?"

"I tried it a couple times."

"Didn't like it, hunh?"

I shrug. "Gives you cancer."

"Oh, yeah. Bad stuff, that cancer." My father twirls one end of the cigar between his pursed lips. He squints down its length, touching a flame to the other end with his worn gold Zippo.

For me, as a boy, that gold lighter, simply engraved with my father's initials, was a talisman. Even lying on my father's bureau beside his car keys and comb, it was mystic. I used to rub it, feel its weight in my fingers, thumb it open and plink it shut over and over. It seemed to embody the stubborn impetus of history—and history-yet-to-come, for they were my initials, too. On his sixteenth birthday, before my father had ever lit one cigarette, the lighter was presented him in a plush case, "a little gift," said the card, "from your staunch friend, Bill Tilden."

As he sucks on his cigar, gazing over the courts, I tell him I can't help it, I really do feel great, *really* great. So it's temporary, so what? Isn't everything temporary? "See, the important thing—the stupendous thing—is my tennis," I say. "I have it, Dad. I always have had it. It's still in me. Dust it off a little, and it's good as new. That is one great feeling, let me tell you. But shit, I don't have to tell you—you're a witness. It's Mom I have to prove it to. But anyway, the big thing is now I know I can make it. You see, Dad? With her or without her. I can *make* it. That's what's great." I slap my thigh. "*Great.*"

In the quiet air his smoke hangs undulating on a plateau beside his ear like a pet. He seems deaf to me, gazing and puffing away. The knobby hand propping up the cigar is pale and flecked with age spots. Perspiration sparkles in the combed rows of his hair. How has he got so old so fast?

Finally, he breathes out, "Why?" And then, "Why, why, why, why, why?"

I finish my collins, the cubes against my lip. "Why what?" I say.

"Why . . . are you here?" he pronounces, turning to me, his bushy brow lowered.

"Here?"

"Why," he says, "with the world wide open to you, have you slunk back here to cast your fate among the dregs and failures?"

"Here in good old Balboa?" I say, glancing around at the other tranquil drinkers.

"Failures," he repeats. "All of them. Failures and forlorn seekers, the whole sick lot."

"OK, Dad, I give up. Why am I here?"

With a rueful compressing of his lips, he sighs. "That's an answer I shrink from, Will. But here goes. And look now, by the way, if this should strike you as too simple, as too bald and simple, well, I say goody. Because that's how the truth *ought* to look. OK?—

"It's the seventeenth century. America the Beautiful is empty of people and full of promise. Europe, the Old World, is all civilized and cozy. For some. For the richest, the fittest, the survivors of long struggle. So who is it who's chucking the good life there for dreams of gold and glory in the New World? Not the clever merchants, not the silk-clad ladies, not the noble noblemen gorged on squab and brandy—no! Who would trust his last heartbeat to the wretched crew of some rotting oaken nutshell of a boat and a weeks-long nightmare of a cruise just on a gamble, a whim, a hope? Who? Bums! Misfits and wild hairs! *Failures*, that's who. Sure, among them were a few with strong backs and brains who could cut it in Boston, or New York, or Charleston, or wherever they got dumped. But the luck-less and the shiftless rolled on to Chicago, Topeka, or Dallas, before those places had names, into the hollow, Christ-bitten Midwest. And the truly rootless, the depraved, those that *no* end would please, finally hit bottom . . . where? Where another ocean stopped them. Right here!" He jabs a finger down at the terrace and drains his Gibson. "It's a head-shaker, isn't it? It's a sad tale. And the saddest part is its conclusion, a conclusion no man can dismiss. Which is this: all native Californians carry

the genes of failure within them. *Yes!* Oh, yes." He rises half-up from his chair, eyes wide and teeth bared. "All of them," he breathes. Then he sits back, the tension going out of his shoulders. "Ahh, balls. Will, for what it's worth, I apologize for fathering you on her. You're half a failure, Will. But you're half a Muldoon, too. That alone can carry you further than health and prayers. Maybe it won't—there's that chance. Maybe you'll just sink with the rest of the scum. Maybe you'll stay here, wallowing along, floundering in this unforgiving game, or soaking out there in that great trough of brine and oil and dying fish, and gulping down vitamins and breathing poison, and mostly waiting, like a goose for Christmas, for the crack and spasm of the planet to come for you all . . . but so help me, Will, I'm going to do my goddamnedest to wrench you free. I'm going to save one half of you from the other half. You'll help me, too, by the blood that's in you. I know you will."

"You're full of shit, Dad."

"Hah! Not quite. Up to the chin, maybe, but my resourceful brain remains clear of the tide."

"And for that I should be grateful? Is that it?"

He shrugs. "We'll see." He waves to the waiter and gestures for two more drinks.

"We'll see what? What are you here for anyway? And where do you come off, swooping in here like the Lone Ranger—so you can rescue me from me?"

"Now, Will, even if I had a plan all planned—which I don't— do you suppose I'd lay it out for you in advance and ruin the surprise?"

"You gasbag! Jesus, Dad, you been gone five years! You bugged out! Meanwhile, I grew up. By myself. Whatever I make my life into now, I'm making it by myself. I'm on my own, Dad. I don't need help from anybody, and I don't want help from you. You can keep your surprises under your sombrero, OK?"

He laughs. "On your own, eh? That's a good one. On your own in a waterfront shack with a mortgage you couldn't cover with ten winner's checks from Forest Hills. And leave us not forget beer in the icebox and cornflakes in the cupboard by the mysterious grace of Alcoa and I, T, and T, and Anaconda Cop-

per and Lockheed, and other bonds and issues too nebulous to mention." Our waiter interrupts with our drinks and two shrimp cocktails, compliments of Mr. Thatcher, he announces. "*Well*," says my father. "Isn't life just marvelous? You never know what pleasures lie around the next bend." He dunks a shrimp in the sauce and eats it whole, tail and all.

"OK, Dad. All I want to say is this. I explained to you once already, over the phone, why I'm here, why I came home, and it has nothing to do with failure. It has to do with the opposite of failure. I'm here for tennis. I'm here to work—"

"Crap!"

"Listen, will you? I'm here to make it, whatever *it* is for me . . . and I'm *going* to make it."

"There. You betray yourself there, Will. 'I'm going to make it,' you say. Yet you just admitted you don't know what *it* is!"

"Oh, God. Do you?"

"You're goddamn right. I'm here because I know what *it* is. You're here because you don't."

I glare at him. I feel furious. I have nothing to say. Nothing I have been saying can be turned to understanding. Not for him. Then suddenly and fiercely, I wish him dead, my father. Dead, just like that. Well, isn't his death what he's after? Look at him! On the boneyard freight. Bought his own damn ticket. There he goes. Off the cliff. Everybody wave! And still he can do this to me.

More softly he says, "May I tell you another reason I'm here?" I just sit, poking at my slice of orange.

"I'm here because I love you, Will. That's why. That's the last reason—and the first." He reaches across the table to curl two of his long dry fingers gently around my wrist. But I hold on to my drink, and I do not look up at him.

After a moment, he takes his hand away and says, "Want my onion?" He offers it impaled on his little plastic saber, with the same twirling gesture and the same inflection of his voice that I responded to a hundred times as an adoring boy. One Christmas I found a jar of cocktail onions in my stocking. They were delicious, but not as tantalizing as the vodka-soaked few I was presented on nights out with the old man.

I meet his eyes, that's all. The onion stays where it is until, with a grin at me, my father eats it himself.

We munch our shrimp and watch the courts slowly take on players as the sun slips behind the pavilion and the heat drops. My father comes up with some congenial question about college and my years in the East, which I scarcely answer. I am following the flying balls below us and trying to savor still my own recent sterling play, rolling it around in my head like a cocktail onion. Too bad old Lou couldn't have seen me out there, though really, the more I think about it, her help seems too much to expect. To her, I must look like a lost cause, and more completely lost now, with that big goon Barry Glines taking up what small space my mother has in her life for anybody besides herself. Still, when she gets here, we'll hit. We'll have to, and then she'll find out. She'll see I still have it, and what's more, she'll discover she still wants it for me, Bad Barry or no Bad Barry.

That heartening awareness reached, I swing around to the old man and ask, a bit too brightly, "So what's the scoop on happy-go-lucky Mom? What is it you guys still have to talk about after all these years?"

He shakes his head. "What we have to talk about and what we *can* talk about are two different whats," he says. "You know, bygones are emphatically bygones. You'd expect anyone to accept that. The fire is dead. Say what you want about the smoke that lingers, but it's dead. You'd hope she and I could be easy on each other—in memory of bygone warmth. But no . . . Ahhh, Christ. You wouldn't remember, but we *loved* each other, Will. Deep and true. And now what binds us together is like the string that ties a pair of alley cats by their tails. Pretty sad, eh?"

"Maybe you still love each other," I say.

"Smoke," he says. "Just smoke." He illustrates with a puff of his cigar.

"Am I the string that ties you together?"

"*Hah!*" he barks, startling me. "You're just a strand in the braid, Will, a strand in the braid." He dips the last two inches of his cigar into the hot sauce. "What say we beat feet, Will. Celebrate. Get us some chateaubriand and fresh asparagus. Can I sign for this? Our name still magic at this joint?"

"I don't know. Sign Skippy's. He'll pick it up."

"Gladly."

"But I can't go anywhere until I change, Dad."

"Boy, you said a mouthful there. You sure have to change." He gives me a big smile. "Nice as you look in those pretty shorts."

"Thanks," I say, smiling back. I get up and twirl on my toes. "I'm all dressed up for my date with destiny!"

He says, "Yeah. All dressed up and no place to go."

We end up buying a slab of beef on the way home, and some mushrooms and salad ingredients, dessert, and some Chianti. When I set the wine on the check-out belt, the old man suggests I not forget that alcoholism is hereditary. He is sincere. For emphasis he purchases a half gallon of vodka and a bottle of vermouth.

The meat is London broil, but one look at the broiler pan would make anyone wince, even Lou, so we fry it. "A travesty, but we have no choice," says my father, nimbly slicing the mushrooms to sauté. I peel cloves of garlic for a dressing made with milk, mustard, and dill that I learned from a girl at Syracuse, a compact and muscly gymnast from Poughkeepsie who had a mustache that she shaved, I discovered when I first kissed her, and amazingly hairy little boobs, I found out later.

It is like old times. We have Fats Waller on the hi-fi (Lou has removed the stereo to Berkeley), many lights and candles ablaze, and a few promising television shows picked for consideration during the evening ahead.

Midway through dinner, which is tasting splendid to me, as we converse idly about the fool, Agnew, and the exciting nonsense of the manned moon mission filling the papers already, my father lets out a surprised grunt, hooks a finger into his mouth, and pulls out a brown chunk of something, like a peppercorn.

"Christ, see?" he says, working his tongue into the gap it made. "I'm falling apart."

"What is it?"

"Got me. Piece of tooth, I guess. An artifact from a forgotten age of dentistry, I don't know. That's why I'm back to steak now, see? So I can enjoy it while I can still chew."

Just that puts our good mood to rout. For dessert we have perked coffee and Sara Lee orange cake, chosen in an ebullient moment at the market, but we fork at it disinterestedly, thinking of ourselves.

Last summer Cici and I shoved the giant RCA out of the kitchen into the space in the living room left by Lou's seizing of the stereo, where my father was at first alarmed to see it. "A television," he used to say, "is not furniture. It is not a decorator item. It is an appliance, like a clothes dryer, a *machine*, like a typewriter or a band saw. When you're doing a tough, necessary job like watching the tube, you do it where you do your other jobs—in the kitchen, in the basement, in some specially appointed spot. You don't do it where you relax, or where you think, for God's sake."

Nevertheless, now, coffee cup in hand, with no sign of reluctance, the old man stretches his swollen yet diminishing yet forceful self out on the creaking sofa. And I likewise on the floor. What I don't realize is that my father has not watched television for five years. He is only curious, and not for long. We watch "Gomer Pyle" and part of something else before he springs up and switches it off without hunting through the other channels.

"Christ!" he shouts. "Is this the peak? For shame. For shame." He turns it on again for a few seconds, then off. On, then off. On, off. On, off. On, off. *This* is how it's used, Will. Like this." On, off. "You make it blossom, you absorb the image, then you cancel, you exhale. You take control." On, off. On, off. He comes over to me and squeezes my shoulder. It aches from push-ups. "You're solid, Will. A blessing of the genes to balance the curse. I hope. She's coming. I can feel it. Walk outside with me, OK? I have to level with you."

We cross the patio and shuffle down the walkway to the boat dock. Across the channel the lights of Corona wink on the water. At the end of the planking, he turns.

"Will," he says in a strangely high-pitched voice, "did you

ever imagine your old man a suicide?" He holds up his palm. "Don't answer. See . . . goddamn it—I'm in plenty of trouble, Will. Oh, I can manage, don't worry. But I just want you to know, in spite of what you hear, blowing out your brains *is* a solution. Sure, it's a last resort. As far as we can figure. Anyhow, it's a cruel burden to load on a son. I want you to know I know that, just in case—*just* . . . in case."

"In case what? What kind of trouble are you in?"

In reply he digs into his pocket and brings out a lot of jingling coins. He keeps them jingling in his open hand until they all dribble and bounce away onto the warped boards under our feet or into the water.

"C'mon, Dad—money? You'd never blow out your brains over *money*."

He laughs. "That would really disappoint you, wouldn't it? Your old man eating lead for want of gold. Pretty small, right? Well, how small is small, Will? Do you know? Look up at that sky there. Stars, all kinds of stars. That sky has more stars than we have grains of sand on this earth. Yes, that's true. And here's another one: those Apollo spacemen, Will. Do you know how long their junket's gonna take? Three days. Boom, zoom—three days to the moon. At that speed how long would they have to spend zooming to get to the nearest *star*? Can you guess? Go on."

"I don't know," I say.

"Nine hundred thousand *years*, Will, that's how long. That's how small small is. It's pretty goddamn small. It's so small it makes *big* small. OK? OK. Here's another number for you: thirty-five thousand. How's that hit you? Dollars, I mean."

"Dollars?"

"Yeah."

"What do you *mean*? You mean you gotta have this money or you'll kill yourself?"

"Oh, Christ," he groans. "Why am I trying to shroud all this in its lovely meaninglessness? Just so you can strip it bare-ass and ugly."

"Sorry, Dad, but you said you were leveling with me, right? That's what I'm waiting for."

"Hell, Will, if you're still waiting, then you missed it. I need thirty-five thousand bucks. That's as flat as it gets."

"OK, but what for? How come?"

"My old age," he says dryly.

"Your old age," I echo. "Sure. You call that leveling?"

"Will, please. It's rude to inquire into somebody's money matters. The upshot is I need a little help. And *you* need a little help. What I'm hoping is that you and I can somehow dovetail our needs and both come out ahead." He pauses. "*Comprendez?*"

I'm leaning against a piling. The tide is in, so the top of the piling is about even with my chin. I'm leaning against it, picking the crusty gull-shit loose with my nail and flicking it into the slosh. In the channel the ruby port-side lights of the boats chugging back from their little jaunts to Avalon or Ensenada ease through the half-dark, and voices float in. I am saying, "Listen, the *only* help I need, now and forever—" when all at once I understand what the old man wants. He wants my money. "*Jesus*," I breathe, shocked. "You want it from *me*, don't you? You want *my money!*"

He sighs. "We're not there yet, Will, and the word is *need*, not want."

"Jesus, Dad, I don't give a shit what the word is. The word is *eat it*, that's what the word is. First, I have zero right now—I mean, I haven't even *talked* to her. And second, I don't even know—"

"Whoa, Nellie," he sings out. "Save your breath, now, Will. C'mon. Relax. I don't want to crowd in on your inheritance, brandishing a cutlass and with a dagger in my stubby teeth. See, I got options all over the goddamn map, OK? All right?"

I stand there seething. Options! Fuck that. He wouldn't have flown his decrepit ass out here to hand me this solemn shit about stars and suicide if he had options. "So now it comes out!" I yell at him. "That's what I am to you! A bank, right? A big, fat, easy touch!"

"Discussion's suspended, Will," he says with a quick shake of the head. "Went on a shade too long, I'm afraid. . . ." He slaps a piling. "Hell. It's been one bastard of a day, eh? I'm in. So—as host of the manor, you got someplace special for your daddy-o to dump his corpse?"

I feel baked solid. I don't move or say anything. He waits a moment with that old incongruous bright moronic look on his face (I know without seeing it), which he lets melt into a look of amused scrutiny, and then he gives me his wish of "sweet dreams" and a brush of the neck as if it's still 1959 and tomorrow we're going down to the zoo. He makes his way up the planking slowly, loafers scraping, into the house. I stay.

After a while my legs will just buckle. I will tumble off and sink headfirst into the inkiness, down and down without a gurgle, straight down to the muck, where I will stick like a ketchup bottle half-full of ketchup. What's down there? Nothing strange. Nothing pleasant or useful. Years back often you would come out here and see a seal paddle by close to shore, an easygoing seal with beseeching eyes. You don't see them anymore. Though you do still see whales, not here but in the sea, far out, bucking and spouting, and if the surf is quiet enough you can duck under and hear them creaking at one another. Let them all die, I don't care. If that's where evolution's taking us, it's fine with me. We do all right without buffalo, and we'll do all right without whales and seals and elephants and eagles and everything else that's hitting the skids. It's beyond judgment. I mean everything that happens is beyond judgment because it's happening, it's part of the imponderable cosmic design. So I don't care. I'll be the ketchup bottle stuck in the muck. You save the whales, if you think they're worth it. Just remember dinosaurs had a good grip once. We'd really be in trouble if somebody had been around saving them. Luckily, they went. Everything goes.

As the old man says, you have to see the big picture. The *big* picture. In the *big* picture even God is small. Because everything goes, plants, and animals, earth and water, moons and stars, myth and fact, time and motion, everything that God created. It all goes after a while. And when everything's gone, all that's left, besides God, is Nothing. Maybe God will be disgruntled to be left with Nothing. Maybe He'll try again, start over. But my guess is God will go, too, and Nothing will be left alone, though *alone* won't mean anything. And meaning won't exist. Nothing will be all that matters.

My legs don't buckle. My feet fall asleep. In the Middle Ages, pillar saints were guys who would crouch nearly motionless for decades, high on marble columns, waiting for something as pure as the death that eventually took them, while maggots burrowed into their long-since unfeeling haunches. I keep upright on my numb feet for a long time, letting my thoughts drain out. When I begin rising loose from consciousness to come down to it again a bit later, like a skipping stone, I decide to sit and fall over. By the time my feet stop sizzling enough for me to move, I've conked out. I don't restore myself with sweet dreams either. I only join up briefly with the great Nothing.

Later, I find the old man snoring away like a cartoon character in Lou's fresh-made bed and half the houselights on. Mad as that makes me, I don't wake him, but go back downstairs for a soporific beer. I am exhausted. Yet sleep, when I did finally drag in stiff and sore from the dock, wouldn't come to me, I don't know why. That's when I wandered upstairs to see where he'd stashed himself.

The sky above the bleak eastern mountains is turning rose. I open a second beer and fry three eggs in the steak pan. They are awful. Twice I lower myself to the linoleum for a set of push-ups, but my shoulders tremble and won't work, so instead of going up to bed I rebandage my heel and trot to the beach for a sunrise swim. Since nobody's around closeby, I go in naked and feel ten times better right away. When the ocean does that to you, it's a wonder drug. From the water, I watch the sun climb, changing from a pale disk to its usual blinding self.

I feel great again. Hoo-*eee*! I thrash in the water, celebrating my new confidence and determination. Dawn of a new day, fucking-A! My star is on the rise, and it is brilliant with promise. Even Cici has to see the light. With a rush of joy that I feel in my throat, I decide I'll even lend my father some big money, not all of it, but say ten thousand. That will clear the air between me and him, and he won't have to tell me what it's for, either. He is my *father*. Shit, I can afford it. It's only money, right? And anyway, before too long I'll be raking in heaps, the way promoters are kicking cash into the tour—and even if I break a leg next month, I'll still have enough in the bank so Cici and I can buzz off to Maui and live for years in some tranquil cove on baked fish and papaya juice.

I scramble into my tennis clothes and trot back toward home feeling like a new man. Around one side of the house Lou had an outdoor shower built in a three-sided trellis covered thick with bougainvillea. It's really been a fine improvement. But this summer, in glum self-denial, I haven't got around yet to turning the hot water on from inside the house. Today, whistling and humming, I do, and I find some soap and towels to take outside. Just as I'm screwing on the old brass showerhead, I hear a car pull into the drive. I can see it through the greenery, a maroon Mercedes. The motor stops.

"Not yet, not *yet*," sings a voice. It's Lou.

I stick my head out around the trellis to see better. I am undressed.

Lou, her hair cut short and gleaming, wearing all pink, slides out of the car, skips to the passenger's side, opens the door, and helps somebody out by the arm. He is a giant with his hands over his eyes. He has a coal-black head of hair cut just like hers and a black shirt.

"OK, Bare," she sings, yanking his arms down, "welcome to our summer dump!"

He stares at the sun-washed stucco, the lush plants and tile-work, the tall windows and varnished front door. "Unreal!" he says. "Hey, this is really *unreal!*"

"Well, you're lookin' at it," says Lou.

"Outrageous!" says Barry. "Hah-see-en-*dah!*"

Lou laughs. "Like it?"

"Oh, *babe*," he shouts. He drums a loud tattoo on the fender of the Mercedes. "Not too *shabby!*"

"Hey, keep it down, sweets," she says. "The kid's probably asleep."

I duck back behind the trellis and crank on the shower. "*Oh sole oh meee-ohhh,*" I blare out hoarsely. I don't care, I'm thinking. I'm a new man.

After her own morning shower, a ritual of mesmerizing length and heat, Cici stepped out of her little stall of pink Fiberglas into the steam-shrouded air of the pink bathroom, clean water coursing down her flanks to the floor, humming and ooo-ing through part of a new song she hadn't learned all the words to yet. She shook open a towel and wrapped her heavy hair in it, squeezing, dancing this way and that, daintily, on her toes.

The week before, Cici's mother had stolen Cici's white enamel scale, the kind with a fan of old-style numerals floating under a bubble of glass. Cici knew then there was no use finding where she'd hidden it (probably in the trunk of the Bonneville), because the fat bag probably checked every day to see if it was still there. But now as she dreamed, shuffling in the wet, Cici did not remember the scale was gone, and so she pressed the water out of her ropy hanks of hair to keep its extra weight from affecting her reading. She was dreaming about Paul McCartney. Over her humidifier she had taped another picture of him, the one that had come like a prize inside the new double-album. He was whiskery in it and so pale that you wanted to just hug yourself and snuggle your head down between your shoulders and just wonder what his open lips were about to say to you. Again Cici was imagining that if she could teach herself to sing a flutey counterpart to Paul's liquid melody, she could maybe mail him a tape of herself in care of Apple Records, and he would listen to it shaving, at first carelessly—but then he stops his razor midstroke, shuts the faucet off . . . the voice of a bloody *angel* is what that is, and he rushes to twist up the volume, leans down to her singing, with his soft whiskers still under the tufted cream, and he thinks, She sounds like me own *twin*, she does. And then he mails the tape back to her, a duet now, with his boyish tenor dubbed in—along with a letter. And a plane ticket.

Sugar! thought Cici, hurling her towel into a corner. It's my scale, the fat *bag*. She rammed her fists through the sleeves of her bathrobe. It's my *life*. Why can't I run it how I want? She felt the tears pushing behind her eyes and a rising bulge of misery in her throat. "Man oh man. Man oh man oh man," she breathed at her shadow in the fogged mirror. "Man oh man oh man," a net of sound to keep herself in. God. Her surface was so crumbly and thin, like the crust on sand. She lifted her hair out from under the back of her robe and shook her head. Whew. OK. Spend it, she would spend it then. She had over two hundred dollars in her ballerina music box. She would walk to Archway and buy another one. And another one if she had to, fill up the damn Bonneville if she had to. But . . . she had to save it. Her allowance was cut off, the *bastard*. She *couldn't* spend it. OK. It didn't matter. It didn't matter.

"Cici?" Her mother was calling from the bedroom. "Cici? Are you OK in there?"

She wrapped her robe tight around her, yanked the door wide. "*What?*"

There was her mother over on the rumpled bed. "Excuse me for barging in, but I got sick of waiting." Her mouth tightened. "That was an hour and twenty minutes in that shower, young lady, an *hour* and *twenty minutes*."

"So maybe I was dirty," she said from the doorway.

"Cici, I'm *not* telling you again. I'm not going—"

"Where's my *scale*? You *bitch*!" She slammed the door and locked it. Man oh man oh man oh man.

There was a short silence. "You have a packet here from the high school," said her mother. "From guidance."

Cici pushed her fanny against her hands on the doorknob.

"From Mr. Armstrong," said her mother. ". . . *Cici?*"

"So?" She heard the bedsprings squeak as her mother stood up.

"Do you want to come out here and open it, or do you want me to open it?"

Cici spun around, jerking the door open again. "Don't you dare *touch* my personal private mail! It's my personal mail! You're making a federal offense if you even just *sniff* it!"

Her mother tossed the big envelope onto the bed. "There it is, then. You open it."

"Don't worry, I will—when I feel like it."

"I've had just about enough snappy guff out of you, you understand me? If he's sending you those take-home tests in there, young lady, like I requested, then you write them out—today. And if you need books from your locker, I'll fetch them for you. You are not letting your poopy little problem keep you out of graduation, understand? Or else there'll be hot hell to pay when Daddy gets home if you don't."

Cici flounced to her bed and threw herself across it on her back. "Ask me if I care," she pushed out in a breath, overcoming the trembling in her throat.

Her mother said, "You don't care about anything anymore, that's your whole problem right there. *We* have to care instead, Daddy and me, just like you're a baby again, or a case for the booby hatch and bars on your windows."

"*You're* insane!" Cici shouted. "I'm not insane, *you* are! Get out of my room!" She hopped to her knees on the mattress. "Get *out!*"

Her mother strode fast across the carpet, then paused in the doorway. "OK. But when you get around to opening—"

Cici slammed her hands and forehead into the sheets and stayed in that position, like a Muslim praying. "Get *owwwwt!*" she yelled.

The pressure of the bed against her face made her vision blurry, so when she looked up it took her a few seconds to see she was alone and the door shut. The fat *bitch*. She rolled onto her back, letting her robe fall open. She was still hot from the shower. She really was, she was sweating. She let her thumbtip glide from the wet hollow at her throat down her breastbone into the dish below her ribs to her bellybutton, around it like a skater, faintly tickling, and over the tight roof of her tummy, down to brush her damp thicket of hair, back and forth through the curls, letting cool air in to the skin.

Her other hand reached blindly behind her head for the radio and switched it on. Into the room at good-song volume came the brutal noise that foreran the news—the wire-service machines, gnashing their hard facts together. She switched it off. Her arm flopped back onto the envelope, making it crackle.

Tests—bull! Cici knew her guidance counselor wasn't sending her any tests. What would that solve? The three big ones she missed—calculus, English, and history—were state exams. You could only take those in school, and at specially designated times. Armstrong, that bald dope, he was disgusting. He had impetigo, some rash on his wrinkly neck. Whatever he was sending, it was bad news for sure, maybe registration forms for summer school. Because no way was she graduating, that was out the window, bye-bye like a canary. Her mother, God, if you dropped her brain into a cavity in a gnat's tooth, it would rattle around like a BB in a boxcar. She gave a little laugh. She heard that one in study hall. From Maggie Chaffee. God, now she was going to miss Maggie's graduation party, and also Janice's. But so what? She hated those parties, she *did*. They were just for getting wiped. Really, that was the only way to have fun anymore, get wiped. Beer, pot, pills, vodka . . . even Janice was into it, dippy Janice, with her culottes and Capezios and seed pearls from sixth grade. Sure, wipe out blind on whatever your boyfriend handed you, and then you bomb to the beach for some nooky—if you had a boyfriend. Forget it, if you didn't. Then you would get skags wanting to dance all night long and play "Moon River" or some slow junk so they could bump your chest up close. Like Rory Alloway, that dufus, what a faggot dufus, maybe now he would stop calling, now that she was grounded and Daddy ripped out her extension, her baby-blue Princess, that she got for Christmas. . . . The helpless anger washed through her again, making her brain feel bruised and her Adam's apple feel like a grapefruit.

God. "You don't care about anything anymore." How could

she *say* that, the bitchbag. Cici knew really she cared more than ever. She *did*. More than Janice and those other dips—more than anybody. She cared so much she got like paralyzed. She wanted her life to come out *so perfect* that . . . that she was flubbing it up instead. But school, cripes, what good was school when you really thought about it? School could go suck doorknobs. . . . That's when things got more serious and awful, in November, when Daddy found out she wasn't applying to any colleges. Because, she *told* him, she was sick royal of lectures and projects and quizzes and that garbage, the thrilling yearbook, the thrilling student council. . . . And, man, did he hand it to her then, he got out the jumbo shovel, the crap about her opportunity and her future. But what hurt worst was Gwen, when he said Gwen was better off than she was if Cici didn't go to college and just floundered around Orange County for the rest of her life waitressing or something, as if that was her whole goal all along, the bastard. You just didn't talk about Gwen, either, that's what did it. Gwen was her sister, who was out at Sunny Haven, in Covina, the home for retards. It was like a rest home, where you went for the rest of your life, Cici thought it meant. They were supposed to visit Gwen every other Friday night, only it was dumb because you were never supposed to mention Gwen at home, never, not even on her birthday, May 10, that was just two days before Cici's, but you were always supposed to go up there every other Friday and visit with her in this like indoor garden full of retards and talk with her like your whole wacked-out family were panelists on a TV show. So she quit going. Her mother about checked out over that, sobbing at night alone in the living room because of how Cici could have everything, everything, and now she wanted nothing. Which was very scary, because what if it was true?

What Cici sensed was that she did want something, only nothing she could name, it was nothing she could even imagine in a way she could discuss with anybody she knew. Except Will. (Me. She was thinking about me, and she told herself, stop it, stop it. Her parents would never let her see me, never in a zillion years, no matter what dumb, wild things I did to get attention.) Anyway, she was all changed now, so who

103

cared about Will? God. She didn't, that was for sure. Man oh
man oh man.

She stretched back for the radio. It was a shoe store ad. Sometimes Cici thought the radio was like a country in revolt with
three factions fighting for control of the government: the news,
the ads, and the music. But the music was winning. Luckily.
Then—finally—a song came on, *bomp-bomp, a-bomp-bomp*, and
Cici let loose a perfect echo of the record artist's heartbreaking
tremolo.

As she would on any special morning of old—Sunday, a birthday, or a homecoming—Lou is whipping up a batch of pancakes.
When she discovers furry colonies of mold established inside
the syrup jug, she dispatches me after a fresh supply, "the real
McCoy, from *trees*," she says, because poor Barry has never
tasted it. She tosses me the keys to his Mercedes in a high arc,
the way she always used to toss me things so I can dip, let them
pass over my shoulder, and catch them behind my back. It is a
gesture like my father's with the cocktail onion, one as close to
genuine intimacy as Lou has allowed herself (her greeting kiss
was just the seal of recognition), and I felt pleased, the keys
clinking into my clever fingers, and then irked at myself for
feeling pleased; I am too easy to manipulate, like a kid.

"I need a few pesos," I tell her.

She frowns and points with her chin toward Barry, who has
his forehead resting on his plate at the table. "You'll have to
siphon the exchequer," she says. "I'm flat."

Somehow the unmoving bowling ball of Barry's head does not
have a generous look to it. "He's a tired, tired boykins," Lou
said a few moments ago, rubbing his shoulders, "isn't he? Tired
and grumpy." To me, more than tired and grumpy, he is a simple prick (true to his advance billing), and I've known the boykins for almost an hour. But Lou has been apologizing for him,
explaining they've driven ninety, ninety-five all night all the
way from Berkeley to beat the sun, and they lost, so I am not to
be insulted by his not shaking my hand, or talking to me, or
looking at me. He is just tired and grumpy.

104

I watch Barry for signs of life and then tell Lou, "Well, I will get what I can afford."

"Hey," she calls after me, "are you a pauper now, or what? C'mon, I'm good for it. Syrup's on me!"

I snatch my wallet off the hall bench and go out into the heat, gritting my teeth, knowing I'll do what she wants, I'll come up with the goods, as always. Another old tune—why am I surprised it's still on the charts? Lou makes sure she's cared for. Cash is vulgar stuff, she never carries any. After a lesson with Lou I'd be heading for the Coke machine, and she'd sing out, "Hey, pack of Benson and Hedges for the coach. I'm good for it!" By *good for it* I used to think she meant she deserved it, a fee for the lesson, or a tax due for her special maternity, or just a gift. I never asked to be paid back, and she never offered me a penny. How would she feel now, I wonder, if she knew the state of her account with me, how for years I'd toted up on the inside cover of my social studies notebook all the cigarette packs, cab fares, ice cream bars, and ferry tickets, the drugstore delivery bills for roll-on deodorants and jars of Noxzema, and every got-a-loose-buck-for-the-old-lady loan that she's touched me for in my short life? (All multiplied by three and a half percent interest.) She would feel disappointed, that's all—in me, because I've had to keep that little flame lit under my petty resentments: besides, come *on*, it's all been her money to start with, right? Right.

02314.2 reads the odometer in Barry's Mercedes. The damn machine's brand-new, but you'd never know it. Dust-covered already, and full of crumpled tissues, doughnut bags, yogurt cups, clothes, newspapers, tennis balls, smoke-stale air. Most of the delivery-price sticker is still glued in strips to a back window. They probably did a job on the motor, cranking it up to ninety for eight hours before it was broken in. That depresses me. A shithead for sure, this Barry Glines.

I jam in the key and turn it over. What a great thing to have a car that starts, a luxury. I make up my mind to get the Porsche fixed, take it to Karl's Auto Werks. Now I hear my name from somewhere, in a shouted whisper:

"Will! Wait! Will!" It's the old man.

I stick my head out the window. I can't see him.

"Up here!"

Thrust between two slats in the attic ventilator, a flyswatter is swishing impatiently.

"I got you," I say. "What now?"

"*Shhh*," he whispers.

"What now?" I whisper.

The flyswatter is withdrawn, like a tongue. "Get me some cigars!"

"OK—what kind?"

A five-dollar bill, folded lengthwise, is poked through the ventilator and falls spinning to the concrete. "Long and cheap," he whispers. "They're all the same."

I give him the OK sign and back the Nazi-mobile into the street. It feels like an ocean liner after my little speedboat.

Well, shit, I'm thinking, not an hour past full bloom and already this family homecoming scene's gone buggy and wilting. The only fruit it can produce now is bound to be some pulpy, split-skinned garbage, the kind you throw at bad actors.

After cutting short Barry's overstated awe at the sight of my home with my yodeling song from the outdoor shower, I appeared before him and Lou, beaming, a towel around my slim waist, and, to keep myself from betraying any surprise at the manifestation of Bad Barry in three laughably exaggerated dimensions, I mingled my gaze with Lou's, bowed, and said, "Long time no see."

Just as she said, "*Moe feece!*"

It was French, I realized a second later. She looked good somehow in her pink bell-bottom overalls and jersey T-shirt. She threw out her arms and I went up to her, and we lightly kissed cheeks. When she stepped back, she kept hold of a good hank of my hair. "What's this?" she said.

"Looks better dry," I said.

"Seeing's believing," she said, letting go. "Barry, this here's wonderful Will Muldoon, my one and only, and Will," she said with a sharp look that I couldn't interpret, "this is Bad Barry Glines, the Tennis Court Oaf himself."

"Hi," he rumbled.

"Gladda meecha," I said. I was looking up at his glittering black throat and chin, covered in whiskers like iron filings on a magnet. His dark eyes were aimed past me, toward the house.

I excused myself to put some clothes on, dashed through the hall, up the stairs, thinking the gigantic jerk-off was my age but he looked like he was from another planet or the twilight zone, where they play tennis with bigger rackets and bigger balls on a bigger court with a higher net; shit, no wonder he was good— "So, how're you enjoying Earth? Pretty nice, hunh?" That's what I should have said—when my father lunged out of Lou's room hugging his World War II suitcase to his chest, its jaws clamped on an indigestible tangle of sleeves and cuffs with even the bedsheets trailing out behind.

"Top o' the mornin'," he heaved out in a breath.

"What's up now?" I said.

"The attic," he said, chuckling nervously. "Look, Will, she doesn't know I'm here, does she?"

"Not from me."

"Good. OK, mum's the word, hey?"

"Sure."

"I think I got everything," he said, shuffling by me. "Double-check for me, will you? And flip the mattress—can you do that?" He turned and slipped through the narrow door leading to the attic, the sheets slung over his shoulder like a bride's train.

He'd left nothing in Lou's room but the smell of sleep—I lifted the windows wide to the channel breezes—and a dappling of blood across the floral pattern of the mattress cover.

A stop at Brighter Day, the only place to go in Balboa for real maple syrup, will put me in range of watchful Mr. Busch, who always sits gazing out through his display window when the hardware trade is at low ebb. This in mind, I park the Mercedes beyond the post office, so to perform my errand, car-to-store-to-car, at the dead-end of the shady street, where he may not spot me, away from the action on the avenue.

It's the sloping snout of the curbside mail drop that reminds me of Cici. Or, specifically, of my hopeful deposit there yesterday of the manila envelope containing the photos (of Lou and dickbrain and of golden Cici and me) that are supposed to thaw her heart. But with a rush of despondency now I see they will do no such thing. The one of Barry committing assault will mean nothing to her (what did I think it would do?), and the one of us will only perplex her, embarrass her, or make her feel sad—it will not arouse her, no—Jesus, she is too young and still shy. For her to warm, to melt, she needs sound and touch, words, scent (the Canoe), slow smiles, sighs, and the beat of the moment . . . sparks. She needs sparking, as they used to call it. And that photo is just flattened history, it is ashes.

Me, she needs *me*! But as I half-speak this silly conviction, beating my palm on the dashboard, I realize its reverse is the harder truth, the fervent truth: I need *her*. I am lonely. Yes, I am lonely as the godforsaken Sphinx. And all the lonelier with my parents reinstalled on my flanks like a pair of ravaged pyramids, as if only to serve as points of measure for the drab waste stretching, with no other definition, to my horizons. Yeah. Shit.

I grab a Berkeley *Barb* out of the backseat so I'll have something with which to shield my unmistakable profile from Mr. Busch, and I dash down the sidewalk into Brighter Day Foods, safe. I tuck the paper under my arm. There's no one behind the counter. I look around at the shelves of jars, the bins of dried fruits and beans and grains. In spite of myself I half-expect and half-hope to catch sight of Cici at the end of an aisle, hanging up ropes of garlic or sweeping up the sand from the surfers' feet in front of the yogurt cooler. But no, I see nobody at all. Probably the clerk's back in the kitchen, or the stockroom, the stockroom, where Cici and I were once tossed into passion, like two boats torn from their moorings in a storm, swaying, clunked against each other, sinking to our knees. . . . Shit. She has someone else, that's it. But on the phone, what did she say? *It's all changed, you can't fix it.* Fix what? Why isn't she going to school? Another guy— Hell, she'd admit to that wouldn't she? That made no difference last summer. And what about this doctor crap? Does she have mono? Shit, maybe she's *pregnant*. That would fucking well do it, all right. But I've got to know, I've got to find *out*!

I'm stalled here by a display of wooden kitchen implements—beaters, spoons, pie-crust shapers—and still no one's appeared to tell me where in this maze they hide the maple syrup. "All-ie all-ie in-free!" I sing out.

Christ, I'm on my own. I round the spice and condiment shelves at the end of one aisle and there below a dumbfounded herd of honey jars are the maple syrup cans, just like that, easy. I pick up a hefty pint-size can to inspect. The stuff's from Vermont, from Essex Junction, says the lettering superimposed over a painting of two horses dragging a syrup wagon, or sled, through the snow, with a shack among trees in the background and smoke twisting up out of it. "Cheesus," I hiss at the price—over *five bucks* for this elixir, and what is it but sugar, right? That's all—sugar. You know those dour hicks in the Vermont woods don't share in the monster profits that slick sharks like the owner of this place gouge out of their indifferent California clientele. If this dinky can's worth five dollars, that one syrup-wagon load in the painting is worth five thousand. I'd be surprised if the Vermonter who slogs that team through the winter snow harvesting dribbles out of the frozen trees makes a thousand all season.

"Need help?" A girl in a burlap apron is speaking to me over the louvered swinging doors of the kitchen. She's the same one I spoke to about Cici, and I wonder if she remembers me.

"I will in a minute," I tell her, meaning I intend to buy. Then I realize I've left the old man's money in the car and it's for cigars anyway. Maybe my wallet will just cover, but now I'm damned if I'm going to break myself in this clip joint for Lou's gratuitous indulgence of her moose of a boyfriend. I return the can to the shelf, but I don't move off. What do I tell her when I come home empty-handed? There's a syrup strike? Some hillbilly Chavez in snowshoes has gone and organized all the syrup-croppers and you can't get any? No, it's too early in the game to chance priming Lou with needless disappointments. That would gain me nothing, and besides, you wretch, she's your mother. Some sons would sooner live on green water and weevilly bread than hold back a nickel from their mothers, their precious, silver-haired mothers. Lou's birthday's in March,

March 8. I try to remember if I sent her a card or a present. I can't even remember where she was in March, so I don't think I did.

OK, I decide, I'll steal the syrup. Somehow this makes perfect sense: everyone will get what he deserves, the downtrodden Vermonter, the greedy shopowner, my insouciant mother, and malevolent me, too—I get a bargain in the short run, forgetting for now the karmic long run. I look around for the girl in the burlap apron, feeling wily and excited.

She's gone behind the counter, I figure. Then, sure enough, in the great shiny hubcap of a mirror that's suspended reprovingly from a corner of the ceiling, I spot her up there stacking carob bars by the register. With my back to her I swiftly crouch and whisk the can into my folded Berkeley *Barb.* I straighten up. The lump under my arm feels about as inconspicuous as a sheep just swallowed by a boa constrictor. Giving the mirror another glance, and the kitchen doors, I tug my shirt out of my shorts and slip the syrup inside my waistband. The loose shirt disguises it nicely. I shiver. I'm not wearing any underpants.

On my way to the front, I stop to lean into the cooler for a carton of kefir, peach, my favorite flavor of last summer. Just the primrose hue of the carton is enough to return the taste to my mouth. But now I put it back and take a black cherry instead: see?—the future is unknowable.

"Will that do it?" says the clerk.

"Yeah. Let me know when you have a sale in here, and I'll buy what I really want."

"Really," she says with a serious sort of half-laugh. "Dig it, you know what I get in here mostly? For big customers? Chauffeurs. Yeah, in uniforms and all, and those *hats.* They walk outa here with a hundred dollars' worth of this-and-that, all in one bag."

"Lotta dough in this neck of the woods," I say.

"That's the truth," she says from behind her molars. She snaps my bill into the cash drawer and fingers out some coins. "Stay healthy," she says, in warning.

Out on the sidewalk again I have to walk slowly, and stooped over, because the can has slipped down onto the root of my penis, which is now the last bulwark against my losing it out my shorts right in front of the store.

What better time for Mr. Busch to shout, "Will!" (as he does), slanting from his doorway across the street, one fat arm wildly waving above his head.

When I look over, the waving stops, and the arm makes a few imperative *come here* sweeps. The guy's a dodo all right, in Technicolor—if I were Andy, I'd be sucking a hookah in Morocco now myself, or in the caves of Crete, or wherever.

But I'm me, and I can't say why I feel sorry for the old bean bag. I do, though. So I hitch up my maple syrup with my forearm, hiding this strange motion with my newspaper, and I amble across the quiet street.

"All I got's a minute, Mr. B.," I tell him. "They're holding breakfast for me. And everybody that I've asked so far about Andy—just only a few people actually, three or four—nobody has an inkling of where he is or why he left. Nary a clue so far, but I'm on the case." This is a total fib, of course. I'm only trying to make him feel better. The deep creases of melancholy on his pudgy face look as though they've reigned there since birth.

"I'm not air conditioning the whole darn peninsula here," says Mr. Busch, urging me inside. "I won't keep you long—I'm right in the middle of inventory. That's the heart of this business, Will—inventory. You can't sell it if you don't stock it."

"Sounds logical."

He eyes me a second. "About Andy—for me you're just a stab in the dark, Will. I don't expect much. But we can't go leaving any stone unturned, is all. Not that I'm expecting you to devote your whole career to this thing, if that eases your mind. Just so you're an extra pair of eyes for me, that's all I ask. What I wanted to say is I hear your dad's back. Been a while, eh?"

"I'll say. Yeah, he *was* back, briefly, Mr. Busch. Nobody can miss him, I guess. He's subtle as a B-52."

He clears his throat and forces a smile. "Well, the reason I saw you, that I went and hailed you out of the health-food place, is, you see . . . I was only wanting you to be aware, that . . . it's

111

Father's Day . . . you know, *Father's* Day, this Sunday."

"It is?" I say, remembering the cigars, and just then, like a trap sprung, my elastic waistband jumps over the top rim of the can sending it past the obstacle of my penis and down one loose leg of my shorts. My quick hand pins it against my thigh, and I say, "Woops." I feel a traitorous blush begin pouring out of my scalp. For a moment of imbecilic suspense, I stand clutching the can to my leg like a poultice, staring at displays of steam irons, kettles, and bakeware, until, with equally imbecilic abandon, I whisk it into full view, give it a little toss, and say, "Syrup!"

Mr. Busch says nothing.

My ears feel like a pair of boiled lobster claws. I tuck the can into my newspaper.

"Ahhh . . . so," he says finally, "Father's Day. That was the extent of my meaning, when I saw you. Just to give you that awareness."

"Yeah, thanks, Mr. Busch. That's an awareness I appreciate. I mean I would have thought of it—probably. But who knows, maybe I wouldn't have. You never know."

"No, you never know," he says. "Well, it's back to work for me. You, uh—enjoy your breakfast now. And keep an ear to the ground for me, and also, any help you need, Will, or spare change, or advice, drop by, OK?"

"Oh, I'll keep you in mind, Mr. Busch, and The Case of the Missing Son, you know, I'm getting curious myself now, so maybe I'll come up with something."

"Fine. Drop by."

"Sure. *Adios*, Mr. Busch. And wherever he may be, from Andy, well, Happy Father's Day," I say, slipping out the door.

"*Sunday*," he barks after me, as if I don't know today's Saturday, as if I'm that thoughtless and dumb. Which I am. I'm a clumsy thief. A ne'er-do-well, and a big disappointment. Sons are supposed to disappoint their fathers—that's my rueful reflection as I trot down to the Mercedes—it's what's expected, it's the dark half of what we were designed for. No wonder he didn't say anything, the dodo. What's to say? Maybe I made him feel better after all, fulfilled his expectations. So now he feels grimly better, in the midst of all his feeling worse. Shit, I don't know.

Late with the syrup, I forget the cigars. I red-line the poor Mercedes in first gear, and then second, screaming back down to the channel.

"How many for you, Will," says Lou. "Two? Four?"

"Two."

"Two," she says. "*Et tu*, Bad Barry?"

"Four," he says, growling. He's like a caricature of himself.

"All I got's four. Start with two."

"Bluto can have mine," I say. "I'll wait." In my absence he has changed and shaved. Now, besides an astonishing pelt of black fleece all over, he wears only new green surfer trunks with white cuffs. And he is dowsed with my Canoe—*Cici's* Canoe, I remind myself in a gust of anger.

"Mama," says Barry, "you better inform this little pecker to watch his mouth."

I snort. "Ooo, shiver me timbers."

"Hey," says Lou, aiming her spatula at me. "Haven't you got worries enough without jerking *his* chain?"

"What, I just offered him my pancakes! All right, I take 'em back."

But she's already slipped the stack to his plate, where they steam in the sunlight, tasty-looking pancakes, brown and irregular, like all the Sunday pancakes of my childhood.

"Relax," she says. "Second batch comin' up."

"So where's this famous maple shit?" says Barry.

With her spatula Lou raps the side of a silver pitcher that sits like a vase in the center of the table. This pitcher, large enough to use on a lectern during a filibuster, is where Lou has dumped my pint of syrup after heating it in a saucepan. Engraved across its stately belly is QUEENSLAND CHAMPIONSHIPS 1955, a few fancy curls and swirls, then, LADIES' SINGLE WINNER, and her name. Once the house abounded in junk like this, the spoils of sport, but I guess Lou's lugged most of it home to Berkeley.

"Well?" says Lou.

Barry is assiduously chewing. "It's weird, like . . . like I can't get much taste out of it, like it's watered-down."

"Watered-down!"

"Well, yeah. It's got no taste."

"Sweetheart," she says, "you're the one with no taste."

I laugh. "Maybe he'd like molasses."

"Maybe you'd like a trip to the oral surgeon," says Barry.

"Jesus, Lou, this guy's quite a comedian."

Barry shoves back from the table, and I feel my underarms prickle. "Mama, two more words and I'm gonna glue his face to the floor with his own snot."

"*Boys!*" she shouts. She unloads a pile of pancakes in front of me. "Here! Eat! My, my, what a coupla farts I gotta contend with. Will, listen, break out your good manners, OK? We have a guest here. Like I said, he is tired and he is grumpy. And he is also just a trifle nervous this close to Malibu and his fire-breathing daddy. And his daddy is a big problem right now, I think you should know, because of one little nympho in the—"

"HEY—Lou-*eeze*," yells Barry, clenching his teeth. "You don't have to tell him my big problem. Tell him his own big problem, hunh? How about it?"

"What's *this* now?" I ask.

"Let him *eat*, Barry," says Lou.

"What's this?"

"You been drafted, cocksucker."

"Oh, for Christ's sake," says Lou.

"*What?*"

"Yeah-yeah. You are booked on the Saigon shuttle, buddy. Sayonara!"

"Mom, c'mon. What's this bullshit?"

"Barry," she says fiercely, "you just dug yourself right back in the goddamn hole, is that what you wanted?"

"Get bent," he says.

"Oh, hell. Will, this is your fault. That mailbox was jammed with crap. Why the hell do you resume our deliveries if you're just gonna let it sit out there?"

Now I see the emerging sense of this. Two days ago when I rejoined the Bell System (it's wonderful, I was thinking that day, a *bell* system—you can reach anyone you want in the world just by ringing his bell), I called the postal service to ask for my summer mail to start, hoping Cici would maybe contact me that way, but that was before we talked. Then I knew she would never write to me, not Cici. What would happen instead was that every piece of paper with my name on it would find me, including my notice to report for a preinduction physical, a piece of paper I've ducked twice already. Well, nothing would find me, I decided, unless I let it find me. So I would not get my mail. That was simple. What could they do if I didn't get my mail? They'd think of something. But whatever they would do, it would take them extra time to do it. And time is all I've got. (In enough time anything could happen. The war could end. Or the world.) Stalling has been my flimsy tactic from the start. At Syracuse in December, when the notice first cast its greenish shadow through the window of my postbox, I took it to my room and steamed it open to be sure it was what it was. Then I took it to Gordon Higbee, a J-school friend, a graphics major who had a huge collection of old type and rubber stamps. He picked out an eight-inch DECEASED stamp and thumped it crosswise across the face of my notice. Then I resealed it, stamped the envelope RETURN TO SENDER with a hand pointing up at the Long Beach return address, and fired it back. Though the board was not convinced my death really had found me without their help, the notice took until May to reappear in my postbox. It directed me to proceed to an induction center in Albany, but I applied instead for a change of venue, to San Francisco, where rejection rates are highest in the country. Apparently, this dodge has given them less trouble.

"Mom, you're not saying you opened my mail. Are you?"

"Will, honey, it was . . . it was obvious what it was concerning, and it was not a *personal* letter, so—"

"You mean you *did*? You *opened* it?"

Pained as she looks, still I cannot believe she would. Lou was always scrupulous about the mail. She made a big deal of the sanctity of correspondence because she used to accumulate piles of it while she was off touring. I felt weaselly, back then, just reading a postcard addressed to her.

"I didn't," she says leadenly.

"What's the difference who opens it?" says Barry. "The message stays the same, right? 'Greetings' is 'greetings,' right?" He tips his juice to his mouth, taking in a long swallow.

Lou's back is to us. She's peeking under cakes on the griddle.

"Mom—Jesus. This is too *much*. Can't you control the animal? You gotta chain him to his unicycle and make him play outside. He'll be crapping on the rugs before you know it."

Barry jumps up, knocking his chair all the way back into the broom closet. Lou whirls, yells "*Barry!*" and slings a half-cooked pancake at his face. He ducks. "Get *out!*" she yells. "Go to the beach! Go down and sleep on the goddamn beach for a while, will you? You're too frazzled for normal adult civilization. Get some rest, sweetheart, OK? Please?"

He sways above us for a moment, like a tree, trying to transfix me with his most wrathful glare, I can tell, even as I contemplate my palm's peeling blisters. He thuds out down the hall. The door slams.

"Holy Christ. . . ." Lou sighs. She aims a forefinger at her temple and kills herself: "Bang."

"Where's my mail?"

"Will, let me apologize for that big ox, can you? I mean, he's mentally just beat to hell. You don't know all he's been through. It came down like bricks."

"All *he's* been through! Shit, he's a rich and famous tennis star. What about all *I've* been through? And all I still got to go through. Hey, Mom, remember me? I'm your blue-eyed son. *Me*. Will Muldoon. Who's *he* anyway? He's a jumbo economy-size jerk."

"He's my lover, Will. Get used to it."

"Yeah, well, I hope his dick's a lot bigger than his sense of humor."

"Hey, cut the vulgarity. Listen, he's young, that's what people tend to forget—no, now you listen, Will, sit here and *listen*. Where you going?"

"I *want* my mail!"

"It's not out there. It's over on the windowseat, like always."

"Two letters, that's it?"

"That's it, yes. The rest was circulars and sweepstakes and junk. You want any more of these?"

Nothing here from Cici, of course, and not till I see there isn't do I realize I'm hoping there is. Like an idiot. One letter is an appeal from the Syracuse Alumni Association, wasting no time, and needless to say, the other is my notice-to-report, its envelope torn raggedly open.

"Come on, you want any more of these? I got three hot ones."

"Shit, Mom, how could you let this happen? That asshole. You know, I could've just boomeranged their little invitation right back, addressee unknown."

"Yeah? Well, then, why didn't you? It must have been out there for days."

At this point through the front door Barry bellows, "Hey in there! Mind if I take along this old purple board in the garage?"

Lou pleads at me with her sculpted eyebrows. "At least he's asking."

I suck in one cheek. "Sure, ox, take it. You better find one for your other foot, too."

Lou smiles. "Thanks."

I nod. "There's no surf down there anyway."

She gives me the three pancakes, drops into a chair, and lights a cigarette. "Eat now, please, and grant your old mom the chance to explain herself, OK?"

I say nothing. The lavender smoke wreathes her hair in the same caressing way I used to think elegant. She watches me loop the syrup around the stack.

"He'll soften up, Will, I promise. But what you gotta under- stand—and notice I'm not saying *sympathize*, just *understand*— is that this hullabaloo over Bad Barry Glines all came outa left field, like a runaway truck. A year ago, nobody heard of him. Will, he's your age, but coming up, at clubs, in tournaments, did we ever hear of him? No. You know why? He was a base- ball jock, that's why—a pitcher. The damn Dodgers wanted him right outa high school, but his father made him go to USC. Baseball coach up there threw him off the team halfway through freshman year. Gave him another look sophomore year and threw him off again. Attitude, maturity, dependability, you

117

can imagine the reasons. So three guesses what he takes up. *Tennis*, which he always played his whole life, but he never cared about it, not *hungrily*, not *passionately*, like you need to—until he quits baseball. And, Will, it must have been like lightning hitting the sea and creating *life*, the way he was just born to the game. I mean, imagine Abraham Lincoln as a baby coming into the world wearing a top hat. Nuts—I can't describe it, what it was like last July when I first watched him hit, but it was like God was changing my conception of the possibilities. And I knew . . . and I felt myself wanting to . . . oh, hell. So, wait, anyhow, this was last July. His daddy, the movie dictator who I'm sure you heard of, from Holly-weird, his daddy was kicking down the stable walls over me taking his iddy boykins out of real estate school to become a world-class pro athlete. He's still kicking, only now he's got other problems. . . .

"But what I mean basically is, OK, a year ago, who was Barry Glines? A rich kid. A college dropout. And now, today, he is number twenty-six in the world, and on a *tear*. And for his talent, his own raw talent, *but* with the press attention they'd give a rogue elephant. Until just last *week*, when he screws up the elbow, which, I now find out, was already screwed up from throwing baseballs. So, bang, he DQs out of his biggest tourney to date, then gets sued, for God's sake, and maybe now he has to back away from Wimbledon. Combined with *two* six-hour plane flights in a few days, plus an eight, nine-hour caffeine jag barreling down the San Joaquin Valley, *plus* Daddy the dictator waiting offstage to slam his balls in the vise over some teenage nymphomaniac, this dreamboat in hot pants, who is Daddy's little diddle to begin with. So all I'm saying is, OK, he's rude, he's crass, he's rowdy, and maybe this expresses his personality type, but you gotta appreciate what he's been through that has rattled him and made him worse. He's on edge. He'll soften up, like I say. But for now, Will, I'm asking: show some tolerance, OK? Just for the sake of a peaceful vacation. You dig me?" She tries to smile.

"Sure, Mom, I dig you. Do you dig me? Why should I show any more tolerance around here than your King Kong? What makes you think my life hasn't been just as much torture as his?

Shit, the guy is rich, the guy is a tennis star, *forget* his father, the guy is *on his own* with a future that'll keep silversmiths employed for decades, if he wants to grab it, that's all. And he has love, he has you, Mom. Meanwhile, I have about ten bucks to my name, a car like a bathtub on wheels, and a future that looks like a choice between Vancouver and Dien Bien Phu." I pause for breath, watching her face, her rosy lipstick, her cerulean eyeliner, the fine blonde filaments on her tan cheeks, about to go on, to say I've got a boo-boo, too—See my heel?—but fuck me, what's the use? Again it's the old rutted story, me hopelessly trying to draw out a measure of her sympathy, which she was always so tight with, having the stuff in such short supply, and Lou patiently sitting there, or standing there arms akimbo, or reclining on the divan watching me with feline detachment, almost thoughtfully, waiting to speak her well-reasoned piece. I stop and laugh out the breath I've taken, as my throat constricts around it.

She blunts her long cigarette on Barry's plate, carefully crushing all the orange bits of spark. "But, Will, honey, the difference is, you're solid. You're independent, you always have been. Christ, don't think I don't know you have it rough. But wake up, everybody has it rough. Some can take it, some can't, is what I'm saying. And some, like Barry, who God knows *should* take it, make taking it harder and harder and harder on themselves until they bust up on it, and it beats them. But that's not you, Will. You got an iron grip on the tiller, which I wouldn't say if it wasn't true. And hey—Canada or Vietnam, that's not your only choice, is it?"

I groan. "I don't know. Maybe not, but the position it puts me in is for shit."

Lou shakes her head. "Nuts. You have time, right? You got until Monday."

"*Monday?*"

"Sure, Monday. Isn't that what it says on there? You got two days."

I unfold the paper. She's right. This Monday, at some United States Navy yard on the Bay. Ten in the morning, too. I'm fucked. I crumple it up. "Well, I'm not gonna be there. They'll

119

just have to beat back communism without me."

"Will, come on. What kind of feeble move is that? Then when they come here to the door, are you gonna bend over and point to where they can put the boot? That's not you. You're a scrapper."

"Right. So don't worry. The boots'll never get in range."

"I know, but what I'm saying is why not go? Go up there. Go through the procedures. Fill out the questionnaire. Step on the scales. Pee-pee in the bottle. Just be sure and flunk the thing, got me? That can't be so tough."

"Why, you think the army's stupid?"

"Not exactly," she says dryly, "but if you could slip a bread-knife between the *army* and *stupid*, I'd whistle. And if you're not smarter than the army, maybe you should join up. Oh, hell, look at it this way: why not stay in the game until the last out, you know? You have last ups. They got to make the plays. It's only over when it's over. I mean, come on, can't you think of something? Sure you can. We'll think of something good, and if it doesn't fool 'em, OK, then you can scatter. But if it *does* work, hey, marvelous! See?"

"Marvelous," I say. But I think she's right. She is. I do have the time to invent some ruse. Maybe. And putting off any last-minute maneuvers until the last minute is advice that squares with my established strategy anyway. Still, flunking that physical is no kind of cinch. Even though, sure, you can poke out an eardrum with a pencil, or have "Fuck" tattooed across your forehead, those aren't the moves of a smart guy like me either. And even if sticking a dead mouse up your ass for the doctor to find is often a dependable tactic—and sort of an appealing tactic, too—I could not stoop to that one, figuratively speaking. What's more, it's futile to take serious drugs or get puke-drunk before you amble in there, because they can lock you up for three days if they think you'll look more soldierly after a rest. Those induction overseers have seen it all, especially up in Flower Child City. Yet guys bluff their way out every day. Jesus, *sure* I can think of something. "OK, Mom, suppose I turn myself over to these bloodsuckers on Monday morning. You're the one daring me to gamble with my life and future. Just what can I do

to myself between now and then to make them believe they'd be better off without me?"

"Raise your blood pressure."

"Raise my blood pressure?"

"Yeah, your blood pressure. Your heart. Your pulse."

"That's real good, Mom. How? With a bicycle pump?"

She rises abruptly and begins clearing away our plates. "OK, Joe Sarcasm, I butt out. One minute you're bemoaning your entanglements, and the next minute you're sneering at them. That's your old man's formula. When you wanna get serious, come around again."

The plates clash in the sink, and the pipes rattle with the sudden rush of water. Lou's vigor has always made her wantonly hard on things, furniture, machines, clothes. In a bathroom she's a splasher, in a car a heedless grinder-of-gears.

I say, "Relax, why don't you. I *am* serious. I just am very aware of what I'm up against. At school I talked with draft counselors and conscientious objectors—people who've been through this. Beating the draft is no simple proposition, Mom. It can be done, sure, but every cute scam you may—"

"Did I say it was simple?" Lou cries, spinning around. "I know it's not simple." She sighs. "Listen, honey, this isn't some chuckleheaded gimmick I read in *Good Housekeeping*, this is the real cheese, this is a point-blank medical fact. Time may be too short now to bring it off, but it's worth a shot. Can't hurt, anyhow, and so far your arsenal is bare. So listen, what you do first is you start smoking . . . here—" She flips her Benson & Hedges off the counter for me to grab out of the air. "You smoke like a steel mill, three packs a day. Then you buy Contac, those cold pills, and take two of them every day. And also you consume as much salt every day as you can, at least a tablespoon. Bang-o, up goes the old BP like a booster rocket, OK? That's a start. That's something. And it doesn't exclude other stratagems, which is the beauty of it." Out of a shot glass on the counter she pulls a kitchen match and scrapes it lit on a skillet. "You get all the health benefits of nicotine, too. Light up." She holds out the match.

I blow at it, but she lifts it away still burning. I say, "First tell

121

me whose point-blank fact this is and how you're so sure it works."

"Will, to me this is firsthand medical advice I'm giving you." She shakes out the match. "This MD who's a friend of the family, Barry's family . . . these three requirements are what he gave Barry. If they'd work for him, they'll work for you, right? Right."

"That's how Barry got out? This blood-pressure number?"

"He didn't have to. He used bee stings, a bee-sting allergy. All he needed was a doctor's letter certifying this allergy, and he was home free. It was the same doctor."

"Well, shit, Mom, don't you know a doctor who could give me a bee-sting letter?"

"No, honey, I don't, and even if I did, you have no time for that route. We're lookin' at Monday morning. So light up."

Never, believe it or not, have I smoked tobacco. But now when Lou extends her second offering of fire, I do. I inhale and cough. "Jesus." I cough again. It's bitter and dense, not half as mild as I expected it to be after all my happy-weed. I take another, smaller toke and sit back, exhaling like a fish.

Lou laughs. "Old Walt Raleigh wasn't such a bad guy after all, eh?" She screws the lid off the saltcellar and dumps its contents into my glass of juice. "There. That's probably a double dose, but we're on a condensed schedule here, so stir 'er up and drink 'er down."

I sink my finger into the juice and swirl it around in the murk at the bottom.

"Quit stalling and start guzzling."

I take a short gulp. *Bleeh!* This is poison!"

"Of course it's poison. Anything's poison in the right quantity. That's the whole idea."

"Well, shit, couldn't I just gobble down nine or ten bags of pretzels?" I pull in a draft of smoke and cough.

"OK, pal, make jokes. This is verbatim medical orders. This is a goddamn prescription for your exact plight. How easy do you think it should be?"

"A bee-sting letter sounds pretty easy."

"OK, think up your own divine rescue if you can't stomach

mine. But, like I say, the old garrison's surrounded, and you're out of musket balls." She goes back to the dishes.

I puff away gingerly on my new toy, already exploring ways to fiddle with it, tapping ashes into my juice. "Mom, I don't mean to sound thankless. I agree you're right, and I'll go with this blood-pressure number, but you have to recognize the likelihood is I'll end up being run out of my own homeland anyway, by my own screwed-up government."

She grimaces. "Oh, *horrors*—is that what I'm supposed to say? For your edification, William, Canada is a very very nice country. Vancouver is one of the most advanced and beautiful cities in the world. And the USA, I am afraid, isn't so damn special—which, when you travel and see some of the world, you find that out. You may be too young to appreciate it, but your sugarplum homeland has been on the skids ever since they ventilated JFK's cranium. Hell, this may just be a good time for us all to hop to a new lily pad, I don't know."

"It's not hopping that bothers me, Mom—O woman-of-the-world—it's *having* to hop. But all right, that's a problem you can't help me with. *But* what it finally brings us to is the problem where you *can* help me."

Her hands are quiet in the sink. She's gazing out the window toward the gleaming, sun-struck aluminum wall of the neighbors' pool house.

"Lou?"

"Fire when ready," she says.

"If I *do* have to hop the border—which I could be pushed into doing any day—you know Grampa Jack will slice me out of my inheritance like gangrene. True?" I pick another cigarette out of the box and light it with the smoldering end of my first. "Mom?"

Softly she starts to sing. "Three cheers for the red, white, and blue. Doo doo-doo, doo doo-doo, doo doo-doo, doo." And she rolls her head around on her shoulders. "You know what I sometimes wish, Will? I wish it was 1919 again. 1919—and we had these last fifty years to make over the *right* way, as a *nation*, you know? Dedicated to the sincere, positive, obvious good of mankind. Dumb, right? Wish in one hand, crap in the other. See which one fills up first."

Dizziness starts to rise through my neck like a sweet liquid drawn up by the sponge of my brain. I clear my throat and dunk my cigarette in my juice. "Ring him up, Mom. Please. One quick call to say, 'Hi, Papa—oh, and by the way, could you send Willie's inheritance money all in one big check right away? He wants to invest in his future.' Lou, Grampa Jack would spit in his own face if you asked him to. Why should I chance losing all that money when it's practically mine now anyway? And when I may need it. To live on."

She turns to me. "Well," she breathes in a sigh, for the first time now gathering me in her amethyst gaze as she used to do when I would surprise her, or make her proud of me, seeing me now, sizing me up, how I'm older and harder, her grown son, and she says, "Well, Will, if you're not on top of this one, you can dog my cats. If I called him today—and that's what I was about to do, today or tomorrow—I could broach this subject, and he could have the whole figure freed up on Monday, I'm sure. But I'm *not* sure he'll do it, even if I ask him. You know, Jack's not near as conducive to my arguments as you think. Let me sit on it awhile, and I'll RSVP later." She cocks her head. "Say, your old man wouldn't have anything to do with this request, would he?"

"What? Why would he?"

"Because he's in a big bind with a dollar sign in front of it. He must have really crapped out this time, because over the phone last month he tried to stick *me* for a loan, and it would not be unlike the old souse to pull his heartbreak performance on you."

"Hell, Mom, if Dad calls me, I'll just say what I said to you. It's my money." I light a cigarette. "But here is one consideration I want to remind you of. Since I was seven years old, you know Grampa Jack's been promising me all this money. He's given me dreams about money as a kid. 'When you're one and twenty, Willie, and a man . . .' Remember how he would say it? And 'financial responsibility,' remember, Mom? 'You'll feel the weight of financial responsibility.' A pure promise to me. So just tell him I'm one and twenty and a man. He'll remember, if you don't."

"Honey, I'll sit on it, like I said. Are you gonna drink

your salt? There's no sense smoking if you're not gonna drink your salt."

"In water, I'll drink it."

"OK, see you do that. I'll finish these up, and we'll go knock some tennis balls, hey? For old times' sake?"

I pour my juice into the dishwater. "For *new* times' sake, Mom. *New* times' sake is the only reason to do anything."

She smiles. "You know, you're just like Barry—full of these broad statements. Don't be so sure of everything. It isn't becoming."

In Barry's Mercedes, Lou drives us not to the club, but to the two cracked public courts along Balboa Boulevard in a small, dried-up park that cures itself in carbon monoxide on still days. She doesn't want to be seen yet by anyone she knows until she and Barry can discuss some plans, because if word gets to his father that he's in the state, a *lot* of legal hell could break loose. She won't say more than that.

Both courts are taken, but fortunately no one's waiting. We've hardly set down our equipment when one foursome of large brown women, like Jersey cows, plod off, and we start hitting.

Though my taped heel gives me no trouble after the first fifteen minutes, and I'm clearheaded and feeling quick, I can't summon up that laser-beam confidence of yesterday's match with Skippy. True, it was a match, which definitely makes a crucial difference—and for half that match I was lusterless as I am now—but still, why can't you ever stay at the peak? I know why. Too many rare abilities must support you there all at once. So the old man's told me often enough. "Your *best* play rejuvenates your spirit," he would say. "But it's your *average* play that pays the bills." Right now my average play wouldn't buy a peanut butter sandwich.

Lou's making no comments. It's a professional courtesy. Even during lessons she dispenses no advice during the first half hour. She wants you to warm up relaxed. Her play, I note with an odd sense of desperation, shimmers with the old concinnity of yore, like a reproach. Every ball flies two clear feet over the net to within a foot of the baseline, again and again.

Three fairly fat men, who could be husbands to the departed cows, have come in and dragged the bench to the shady corner next to Lou, where they're joking and blowing wind. Before long, as he sends a couple of our balls rolling toward Lou with his foot, one of them asks her, "Any idea how long you'll be?"

"Hard to say," she replies, tossing me a sidelong glance. "Years at least."

Like a jerk, I take this slight as bait and immediately begin to overhit. Lou, who must recognize my collapse, doesn't chide me about it. But any out-ball, no matter how close, she ignores, letting it bound off into the fence as she reaches under her skirt for another one. She holds two in a pocket beneath one buttock, requiring a risqué act of retrieval that no woman until Lou would dare perform in a tournament. Seeing it again makes me realize I never did get used to it. That hand fluttering at her ass always distracted me.

Lou comes to net and I slow the pace for her. She works me side-to-side for a few minutes, then catches a ball on her racket and motions for me to trot up there. I wipe my brow on my shoulders, one temple at a time. She leans on her forearms over the net-cord, and I do too, stretching my back, which aches from all that strenuous serving yesterday.

"Bushed?" says Lou.

"Not bad. You?"

"Well, you know I was up the whole night."

I look down at the brown bloodstain like a fringe around the back of my sneaker.

"Well, I *was*," she says. "Really, it's not like I'm not enjoying it out here. I am enjoying it. We're hitting fine. And very grooved, too, like days gone by. But, honey, I been through the wringer this week, you don't know. Give me a couple days' catching up, and we'll have at it again, six-guns a-blazin'." She pats my arm with her racket. "Maybe I'll set up some dubs tomorrow in Pasadena, hunh?"

"Mom, I can guess how I must appear to you after all the razzle-dazzle tennis you've been immersed in lately, but remember I've been back at it only a week. And really I *know* how much work there is between where I am now and where I'm going, but I'm going anyway. And I'm making it. But I would deeply sincerely welcome your help."

"I know you would, Will. That's what you told me on the phone. For starters I would say, cut off about nine-tenths of that hair so you could have it off your back. Hey, I've played with hair down my neck and I know where I'm talking from. All those wisps in your eyes—you gotta get rid of that stuff. Cut it the way I say, and you can still look like a hippie, I don't care. That's not my motive. Athletics is my motive, not politics."

"Baloney, Mom. You sound just like Skippy. I need my hair for now, and it's no handicap. Shit, Barry's hair doesn't bother him, does it?"

"You through?" calls one of the bench warmers.

"*Une minute,*" answers Lou, holding up a finger.

"And that's the other thing I want to mention, Mom. It's no feat of glory, but I beat Skippy in a match yesterday. I played truly great. *Truly* great. See, so it's still in me, Mom. I have it, and that's what I've got to get you to believe."

She smirks. "Skip Collier—whew! Right up there with Rodney Laver, isn't he?"

"Skippy sucks!" I yell. "I know he sucks! It's me I'm trying to describe!"

"OK, OK, honey. I'm teasing, that's all. C'mon, let's scoop up the balls here and go get us a soda, OK?"

"The hell with dubs in Pasadena. Tomorrow you get me out here with your woolly mammoth of a boyfriend, and I'll show off the whole line of goods."

But she's moved after the scattered balls. Holding her racket in two hands like a putter, she bends over and strokes them one at a time toward our basket. (Lou is an excellent golfer.) She mumbles something.

"What?"

"I say you'll hafta gird your loins for that tilt." She straightens. "Listen to me. You got nothing you need to prove, Will, not yet. Me and you'll spend more time out here, don't worry. I'll frankly give you my help and opinions, too, cross my big heart.

But . . . patience, right? Hell, patience must have been your first lesson after the forehand grip—you didn't forget, did you?"

I shake my head.

The waiting men get to their feet. One of them says, "Say, you two are sure a treat to observe. Ever play in any tournaments?"

"Oh, no. No, no," Lou laughs, ducking out the gate.

The car is baking. "Yikes!" says Lou. "Here—no, don't roll that down—I'll have it cool in here in a jiffy." She turns on the fan, tugs all the switches to "arctic gale," and leans back. "Whew. Let's rest a minute, OK? No, that's all I need, for some clown to recognize me down here. Jesus. Poor Barry, you don't know how overwrought he is. If some pipsqueak sportswriter sniffs him out now, slaughter could be the outcome." She sighs. "But admit it, Will, he is a cutie pie, isn't he?"

"I don't know. For a cutie pie, he has one monster pair of legs."

"Oh, God, yes. Do you remember Darlene Hard's legs? Pillars! They terrified me. Now Cliff Richey's got some set of pins, too, but next to Barry he looks like a street urchin. Oh, Will, I know you can't see it yet, but Barry's a prince, Will. He's a jerk, too, sure, but inside he's a prince. He's got it all. He could own the game. He could *rule* the game, and I think he knows it." She swerves around in her seat. "I *swear* to you there's been nobody like him on the court, *nobody*, not Perry, not Budge, not even Tilden! Command! Style! Control! Power! Lord, if the vultures of the press would get off his case, you know, and give the boy a chance . . . Will, he is history. In the magnificent flesh. I know. I have seen it all, and I swear to you, he is *it*."

I stare at her a moment and look away. Lou's eyes are like neon in the desert, a consistent, but foreign spectacle, impossible to get used to. But her vision, like mine, has always been prey to her enthusiasms. And understanding this, still I cannot forgive it. Just to mention that mutton-headed moose in the same breath as Big Bill Tilden is a sacrilege I'll hate myself for overlooking, as now I do, merely gazing off between the boxy buildings at the ocean's mist. The old man would never have let it pass.

Since that sweltering September day in 1924, in Queens, when they met—my father a fifteen-year-old ball boy and William Tatem Tilden II, then as now the greatest player on earth—the old man has borne an infectious devotion for him. This devotion had its seed planted three years before that, though, on exactly August 15, 1921, the summer my father first took work at the West Side Tennis Club tending the club's forty-odd clay courts. The new concrete stadium where he would ball-boy three years later had not been built then, so that Monday afternoon he and a friend were recruited away from their brooms to help set up folding chairs and benches near the center grass courts. The chairs would augment the permanent bleachers to accommodate the crush of spectators expected for the match next day. Suzanne Lenglen, Maid Marvel of France, Empress of Tennis, had come to America for the first time to play in the national tournament. On this day, the day before her first-round match, sprightly Suzanne's debut at the club was to consist of a practice knock-up on the unfamiliar turf with the American Davis Cup Team captain. A crowd of fans and photographers in their straw boaters were on hand to witness the event. The act filling out the bill happened to be a warm-up exhibition between Tilden and William Johnston.

As my father slid the chairs from the cart and snapped them into place, his friend hissed to him. "*Johnston*," he whispered. My father looked around. Sure enough, there was the wiry gentleman, arranging a few rackets and towels on the grass. Little Bill Johnston was the idol of my father's youth. He was from the far, far West—San Francisco. He was wavy-haired and nimble, and he weighed 120 pounds, near my father's own weight at age twelve. Twice he'd been national champion, but the year before he'd lost his title in five sets to the gangly figure on the other side of the net, Bill Tilden.

Just as Big Bill and Little Bill were to dominate the game through that new decade, so did they dominate the old man's attention that glowing afternoon. The Bills played hard and cheerfully, quitting at 12–12 to much applause. That rippling applause, like the black water that closes over the coin that carries the wish, sealed my father's fate. And mine, too, as ripples beget ripples. My father swore he would become a tennis hero, and a swaggering, regal one, like Tilden.

Whatever the reasons he fell short, lack of discipline and good instruction were not among them. From that day he practiced hard and daily, hitting against a wall, inside a gym, or with lesser club players for hours on end, and so, when Tilden invited him to accept a lesson or two, he had a game that could be built on. This astounding offer came that day they met in 1924, just minutes after Tilden's fifth victory over Johnston in the title round of the National Men's Singles. (Though my father had watched the champion in many matches since the 1921 exhibition, and had sometimes been close enough to him to smell his cigarette breath and to note his sweat-soaked high-waisted flannels with the red, white, and blue belt, and to feel the force of his arrogance, he had never held a hand out to him as others did.) As a ball boy, he had worked the Johnston-Patterson semi the day before, so during the final he was a reserve in case one of the boys got sick in the heat. He watched the match from the clubhouse steps. The moment it ended a heavy downpour spilled into the stadium, and the players and linesmen and reporters ran for the clubhouse. The throng swept by and there appeared Tilden, alone, it seemed to my father, all shoulders and stride, with droplets of rain or sweat in his long hair. My father jumped up in front of him, threw out his palm. "Wonderful match, Mr. Tilden," he says he said. Tilden stopped. His hands were full of rackets.

"Are you Muldoon?" he asked.

"Yes, sir," said my amazed father. "W. R. Muldoon."

"I thought so. Vinnie's spoken to me about you. Let's hit tomorrow morning, you and I, all right? Can you do that, W. R.?"

My father likes to say he remembers nothing after that, nothing he saw or heard for hours is left to him. "My brain was filled with a golden light," he says.

Vinnie was Vinnie Richards, the boy wonder of Yonkers, who that summer had won the Olympic singles gold medal the only time it was offered. Five years before, at the age of fifteen, my father's age, Vinnie had won his first national doubles title with Tilden as his partner. At West Side, Vinnie had heard enough talk about the kid's precocious mastery of the court to want a look at him. He saw a natural hitter in knickers. The boy was not a slugger, though, in spite of his dense physique. He was contained. He was no boy wonder of Queens, but he was ascendant. So Vinnie Richards decided that Tilden, the patron of many a hopeful youth throughout his long career, should see the kid play.

My father and Tilden hit for an hour. Some reporters looked on at the beginning. Afterward, Tilden said, "Muldoon, you have the stuff. I'm telling you so you won't slack off when you get discouraged. Don't get discouraged. Do you know what's the key ingredient in the recipe for greatness?"

"Practice?"

"Well, practice is the *bulk* ingredient, that's right. But the *key* ingredient, my fine fellow, is courage—a lion's courage—and heart. That's it, and you have it. Never lose hold of it, Muldoon, all right?"

"I won't, Mr. Tilden," said my father.

Over the next two years or so, while Big Bill remained unassailably at the peak of international tennis, he advised his hangers-on occasionally that they should mark his words: the Muldoon fellow would be a great one. Tilden made far too many similar predictions, and the repeated fizzling of his protégés didn't stop him. Writing about him much later, my father said Tilden was without much discrimination as to a boy's promise with a racket because his discrimination was diverted by the pure boyness of the boy—the verve, the freshness, the keen ambitions, the elastic build, the clear eyes, the peachy skin. . . . He and my father went where their lives took them, but the game kept them connected. The old man was one of the few Bill could touch for money through those last years when he was reduced to giving pay-as-you-play lessons on a junky court in LA near Grauman's Chinese Theatre, and he penned one or two letters of support to the judge, attesting to Bill's good character when they finally got him for fooling with some youngster in his car.

When I myself met Tilden, I was five years old, and Tilden was dead. My father had flown us down to the memorial service, my first plane ride. I remember Tilden wore a white sweater with red reindeer running across it. I wore new black trousers and new black shoes, and I wept into my hands because my father did. I knew then who Tilden was and what he was— what he still is—and I believed in him then as I do now. What this amounts to is another of my father's legacies to me: the worship of greatness unparalleled.

So then, how can I let my mother get off paralleling? Maybe it's just that I know Lou is godless. Her devotions have always run wide more than deep, and also, she has always considered Tilden a flaming asshole. This synecdoche is not hers alone, of course, but I remind her of it now anyway, in a wry tone. It's the least I can do.

"Well . . . yeah. So what?" she says, turning the key for ignition. "Barry's an asshole, too. See, that's the point. I mean, he's no flamer. He's no yodeler from the Swish Alps, God knows. But he's an outcast, see? By his own knucklebrain oddball behavior, like poor Bill. It's incredible, I know, but the shoe *fits*. He is the new black prince, and he is all alone on the road to the crown." With this she hits the horn, *beep, beep-beeep*, the trumpets' tantara.

Supper, by Lou's decree, is an old-time cheeseburg cookout. "Charcoal, chips and dips, gooey coleslaw from Ray's, jalapeño relish to scorch your teeth to cinders, mucho mucho beer—the works!" It's fine by me.

Restored but groggy from his all-day doze in the sand, Barry sits sprawled in one of Lou's butterfly chairs on the patio by the grill cheering on the smokily reluctant charcoal. "Burn, baby, *burn*," he keeps chanting.

In the kitchen with all the beer I watch Lou slap patties into shape. "Don't you worry," she says, "they'll get eaten." She's building a great red mound of them on a platter.

I've bought Camels, to me the most impressive brand, and this afternoon, as I've puffed away, I've been trying to find a subtle and mannerly way to make use of this virile accent on my personality. Mainly, though, like Barry, I hit the beach to brood and sleep among the masses of pleasure seekers, and I am sunburned, and my raw throat aches for icy beer, a palliative I am applying in lavish continuum.

Cici, needless to say, has not called. Whatever the effect of her day's mail on her reclusion, she has not been moved to reopen her heart to me, or I'd have a sign by now. Besides drink beer, I don't know what to do. I can't just forget her and be done with her, at least not without an earnest exchange of pleas and hugs and . . . yes, farewells, if her lips can speak one. But that's just it—they can't. So she hides from me, leaving time to do what she cannot. Yet, some ebbing tenderness for me must still affect her deeds or she'd have heaved me to the crocodiles by this time, after my outrageous blitz on her family home. She has shielded me instead. This may be gossamer stuff on which to pin my lumpish hopes, but what else have I got? Only her graduation tomorrow afternoon. Glumly, I expect this event to prove of slim value to me, since Cici will be all bubbling with friends and attended by her wicked parents, but I'll go—who knows what may happen? I must shrink from no small opportunity.

A chef of no experience and less sensitivity, Barry grills burgers like a cobbler, pounding them, poking them, slamming them over like slabs of leather, enjoying his command tremendously.

"Getcher hot dee-luxe dee-lights!" he cries into the dusk.

Lou and I sit in the flickering glow of many glassed-in candles that Lou was happy to find where she'd dumped them years ago in fruit crates under the workbench in the garage. "I still love these gizmos!" she exclaimed as she lit them. "Some things never change."

Now, as she is volubly assessing the numerous portents of a bright bright future for professional tennis ("for *open* tennis—a toast to open tennis!"), Barry brings around a platter of dee-lights, which I dee-cline, electing to wait for my own crack at the grill.

"What's the matter," says Lou, interrupting her discourse and nudging me with her foot, "don't you like *haute cuisine?*" She laughs.

"I like rare beef. I always did."

133

"You always did," she says. "That's right. Barry, sweetheart, come away from there now. Some of us don't got the fangs to penetrate your rockburgers."

He turns to her. "Hey, you gotta fry the germs out of 'em. You want germs in your meat? Bacteria?"

"We'll risk it," I say. "Or starve."

Lou gestures for his cooking fork. "Come on, let me spell you."

For an instant a look of hurt visits Barry's eyes, then he scowls and says, "Frankly, Scarlet, I don't give a warm shit."

He flaps his huaraches over to the card table after a plate and three buns, which he opens to blanket with Lou's five-alarm relish, fits them with burgers, takes a big chomp.

"Beer?" I say. I'm next to the cooler.

"Yow!" he shouts. *"Hanh. Hanh. Hanh. Hanh—"*

I shove a can at him.

He grabs it and guzzles, pauses for breath, and drains it. "What *is* this shit?"

"Relish." I hand him another beer.

"What's *in* this shit? I feel like my tongue got bit by a scorpion."

Lou chuckles. "Jeepers, Bare, that's healthy stuff. You don't want *germs* in your mouth, do you?"

He's trying to scrape his burgers clean with a Frito. "Really, have you tasted this shit? You musta screwed up the recipe."

"Chaque homme à son goût," says Lou.

He groans and looks at me. "She thinks she's still in Frogland."

After dessert (the old man's Sara Lee cake left over from last night), Lou uncorks a souvenir jug of Armagnac, and we start seriously hitting the sauce. The beer and our snoozeful afternoon have us all feeling pretty good. Lou offers loud toasts to the curative powers of cortisone and to the debilitating powers of tobacco.

Barry bellows a toast to Balboa, California.

I leap up. "Yes! And to Balboa the explorer, in his plumes and armor, *Vasco* Balboa, the first blundering white man to eyeball the Pacific!"

"Old Vasco!" says Lou. "First among far too many!"

"Vasco!" yells Barry.

This is hilarious. We laugh exuberantly and pass the jug.

"Oh, these scrumptious, velvet nights," sighs Lou, throwing a limp arm toward the firmament. "How I missed them!"

Barry leans to me out of his chair, making the frame creak. "But he was a spick, wasn't he, that Balboa. No spicka da Eeenglish, right?"

"Yeah, sure he was," I say. "Or Portuguese, maybe, now that you mention it."

"Well, some kinda greaseball anyway. He wasn't any *white* man, I know that."

"You know, you big Palooka, you put your finger on an interesting irony. The first white man to the Coast was *not* a white man. He was a wetback."

Barry coughs and laughs.

"He was *European*," says Lou disdainfully. "And speaking of peein', excuse me for to go make tinkle."

"Make me some, too," I say.

Lou stops in the doorway. "It was Indians here first anyhow. Little grubby little *nut* gatherers!"

Barry laughs.

"Piña nuts!" calls Lou from the living room.

"The lady's berserk," Barry says happily. He shakes his head. "No, but this is a groovy, complete community, Balboa. You got it all! Why would you ever wanna leave?"

"Who knows? Maybe you have a nice home back in Spain."

Barry's saying, "Fucking great beach, great weather, great hacienda to base your act. Restaurants, and hey—fishing! And get yourself an outrageous yacht, man, an eighty-five-foot twin diesel job with a crew and a French cook for when you wanna sail to Hawaii!"

"You hardly been here a day," I say, "and already you want to sail to Hawaii."

"Not me, man," he says. "I'm puttin' on the brakes right where I'm at. This is a great place! I gotta lay back and get used to it awhile. Recoup. Sort out my options awhile."

"What about Wimbledon?"

"Shit, fuck Wimbledon. She goes, 'Forget it now, sweetheart.

There'll be plenty of Wimbledons,' but no, hey, it's an option. I'm in the *draw*, man. I'm not abandoning it. No way." He starts flexing his arm.

"You hit at all since he gave you the wonder shots?"

"Shots? *One* shot, man, but the thing's humungous, like God's dick. And the guy does not fuck around. He *wiggles* the mother in there. Deep in there. . . ." Barry shivers.

"But you don't know yet whether it worked, right?"

"Hunh?"

"Did it work?"

"Shit," he says. He rises from the chair into a half-crouch to sweep his open palm through a slow pantomime of a forehand. "Boom!" His knees straighten, and his palm rises to his brow to shade his eyes from the brassy British sun. "You see that?"

"Just a puff of chalk," I say.

He turns and grins at me, a genuine grin, saying, "My man, my man." He brings up the jug of Armagnac and takes a swig. "Ahrrgh." He passes it to me. "Hey—hey, know what? Let's do something. You and me shake the lady and we go sniffin' and scratchin' around the scenery. Gimme the tour, right?"

"No shakin' necessary," calls Lou behind us. "I just started filling my bath. You cub scouts can go collect merit badges, but Barry, you stay low. Any kind of squall you raise out there could lead to evacuation, understand?"

"Ten–four, Chief. Junior here'll run my interference. Hey, Junior?"

Lou says, "Will, you know the sawdust joints to stay clear of. OK? First sign of any entanglements, you make him walk. I'm counting on you."

To this what I want to reply is something acid or inane because obviously I have as much influence over Barry as a kite does over the wind, but my throat is full of brandy chased with beer, and I can't think, and anyway now Barry belts me on the back, roaring, "Outasight! Come on, Junior, let's bust loose before she sees how drunk we are!"

Strange as it may seem, I want to go. Barry's invitation flatters me, moves me, even as I perceive its self-indulgence. Besides Lou, who else has he got? Then again, who else have I got?

Barry's supercharged vanity has no small measure of hypnotic appeal to it, partly because, Jesus, if I looked into the mirror to behold what Barry beholds, would I not also be smitten unto insolence by the same gloating conceit? He is the just avatar of ego, invulnerable to mockery and careless of every lesser mortal's worship. So, as Barry propels me down the walkway through the veil of Lou's last admonitions, I am lapsed into unprotesting, uncomplicated wonder, and I am saying, "The Asteroid Belt, we could go there. Or Phil's Hideaway, or The Broken Spoke, or 1786, where they have these waitresses in wench costumes. . . ."

"Skin!" Barry's saying. "That's my denominator. The place has gotta show me some skin, some raunchy skin—boobs and bushies, hey? Set my soul on fire!"

"Yeah!" I sing. "Tits and tushies!"

"My *man!*" thunders Barry.

We whine away in his red sedan, my spine pressed by eager speed into the leather. Lights blur. Wind whooshes. Such a cataleptic daze possesses me that Barry has to whack my arm to make me give up the brandy.

He says, "Hey, loosen up, dork-nose. This is my night. My night to hoot."

I laugh crazily and then remember, shit, my wallet's home on the hall bench. "Barry, can you lend me a few bucks?"

"Hoot and holler!" Barry shouts. He clacks a Doors tape into the slot. "Sure, man. Fuck, man, I can front bread to the Syndicate, man. I am *loaded*, flush royal, and that is all she wrote. How much ya need?"

"Say a hundred?"

"A hundred doesn't even slice through the icing, man."

"Far out!" I say.

"Arrr-*ooo!*" goes Barry, stretching his throat.

The Doors start to chant, "Hello—I love you won't you tell me your name?"

Rocketing up Harbor Boulevard to Phil's Hideaway, a destination I've recommended because it's got no go-go crowd, no nauseating strobe-light bullshit, no muscle-car mania in the parking lot, and free nachos with your third pitcher, Bad Barry manages to fasten on one blinking yellow word in the electric blaze that envelops us: NUDE.

He wrenches us through a squealing U-turn and swerves in under it. "How's *this*?" he says, delighted, craning his neck at the sign, where two ludicrously chesty depictions of what we're promised within cavort like fawns parenthesizing this enticement:

NUDE ★ Girls ★ Follies ★ GYPSY CLUB ★ Follies ★ Girls ★ NUDE

"I don't know, Barry, you like follies?" This place, I now remember, used to be a supermarket—and not long ago. Its plate-glass front is boarded over in black plywood.

"Follies! Fuck, man, I like pink meat! You comin'?"

I swig at the brandy. "No—just breathin' hard."

"Asshole!" he says with a laugh. He raps my knee with his knuckles. "What d'ya say? Let's move 'em out!"

We pound the doors shut and swagger into the Gypsy Club, Barry in the lead. A placard at the bouncer's station reads, "21 or 'Scram!'" Barry gets by, but two beefy goons lurch out of the dimness at the sight of me.

"Hold it up," says one. "Picture ID."

"Hey, hey, hey," Barry says scoldingly. "The man's cool. The man's with me, hunh?" He glances behind him and waves a bill in the ruby glow of the Exit light. "We got all kindsa ID, right?"

One bouncer takes the money. The other moves his hand like a flipper, waving me by.

"Very smooth," I say over the percussive din of music ahead of us. "What kind of ID *was* that, by the way?"

"Green, man. That was green ID. I can't keep squintin' for the numbers."

I laugh. "Sure, don't strain your eyes. Say, maybe you should start a foundation for struggling young tennis talents."

"It was a ten," says Barry. "Owe me five, how's that?" Then, "*Heyyy!*" he says, swinging his arm across my chest like a rail-road barrier. "My achin' *nuts!*"

In an orangeish light, through milky eddies of smoke (which remind me instantly to light up), prancing and swaying on a sort of gangplank above a dark phalanx of heads, are two girls in spangled bikini panties and high heels. They're doing the Pony, and their rapt, stoical audience is keeping close watch, like a jury.

Barry hustles us to a free table at the rear of the crowd where we can scrutinize these proceedings from afar, waiting for a breach in the front ranks. A bony, raven-haired waitress wearing a low-slung harness that's connected by straps to a mesh skirt sidles up even before we take our seats. She bends low.

"Your pleasure, men?" she coos in a ratchety voice.

Ogling the stage action, Barry does not respond, and as I tell her, "Beer—two beers," I notice one brown nipple peeking through a fringed opening in her halter top. It's so close—at about nose-level—that when I glance reflexively toward her other boob I swivel my head. But though there is a similar porthole on that side, too, I quickly note the nubbin is not availing itself of the view—there's only a pale blister of flesh behind the fringe.

"Quite the costume you have," I say.

She rattles off several brands of beer. She has steel-blue eyelids.

139

"Budweiser's good," I tell her. In bars back east it's all I drank.

Off she goes. I think maybe all she's got is one nipple. I feel not at all aroused, only strangely oppressed and guilty, and suddenly I remember Cici's touchingly mismatched nipples, and a sickening melancholy floods my chest. I light my cigarette, only four more to go in my second pack. "Barry," I say, "this is a very sordid place."

He has risen to follow the ponies' cantering exit. They duck behind a crimson curtain that someone's parted from the other side. Barry beats his hands together a few times and howls: "Arrr-*ooo*!" We draw some curious looks. "Righteous!" he says, sitting down. "Is this righteous, or what? My kinda titty bar, man."

"This place is bad news, Barry. It barfs and smells." I blow two smoke rings.

"I know." He surveys our surroundings with a stare. "We gotta claw for that pole position. Hey, did you see that sassy redhead dancer? Hunh? Man, my target-goal's to check out the split ends in her *bush*, man."

Our waitress dips between us to plunk down our bottles and glasses.

"What's your name, little doll?" says Barry.

"Call me Gretchen," she says, flashing a grin. Her crooked teeth embolden me.

"Gretchen?" I say.

"Yeah. That'll be four dollars."

"You only have one nipple peeking out its window there—just so you know."

She sneers. "What are you, Peach-fuzz, some kinda designer? You wanna make alterations? Come on, I collect four dollars, I do not pass Go."

I slap the table. "You heard the lady, Bad Barry. Four Washingtons. And tip her one for friendliness."

He finds a five in his wallet, which she clips with two fingers, and tells her, "You can bring two more, while I'm thinkin' of it."

"Intermission-time," says Gretchen. "You ain't the only no-mads dyin' of thirst."

"We're your favorites, though," I say.

"Huh!" she pushes out. "A lot you know." But she squeezes off an incongruous wink at me before slipping away sideways between the tables. There is something exciting about her, I think. Or else I'm so lovelorn that any hint of flirtation can unhinge me.

"Now!" says Barry. "Break!"

I grab my beer and surge after his black-shirted back like a scrap of paper in a truck's turbulence. We meet no solid resistance—a little jostling is a tolerable mode of introduction up toward the rail, and since the carpeted walkway on the other side of the rail is vacant, the congestion has thinned enough to let Barry bull through.

"Gretchen'll never find us again!" I yell at Barry. We've stopped railside at a corner right under a shuddering speaker.

"What?" he yells.

"Gretchen'll never *find* us again!"

"You think she cares?" he shouts. "Fuck!"

There's nothing too savory looking about the men pressed around us, not that very many appear dangerous exactly, or depraved, but they all have something inward and feverish about them, they all seem to wear the same twisted, shell-shocked expression.

"What?" I yell at Barry. He just said something.

"I say, hey, I think we got it licked now, hunh? You got me? We got it *licked*, dig it?"

I nod and waggle my tongue at him.

He claps me on the shoulder.

I fire up another cigarette. Now that we're up here primed and in place, I'm starting to think, *Yeah*, bring on the action, what do I care—it's great entertainment, right? Hell, *classical* entertainment. Next to me some half-bald sunburned slob chawing on a cigar sends me off on the old man again. I never did pick up the cigars for him because after breakfast I decided if tomorrow's Father's Day I should splurge on a cedar box of fine aromatic imports, each in its separate glass tube like a laboratory specimen. For splurge money I stopped by the pro shop on the way to the beach (already having blown the old man's five bucks on my Contac and Camels) to hit up Skippy for his wagered hundred. I was sure I'd squeeze some cash out of Skip, not the whole sum maybe, but enough. Little did I imagine, however, that he'd have a check drawn up when I popped in there—all Skippy did in fact was tug it out of a pile of other papers weighted by a pair of pliers and hand it to me.

"Skippy," I said in surprise, "thanks . . . you know, thanks, but I need some cash."

He said, "Do I look like a bank? We're square now, and I got no use for you—*zilch*, get it?—until you join the human race, OK?"

I stood there folding my check. "Shit," I said. "If it's a race, I must be so far ahead you can't see me."

I was oiled up and stretched out in the sand immobile as a desert plane-wreck before I realized any bartender at the club would make good on Skip's check. Well, fuck it, tomorrow I'd cash it, sneak upstairs with a luxury cigar box wrapped in colored foil and a ribbon . . . the old man's disappointment in me today would only sharpen his delight on Father's Day.

"*Hey!*" I yell at Barry, tapping his biceps with my bottle. "Tomorrow's Father's Day, you know?"

"What is?"

"Tomorrow! Father's Day!"

"Hey, my father can honk my tuba, man. What's this, you know him?"

"Who?"

"Who! Who we talkin' about? My *dad*, Chief Sucks-the-Dick."

"Me? Shit, Barry, how would I know your dad?"

"Because any dry little pop-fart with any kinda line on me is bein' sniffed out by his pack of lawyers. They're tryin' a bust my drawers over Louise and everything else along the way."

"Lou?" I shout. "Oh, hell, Barry, he can't shake you down over *Lou*. You guys are two consenting California adults, right?"

He squints fiercely down at me. "Yeah, well, he's weirded-out,

OK? Because there's this chiquita in Burbank I was engaged with before I came on, right? Last year. History, man! The Dark Ages. What's he want from *me*? Now he's got her in this apartment, this fucking *house*, in the Valley. Because, OK, she's pregnant. And he's a fucking eagle scout. But no blame's passin' onto me, man, negatory! That girl'd hump a coat hook, man. He knows it, too. So what's he *want*?"

"Maybe her!" I shout, remembering some of what Lou said about this mess over breakfast.

"Hey, fuck—tell him Happy Father's Day, he's *got* her. No, man, he wants my dick boiled on a plate with sprigs of parsley for my pubes!" He pounds his fist on the rail.

I yell, "But why?" just as the waterfall-roar of music ceases above us, leaving my ears clogged with buzzing. In my normal voice I repeat, "Why?"

"I told you," growls Barry. "He's weirded-out. I mean, that kinda says it, right?"

Indian tom-toms erupt from the speaker, and Barry elbows me so I'll turn my eyes to the stage. A husky, strutting MC in a headdress and leggings and a red velour shirt has beaten his way through the curtain and is now half-dancing up there and lashing his microphone cord around. . . . *DUM, dum dum dum. DUM, dum dum dum. DUM, dum dum dum. DUM, dum dum dum.* Then they stop. He freezes. At half-volume the tom-toms resume.

"Kowa-bunga!" says the MC, pushing his headdress higher on his forehead. "Well, didn't you shrewd dudes do right tonight! Made the right choice! Oh yeah! You hard-drinkin' bronco-bustin' panty-rustlin' rowdies on top of it tonight! Won't find the Magical Maiden *no* place but where you're at right now. Yeah, yeah, the whole world wants her, and damned if you desperadoes don't know we *got* her! The one and only Queen of Quivering Quim! Yes! Yeah, yeah, the Magical Maiden is the *most* unique piece of passionate pulchritude that the Great Spirit has dared set loose on this poor globe. Because if *every* squaw could do what the Maiden can do . . . why, no handsome brave would ever leave the tepee to hunt meat again. You'd *starve* in there! Die of *love*! Set your loincloth to steamin'. . . .

143

Yeah, she is a pureblood Cherokee princess from wildest Idaho, granddaughter of powerful medicine men and vo-luptuous In- jun vixens, raised on bear steak and mountain water, a true royal ambassador from enchanted history. She's the luscious lassie with the Cherokee chassis, the high-voltage hussy with the PhD pussy, our Magical Maiden—*made in* heaven—the reigning Queen of Quiff, hear me now, Shhhhhhhhh-Sheila Honeysweet! Eat your *hearts* out, men!"

A flurry of spotlights convenes on the center of the curtain, where through the folds a long leg appears, hesitantly circling in the air, like a bug's feeler. On the end of it is a glittering moccasin. There's some applause.

"Is that yummy you? Princess Sheila?" says the MC.

The leg withdraws. The drumbeat quickens, and horns swell in the background.

"Oh-oh," sings the MC, "*oh*-oh. Men, now, Sheila can be shy. Or she can be coy. She wants a little coaxin'—to bring her in the open!"

The drooling, empty-eyed crowd around us begins emphasiz- ing the rhythm with heavy clapping. Barry joins in, too, elbow- ing me again, urgently, for my abstention.

He shouts, "Man, you stoked, or what? Fuckin' *stoked*, man!"

So I clap.

And now the leg returns accompanied this time by a slender arm, bracelets around it in coils, sinuously waving. It extends two of its fingers and twiddles them.

"Whoa!" cries the MC. "Any you bronco-busters read sign language? No? Princess wants a paleface that speaks with forked tongue! That's the Quest of the Queen of Quim! Any forked tongues in the crowd?" He cups his ear, a few voices call out, "Yeah!", and he executes some pelvic bumps, singing, "Love it, love it, love it, don't ya know!"

The Princess has disappeared again, but the MC is grasping the curtain edge. We're all still clapping. "Men, now I give you . . . I say, I *give* you . . . Shhhhhhh-Sheila Honeysweet!" The horns blare, the drums tumble, and. . . .

Out she comes, the Maiden herself, a tall dusky girl got up in a little buckskin vest with spangles and glittering red flaps hanging from her belt that match her moccasins. She's wearing a red plume in her headband. She dances past Barry and me out along the ramp, bobbing her head and chugging her arms like a boy playing freight train. Her bracelets flash. Some isolated clappers keep the beat, but the crowd has largely lapsed into its strange attitude of truculent supervision. Necks stretch as she bounces by.

At the end of the ramp the Maiden begins shrugging out of her vest. She elicits some war whoops. Slinging the garment around on her fingertips, she aims her breasts out over the dark crowd toward the banks of lights in the rafters. More war whoops.

"She's no fucking Indian," yells Barry, nudging me. "Wadda you think? You think she's an Indian?"

"Nah. Maybe she's a Gypsy!"

"A *what?*"

"Remember the Gypsy Club?"

"The *what?*"

"That's the name of this establishment!"

"She's a *Mex!*" Barry yells. "A Mex whore!"

I laugh. He could be right. She is slick and strong with an oiled, wickedly rippling body, and she is sexy. She's sexy the way a car can be sexy, or a gun. On her mean-sweet face she wears more of a wince than a smile, but her deep, lidded eyes convey abandon and sly lust.

As the music slides into a rock 'n' roll arrangement, the Maiden Princess sashays her way back along our edge of the ramp, dipping now and then, or thrusting one brown thigh akimbo to show us she's got nothing but the acclaimed goods beneath her sparkling flaps. Her stubbornly conical breasts leap up, down, right, left, like a stadium cheering section. Barry is straining at the rail. On she comes, her gaze passing over us tepid and searing at the same time. Barry purses his lips at her and works his jaw.

The Maiden turns at the curtain and swirls half her ass, then the other half. She sets up an ocean-roll in her shoulders, and now she dreamily spreads into a split, drawing her twirled-up vest back and forth tight against her crotch.

145

"*Caramba,*" I say to myself.

She straightens into a shimmy with her arms entwined above her plumed head and the vest still drooping from its new home, obscene as a penis. But now with a dip and a flourish she snatches this away and flings it through a gap in the curtain. The drums give exclamation as, in the same motion, she plucks from the hand of a hidden accomplice (the MC?) a baton of some kind, which she starts spinning in her fingers, around her taut neck, between her legs. She has no hair there, only sequins. She dances down the other side of the ramp.

The baton, for Christ's sake, is a flute. What makes this revelation so amazing to us is that she is somehow tootling it with her nether lips. The speakers' cacophony has abated so we can appreciate such virtuosity, though except for some grunts and muffled guffaws, everybody seems bound to keep up a stony front. Why? What must she do to *move* this bunch? And me, too—why do I feel so flickeringly little? Twinges of excitement, like half-remembered parts of an old nightmare, that's all I feel. I feel sodden, distant, too awake. Another beer might help. Peering back through the assembly of faces for Gretchen, for whom I am insanely developing an attraction, a need, I miss the Maiden's unclasping of her flap-string. She has it in her teeth when I look again, and the flute depends, tweeting, from her scintillant pudendum. Jesus. Is it a special instrument, I wonder—a twat-o-phone? Barry is awestruck and, by his foot-to-foot rocking, seemingly distressed at being so far from a good view. But already she is favoring our side of the stage with a squat here or a stiff-legged bow there to offer peeps at her cleft. Its flute now disengaged, it makes a poofing sound and flexes its galloons like a butterfly trying new wings. I shake my head. I stare. I lean in with the rest, drawn to her.

When she arches her back, limbolike, to begin crabbing sideways along the ramp, the Maiden Princess, as a whole woman, as a person, folds herself away, and she is as detached from those fluttering cerise petals and sequined mound as an organ-grinder is from his monkey. What tiny muscles has she learned to put to work, and how? Is she a freak or just an esoteric sort of contortionist? Could Cici do this if she would practice? And practice?

Ahh-gh, this speculation makes me feel sick. My kingdom for a beer! "Barry!" I yell, "I'm fading for a cold one."

His head twitches, but he doesn't answer.

Out of the blue I remember the night Andy Busch gave me Auto-Suck, as a joke. It was the April before high school graduation, and we had turned in our coupons for winnings after a long evening of Skee-ball at the Bay Arcade. It was raining, a steady soaking rain that left lakes at intersections along the boulevard, the rare kind of Southland rain that would make me miss San Francisco, or my childhood. We were just standing in an archway, not in any hurry to make a run for Andy's father's Comet wagon out in the street, propped against Mobland, the last in the rank of pinball tables, and Andy was making his prize, which was a wind-up mummy that shot sparks out of its eye sockets, stalk up and down the glass.

For maybe the eighth time that spring I was nattering on about what a cool bitchen trip it was gonna be to drive across the whole giant country, one corner to the other, smoking pot, picking up miniskirted girl hitchhikers, camping on grassy hills beneath the prairie moon, taking adventurous detours through Vegas, the Badlands, Chicago, Niagara Falls. . . .

Andy was listening with a solemn look on his face, as if he knew I was only trying by reiteration to convince myself I really should do it, spend weeks alone vibrating behind the wheel when I could fly east to college, and that I never would.

"Will, you know," he said, "I got something for you, like a going-away present."

"You do?" Andy had never given me anything. He would not even look glad to lend me his board wax.

"Yeah, well, I wasn't gonna," he said. "I mean, I was, but not right now. But I ordered it and it came, so I got it now, so I might as well give it over. It's nothing humungously great or anything, so don't get excited. You want it? It's in the car."

It was cushioned in the kind of spongy mailer that a book would come in, with postage on it and Andy's address. Despite my surprise at his troubling to treat me with any small keep-sake, I was let down that he hadn't cared to wrap it.

"Don't you want to look at it?" said Andy.

I had the package in both hands like a hymnal. "I'm trying to guess what's in it."

"It's for your long journey," said Andy. "It's like a driving aid." He held his arms out and pretended to steer.

We weren't moving. We were parked under a street lamp that was trying to untangle its light from the tossing shadows of a palm. Pattering gusts of rain blew across the windows and over the hood.

I narrowed my eyes. "C'mon, A., what is it?"

"Have to open it, I guess."

It was a sort of cup or tube of black dusted rubber with a long cord attaching it to a metal knob at the other end. Something to do with a spark plug is what I was thinking. The slip of printed instructions said:

AUTO-SUCK

3 Simple Steps for Satisfaction:
1. Plug motor/activator (A) into cigar lighter on dash.
2. Insert member in receptor (B).
3. Sit back and "tool" along!

(For added security, enough cord
is supplied to string down trouser leg.)
Clean *receptor only* with soap and water.

Diversified Products
Box C-104
Long Beach, Cal.

(Over 21, send 50¢ for picture catalog.)

"What is this?" I said, laughing.

"It's *great*," said Andy.

"Does it work?"

"I'll send it back if it doesn't."

"Yeah, but what if you electrocute your pecker with it?"

"Have to sue for damages."

"Sure. Lotsa luck."

He said, "I think it's great. You fuck your car, you know? That's neat. And probably you're gonna want it, too, 'cause girl hitchhikers, that's bullshit." He flipped the key. "So, you wanna plug 'er in and let 'er rip?"

"Not on *my* beaver cleaver."

We let it grasp our thumbs, though, or a couple of fingers, and it pulsed like a milking machine at a farm. For all I know, it *was* from a milking machine. I never did use it. When I flew east I left it home and forgot about it. Until now, until the Maiden, I haven't really thought of it much. Now I realize the reason it seemed peculiar of Andy to send away for that Auto-Suck as a gift was that *he* wanted it himself. But he couldn't allow himself to have it. Maybe he hoped my happy ownership of an Auto-Suck would validate his buying one of his own, and as I think this, a little arrow of sadness zips through me.

In the sparser crowd away from the ramp I spot a waitress, not Gretchen. She'll have me another beer in two shakes, she says, if I stay put—she isn't going to roam the floor hunting for me. I wink and nod. She is trussed up like a circus horse in a harness-and-fringe costume similar to Gretchen's, though with both her nipples in isolated display. I light a cigarette, chuckling in wonder: it's a screwy, screwy world. Still, the musical bedlam prevailing in this corner of it is becoming too much for me. How do the rest of the patrons stand it? Maybe the hammering sound waves have already tenderized their brains. Barry, I see, remains transfixed by the show. In some splayed pose, the Maiden is exercising out of my view, except for her bright plume, which jiggles above the row of heads.

I glance around for my new waitress, but she's not in sight. I am suddenly very thirsty—the salt is what it is, all the pure salt Lou's making me swallow to confound my heart. On nights out with my father in years past we'd be drinking tomato juice and vodka (I had the juice, he had the vodka), and I remember how if our busy waitress stayed away too long, when she returned he'd tell her there was dust in his glass. It was funny no matter how often he said it. My father always got along well with waitresses.

Me, too, until now. I'm pressed over here into a corner hiding from my waitress because I just realized I am penniless and Barry is unreachable beyond the pale of snatch watchers. I could hit the men's room for some water, but there I suspect I'd have to dodge overcome patrons in the grip of their five-fingered dates—and water's water. Lou's Armagnac, however, is jammed under my bucket seat in the Mercedes-Benz. I make my stealthy way toward the Exit sign, slip down the vestibule, half-nod to the monolithic bouncers without really being able to see them, and push out the doors into the bright night. In the soothing shush of traffic my eardrums seem to pant in relief.

The car's open. I find the bottle, toss back a swallow, and shiver. All these automobiles. Auto-mobile. Going by themselves . . . somewhere, wherever they please. *Zoom. Zoom. Whoosh, zoom.* Ahh, I was a chickenshit kid back then not to go do what I told faithful Andy I'd do, roll alone and free across the forty-eight, hot on the trail of tomorrow. Careless—that's what I wanted to be, careless in the cockpit, top furled back, hair wind-washed and eyes goggled, just barreling along, with my raffish smirk aimed out over the onrushing roadways. Instead, I was careful. To Lou my moving east was stupid enough without my insisting I had to drive there. And she wasn't past snapping shut the family purse if my plans started to look really unsupportable. Then I'd have been truly alone and free, kicked from the nest with unfledged wings. But actually there wasn't much risk in that. Lou loved me. She would have groaned and let me go. She would have let me *bicycle* if I'd demanded. No, a chickenshit kid, that's what I was.

Or else I sensed that undiluted adventure wasn't what I really wanted (even if it was out there waiting, tapping its big foot), but that wanting it was a way to express a more fundamental wish: to end my childhood, to be done with dependence. College had painlessly taken care of all that—so I used to think. But now that I'm back in the middle of the old fettering attachments, I see I'm *still* a chickenshit kid. What did I expect? College is no route to independence, it's a diversion from it. Anyway, you

150

can't ever end your youth. Not in your parents' eyes. And independence—at least the isolating kind I was drawn to—can't be so wonderful. You'd be lost, a miserable bum. Hanging out in laundromats and libraries, camping off in the weeds somewhere, trying to pick up giggly small-town girls, drinking strange brands of beer. And what if you blew a valve or caught the flu? Who would give a goddamn? Nobody. Well, OK, there's some half-assed romance to such a tragic posture. That I recognize—and recognizing it, I soften to its appeal all over again. Because, to come to cases, I don't know what I want, and I never have. So all bets are hedged. Golden-boy tennis pro. Canadian lumberjack. Garbage man in Pittsburgh. Gigolo in Rio. What difference does it make? From this protean mess I can descend into decadence or rise to exaltation. Either way I am fulfilled, joined with my unflinching destiny.

The brandy is gone. I light another cigarette. Cigarettes go pretty well with drinking, like pretzels. They keep your thirst unslaked. Really, I am so full of shit. I mean, here I sit hoping my healthy blood pressure will succumb to my attack on it, so I won't have to skip the border for haven in that northern facsimile of the good old U S of A, my home . . . Jesus—my bets may be hedged, but I know what I want. I want security. I want cash, fame, happiness, and wisdom later on. It's the same shopping list of wishes I had when I was sixteen the morning the old man coaxed it out of me as we cruised to Tijuana for breakfast—wishes I was then about to renounce or repress. Now the circle is closing, I am beginning to see, because here I am really wanting to be a tennis pro all over again, hoping that those other bonuses will come in the bargain. Like a jerk. Even if I did make it, against the odds, what have I got? A job, a fancy job—so what? You won't survive the madness, that's how the old man put it. He was right, I guess. You have to see past jobs and even goals to, to *ideals*. Ideals? What ideals? Even if I knew, even if I could map out my life's path guided by clear, fine ideals, wouldn't it still be perilous? Yeah, but your ideals protect you—that's what they're for. They clamber around you like bull mastiffs.

But fuck, lacking fine ideals, I still want to be a tennis pro, I can't help it. Anyway, I probably wouldn't know an ideal if it bit me on the ass.

When at last Bad Barry bounds out of the Gypsy Club, I am half-asleep, but I jerk up at the commotion.

"Come *on*, cocksuckers!" he shouts.

Oh-oh. I swing open my door and hop out.

A few guys emerge from the club doorway, fanning out to give Barry room.

"*Hey!* You cock-sucking, dick-licking scumbags get *out* here!"

Two more guys hurry out. Barry ignores them.

"Hey, fuckers! Bring it to me, fuckers! I'll knock your teeth so far back you're gonna hafta chew with your asshole!"

"Cool down, you ape," says somebody.

The little crowd backs off when he spins around.

"Barry!" I call out.

He looks startled to see me.

"Barry, listen! Lou's in serious trouble. We gotta get movin'!"

"*What?*"

"Let's move, big boy! Hustle!" I dash for the car, hoping he'll lumber after me.

He does. We slam our doors in unison like a team of good cops, and Barry, whose instincts are right, roars us around the lot and back down the boulevard toward Balboa.

"What kinda trouble?" Barry's yelling. "*Hunh?* They find us? Hunh?"

"Pull over!"

"*Hunh?*"

"She's not in trouble anymore. Pull over!"

Barry brakes and squeals into a Taco Bell, our rear end tailing around just short of the garbage cans. Customers flattened in fear against the service windows glare at us.

He clutches my shirt at the shoulder, and I hear it rip someplace. "What fucking trouble?" he says slowly.

"Let go of me first."

"Talk!"

"Let *go*, he-man."

He lets go, shoving me into my armrest.

I pull up my sleeve. "Thanks. OK, so Lou's in trouble when

you're in trouble, get it? Now you're out of trouble, right? So she's safe."

"What the fuck? . . ." he growls.

"That's the story, Bad B. See? Short and sweet. C'mon, steer this tank out of the way here—you're obstructing traffic. Want a burrito?"

He curls his lips. "You little dork, you're too much. You're just like she is, full of these fucking *tactics*."

"I'm your guardian angel, right? I got recruited."

"Yeah, shit. . . . That cunt-show joint oughta be touched off, man. Gas-bomb, you know? Fuckin' blown into orbit."

Somebody swings in behind us from the street and honks. Barry honks back. He says, "You didn't even catch what went down in there, did you?"

The other car honks again, and Barry honks again.

"Barry, c'mon, crank your piece of crap out of the way! Why are you such a prick?"

"Hey, I don't eat this Mexican dogshit, man. I'm bustin' outa here. Cool with you? Hunh?" He finds reverse and backs up, watching me. "So who's in the way, man, hunh?" He straight-arms the horn.

Behind us the other car creeps backward along the curb to let Barry swing out. The boulevard flow bunches around us. The Mercedes jumps ahead. "Off we go," says Barry. "Hey, was that so tough?" He taps out a few toots on the horn. "You're a dork-nose, though, 'cause I can't stop remembering Lou's in trouble some way. And she never was. It was your shithead *tactic*."

"I'm taking that as a compliment."

"Fuckin' numbnuts. . . . You know, that joint probably cleans out maybe ten, twenty guys a night. She's still wigglin' up there at the end, right? Guys are eatin' her and all, or you can fold a bill in half, and she lowers down in front of you and scarfs it with her thing, and what they got now also, as she is gobblin' up your government money, is the other two dancers, right? They're out in the audience with their tits still hangin' out, easin' around in back of you, *nuzzling* you, right? And begging for donations. You got everything goin' at once, and if you're just some dead-ass shithead, before you know it, before you can

153

feel it, your whole wallet takes a walk, right? Kiss it good-bye, because you—"

"Jesus, you mean they got your wallet?"

"Fuck no, they didn't get it! She barely gets her claws on it before I give the bitch a ride to the wall. But that's the procedure, see? And then it's like the Green Berets've landed, man. Everybody wants to be a hero, like she's their little sister! But that lasts about two seconds before those two bulls wade in there, and I'm in the corner like it's King of the Mountain and you're in third grade, and so they just invite me to leave, right? They do not wanna get busted up, so they just say, 'Out, buddy,' and I go. Only then it hits me, why the bitch picked *me* to hook. The fucking *bulls*, man—I was fingered! Dig it? The scumbags. But by this time I'm out past the cigarette machine, and when I turn around everybody else is shovin' along behind me, and when I start hollerin' to those big scumbags to get their attention, you know, they say, 'You wait, buddy, we're comin',' only are they comin'? Fuck no. So I'm waitin' there for 'em, and outa nowhere you show up all scared and excited. You made me look like a pansy, man."

"Shit, Barry, I saved your fucking life. Those two goons know karate and everything else. They would've turned you into tapioca."

He snorts. "Fuck, you think *I* don't know karate and that shit?"

"I think you don't know how Lou deeply cares about you and *worries* about you, behind all her gruffness."

Barry glances at me, then out at the traffic. "Ahh, she loves me." Then he sings "She Loves You," with a lot of *yeah*'s thrown in. "So what? Is that so great?"

"She more than loves you. She *respects* you. She has these enormous hopes for you, Barry. Today—if your ego can bear the load, I'll tell you—today she was comparing you to *Tilden*. She was. She believes you could dominate. Become a unique *legend*, how's that? A chapter in sports history! And she can't feature you kicking it away just because you're such a Stone Age prick."

A look of disgust sweeps his face. "Tilden! Who was he? Somebody's grandfather, man. Hey, I could—"

"He was nobody's grandfather. He never even kissed a girl his entire life."

"Do I care? That was fifty years ago. Gimme a break! What did anybody know back then, hunh? They thought *biplanes* were fast, man. Nothin' on top back then would look for-real today. Tilden . . . fuck. Maybe the guy could play badminton today, you know? Bust the little birdie."

I have no reply to this bloated nonsense. But Lou is right: like Big Bill, Bad Barry is an asshole, a narcissistic oddball. Who knows, maybe he will wear Tilden's crown. Somebody's bound to. Don't old stars dim, along with memories? Maybe he will come up in thunder, the wizard-king whose uncanny powers will make us wonder whether such a greatness was ever truly known before now. Or me . . . shit, why not me? Really, a few years' hard practice, sharpening, building discipline. It's such a simple game! You just keep hitting a ball consistently through the clear air to the back of a big box. Easy! I chuckle to myself: I'm pretty hopeless. A *beer*, that's what I need right now.

Instead of charging on through the yellow light ahead, the car in front of us slows and stops, so that Barry has to jam on his brakes, cursing. "Who'd you suck off for your license?" he yells.

"How about a beer stop, Bad B.," I say. "You could use one, right?"

"Heyyy, right on." He reaches over and pokes my head with a finger. "Always thinkin', hunh?"

I direct him to the El Rancho open twenty-four hours, and he hands me ten dollars, telling me to get a roasted chicken, too, if they have any. But I wheel straight to the cooler and lift out four packs of Coors. Then I get a fat liver sausage and a loaf of pumpernickel. It's too late for cooked chickens in here anyway.

Sliding into the car with my heavy sack, I expect him to make some crack about all the beer or else to ask for his chicken, but after I open two beers, he continues to sit there, staring at the old tennis ball he's squeezing rhythmically in his hand. I take a couple of long, stinging swallows. The windows of El Rancho are plastered with "Moon-shot Specials," big posters with rockets roaring up through the middles, belching fire. "Seedless grapes! 39¢ lb.!"

Barry starts up the car, revs it once, and shuts it off. He pours down half his beer. Foam spills out of the bottle when he thumps it on the seat. In a low voice he asks, "She really say that?"

"What?"

"What you just said! About I could dominate. A legend in my own time, like Tilden and that shit."

"Sure."

"She's . . . was she, you know, serious?"

"I don't know how serious she was. She compared you to Tilden, like I said. 'The shoe fits.' That's exactly what she said."

" 'The shoe fits'?"

"Right. Exactly."

"Yeah, but like I could dominate the game—she said that?"

"Yep. That was the gist of it."

He nods. "Fuck. . . ." he says ponderingly. He finishes his beer, gives the key a quick turn, and sends a blast of gas to the engine: *brrrRRRRRMMMMMmmm*. "Hey-hey, know what, Junior? You and me're gonna play tennis! They got lights some-place around here?"

"*Now?*"

"No—*yesterday*. What d'ya think, dork-nose?"

"Barry—shit, I don't have a racket or anything."

"I got rackets, man!"

"I can't play in these sandals, either. Come on, Barry, it's *late*. What about your elbow?"

"My elbow—hey, you got elbows, right? You worry about your own elbows. You and me're hittin' some balls, and that's all she wrote."

Cruising down the peninsula to the channel to fetch my sneakers, I have a chance to get used to this idea, and what the hell, I do want to hit. I want to see what the big mastodon is made of. Also, we pass the park courts, where Lou and I played this morning, and we see they're empty—the lights are out. This is not surprising, though around here you never know; some people wander out there at three in the morning. It is cooler then, but the lights are so bad you can't really compete. And

156

they go out every twenty minutes, throwing darkness over everything, usually in the middle of a point.

My sneaks are out on the patio, where I tossed them to dry out, so it's no trouble creeping up on them without arousing my mother, who would doubtless not be pleased at Barry's intention to test his arm away from her scrutiny.

Barry waits idling two houses down while I perform the mission. The remains of our cookout dimly adorn the picnic table. A wind off the water is flapping the tablecloth. I eat some potato chips, still crispy, and gaze off at the lights of Corona across the channel. There's diesel exhaust on the breeze from somewhere, and catching its thread through the low-tide odor of weedy pilings and rocks, I discover I am crossed to the other side of drunkenness, I am planted again on sand, and the surrounding opacity is part of the night, not me.

Rounding the house to the driveway, I peer up toward the attic ventilator, hoping, I realize, for a faint glow, a sign of life. But I can make out only the denser dark of the roof's peak against the sky.

We speed back to the courts, dig out a basket of balls and some rackets from the huge trunk—which is brimful of crumpled clothing, racket frames, and yellow Wilson cans—and Barry slams a quarter home on the tongue of the light box. The beams flare above us, humming.

"Hey, you call these *lights*? These lights eat it, man."

"So whose idea was this in the first place?"

"I know, but . . . fuck. If Nixon got shot today you couldn't read the *headline* under these lights."

"Well, maybe they'd mention it on the radio," I say, and he stares at me. "You sure you want to do this, Barry?"

He raises his stack of rackets to his shoulder like a shotgun and aims their butts at my face. "Get your ass on the other side of the net."

I feel pretty good, loose and shambling in a lively way. From over here on my baseline, Barry still looks enormous. He looks big enough to be a doubles team all by himself.

"Forehands!" he calls over.

So we start out stroking gently cross-court. This is easier since we have beers in our left hands. After a few minutes, I let go and pound two or three, but Barry slows those up with under-spin to keep the pace down. Fine by me. Bad Barry's hardly been so peaceable all day, and our ruminant pace makes me wonder how I ever could have given up tennis so totally for so long. Isn't this just the kind of moment I loved as a kid, shuffling and pokking, looping the ball into soft flight sweet as a Frisbee's? No. I can remember it as though I loved it, but I didn't. Or if I did—just a little—that little love was smothered then by my impatient aggressions: you couldn't *beat* anybody with these shots; these were not the bullet placements that would work some panting sucker side-to-side like a mad dog on a chain until you drifted in for the coup de grace, probably to his relief. Maybe I played too many tournaments too young. For me by age twelve, when I was strong and steady enough to gain confidence with easy stroking, tennis was not the ethereal dance I first took it to be from my parents' early example. It became battle. It was a contest always, in no shades of gray, and from practice I wanted to learn how to win, that's all. Is this why I quit? Because I sensed I could not love the game for its grace but was instead doomed to measure myself against its perfect standard over and over, forever? Maybe. Yet isn't winning a pleasure? What *is* a game, anyway, for Christ's sake? Who plays a game to lose?

At this point I note Barry has upped the tempo. The balls are flying flatter and bounding with determination. As he ups it some more, I stay with him pretty well, only missing a few, overhitting. Then he really starts to muscle, carving his shoulders through each stroke, and the blurred object of our attention jolts my racket like a baseball. I can barely handle it. I can block it, but not comfortably. I'm behind every ball, as if he's scrambled my timing with radio waves, and when I hurry my swing, my control just bails out.

We stop to pick up balls. From the net I say, "Hey, you ox, do you always clobber the poor apple like that?"

He glances up, smiling. "Come on, don't insult me. We're

groovin' it, right? I don't hit nothin' *hard* unless I'm under pressure."

I can't tell if he's serious. "Really? Far out." He probably is serious.

I watch him pry open two more beers on the gate latch. "Thirsty?" he says. Underhand, he tosses me a bottle with enough arc so it loses just some foam in flight. His own he pours right down, head back, throat pulseless as a funnel.

"OK," he coughs. "Get back there. Same thing, other side."

The lights go off with a hollow-sounding clink. Barry shoves in another quarter.

"How's the wing holding up?"

He pauses as if he has to think about it. "Good," he says. The unguarded pitch of his voice exposes the relief he feels, and I am swept by a brotherly tenderness for him. He's really such an innocent, for all his stupid bluster.

And I won't deny it, his talent is whopping. We run through a twenty-minute progression of backhands, quitting, as before, at a plateau of bruiser-balls that I have to slice and float to stay in the rallies. I feel wobbly out here, as if my daddy just took the training wheels off my bicycle.

But shit, three weeks' work against his bludgeon, and I'd be matching him, I'd be on it, sending those bruisers back with interest, right? *Right?*

Once more, darkness floods our little arena. It's so late headlights on the boulevard are only occasional, bartenders going home.

"Let there be light!" yells Barry. He feeds the machine . . . just to see to gather the balls, I'm thinking, until he says, "Up for some games, Pancho?"

"You serious?"

He crouches, lashing the air with his racket. "You know it! Gettin' up for *England*, man. Dig it! Strawberries and cream!"

"C'mon, Barry, under these lights?"

He frowns. "Hey, no grudge, no gamble, right? Nothin' on the line. Relax and serve 'em. And you can take thirty."

"What for?"

"Just for the halibut." It's one of Lou's expressions.

"Fuck you, Barry. We play even or we don't play."

"What a dork. OK, dork, serve."

Even at my peak (whenever that was) my serve was not impressive. It was firm, and I could move it around the box some, but it was no can opener. In fact—and this is the key to the trouble—my serve was the first issue of conflict between my father as coach and my mother as coach. My father wanted me to have one, and Lou didn't. That's not true, but my recriminating hindsight is sharp. What Lou gave me early on was a kid's serve, a woman's serve, a crisp, artful tool, mostly flat with controlling sidespin that kept it deep and low. One summer during her touring years, as I grew taller and stronger, the old man began tinkering with it, angling my left foot more acutely to the line, pushing the butt end of the racket up inside my palm, exaggerating my backswing, raising my toss, urging me to paste the ball toward a corner and storm the net for the kill. Lou's autumn return to these developments was traumatic. Granted, my new weapon was a long way from crushing, but so was I a long way from menacing opposition. For the old man, watching me grunt my manly cannonball into play must have been like a father watching his son at the wheel of the family car knowing the hellion he'll be some day. For Lou, standing hands on her white-skirted hips that misty morning in October 1957 (having arrived the night before on a puddle-jumper from Idlewild, O'Hare, and Stapleton), the sight of me rearing up to pound my "surprise" at the old man's cooperatively vulnerable backhand was a source of stunning consternation. When I turned to her, my heart plummeted. She was slowly shaking her head.

"Mom, I can hit it harder. I can belt it, Mom! Watch!" I tossed up another ball, but my father was now crossing by the netpole.

"Louise . . ." he began.

"Think he's Jack Kramer, is that it?" she said. "Who is he? Gonzales?"

"Louise, you have to give in on this one. Every coach in the country's pushing serve-and-volley. You should see some of these kids we play. Pint-size kamikazes."

"I want to know why you can't stick to the *simplest* little program, which we set up so nicely—with agreement all around—in May. Why?"

"We *have* stuck to it. And we've embellished it! Right, Will? You tell her. Haven't we been good boys?"

She moaned.

"Mom, serve-and-volley's been around since the dawn of time," I said, quoting my father. "Kramer didn't invent serve-and-volley."

"Yes, Willie, I know that. It's a fad. It comes and goes. *We* don't fall for fads, remember? We stick to the basics."

"At the boy's age, Louise, every nuance is the basics. Besides, he's absorbed the *basic* basics anyway."

"Is that our plan, William? Now are we building nuances? We were building a simple winning game. That was *my* understanding. We're giving the boy what works, not whatever the fashion of the day happens to be."

"But be reasonable now, Louise. If he has a serve he can follow to net when he wants to, you see how his wider choices give him generalship?"

"Here's 'reasonable'!" barked my mother. "Look, number one, he's too small to hit the damn stroke in the first place. Number two, it's too much effort for too low a percentage. Number three, he does not need it. Number four, we already settled this months ago, and you both know it." She turned to me. "Will, you can take charge of *every point* with your first serve. All you need is . . . what?"

"Consistency," I said.

"And?"

"Placement."

"What placement?"

"Into the body or off the court."

"See? You do remember."

"Yeah, but Mom, I'm good enough at all that now. Me and Dad are making it *effective*."

"Honey, the way you make it effective is by practicing it. And

161

if you can't get it where you want it every single time you try it, you're nowhere near 'good enough.' "

True to the old man's prediction, however, Lou did have to give in on this one. Over supper, between bottles of wine, as our reunited little family got used to itself that night, trading funny stories and warm glances, the talk turned again to my hopes— and to my parents' hopes, then both the same.

My father was saying, "So I left. I was furious, I was miserable. He's a game into the second set, and suddenly I very simply can stand it no more, and I left. Did you see me disappear?"

"No," I said. "Well, yeah, but not right then. You walked kind of . . . you know, you looked sick."

He laughed. "I *was* sick. Imagine my frustration. An entire morning invested in sure-fire ways to pick apart this goony kid's offbeat game, short-balling, smashing for angles. We knew what was coming, and we had the goony kid skinned in advance. But then bing-bang, in twenty minutes we're down seven games to none, and the goony kid's entire goony entourage is hooting and stamping their feet, and so I left. I meandered down through the trees and the parking lot and wound up sitting on the bank of a babbling brook that runs by the fairway there with my toes in the water. I thought, Well, hell, we got three good matches out of this trip anyway, and when we meet this kid again in the city we'll have the solution all doped out, we'll be really ready. More than an hour I perched there, listening to jabbering golfers strolling past me and the chirping birdies and tossing pebbles at water bugs, trying to give Willie time enough to shower and gargle a couple of Cokes before returning to the scene of the crime—and wishing I had a bit of gargle myself, actually—and then I meander on up to the clubhouse to perceive a rapt throng still surrounding number one. Well, it's definitely too early for the finals, and then when I spot the pinched faces of all the goon's fans—they must've uprooted the entire family tree for the occasion—the terrible truth knifes through me: he's still in it! I propel my bulk to an opening just in time to catch Will standing in the backcourt like a cigar-store Indian as the ball sails by him over the baseline for the match. Ye *gads*! I have missed it—the triumph of his budding career, and I, his reprobate father, have *missed* it! Well, dear listeners, I was so ashamed of myself then, that I put the accent on my spinelessness by not owning up to it. I jumped up and down—"

"You congratulated me," I said. "And you said . . . whatever it was that I did to him."

"I said you *eviscerated* him. I didn't know what the hell to say, I was so upset with myself. And you were so pleased with *your*self it was truly painful to see it, to be excluded from it. But then I admitted my perfidy, didn't I?"

"Not *right* then."

"No. You're getting to be a stickler in your old age, aren't you? Anyway, Lou," said my father, grinning at her, "the lesson I learned that day is not the obvious one. I'll always find appeal in the most sinister omens—usually with good reason, naturally—but the lesson I *did* learn—"

"Dad's warped," I said.

They laughed.

"The lesson? . . ." said Lou.

". . . is that it's high time Will took control of his own game, evolved his own strategy. Louise, he won that match without me. He abandoned our wrongheaded scheme, and constructed his own—on the spot."

"I played *his* game, and I plastered him."

"True, but also you mixed it up, right? You looped him, you lobbed him, you sliced him, you dinked him. You had him chawing splinters out of his racket by the end there. He was a basket case. Lou, here's my point: if he wants to try serving a thunderbolt to go along with that banana-ball you've talked him into, we *must* let him. We must give him generalship. Do you see?"

Lou was smiling at us. She emptied her wineglass and threw up her hands in surrender. "OK, OK, OK! We let him develop it, we let him practice it. . . ."

My father and I shook hands across the table.

"*But*," she said, "there's gonna be rules. First, he doesn't drag out Big Bertha until he can put six of ten in there during practice. And then he doesn't boom 'em more than twice in any one game—and never unless he's at least one point ahead. Agreed?"

Did we have a choice? Yet I wish I'd had the stubborn presence to say, "No, Mom, I'll develop it. And I'll decide when to put it to work." The crimp Lou's strictures put in my newly acknowledged generalship did not trouble me at first. Three and four years later, though, after we had moved to Balboa and I'd stopped gaining in the rankings (I never cracked West Coast top three), and after I was tall enough to really crank a first serve when I felt like it, Lou held me to our agreement. I did not petition her, in fact—I knew that would be pointless. Instead, I welshed. Not with conviction, either, but sneakily, with a paltry, furtive daring that only left me feeling guilty and resentful. But I was under pressure. Some of these guys were *good*. And I was handicapped. So in match after tough match, behind a little, or tiring, or bored, if Lou was not close by to see it, I'd slip in the big one where I shouldn't, serving for the ace.

The sad, perverse irony was that I believed my mother was right. "Your big boomer," she would say, "is only gonna beat those slow dodoes you'll beat anyway, without it. Players who're giving you trouble are gonna handle it enough to *keep* giving you trouble. And you're gonna start faulting trying to bust gut with the thing, and you end up opening too many points with your second serve. Get me?"

Sure. By my teens, however, the issue had come to be not the logic of the winning game, but the command of my game, the command of *me*. So I rebelled. And the focus of my rebellion was my serve, which then became my Achilles heel. Toward the end, just before my unforeseen (if not unforetokened) break with tennis at sixteen, in tight matches with Lou on the sidelines, I would come inevitably to that crucial ad-out when I'd suddenly think, Shit, if she weren't over there chewing her thumbnail, I could rocket this ball for deuce! It got so I didn't like my serve anymore. Because Lou always knew what I'd do with it, I began to believe every hunched receiver across the net knew, too. During matches, against the firmest tactical standards, I would experiment. I would change my motion in little ways, looking for a bit more spin or speed, thinking, *This*'ll get him, but beyond that knowing it wouldn't—it would get me. (Of course, it got Lou, too.) What's more, it's no coincidence that on that afternoon five years ago when Lou blew up at me, and I cracked, and tennis drained out of me like blood, I was practicing another forbidden service.

Shit, I'm thinking as I warm up the same queasy old serve, tossing balls up against the night sky . . . why do I want to play this game? It was the glory and blight of my boyhood, and it's gone. Gone! How can I pretend that now some amalgam of desire and brushing up will ever carry me onto the same court with Laver, Pasarell, Santana, Newcombe, Richey, or even Barry Glines? Admit it, Muldoon: you quit the game at sixteen because in your heart you knew that it had quit you. Not only is it gone now, but it was gone then. Jesus, is that true?

"Anytime you're ready there," Barry says acidly. I've hit about twenty in practice.

"I'm ready for a beer," I say. I go over and open one. I pour down as much as I can, burp, and return to the line. "Now I'm fortified."

"These good, or what?" says Barry.

"Good for nothin'," I say.

I serve. Goliath drives a backhand down the line which I try chipping back the same way, only the brute looms above the net for the easy volley. So it goes. I double-fault the last point away looking for something extra. What's new?

We change ends. Barry's all set, he tells me—no practice.

I say nothing. He still wants to impress me, the big, dumb kid. He has a towering motion . . . *Thwock!* Then, *chang*, the ball smashes the fence behind me.

"Out!" I say.

He's up at net, grinning. "Come on, dork-nose."

"That ball never bounced, Barry. There should be a little crater around here someplace, but I don't see one."

He laughs. "OK, second service." It's a twist to the forehand corner that kicks two feet over my head. I get my racket on it, and I push up a lob that bounces about where his serve did with enough spin still on it to send it slithering to the net.

"How was that?" says Barry.

"Superb."

His rocket to the ad court is again invisible. *Chang.*

"Out!"

"*Hey!* Cut the shit!" yells Barry.

"My call, big boy. You think I got radar? When I can't see 'em in, they're out."

He grumbles something with *fuck* in it, but he's relieved and happy with himself, it's clear. Really happy, no doubt. Why not—he's going to Wimbledon, for Christ's sake. Lou is, too, I realize with a pang in my chest. In fact, if she's convinced the stud is cured, they'll be heading out for the grass forthwith. Soon as they can get reservations.

Barry puts a leash on his big one for me so I can handle it in this feeble light, which does me no good at all, since any of my returns that happen to reach the net also reach Barry, who, if he had a saber instead of a racket, could slash the ball into sixteen pieces and have them all fall on my side of the net.

We play two more games. I get exactly no points. He gives away nothing, even when he starts feathering cute dropshots and parabolic stop-volleys that are stone-dead on the asphalt by the time I scamper up there. I am awed and done in. Really, the galoot flicks his racket around like Lou and her spatula. He could decorate a cake with it.

He's swatting balls back at me to serve, but I've left the base-line. I drop my weight on the bench and uncap another Coors.

"C'mon, Junior, you cashin' in already?"

"Gee, I didn't think you'd notice."

"Hey, c'mon, it was just gettin' *fun.*"

"That's what you think. One man's fun is another man's pathos."

"Well, fuck, you gotta finish out the set. Where's your manners, like a gentleman?"

I down a big swallow. "Aw, you don't need me, Barry. You're so fast you can take a little more off your serve and play against yourself. Go on, I'll root for you."

He walks over. "You're bent, you know?"

I shrug. "If I didn't know it a week ago, I sure know it now."

"*One shot*, that's what's so outrageous. One humungous,

mother-humpin' shot, and I am back in the saddle. Give that doctor a raise, man. Hey, I'm gonna send the guy a magnum of champagne, *and* box seats at Wimbledon." He pauses and snaps his fingers. "Hey, what're you doin' this summer? You can bum along! You wanna? We could use you. You can get my rackets strung up and shit like that, hey?"

"Fuck you, Barry."

"Hey, I'm *serious*. You get your own money to spend, and fuck, your own room! Bitchen, right? Listen, I'm gonna say something, OK? You told me what Lou said about me, and that was great, and then we get down here, and hey, I learned a lesson from you, man, you know that? Dig it, when you called those two faults out there . . . the second time I was ripped. I coulda given your nuts a ride, you know? But when you go, 'If they're not in, they're out,' I get this new attitude—like, all right, do I control everything? No. I hit 'em, but other guys call 'em. Let it happen. Stay on track. It's what she's been raggin' me about for months—'Direct your energies at the ball! At the ball and *only* at the ball.' But it takes you to make it sink in. I mean, no linesman makes a for-shit call on purpose, like you. And so like what matters out there is what *I'm* doin'. I just gotta play my game and let the shit slide by. That's my future act, right there, like I got a crystal ball. But wait—I forget why I'm blowin' off now. . . . What was I gettin' at?"

"You were getting me to fly to London and be your valet."

His face darkens. "What's your problem anyway? Is it 'cause I'm dicking your mommy, hunh? So you don't like me? Or 'cause I can play this game, and you're a rabbit?"

"Both—I'm full of problems." But with that, I relent and tell him, no, I like him all right, and Wimbledon sounds far out, but there's too much going down at home for me to consider leaving.

He scoffs at this. "Like what? The draft?"

"Not just the draft."

"What else? A girl, right? So what! Bring her along. She cute?"

I say nothing.

"Hunh? Hey, you know we're goin' to Paris after."

"Groovy. Send me a postcard of the Eiffel Tower." I get up to gather our balls before our lights shut off.

"OK!" he says behind me. "Kiss away a free trip to Europe. Hope your chippy's worth it—but I doubt it."

As we leave the court, Barry wears a petulant scowl. I light my last cigarette, leaning in through the car window for the lighter, and jump when he slams down the trunk lid. This machine will be lucky to last ten thousand miles.

Halfway home to the channel, Barry suddenly switches off the jangling Jimi Hendrix tape and swerves to the curb. "I'm just gonna say this now: no little pop-fart like you is gonna get me into a bad mood. All right? 'Cause I'm in a fuckin' *good* mood. And you got your head wedged."

I'm looking the other way, out at the darkened houses, smoking. It's quiet. I can hear a party still going on somewhere. And the ocean behind it.

Barry's saying, "It's 'cause she came out right to your face and said how great I am. Isn't it? And back there when you witness the evidence, you can't stand it. 'Cause I'm so far past where you're never gonna be it makes you sick. You hate me, right? You hate me, and you wish you could have everything I got. 'Cause if *you* had it, *you'd* be a class athlete. *You* wouldn't have a fucked-up personality like me, right? So where do I get off bein' great, right?—with my fucked-up personality? Well, that's how it works, man. Sometimes bein' great fucks you up. Ever hear of that?"

I open my door and slide out. "Guess I'll walk it from here, Bare—get me some air." Glancing back at him, swinging the door shut, I'm shocked to see two shining rims of moisture low in his eyes, and then the door closes, and the light's gone. "I don't hate you, though. You're in a good mood, I'm in a bad mood, and there's the rub, bub." This is another expression of Lou's, which I hope he'll appreciate. "I'm really glad your elbow's better, too. Shit, if you win Wimbledon, I can tell everybody I got you in shape for the epic victory."

"*When* I win Wimbledon—dig it."

"Yeah, you better," I say.

"Hey, I just wanna know, though. Like, is it a girl? Some hot honey? Why you gotta hang around here?"

"I hope so."

He laughs. "You *hope* so. That's pretty good. No, really—is it?"

"Her name's Cici," I say. "She's really beautiful, young, blue eyes, nice high round boobies, smooth smooth tan skin that she's never shaved, body all toned up from yoga, lots of blonde hair, blonde pussy, and perfect everything else. Only now her crazy parents won't let me near her. I haven't seen her since I got home. I even broke into her house, but her dog chased me away."

"You did? Fuck. That's weird, but I would think, it's a free country, you can *see* the girl if you want to. Stand out in her street till she comes out. Girl's gotta come out sometime, right? Then you go up and talk, right? Easy? You take a car aerial, also, you know, and you can whip the ears off any dog before he yips twice. Fuck, I'd go up with you, man, run your interference."

I chuckle at that. To stop Barry, Colonel Bamberger would have to call in the Strategic Air Command. I can see him there, high on the electricity tower, swatting B-52s out of the air with his paws.

"Thanks, Barry. If I really decide to attack, I'll recruit you, don't worry."

"Or what we do is we order a big combination pizza to be delivered to her house, and then her parents get mad and think she did it, and we're in the bushes, and when she comes to the door, you grab her. Hunh? Easy?"

"I got an idea, Barry. You think up, say, three or four of these plans, write them down in detail, and when D day rolls around, I'll pick one."

"You fuck," he says. "Your head's wedged worse than I said before. What do I care if you see the blonde pussy? I don't give a fuck. If you want to, there's always ways. That's my motto."

Bending and reaching into the backseat for six beers, I say, "Well, dreamboat, thank you for a beautiful evening. I hope you get home safe from here, or Lou will boil me alive."

169

He laughs. "I'm gonna go back to the cunt-show . . . throw a bomb in there."

"Lob one in for me, too." I step back and watch him vaporize a quarter-inch off his Michelins on the way down to the channel.

Like a starfish I am stretched flat on the sand in the moon-shadow of my old elevated guard box at the foot of 11th Street. Last summer I would show up here very early, at six or so, when only some surfers would be bobbing out there, even in the fog, and I would sit with my spine against this stanchion and smoke hash. Those were the best moments of my days. How can they seem now so irretrievable? How can my past seem so broken from me, all its links uncoupling, under what strain?

The moon is almost half itself and going down. It is a perfect thing, measurable but mysterious, beautiful as a ruin, and I don't want anybody tromping around on it, trashing the place with a load of explorer junk. Why can't we just skip it? Go on to Mars. Look, first, being a planet, Mars is equal and unnecessary to Earth. Second, it's merely a pink speck in our sky, but it has an integrity that's always beckoning, and third, our spacemen could find true surprises there to justify the venture. On the moon, nothing will happen to those guys, that's the trouble. They'll be like firemen at a false alarm, standing around with their axes drooping. It won't take the rest of us long to realize the whole trip was a waste, either, and from then on how will we be able to look at the moon without twinges of guilt? Thinking this way makes me see how much like my father I am sometimes, a soured romantic. I'm a loner, too, an escapist, and a resolute drunk. How is Bad Barry like his father, I wonder. How is Andy Busch like his? Could we change these qualities if we wanted? No. Yet aren't we better than our fathers, generally, overall? Sure. But if we have no influence over the changes that improve the old models, as we feel our way, fashioning our young selves, what does? That's what I'd like to know.

Wandering home along the shore, shoes in one hand, last beer in the other, I decide—and the moon smiles at this—that the Russians really could save the world. I mean it, they could. A

170

grand sense of humor is all it would take. The American moon-ship descends to the pocked surface, nestles its pie-plate feet in the dust, and then *boom, pow, shoosh*—fireworks! Roman candles, catherine wheels, a banner spewing colored sparks that says, "Congratulations, USA!" Little spotlit busts of George Washington popping up in the craters. A few tables decked in crepe and spread with caviar and Ritz crackers and vodka for toasts. What a gesture! It could save the world! I should cable the Kremlin and propose it. . . . Shit, this is not the way my father thinks. This is the way a hippie thinks. Hippies are founts of irreverent whimsy. Still, for the Russians, shouldn't this idea have a lot of charm? Yeah. Let's all laugh and be friends, they'd be saying. They would set the tone for the new decade, the Jolly Seventies—and the future of all earthly life would brighten.

A slivered glow seeps from the attic ventilator at the peak of the house. I stand below it, thoughtless, dizzy with beer. "Dad!" I call in a whisper. "Dad!"

Waiting, I wipe sand from between my toes. "Dad! Daaaaad!" I breathe, "Daaaaad!" and then I dash inside before he can answer because I suddenly don't know what it is I have to say.

A jackhammer hangover rips through my tarry sleep, punches apart the cobblework of my dreams, and wakes me. The bed shudders. Sunbeams sink their claws into my eyelids. I lie curled and still, trying to slow my blood's rush, but I have a thick, stubborn heart.

OK. I sit up.

Nope—I lie back and drag the sheet over my head. Why did I do this to myself? Is my life in such turmoil that I have to be drugged to endure it? I guess so. It was yesterday, at least. But *today*, today I'll do much better. Fuck, is it today already?

Let me just rest. Rest. There. Rest, rest.

I can't.

I can if I try. Try!

. . . It's no use. I swing my legs off the mattress, and my feet hit the floor like shot birds. Keeping the wall close by, I plod along to the bathroom, twist on the water, and drink from my hands. Lou's smoke floats sickeningly up the stairway. And the awful smell of coffee. I take a few aspirin. My throat burns from all those cigarettes. I piss into the sink and go back to bed.

There's a magenta world of swirling pain behind my closed eyes, and if I open them, all the too-straight lines of my furniture vibrate. Get to *work*, you goddamn aspirin. I'd shoot up a couple quarts of morphine if I had it.

But all I can do is ball up beneath the sheet with pillows over my head. The punishments slowly subside.

Then—Je-sus *Christ*—comes Lou's same old *knock-na-na-knock-knock, knock-knock.* I don't move. She'll crack the door, stick in her face. . . .

"Rise and shine," she sings. "Day's a-wastin'!"

"Go away."

"Oh-oh. On a toot till all hours, hey? Fun, wasn't it? Should I call a priest?"

I groan.

She chuckles. "I wouldn't've come in, except you got a phone call which they said was important."

"Now? Who?"

"Got me. Definitely female."

"OK."

"OK what? Want me to say call back later? You're indisposed?"

It must be Cici, I'm thinking. It has to be. She finally knows she needs me. She wants us to meet at graduation, maybe, up in the auditorium loft behind the stage lights. And now she has only a secret moment to talk. Shit, pull it together, boy. You have to talk to her. Now!

"Hunh?" says Lou. "Rigor mortis setting in, or what?"

"No, I'll, uh . . . I'll take it in the study, if I can crawl that far."

"Join us for breakfast after. Fresh musk melon and limes."

"Barry's *eating*?"

She laughs. "He's giving it some thought."

With my sheet around me, I shuffle to the study, shut the door, jerk up the receiver. *"Hello?"*

"Hello, Will?"

"Who's this?"

"Is this Will?"

"This isn't Cici, is it?"

"No! Will, is that you?"

"Yeah, it's me."

"You don't sound like you."

"You don't sound like you, either. Who are you?"

"I'm *here*! I'm in Venice!"

"*Susan?*" I hear Lou hang up downstairs.

"Come on, you knew it was me. I just got here an hour ago, and I love it! All these little houses and everything. Cafés, palm trees, the beach. It's fab-a-dabulous! How far is Balboa from Venice?"

"Susan, let me call you back, OK? Things are very crazy down here at the moment."

"What do you mean? You're stoned, aren't you? You're stoned out of your tree."

"I can't talk now. Give me your number, and I'll call you in a few days."

"Days! Oh, criminny, I knew this would happen. I don't know a soul in this whole state but my sister, and she works. I thought you wanted to see me and teach me surfing and everything. But now you can't even talk." Her voice hardens. "But I guess situations are quite different off campus, aren't they?"

"Susan—shit, it's a bad time, I'm sorry. Are you going to give me your phone up there, or not?"

"Not if you're swearing at me."

She reads off the number—three times—and I apologize again, and she makes me absolutely positively promise to call ("OK, now, you *promised*!"), and we hang up.

I press my forehead to the cool glass top of the desk. My ankles ache. I can smell dust and the roof's shingles heating in the sun, and my own breath reflected up at me by the bunched sheet in my lap.

I can't help it. I want to be a tennis star. If this makes me a jerk, OK, I'm a jerk. But I am not a jerk. After you get to a crossroads in your life that demands a hard decision, and once you have made that decision, if you allow it to crumble under its first tough tests, *then* you're a jerk. Where's my slit-eyed resolve? When the leathery old gunfighter sneeringly blasts the fancy shooting iron from the hand of the callow kid, doesn't the kid retire to a hut in the canyon to practice for five years until he can put a bullet in each sneering nostril before the old gunfighter can think, *Oh-oh*? How do I dare consider quitting just because I can't return Barry's supersonic serve in the dark? What do I expect? The big asshole's a seasoned pro! For months he's been out pounding balls with tennis whizzes around the

174

world, and what have I been doing? Dropping acid and marching on the Pentagon. Yet, I'm young. I'm the callow kid, and years of discipline and practice are all I need. I lift my head and smack my fist into my palm. Yeah! Goddamn it, I can't be letting little doubts and setbacks turn me off the path to what I really want in life!

So now in a sudden sweat, heart racing, I grab the telephone and feed it Cici's number. Then immediately I hang up. My skin prickles with fever. What am I afraid of? If the horrible mother answers, so what? I can handle her. I can tell her she's won some panty hose. But if Cici answers . . . That's it. It's Cici I'm afraid of, her voice cool as milk, telling me, "No." Calmly this time, without countervailing hysteria, telling me, "No, I *don't* even want to see you. . . . No, Will, it's over. . . . Because it's over, that's why. You understand 'over'?" And me begging, me blubbering. . . .

Well, shit, if it's going to come to that anyway, what's the sense of waiting? So again I jab in the magic code, and the dial whirrs as it used to, spelling a C with its fingerholes. *C . . . C. . . . C . . . C. . . .* I do love her.

One ring. "Hello?"

Jesus. "Cici?"

Nothing.

"Cici Marla Bamberger?"

"What?"

"William Ryan Muldoon the Second, at your service." Why am I talking like this? "Cici, don't hang up! I have to see you."

Nothing.

"Come on, Cici, please! You know how determined I am. You know what I'm capable of."

"I can't." The stress in her voice hurts my own throat.

"Why? What's *wrong*?"

"I can't have boyfriends."

"*What?*"

"Oh, Will, I . . . you don't know! I can't talk to you."

"Bullshit. Listen, meet me today after your graduation, OK? Out on the cafeteria delivery dock, OK? Got that?"

"I'm not going! I can't do anything! They think I'm sick. But

I'm not. But . . . oh, God, Will, my whole—*shhh*! Wait!'' she whispers. ''I have to go.''

''Cici—''

She's gone. I beat the phone against my father's foam type-writer mat, and then hang up.

''Trouble in paradise?''

I spin around, my head throbbing. ''Dad! Jesus Christ!''

''Make up your mind,'' he says. He's in the corner sitting cross-legged on the floor in his underpants and an open suit coat. His legs are hairless and bruised-looking. ''Sorry if I snuck up on you, Will. I didn't mean to eavesdrop, but I got caught in the hallway when your mother started up the stairs to your room, and I had to scuttle in here out of sight, and then you were on the phone—I was touched by all the drama. Anyway, sorry to intrude. Say, any chance I could scare up those cigars?''

''Uh, not right away.''

He nods. ''They're still on the rack at Ray's Market, am I right?''

''They slipped my mind, Dad. I've been distracted. But don't worry, they'll come through eventually.''

''No harm done. I think I can survive a few more hours without a panatela in my teeth. I'll tell you, though, if you could make off with a couple of those limes your mother mentioned, and some tonic water—and while you're at it—'' he clears his throat—''perhaps six or eight hard-boiled eggs, a few tomatoes, salami or liverwurst, pumpernickel bread, that Diablo mustard, a cucumber, and a few beers—boy-o-boy, would I be obliged. I got a list right here. . . .'' He tries his pockets. . . . ''Oh yeah, that old Pepsi cooler out in the garage—if you can find dry ice for it—a roll of toilet paper, a flashlight, and vermouth, and a jar of olives. You know, scrounge up what you can, use your imagination.''

''You're fixed for liquor, I presume.''

''Indeed. Never mock an addict, Will. 'Let he who is without sin . . .' and so on. You could restock your mother's booze cabinet, though. I hit it pretty hard before my retreat.''

''Dad, this arrangement stinks. I have too much to do already without running these piddly errands because you're in this half-assed exile in the attic. Do you really think Mom would give a damn that you're here? She and Barry—"

"Hold it, Will! My exile is my business. All I've got—after *you*, my *son*—is my judgment, and a few pale hopes. Your mother is convinced I'll show up here after Jack's money, *your* money, excuse me. She believes I'm desperate. However, I am not desperate. I am coolly playing out my last card. Don't you see that the main reason she's here fouling the air is to defend you and outmaneuver me? Listen, if she got wind of my dread proximity, she'd have that human cement mixer turn me into three feet of sidewalk."

"I don't think so, Dad. She and Barry really—"

"Never mind! Whatever you think, for now I'm stuck. But if you can't find the time in your 'distracting' routine to look into your old man's 'piddly' requests, I'll understand. I got half a box of Cheerios I can subside on up there until this little game's over. Those cigars would be nice, but you can forget the groceries and the rest—"

"Oh, come on, you don't have to lay it on me like that. I can smuggle you your supplies and shit. I'll do it, but you've got Mom all wrong."

"I do, do I? Tell me, have you asked her for the money?"

"Yeah, I asked her."

"And? . . ."

"She said she'd have to call Grampa Jack and see how he feels."

"Crap! Jack'd buy her Arizona with a pink ribbon around it if she told the buzzard she had a hankering for her own state. Stay sharp, Will. She's not going to make it easy for us."

"*Us!*"

"Shhh!"

"I don't feature this *us* stuff, Dad. I mean, Christ, what about me? The other night on the boat dock you worked me over pretty good with that shit about blowing your brains out because you mysteriously *need* all this money. Well, brains or no brains, what I said on the boat dock still goes: every damn nickel of that money—if I get it—is *my* money, and I've got plans. It's *my* whole future out there, not yours. Talk about

177

your pale hopes—I've got some hopes of my own, you'll be amazed to hear, and they're pretty damn vivid hopes, too."

"Of course you do. Of *course* you do." He heaves a sigh. "Hell, Will, I apologize for that manipulating diatribe on the boat dock, if that's how you took it. That's not how I meant it, but never mind, I should have known better. But I was sauced, you realize, and—"

"You been sauced for years."

He rubs a hand down his face and blinks. "I'm not excusing," he says. "I'm explaining. That day—it was seeing you that day, watching you run and hit, listening to you again, feeling your pride, your strength—I got eager, see? I got ahead of myself, and I made you mad. But the reason for that is not boozing, it's *glory*. Glory! Can you accept that? See, I am so heedless in my purpose, and so blind in my, in my *vision*, and so haunted by my regrets, that I . . . I . . . Balls. No, Will, listen—what a relief it is to discover that the biggest questions have the smallest answers. The tiniest flicker of glory is still light! And it *shreds* the blackness at the center. At the center!" He stops, his chin falling. "No, no, no, no, no," he mumbles. "I'm doing it again. Now isn't the time for this."

"I'm listening," I offer.

"I know, that's what's so tempting. I must be afraid the time will never come. Ahhh, Jesus. No use pushing it, Will. But here—until then, what you can do is try bending your mind to the possibility that your hopes and my hopes may *converge*! Can you?"

"Sure. You and I could make a great doubles duo."

"I'm reaching for you, Will," he shoots back in a whisper, "and you retreat into sarcasm, like your mother."

"Well, what do you expect? If I had maybe one notion about why you're here putting the squeeze on me, and now spouting off about glory and all that other shit, I'd—"

The phone rings.

I watch it squatting there on the glass, and it rings again.

Again, like red-hot beads streaming through my skull.

Again.

Then it stops. Lou shouts my name up the stairs.

The old man and I stare at each other.

"Will!" she shouts. "You conscious?"

I tug at snags in my hair.

The stairs give out dry cracks as she climbs them. "Where are you? You in the tub?"

"Here I am. In the study."

She shoves the door open. "What's wrong with you? You can't answer the phone?"

"Is it for me?"

"No, it's for Stokely Carmichael, but you're their second choice."

"Who is it?"

"I didn't ask. Sounds like your harem again, getting anxious."

"Mom, would you tell whoever it is you can't find me? I'm out surfing or clamming, OK? I'm feeling kind of rocky at the moment."

"I'll take a message, how's that?"

"OK. You call Grampa Jack yet?"

"I will after breakfast. But you know what Barry informed me? It's Father's Day. If you ask me, it's an insult we even had to invent the occasion, but Grampa will appreciate it. You want to get on and say hi?"

"Not if you'll be asking him for my inheritance money. It wouldn't smell very good."

"Right—smart thinking there, for a hung-over hippie. He does get noodgy about his capital."

"But—so you will try making the touch."

"Try, sure. No guarantees. But last night, Will, as I pondered your sick-looking future, I figured, how right he is. The kid scoots off to Canada, and Jack, who still thinks Goldwater oughta be elected God, is gonna slam the lid on your pinko fingers."

"Just tell him I'm one and twenty and a man. He'll cough up."

"Roger. You come down for lunch, and I'll give you the battle report."

"Thanks."

"Roger," she says, shutting the door.

"Very, very cute," the old man breathes. "You have no idea what you're fooling with, Will. Two more steps in here and she would have jabbed the destructo button, and don't imagine you wouldn't fly to pieces with everything else."

"Sorry. I guess I'm just so fogged out I don't care what happens to anybody."

"Baloney. You care like crazy, like me, and you're just afraid caring won't make a bit of difference. Say, you didn't tell me the army was baying at your heels."

I shrug. "Did I have to? You read the papers."

"I read what I want to read. But, Will, come on, Canada is a piss-poor option."

"OK, what's your advice—join the marines?"

"No, the navy."

"Oh, shit."

"No, listen! I'm serious. You run away to that wasteland up there and you'll end up in some pine-board shanty staring out at moose all day and swatting mosquitoes and reading Thoreau by kerosene light. You'll *Thoreau* your life away, get me? But enlist in the navy and with any luck at all you can serve out your hitch teaching tennis to officers in Honolulu. No stigmas attached, see? You can come home afterward. *Then* if you want to head for the wilderness, go. But if you let this thing chase you from your homeland forever, you'll become one more desolate outcast with a broken heart."

"Like you?"

He slowly shakes his head. "A comedian we got here. I, my son, am free. I'm becoming freer with every dawn."

"Hooray for you."

"Hooray indeed. Nothing should be more desired. Freedom's the road to glory."

"Sure, freedom and several thousand dollars of somebody else's life-stake."

"That's the pity for the moment, yes. But in *my* misbegotten existence, not yours. And quit being so ironic, will you? Christ! Youth is as detestable a condition as it is precious. Someday you'll see I came to you because I loved you. You, above all else. And when you do see that, whatever happens between us from now on, just don't be hard and bitter with yourself. Be glad, OK?"

I get out of the chair and plod to the door. The aspirin makes my headache feel like a soft clay weight. "I know you love me, Dad, and I'm glad already. Our hopes are never going to converge, though. So you can junk that idea along with the one about the navy. I'm going to have to screw up my life by myself. But even if I do bad as you, it's good to know I won't be totally past rescue. See you later."

"Righto," he says dully. "I was just kidding about the navy."

I go slip into bed again, but sleeping's impossible. I have too much to do. I should be smoking now and eating salt. I've got to get plane reservations up to the Bay tomorrow, and there's still Cici's strange obstinacy to pierce through. And the old man's Father's Day requests.

Dressed again in my faded baggies and sandals, I wish I had some shades. I really need shades—my eyes are burning up. So I rummage for a few minutes in my closet until I find, in a drawer with a box of rubber dinosaurs and my old orthodontic retainers, a pair of seaweed-green Donald Duck beauties from Disneyland. I look really nuts wearing them in the mirror, but they do the job. They make me feel defended.

The lovebirds must be out on the patio, because the kitchen, as I peer toward its doorway across the dining room, sounds empty. I duck in there for a few slices of melon, which I wrap in a paper towel.

The club bar isn't open yet, I know, but with the courts hopping on a Sunday morning I should find somebody around with a key to the safe who'll make good on Skippy's check.

All the collisions of strings and balls get sharper when I turn off the boulevard down the club drive between the hedges that funnel out the pokking. Walking past the club the last few summers, I'd cross to the other side of the boulevard well before the entry just to keep these heady rhythms from getting to me. Now I can admit that.

Ramon, one of the grizzle-haired groundskeepers, tells me that at least three of the officers are around because there's a masters doubles round-robin this weekend. I find an umbrella on the club deck and order a glass of milk and some sourdough toast.

Most of the portly doubles players jamming the courts have on those conical white hats, to cover thinly protected scalps, I guess. Mason Thatcher isn't out there, which is fine—I don't want him quizzing me about Lou or the old man or anything else.

The waitress brings my order. She's a stooped-over crustacean with brown hammocks under her eyes, and she doesn't give a damn about my Donald Ducks. You hear a heap of garbage back east about how the streets of Southern California are swarming with oddballs got up in gorilla suits or tutus and tights and how on the freeways Cadillac caravans scream along at a hundred and ten bumper-to-bumper with cocktail pennants flying from their aerials, how half the population is around the bend and the other half is so laid back they don't notice. So you can be wacky as you want out here without raising an eyebrow. Well, I suppose somewhere under that heap there's a sprouting bean of truth, but only because more and more these times are times we all wish we could hide from, however we can, and this easy coast is where everything happens first. Or so it seems sometimes, to me—because I'm young and I haven't seen much, and I love California.

Of course, in reactionary bastions like the Balboa Club the turbulence of the times hasn't stirred up anything to cloud perceptions. Even with the joyful love-garden up north along Haight Street long since withering at the edges and Tim Leary gone loony and Owsley in jail and the Weather Underground laying in ax handles and fruit jars of gasoline, the charter names within these hedges haven't got past seeing long hair as an ugly and stupidly irrational rejection of what's right and good, like a glass of Kool-Aid tossed in Mom's face.

So, when I recognize Gerard Silloway, the club treasurer, ambling off court four—in defeat or triumph I can't discern—and present my irrational self before him, I should expect a crack about the shades, but I've actually forgotten about them.

I let him slurp at the fountain for a while and dab his mouth with his towel. Then, after he finishes warning his partner to lay off the gin at lunch and to be ten minutes *early* for their next match, not ten minutes *late*, and after they laugh, ha-ha-ha, to each other, I butt in to ask if he could spare me a moment or two.

"Willie," he declares, looking me up and down. "Somebody said you were back in the fold. What the hell are those sunglasses supposed to mean?"

"Nothing. They mean it's very sunny."

He takes another drink. "You know, nobody can stop you kids from going around embarrassing yourselves and your families on your own time, but this place has been good to you, Willie, and coming down here dressed that way, with no shirt and with that cereal-box prize on your face is not respectful, and it's not fair to your mother and to the rest of us who used to care about you."

I remove the Donald Ducks. "I'm not trying to be fair or not fair, Mr. Silloway. Really, my eyeballs hurt, and these are the only shades I could dig up."

"Anybody can see you're not trying," he says, walking off. "What can I do for you?"

I fall in behind him along the narrow gravel path to the parking lot, and we proceed that way, *crunch, crunch, crunch, crunch*, otherwise in silence, to his royal blue Buick Riviera. I won't talk to somebody's back.

Finally, he turns. "All right, Willie, let's have it. Is it personal—your dad?"

"Not exactly. I mean, I don't know where he's hanging out, but it's Father's Day, and I have to get him some cigars—in case he reappears. And all I have for money is this check from Skip Collier, which I would be very grateful if you would cash."

He holds his hand out for the check, which I've slipped from my wallet, and reading it, he isn't fazed by the hundred-dollar figure. He has me endorse it to him and forks over two new fifties from a suede-bound ledger he keeps in the console between the seats.

I tell him, gee, he's a regular bank, and it's good of him to be helping me out in this way, considering what a deadbeat I am.

Who I am is the reason he's helping me out, he says—meaning Louise Fraser Muldoon's bouncing boy, I assume. He gives me a grim shake of the head for a farewell.

Fuck him. I return to the club deck to pay for my snack, but my table's cleared already. Wishing I felt rich enough to leave one of my fifties fluttering under the white club ashtray, I think the hell with this place, and I head for Ray's after the groceries and fancy cigars.

I take a quieter walk home, a detour down Jacaranda to Bay Front, where the first waterfront mansions were built long ago and the shrubs are tall, so I can maybe smoke a morning joint in a certain spot I know that's curtained by leaves at the corner of the Trilby estate. Lloyd Trilby must be seventy by now. He made millions by practically inventing the motel, and now he owns motel chains on four continents. His oak-and-stone Austrian chalet is no replica, either. He had it dismantled overseas and shipped to a wharf he ordered built specially to receive it here, along with its eighteenth-century pipe organ, solarium, and outdoor marble baths with fountain. Some chalet. Lou used to blow in here every Sunday one summer to give lessons (on clay) to Madeline Trilby, Lloyd's twenty-five-year-old third wife, who died in Minnesota that next fall of some blood disease. "Nah—he bumped her off," Lou said afterward. "Sure as I'm standing here. That little confection, she had ants in her pants and bees in her bonnet."

Like a fool, I bought a whole carton of Camels. How can I smoke them all by tomorrow afternoon? I have one lit now, as I burrow into the shrubbery. It tastes all right—I hope I don't get addicted. I spread out the finance and real-estate section from my Sunday *Daily Pilot*, sit on it, and coax a flattened joint out of the ID pocket in my wallet. I can just see myself getting stopped by some cop for trespassing here. "Do you have any ID, son?" And I pull out my joint. "That's me, officer, Joe Joint." Hilarious. So I've got two dope sticks burning now, one camouflaging the other for possible passersby. My headache pulses dully. But peace is gliding in.

I can see a chocolate-brown Rolls parked alone by the rose

184

portico, maybe '52, '53, with fat whitewalls and Texas plates—
the symbol of gliding peace itself. If I had that car, I'd drive the
American byways in it for months, *years*, without stopping except to pitch my tent on some grassy knoll, a river bluff in
Arkansas or New Mexico, to grill my London broil over a clean
wood fire, under the spangled sky. Christ, I could *do* that. I
could take half my fifty G's and buy me a dream machine, a
state-of-the-art prairie schooner, and I could *roll free*. I would be
addressless, no government would hassle my ass, I would reach
who I wanted and be unreachable by everyone else. . . . Shit,
here I go again, spinning in my fanciful, bankrupt imagination
some variation—for me—of my father's life. And I would hate it,
I know. I would get lonely and sick of it inside of two weeks . . .
though, you never know, with Cici along somehow for love and
company, maybe not. Cici. Ahhgh, I can't think about her now.
"Peace," I say to myself, forking up two fingers before my
eyes. Peace.

"OK. I am now going to propose to you one very reasonable
proposal, which I want you to hear me out on before butting
in," says my mother, leaning toward me to hand me her cigarette so I can light mine with it. "That sound fair?"

I nod, inhaling.

We're in the cool living room, having left Barry snoozing on
the patio, where he was when I joined them there after stashing
the groceries temporarily under my bed upstairs. Barry has jury-
rigged our broken sun umbrella by propping it on the redwood
geranium planters so that just he can have shade. Anyway,
Lou's warned me that what she has to say is between us two and
us two only.

"Good-good," she says. She retrieves her cigarette and drags
on it. "OK. Now. I had this morning a long go-round with your
Grampa Jack, which the upshot of it was that *probably* he *will*
be able to transfer funds from Bank of America Berkeley to
Bank of America Balboa tomorrow, in the full amount of your
trust, after rewriting a few papers—*and* settling a few of his
concerns."

"About what?"

"You're butting in."

"I know, but this is starting to sound like something I can't help butting in *to*."

She wearily rolls her head around on her shoulders. "Will, listen, I'm going to wade in, step by step, to this deep proposal, and if you go spouting off before you get the full, logical sense of it, I'm not even gonna try to put it to you, because all you'll be thinking about is your own comments and ideas and not what I'm pursuing. This is not your week's allowance we're talking about here, or what you prefer I should fix for supper, this is your position in the family and your goals and your need now for a little guidance."

"Oh, no."

"Oh, *yes*. Hey, this isn't me talking. You know what Grampa Jack would say if he heard you now? 'He doesn't need family guidance, OK, he doesn't need family money. Kids today are gimme-gimme-gimme. They want it all, no strings attached. Well, nobody gets something for nothing—that's life's lesson number one.' Hunh? Can't you just hear him? Grampa Jack's pretty smart. He asks me, 'So—he wants the whole kit and ka-boodle now, does he? Why? Isn't Uncle Sam pointing a finger at boys just out of play school? Nothing he can do with money in the army but gamble.' And Will, here's what I told him: I said you were declared Four-F like Frank Snot-tra in the last big war, and you are just militarily unsuitable for private medical rea-sons, which he had to accept. But you don't think he spent his whole life accumulating capital to flush away fifty thou at the drop of a hat not knowing where it's going. And can you blame him? Will, he's afraid you'll blow it all on a Hawaiian holiday and a fleet of GTO's."

"So what! Is he giving it to me, or not? I mean, I could go buy a trainload of goddamn avocados if I wanted, and he—"

"Pipe *down*, will you? I agree with you, I *agree*. But *his* idea was if you get it in chunks over ten years, you're less likely to waste it. That's understandable, but OK, you and me don't agree with him. We say, give it all over tomorrow. We have our own hidden, surreptitious reasons, but we gotta prove to him this makes sense, see? We have to be diplomatic. We have to sound out his concerns and smooth them over. That's what you expected me to do, isn't it? *You* sure as hell didn't want to talk to him, and that was smart. OK. I worked out this deal then, which amounts to a proposal to you, like it or not, and I believe it's the best deal we could strike under these sudden circumstances, whether you end up scooting to Vancouver, or wherever. Now, knowing Grampa Jack, you don't need half a guess what his primary concern would be—his *investment*. And what's his investment in? You. Y-O-U. Except, as an investment, you have a spotty history. When your whole childhood of costly tennis training went blooey, that was a very disenchanting thing for him. But you got the benefit of the doubt anyhow, and he extended support right through your college years because journalism sounded practical to him, if a little dull and grubby. So now that you're out with this big BA degree, you know he does not want to hear you're trying to swap horses midstream. What are you building up to, he wants to know. What's your magnificent goal? Editor of *Time* magazine? Will, to him the world's your oyster. He does not want to muddy the waters for you. That makes sense, right?"

"Not really."

"To *him* it makes sense. That's the whole gist here, wise guy. Do you have a job? he asks me. No, you don't have a job. But I'm frantically wracking my brains as I talk to him because once he formulates a decision on this thing it's chiseled in granite. What are you? I'm thinking. You're a journalist, a free-lance journalist like your old man—and all of a sudden I *have* it! You need the money because you want to invest it, because the reason is I promised it to you, so you could put it in bonds or high-yield accounts and live off the interest while you work on your free-lance project in your mountain cabin in Susanville or someplace, typewriting your fingertips off. And your project, which I went ahead and divulged to him, is my autobiography."

"Oh, wow," I moan. "Oh, Jesus."

"When it sinks in, you'll see it's perfect. It is! And anyhow, you don't have much choice, if you want the lump sum." She grins apologetically. "I won't call Grampa back until tonight, so take some time and swish it around in there before you say yes.

We can discuss the details later, how to construct it and everything, but Will, just think, this is a break for you. You got that journalism degree, and you can *write*! You know all the adverbs and dangling modifiers and stuff, and this project you can execute anywhere, Vancouver or Stalingrad, it doesn't matter. A few hours a day *maximum*, and a year later you got a book! Also, you still got half the day and all night to pursue tennis and chase girls and whatnot. Unbeatable! And afterwards you're an author! Think about that!"

Too stoned to think about anything, I just sit here staring at the hair on my knees, how it's bleaching white, making me remember Cici, of course, and then Barry (Legs I Have Known), and so I glance up at Lou after a moment and say, "His elbow's all fixed, you know. He tell you?"

She squints. "You mean Barry?"

"We hit some last night. He feels fabulous."

"That rat! He did? Son of a *beaver! Barry*?" she shouts. "Hey, you lug!"

"So I guess you'll be going to Wimbledon after all."

"*Bare!* You grizzly bear!" She sits back, beaming at me. "I knew the lug was het up about something. So you saps were out celebrating, is that it? No wonder! But, still—the dumbo—he knew the procedure, and you're the last guy he should be testing the old wing out with, at night, too, for Christ's sake. What if he screwed it up again? What if he short-circuited his whole damn career?"

"Maybe you oughta put a leash on him. You know—and one of those spike collars."

She bounces to her feet. "Excuse me, Will, while I go get to the bottom of this. Listen, like I say, I won't call Grampa back till tonight, so you just masticate awhile on that hard decision. Oh, and your phone message is on the secretary. She sounded positively despondent when you wouldn't take the call, and she said ring her *right away*. I'm sure it's life-or-death."

"Who?"

"Her number's down there. Cici Somebody."

"Oh, *God*!"

I leap up the stairs to the study.

She answers in a shrunken voice, almost a whisper.

"Cici! It's me!"

"Oh, Will, you—get me out of here. Please. You have to! They're putting me in the hospital!"

"Who are?"

"Daddy and them. And I'm not even sick!"

"*When*? What hospital?"

"The *hospital*! I don't know! And they, they're threatening me, and—"

"Slow down, slow down."

She's breathless and gulping. "Tomorrow. Oh, but Will, they want to inject me and stick me with tubes. And they—"

"*Why*?"

"Because! Will, I'm not even *sick*! It's just mental, and why should they care anyway? Don't let them put me in there and *do* things, please, Will."

"Cici, Jesus, just run away! I'll meet you at House of Pies, OK?"

"I *can't*. I said I would, and they said, no, I won't, and they locked the doors. They would catch me and tie me up. You have to, Will, *please*!"

"OK, Cici. Don't worry, don't worry. I'll get you out of there. When, tonight? After dark?"

"Yes! Oh, good!"

"OK, be ready, then. Put on heavy clothes, OK?"

"OK."

"And get all your money together. And leave them some note, like you're going to Houston or someplace. And chain that monster dog."

"OK, I will!"

"Terrific. You be ready, now. I'll show up there for sure by—I don't know—midnight?"

"I knew you would! But soon as you can, OK?"

"OK—*soon*. 'Bye, Cici."

"Soon," she says, hanging up.

I smack the desktop. Now we're smokin'. All I do now is rescue the beauty from the beasts and she's mine forever! We can escape. We can pass our placid lives by a lake in the Yukon,

189

panning gold, growing corn and tomatoes, picking raspberries, counting meteorites, forgetting the names of days and the reasons for newspapers. Yes! No shit, this *is* what I want. Now I *know* it. And you just load the car and go. It's so simple the thought of it makes me giddy. Up there we won't know how to worry. We'll be healthy and serenely focused as a nest of foxes. We'll have *babies*! Jesus, talk about Nirvana! My brain skips along, listing what necessities I can pack this afternoon: my tent, backpack, and sleeping bag, matches, an ax, silverware, a poncho, candles, fishing poles, pots and pans, a first-aid kit, notebook and pens, soap, shampoo. . . .

In my room, as I rummage through my closet for some of these items, I decide, sure, I'll take my kite, too—a great idea for idle, breezy days—and a couple Frisbees for exercise. Then all kinds of potentially useful doodads occur to me, like fingernail clippers, and a whetstone, and my periscope for clever hunting. Hunting! Shit, I'll need weapons—like a machete, or a gun. No, no, Cici would never accept that. No, *seeds*, that's all we'll need. And a hoe and a spade.

But in fact the thought of a gun appeals to me in a basic, wicked way, and it reminds me instantly of my father. Because when I think of guns, my father's gun's the one I see, that iridescent black .45 automatic swaddled in oilskin, locked in the steamer trunk in the attic, waiting, with perfectly contained patience, like a fire extinguisher, to perform.

This vibrating realization drives me up the junk-strewn attic stairs in a hurry. What if right now he's palming that diamond-nubbled grip . . . ready to BAOW! No more brains! BAOW! The End, like ink?

I pant. My pores pop with sweat in the papery heat beneath the rafters. "Dad?" I can't see him—a row of plastic wardrobe enclosures hung from a crossbeam screens off half the long dim space. "Hey, it's Room Service here!"

"Ahh, my kingdom for an ice cube," comes his voice.

Making my way over heaps of old rumpled clothes and broken furniture, I find him reclining on a low divan built out of luggage and draperies from our San Francisco apartment. To see those draperies again, in their forgotten and familiar autumn-leaf pattern, is a shock. How did they become ugly?

"No ice cubes, Dad. You didn't say ice cubes. I got your beer and limes and stuff for sandwiches—aaaannnd . . . these!" I pull the cigar box from the sack and present it to him. "Happy Father's Day."

He sits up to receive the box. "Well. I am horn-swaggled." He examines the oval picture on the top, a tropical veranda, with lush, blossoming bushes on either side, and beyond, a plantation tumbling away in rows to the horizon. Then he turns up the bottom, which frames a paragraph of elegant print, like a wedding invitation.

"Some stogies, eh, Dad?"

He carefully strips off the cellophane wrap and pries up the tacked-down lid. They're Macanudos, each in a foil sleeve. He opens one to the air, licks it, sucks it, nips off its pointed end. He plinks open his Zippo and lights it. The aroma is wonderful.

Before his appraising eyes, he rolls the cigar between his thumb and two fingers and says, "Ha-rumph! Youse privileged to hereby start referrin' me as Mayor Muldoon the Magnificent. Although my friends call me Mr. Boss."

I laugh. "They any good?"

"I'll say. Opulent is the word. Op-*pew*-lent, in fact. I'm gonna need a fan up here or I'll wind up smoked as well as pickled."

"If it still works, I can snag that fan out of the guest room. And the ice and shit also, but how long you plan to hang out up here, Dad? This is a goddamn sauna."

He leans back, propping his huge fleshy feet on a box. "Crack me one of them thar beers, Will. You hungry at all? C'mon, slap us together some of that chow. What you got? You got liverwurst?"

I spread the mustard with my finger, lay on the Swiss cheese, the slices of cool meat. He's saying, "For you—at the risk of beating the thing into pemmican, I shall reiterate. My mission here is undertaken in the service of a simple cause: to save the world. Putting it less grandly, I'm here to save *me*. Which is the same thing, if you'll excuse my solipsizing, because for me the

191

world is no more than my experience of it. I'm sixty years old, Will. I go whole hog these days, I can't help it." He accepts a sandwich and puts it on the floor. "So, just as soon as I get the help I need, or soon as I learn it's not to be got, I vamoose. And by the squinched expression on your face, another couple hours could do me. Am I wrong?"

"Yeah—I don't know. Shit, you can swelter up here till Christmas, if you feel like it."

"C'mon, Will, you had it out with her. What's the word?"

Bribery, I tell him. He sets his face soberly so that his smoke puffs from a corner of his mouth while I lay out the book deal.

"Well, well," he sighs, "that about queers it. Christ Almighty. Quite a mom I gave you, eh? You laughed in her face, I hope."

"Actually, I'm thinking about giving it a shot." As I say this, I know it's true. After all, why not? Up there in the Canadian wilds, what the hell, I can try. I can sit on a stump with a pine plank in my lap and scribble out the story of my mother in plain language, while Cici brings me mugs of bark tea—who cares if it ever sees print? By then Cici and I will have our fortune buried in Tupperware containers under boulders in the woods, and our simple existence will be secure. We'll need cash, but not for much . . . a sack of flour, a dental checkup, that's all!

The old man groans.

"It's my decision, Pop," I say flatly.

He coughs. "Don't make me laugh! Decision! Five years ago you made a decision when you hung up your racket, and you haven't made another one since. Christ, Will, the other day when you beat poor Skippy you were gonna be a tennis star. Now you're gonna be a ghostwriter, and tomorrow you're gonna be a draft dodger and a fugitive."

"Yeah, maybe. Though I can still play tennis, too, because in *my* life I have *time*."

"Time, crap. You know what time is? A sticky tongue. And you're a two-cent chocolate drop."

"I mean I have time to make choices, Dad."

"You can make choices till doomsday. That's man's curse."

"And besides, I don't *have* to write the thing. I can just say I'll try. Shit, you oughta be happy. I tell her yes, and not only am I following in your career footsteps possibly, but maybe I can even lend you a piece of change."

"Don't be a fool, Will. Say yes, and you're a drudge, and every day you'll have to sweat out three pages before she mails you ten lousy bucks."

"Oh, no. The deal is I get the entire lump up front or it's no deal. She'll put it in savings for me tomorrow in case I have to split the country before she flies to London. That's the agreement."

He puts down his beer can and balances his cigar across it. His sandwich is too fat. Some meat squirms out when he squeezes it for a bite. "Wimbledon, I take it," he says, chewing. "King Kong is cured, is he?"

"I didn't know you cared."

"Just radar. He's a big blip on my screen, Will. He's scary. I want to hang onto the few choppers I got, for just such delectable vittles as these."

I watch him as he eats. His gaze seems directed nowhere, toward his stomach. Now he stops to repair the sandwich, peeling loose the finger-squashed bread. Glancing at me he nods. "Good," he says. "You already eaten?"

"Dad? I got an idea I want to ask you about—a proposal."

"Shoot."

"See, I—I know you're really up against it, or else you just wouldn't be here for the purpose that you're here, which is mainly the money, like you have admitted. . . ." But now I pause, rubbing my knuckles, feeling myself falling back through my accumulated years as through salt water, in soft arcs, back to age twelve or ten, so that my adulthood is only a wavery dome overhead, distant as an afterlife. "And also," I push on, flailingly, "I'm sure you have deep honest feelings for me, too, I *know* you do, and I have those feelings, too. All those many years that you raised me and took care of me, Dad, I could never forget how you were always generous and loyal to me, and I just want to tell you that when I quit tennis and you dropped out of society and disappeared the way you did, it didn't faze me. I mean, it didn't hurt me. Inside, I understood your motivations. I know I didn't show it, but I always accepted what you

193

did, whatever you did, as right. See, Dad, I had faith in you—which I still have, is what I'm getting at. And when you took off, I figured *that* meant, partly, that you had faith in me. OK, where did it go? Now's when I need it. But instead, now's when you come back all wasted and bummed out yourself trying to tell me everything I want to do with my life is stupid. Remember how before tournaments you used to sit me down and encourage me and pump me up with confidence? Where's that old faith now when I really need it?"

"Will, get serious. You think this thing's got rules? Has it got scorekeepers and tricky villains? Who you gonna outmaneuver? You gonna outpsych Time and conquer the Void?"

"You know what I mean. Just listen a minute—"

"I *know* I know what you mean. *You* don't know what *I* mean."

"Dad, will you listen? I'm not finished."

He sighs, clenching his jaws. "I'll try."

"You said that I should consider how our desires might converge to one purpose, right? So, coming up here I hit on the answer to that paradox, and what stimulated my idea was seeing your old steamer trunk there against the chimney." We both look toward it, the scarred black box with its rusty steel studs, scalloped hasps, and corner pieces. "This is it: I go down and tell Lou I'll do the book. She gets Grampa Jack to send me the money. You lend me your manuscript out of that trunk, and I lend you ten thousand dollars. How's that? Smiles and handshakes all around?"

He shakes his head. "You been snoopin' in that trunk?"

"Isn't that where you dumped it? I heard you lug it upstairs the night you split."

"Yeah," he says after a pause. "Yeah . . . well, by golly, that's a very thoughtful offer. Something for everybody, hunh?"

"I think it's pretty good," I say, beginning in fact to think so. "You get a no-interest loan, I get a super headstart on my best-seller."

He assumes his pained smile, part of an annihilating look that I'd forgotten. The big turd. What does he want, then?

He says, "I got the word for you, Will. Know what it is?"

I say nothing.

"*Blithe*. Yup—blithe. Blithe as a butterfly. A little yellow flutter-by."

I get up to go.

He's saying with arms outstretched, in flight, "Your direction is the whim of the breezes. Your inspiration is the dazzle of colored blooms."

"See y'around."

"Just a minute, Will. I heard you out. You can sit through one last loving tirade from your poor old man, can't you? On Father's Day?"

I stop. Through the thinning drug-fog of my thoughts, I sense the waking of small fears and sadnesses, like verminous blobs of fur, squeaking bats in a cave. You can't smoke them out. You have to run, you have to drive fast with the top down, send cold air blasting through for hours straight, for days and nights and days and nights. . . . I lean against the chimney, my sweaty palms pressed to the dry brick by my tailbone, feeling sick again. "That mean you're thinking of leaving?" I say quietly. "Or what?"

"Thinking? No, no. Thinking takes too much time. These days I just stay balanced on the pinnacle of the moment and kinda do what's necessary."

"Yeah? Far out."

"Listen, I'm not about to go shuffling off this mortal coil, if that's what's eating you. Relax. All I meant the other night was a man hates to give in to the creep of rot. He'll take himself before he lets it drag him down. I embrace the *option*, isn't that what I told you? Hell, I couldn't be free without it. Bringing the thing up when I did . . . OK, that was a mistake. I was lubricated, and it slipped out like it was connected to the money problem, which it isn't, no sirree-bob. Money! Let me tell you, Will, money is poison. It's a pestilence. Christ, do I want money? No. I *need* it, Satan spare me. *You*, Will, you *want* money. You got purple Ferraris and gold wristwatches and fancy women dancing in your head. . . . Hell. We came to the right place, anyhow, you and me. Listen, now, about your offer. It's a sincere offer—I see this, and I am touched. But it's also the offer of a nincompoop. An adolescent addlepate. I can't stop you from selling out to your mother. But please, take it from a veteran, the war you really should be dodging is the war between Louise Fraser and sports history. And second, my manuscript—if you want to call that heap of used paper a manuscript—would be about as helpful to you as a pair of spats in a Canada blizzard. Believe me. Third, as for your ten thousand bucks, keep it. If that's as far as you can go, you might as well stop here, with these fine cheroots. In sum, Will, your kind offer is not declined. It is dismissed. But you aren't hurt by this, now that you have my reasons. Are you? You look peaked."

I force a laugh. "Shit, no," I tell him, trying to think of what else to say, what else to say I feel, when shit, yes, he hurts me, he's always hurt me, isn't that what fathers do, by function, by their stern pride and pathetic example? It's a truth too big to acknowledge. Anyway, my words are dammed up behind a cottony nothing, a wad of no-feelings. I want to be gone. Gone and gone. I want to bust loose.

"Good. Good-o," my father's saying, and as I shove away from the chimney, "Don't go yet, Will, now—wait. Give me a couple minutes more while I'm all worked up here. Humor your dying old man, hunh?"

I stop. I push my fingers into my eye sockets, making a polka-dot bandanna in there start to wave. Die then, who cares?

"It's my last duty to you, Will. It's why I'm stuck in this corner of Hell right now! You listening?"

I nod.

"You're dripping there," he says. "You sure you're all right? Beer?" He offers his can. Then sets it down, draws a quick, ragged breath, and caves in, catching his face in his hands. Three great sobs wheeze horribly along his throat.

"Dad. . . ."

He jerks straight. His fingers slip back to his temples, spreading his nose and stretching his eyelids taut. "*Ahhhgh*," he pushes out. He coughs and snuffles. "Whoa, boy. I—*hooo*. Comin' unglued here."

"Dad, hey . . . look, I'll leave and you rest, and I'll come up later. With ice and that cooler, and—"

"No, no, no, no, no. Stay now. Listen, I'm—it's like I'm the racket and you're the ball, and see, if I don't glance off your hide at the right angle with the right spin, you're gonna fly off into the fence. I gotta swing right now, or I miss you altogether. Timing! It's the timing, and I feel a little tight just now . . . the pressure. . . . Just sit, will you? Sit. Let me get a bead on you."

Sighing, easing myself into his backrest of old clothes, dated fashions, trying to subdue me—or both of us—he starts in about himself, his boyhood. Why? And why do I shrink from listening? How little we know of our fathers. How little we ask to know. What mixed fears and needs lie at the root of our indifference? Or do we sons only sense that whatever astounding histories we may hear cannot enhance the draw of our blood?

He, the impulsive racket, must exaggerate his backswing here, he warns me, to be sure of gathering me in his sweetspot.

. . . *Where I was born.* "You know where I was born," he's saying. He waits.

My eyes close. "Queens, New York, April 20, 1909," I answer. Even my voice now is heavy, filmed in sweat.

His mother, *Mother* . . .

"How Mother wanted babies. She must have pestered Dad like a hungry cat, rubbing him and whining. Over and over he refused her, with that flat-handed, palm-down swipe of the arm. No child of mine will take breath in this world until I myself own a piece of it! A pinch-penny half-Scot, not two years off the clipper, and already he was looking to stake out his own fences. He toiled in cobwebby stables first, shoveling muck, and then shoveling feed grain at the railyard, and in time, with that Muldoon fortitude and luck, he founded his own retail grains business. The house he bought for her was humble brick, but new, across from the east boundary of what became the new West Side Tennis Club, more like a pasture to us then, a meadow, and growing up, to me, what was tennis? Might have been polo, cricket, anything. After school, I put in my hours at the granary. . . .

"The rough-timbered floor with cracks where even your shooting aggie could roll away forever . . . the fresh smell of oats and chaff . . . the clouds of sparrows . . . the grainmen with their steel scoops. Six o'clock walking home, we could look back across the tracks and see high up on the clapboard wall of the elevator, in giant yellow and brown letters, E. M. MULDOON, still lit by the sun long after everything around it was lost to shadows. . . .

"Even then the horse population in the city was plummeting. The spring I turned ten he sold the granary and most of the yard, keeping a corner lot out of the deal for himself, where later he built—this was a Christ-awful blow, try to imagine—he built a fueling depot, he called it, for automobiles. A little white shanty with a concrete floor, sharp smells, grimy hoses and pumps—and to see our old brass cash register, with the dust of the fruit of the plains still gumming its works, taking up half the linoleum-topped counter in Muldoon Fuels, Sales, and Service . . . that kicked up a hollow pain in me like lost faith. I lost a faith I didn't know I had: that everything in life stayed the same or got better, and what took its place was a new sense of the deterioration that's part of growth, and worse, of the opening distance between Dad and me. *That*, it was that loss that turned me to tennis, not tennis itself.

"Then, boys I knew worked summers if they could. I would've pushed broom at the granary. But through a friend I got on as groundskeeper's helper, brushing and rolling the clay at the club, toting grass-clippings and sacks of lime. As I fell in love with the place and the game, I came naturally to see my future in tennis. I cast out my father. I replaced him with other heroes. Maurice McLoughlin first, that red-haired Scot, like my father. And then Johnston. Then Tilden. Tilden, Tilden, and Tilden forever, a flawed god, but still a god! He became my father. He *was* my father. He was all I would be. I played and practiced. Meantime, Dad was sickening. I was distant, removed. The June I was to graduate from high school they dragged him into Kings County Hospital with diabetes. Insulin they wanted to give him. It was brand-new then, and it killed him. I hid in the game. Mother wept without me when some little tournament the day of the funeral kept me at the club, in white. Christ, how long did I wait to feel him gone? She sold the fuels business because I had promised Dad I'd go to college—Columbia! Princeton! I reneged, of course, for tennis. Greatness within my grasp and that bushwah. My God, Big Bill had said so, 'The greatness within your grasp. . . .'

"He worked with us then, me and a few other boys of promise, when he was East, and he'd take us out for ice cream heaped in soup tureens and tumblers of ice water . . . ice cream and ice water. Or chauffeured us to his old hotel, the Algonquin, everyone in livery nodding to him as we passed, for steaks up in his suite, and baked potato, and after eating he would smoke and recite verse. He would pace the carpet and soliloquize, flushed with passion, while we shot grins at each other in our embarrassment and love for him, because he possessed us, he possessed us as the game did, and as he possessed the game. The rest didn't matter. His posturing and scolding, his silly vanities, his ventures on the stage, his fickle affections—we didn't care. Down deep, he loved you. He wanted the best for you. He drove you and pushed you because you needed it. Hell, maybe he'd tap you for the Davis Cup squad and take you to Mexico, like he did Junior Coen that year, or to California! The greatness, the greatness . . . nuts, who knows? I was coming, touring the grass court circuit, getting up some polish and confidence. A young Tony Wilding they were calling me, a stroker, deliberate, loose as ashes. But by then some matzo-ball lawyer had hold of the family fortune, and in 'twenty-nine we lost it all, *all*.

"It was finished there. I had to work. Then Dad came back to me nights on end, dream after miserable dream. 'Can I help you, William? Can I help? Can I give you a boost, tell a wee story or two?' He was wanting me to want his advice. He wanted me to make him tell me what to do, and my throat bulged with questions I could not let out because they were all questions like, 'Where are those comfortable overalls?' 'Do we have any more soap?' I lost him. See? So I am saying I know you, Will. You're caught. You're without vision—behind that abounding ignorance that's like a light far too bright, that light of youth. But you haven't lost me. You *will* lose me, and fine, so you lose me, that's fine. But now, lucky us, we have this teensy drip of time, and so, see, so if you can just try squinting past the glare of what you think you know, to me, to. . . .''

I look up to see my father's eyes glaze and blink, and I'm

afraid he'll really break down, he'll crumple in the squeeze of whatever it is, and I'll have to hunch over him like an umbrella, bent into his breathing, the vodka and decay, and say, It's OK, Dad, hey. I'm OK, Dad, don't worry. Don't worry.

But no. "Gimme Christ. Gimme Christ," he's saying. "Vanilla with sprinkles." He twists around on his pallet and digs in the jumbled rags behind him. "And nuts, nuts. Nuts, nuts, nuts. Ahhh, I got something for you besides talk, Will. Here."

It's a very old tennis racket, still strung up with thickened red gut and purple trim, heavy, clublike, with a grooved wood grip. In gold across the throat, it reads, Dreadnought Driver.

"That there is the last of my dad's few gifts to me. He was shy with it because he knew nothing about tennis, but he asked around to make sure he bought the best. Till then I was learning with cast-off junk—you know, some warped antique with a squared-off head that played like a snowshoe. Well, Christmas Eve, and with his rich blood he got too excited to wait. I knew what it was, covered only in brown shop-wrap and twine . . . and I looked at him, and he didn't say, 'Open it! Open it!' He looked back at me, with his lips parted, and his jaw cocked to one side, and his tongue moving slowly against his teeth. . . . We were perched on the sofa together, all the dozens of candles twinkling around the room, and that was it. He was done with me. He got up and left before I slipped the twine."

I sit against the chimney. I am spinning this relic in my hands, spinning and spinning it—the grip feels like five inches— and I know now I'm leaving. I'm going to roll and roll.

"Now it's yours," he says. "It's just as worthy a weapon today as it was in 1921. May it lead you to the glory."

My eyes rise to him. Through a shiver, I suddenly see his face seized by the belief that I'm about to bash him, hack and hack him, wallop him with this club right through his misery and out the other side. Or do I? Or is it only some vestigial mechanism of mine gone haywire for an ugly moment? "Well, thanks, Dad," I say quickly. And I stand up, away from the chimney, smiling, loving him, his undefended life resting below me on the floor. "It probably doesn't have more than a set left in it," I laugh, "but maybe if I had it bronzed and mounted—"

"*Arrrgh!*" he growls, clapping his hands to his ears. "Will, for Christ's sake, you go blithely on! Look at you! You're blithe! What agonies lie ahead? Don't you wonder? For you? For those you love? Don't you consider the horrors? The horrors await you, by God. Horror upon horror. Blithe is no preparation. You age! The years claim you! Day by day you find less and less of yourself to depend on. And it's already begun! Already you've seen the best of yourself, Will. We are all just parcels of doom-bent meat. Your life is the little doom within the big doom. *See?* Your life is just a mimicry of the grand, great, final, justifying, lordly, horrible, righteous, ecstatic, climactic, pure, and ugly *Doom Doom Doom Doom DOOM!*" He groans, falling back again, a forearm over his brow. He rounds his cheeks and blows. "If you can truly know—I mean *know*—that your unprevailing form, your speck of life, is given in the service of the glory, then you will be saved. There. That's it. *Finis.* Go on, go. You can go."

"See you later, Dad."

"Sure," he says.

So, stained as yet by no man's blood, the Dreadnought Driver (Harry C. Lee and Company, New York, USA), my Excalibur, my pilgrim's staff, is the last object I cram butt-first behind the car seats. Well? "Let us absquatulate," I say to myself. Lou's phrase again. Around the house on the patio, she and Bad Barry are packing in an early supper of salad and omelet. They're going to buzz up to LA, where they can play undisturbed on some private court until dark or until Barry proves himself, Lou has declared, though already she's hammered down their plane and hotel reservations for months into their glowing future.

When Lou told me they were definitely leaving, I'd just come down from the attic, the slight breeze from the water cool on my glossy skin, and to Barry I intoned, "You have greatness within your grasp, my fine fellow. May you achieve the glory."

Ignoring me, he gave Lou a sour look, and she said, "Don't make fun of him, Will, what's wrong with you? You coming down with something?"

I was making fun of me, of course, not Barry, but you

201

couldn't expect her to perceive that. Over at Wimbledon, shit, I really do hope he claws to the final, and there whips Laver in three. Fabulous—for him, for Lou, for me, for everybody but Rod the Rocket.

I'd popped out there partly to report my decision regarding her autobiography, which was to go something like, Forget it, Mom, it was a very generous bribe, but till the dust settles around my stampeding destiny, I can't commit myself to any goal that long-range. Naturally, a vigorous discussion would have ensued (all about needs, promises, sacrifices, and talents), to be terminated either by my giving in or by my abrupt ab-squatulation. When I realized this, I figured I wouldn't tell her anything. Why should I? If she was that anxious, she'd ask. And if she asked, I would just shrug. I'm getting to be a good shrug-ger. She did not ask, however, and that was that. And besides, just to illustrate my stormy state of mind, as I procrastinated there on the patio, poking into the bowl of avocado chunks, while the two of them cuddled and cooed, squashed together in one butterfly chair, my forthright reasoning just jibed angrily around the other way, and I started thinking, Fuck her, man—get the money. Tell her anything. Tell her, yeah, your brain is already swarming with fantastic book ideas, *fantastic. Out-asight!* Who cares? As long as you get the damn money. Because you know Cici won't have three coins to jingle, and your cash'll keep you two in cheeseburgers and tofu for maybe a week. But no, I said nothing. Good-bye is basically what I was out there to say anyway, good-bye and fare-thee-well, my lady. I didn't say that either. I don't know, sometimes it's risky giving speech to your bold intentions. A simple announcement like, "Good-bye, Mother-dear, I am off to seek my fortune," can lend the idea an impetus you won't let yourself resist in a calmer moment, should you come to one. Preserve your options to the last—that's my philosophy. Focus on the now. Snitching six or so of Barry's beers, laying them across the face of my Dreadnought, an ar-tifact that excited no interest from the preoccupied lovebirds, I took my leave—forever, I considered weightily. (Well, this is the last time I'll see them. And the last time I'll look out at the channel. The last time I'll pad across this Turkish carpet. The last time I'll climb these stairs. . . .) At my desk I rolled a last joint—balm for the spirit, to lighten the chore of packing.

It's funny about these Camel cigarettes. I love them and hate them. They're so new to me that it's hard to remember to smoke them, and now that I have remembered—so that I sit here on the fender puffing away, waiting for a sturdy soul to come along to push my car—I realize I don't have to smoke them anymore. That is, if I'm skipping my draft physical, why go on debilitating myself? I guess my decisions are coming to me so thick and fast now that I'm not assimilating all their ramifications. What kind of shit is that? The neon truth is that I'm making *no* decisions—I don't know what I'm going to do next, an incapacitation I call preserving my options, focusing on the now . . . Christ. The Mexican weed doesn't help any. Or, how the hell do I know, maybe it does. Whew, I really feel wacko right now, like *dangerous*, flipped O-U-T out. Shit, I have got to collect my wits here. Here's a wit, there's a wit, everywhere a wit-wit. Am I going crazy? Really, *am* I? When you go crazy, do you know it?

In the road a pair of bicycling surfers approaches, and I am rescued from these meditations by the need to act. I ask for a hand. Like a lot of dedicated surfers, they ride rusting, squeaking Sears and Roebuck junkers with coaster brakes, girls' models, too, which are in big demand because they're easy. These bikes you don't have to lock up every time you run into Ray's for a Milky Way and a Yoo-hoo. You bail out of the saddle at a glide and let them clatter to the sidewalk.

Peeking through the windshield, the taller one says, "Whoa—up for some heavy-duty moseyin' looks like, hunh?"

"Yup."

"Hit Death Valley last winter, man. That place is so *weird*—unfit for human consumption, right? Burros all over. Gives y'a charge, though."

"Where you headin'?" says the other one.

"Klondike River."

"Serious?"

"Yup. I got twenty acres of timber on the riverbank, a sod house, a riffle sluiceway, and all my life to strike it rich."

"What, *Alaska*?" says the tall one.

"No, no. The Yukon. Near Dawson."

"You're shittin'. In this?" He slaps my ragtop.

"Better hope the heater works," says the other one.

It doesn't take much—a short running shove, pop her, and off she goes. The surfers grow smaller in the mirror, not waving.

I really do own land in the Yukon. I acquired it years ago through a clever offer printed on a box of shredded wheat, and in fact, that land is the fountainhead of all my long-held fantasies about gold-rush prospecting in the northern wilds—not that you could get in much prospecting on one square inch of tundra, but the idea had its cruel appeal all the same. What a scam that must have been. One square inch. I still have the deed somewhere, probably locked in my little strongbox. What could you *do* with one square inch, I used to wonder—grow spaghetti? I built a picket fence out of toothpicks—just for purposes of demarcation—which I took apart and mailed off to the Big Inch Land outfit with instructions for reassembly.

I worried a lot about that land. It was reasonable to assume, for one thing, that many a visionary youth, having made an investment equal to mine (fifty cents), would together own all the terrain surrounding my property, for inches and inches, and could even prevent (with tiny No Trespassing signs) any access to my spaghetti plantation. And what if, say, half my land lay under a rock that was also across the land of some neighbor who didn't want the rock touched? But the land company had thought of all this, I reasoned, and all disputes would be mediated fairly.

Later, on further—actually *endless*—reflection, I had to jettison those senseless dreams of agriculture with the discovery that what I really wanted to do was *build*. Not only on my inch either. The towering structure I spent one long afternoon sketching would have to be at least four feet on a side to accommodate all the preposterous refinements that sprang to mind at the rate of one every ten minutes. Swept away as I was into the far realms of architectural hallucination, not until that night did I arrive at the crushing understanding that squeezing out my neighbors for four feet around (by some not-yet-devised wheedling scheme) would mean buying up some two thousand inches—to the tune of at least half a buck an inch.

If my father lost his boy's boundless faith when his father sold the granary, I lost mine when I realized that some slick shredded-wheat tycoon had sold off four square feet of Canadian bog for one thousand clams. My fifty cents was good money thrown away, *stolen* away, by a fat adult who doubtless didn't need it to begin with. I imagined him high in an office building in some smoky eastern city, slitting open my envelope, stripping my five heads-up-for-luck dimes from the card I'd taped them to, and chuckling an oily chuckle. Still, in my outrage, I couldn't bring myself to mail back my deed with a demand for a refund, because without knowing it I guess I understood that, more than fenceable property, what my fifty cents had purchased was pure ownership itself. I really did own land, and, well, that was a good feeling. It still is.

This old car feels pretty good, too. I sometimes forget that, though all it takes is a few minutes at the wheel to restore my affection for it. I don't need a Rolls-Royce. This little Dixie cup's still nimble as an antelope, and the shift knob in my fist feels like muscle, like a spear sunk into a great dying fish.

Three summers ago I worked very briefly laying forms for a construction company. Eight hours in a sandy hole. A hundred and ten degrees. It was horrible torture. The best thing about it was how good the beer tasted at four o'clock. The work boots and heavy denims I bought for that job are what I've donned now as armor against canine chompers, breaking glass, shrapnel, napalm, anything the US Air Force might throw at me in my raid on the Bamberger Bunker—though, like the VC, I recognize stealth as my first defense.

Even so, a stop at Busch Hardware for a machete would be a prudent move. A machete will be useful in the wilderness, too. But now, turning off the boulevard toward the pavilion down the tree-lined street of shops, I remember, Christ, it's Sunday afternoon—nothing's open but the arcade, and I also remember I still have Mr. Busch's twenty dollars. The sad old fart's probably at home right now, sprawled out before the tube, clinging to the hope that the next ring of the phone will be me saying,

"Well, Mr. B., you can rest easy. Andy's fine. I've uncovered him in Florida, of all places—Cape Kennedy. He's a coordinating technician for the *Apollo 11* flight. And he's wiring you tickets for the launch, if you're interested. You can stay on his houseboat, in the guest suite."

Groping in the glove box for my bottle opener, I decide, sure, why not, I'll drop in on poor old Mr. Busch, to tender a sort of official farewell to somebody, and also to return his twenty bucks. All day I've been worrying and hurrying, but now that I'm finally cut loose, hell, I have all kinds of time, I have forever. Besides, the fall of darkness, an optimum condition for Cici's rescue, is still hours away.

I slouch in the seat with my beer, soothed by the car's tinny idle. I'm very thirsty. I twist the mirror down to get a look at my beard-growth. I haven't shaved in a while. It's pretty sparse, however, I being so young and fair. I tap my reflection with the bottle's lip. Here's to me, I think. But I don't say that. I say, "Here's to the glory!" Glory. What the hell was all that about anyway? Not that it matters much now. Here's to *me*, surging free from the bonds of the past, free from the future's crooked magnet! Here's to Now! From now on, Now is where you'll find me, just doing what I have to do to stay here! OK! I snap the wipers on and off. Whew-ee, I'm nervous and still feeling a tad unhinged. Maybe it's these cigarettes. It is, goddamn it, they're making me sick. I fling the pack into the street. I dig in back for the carton and get rid of that, too. There. This is wonderful. This is what Now means. You never know what's coming next.

Vroom, vroom, goes the Porsche. I crank into a zippy U-turn, hi-o Silver, away to the Busch home. I feel so honorable, so fair and square. Do I have to return that twenty bucks? No. It's just the right thing to do, I'm doing it for the health of my soul. Then, as I pull into the drive behind their old Dodge pickup, I realize I'm a jerk again. I want to give Mr. Busch his twenty bucks because he knows I ripped off that maple syrup. My soul, my ass. I just want to show him I'm really a good boy. When what I am is a transparent jerk.

Mrs. Busch, paler and dumpier than I remember her from a few years ago, wearing a new yellow hairdo as artificial-looking as Easter grass, declares that I've certainly grown and invites me into the kitchen for cookies. She doesn't bake anymore, but she has three kinds of fresh-bought on her pantry shelf.

"What's your favorite?" she calls from within the pantry.

"I don't care. Anything." Being here again is strange, like stepping into 1963. Nothing has changed, nothing, right down to the potted ivy with the ceramic elf squatting on the rim and the same color paper napkins (blue) ready in their dispenser, a sort of wavy glass pedestal. The refrigerator still has that black chalk board next to it with what could be the same things written on it: cot. cheese, Bab-o.

"I don't know what you like, Willie," she's saying. "These kinds are what old folks like. Pecan Sandies, and Cameos, and then gingersnaps, if you have old-fashioned taste buds. Hope I'm not spoiling your supper." She sets the packages before me in the middle of the table in a row, like courtroom evidence.

"Pecan Sandies I love," I say, so she slides those closer and sits herself down, making air wheeze from the vinyl cushion.

I don't know what she knows of my arrangement with Mr. B., but before she brings Andy into the conversation, reminiscing about his favorite cookie or something, I say, "Actually, Mrs. Busch, I can't stay long. I'm only actually here to see your husband. Is he gone somewhere?"

After a pause, she says, "He's here. The dishwasher's on the fritz, and he's got it spread into pieces out back. See?" She points to a gap between the cupboards by the sink. "I wouldn't let him fiddle with it on my floor. Oh, pooh, I forgot your milk. Pecan Sandies with no milk—they named *them* right, didn't they?"

She gives me the milk in a fuchsia aluminum tumbler. "Will," she gets out suddenly, in a rush, "if you have any—any news, I want to hear it, too, you know. I'm his mother."

At this a wave of guilt sweeps over me. *News?* Jesus, I haven't made one damn phone call to try to get a line on old Andy— not that a phone call would have yielded any clues, but it would have been a gesture of compassion. I swallow some milk. "There's no news, Mrs. Busch. I mean zero, not a ripple. So my final conclusion is that Andy's probably definitely OK, only he just figures the time for him to surface and make amends is not yet here, that's all. But you know how he always talked about going to Florida, the Keys? Maybe you don't, but that's what he used to fantasize about—starting up a sport fishing business and diving for buried treasure on the side. Well, I wouldn't be surprised if that's where he turned up, all tan and happy and rich, living on a neat little houseboat with geraniums in the portholes, leading the life of Riley."

Looking away from me, Mrs. B. shakes her head, then walks over and calls through the screen, "Mitch? Company's here!"

"Who?"

"It's Willie Muldoon."

He clomps fast across the porch, and Mrs. B. opens the door for him. He's wiping his hands on an old bath towel.

"Willie! Say hey, what's the word? You got something?"

Mrs. Busch says, "Willie thinks he's in Florida."

"*What?*" He grabs a chair.

"No, no, that was a *guess*, a wild, wild guess. I tried, but I couldn't find out anything! Zero! All I want to do is give back your money because I'm—"

"Wait just a minute. What's this Florida stuff? What's all this?"

Mrs. Busch whirls to him, shouting, "He sat right there where he is now, with those milk and cookies, and, and just like the *Devil* he teased me, he came to *punish* and *torment* me! He's brought me *Hell on Earth*, and what did I do wrong? *What did I do wrong?*"

"Carol . . . Carol, now, Carol, calm yourself. Calm yourself, now. . . ." He has her by the elbows, and he's resting his forehead on top of her hairdo. She stares at the white vee of his undershirt in front of her nose, pumping out short breaths. Then he makes her about-face, like a wind-up toy that's stalled against something, and she marches out of the room.

All the cookies in their fancy bags look suddenly awful to me. "Really, Mr. Busch, Florida—that was only like a fantasy of Andy's back in the old days, is all I meant."

"It's me you report to from now on, Will—*me*, not his mother.

This thing's eating her up. You can't show up here and gab with her about your fantasies. She's too weak. She can't take it."

"All I came for, Mr. Busch, is to give back your twenty dollars. I'm blowing town. I'm blowing the whole damn country, in fact. So here you go." I stick the money in the napkin holder and get up to leave.

"What is that outfit you wore in here, Will? Is that your SDS uniform? You going SDS on us now, along with your hair?"

"Good-bye, Mr. Busch," I tell him, but I don't move. They're both bananas, I'm thinking.

"Aw, sit down, Willie. Sit down and have another cookie. Take that dough back, too. It's yours. You tried. That was the deal, and you know it."

"No, it isn't, Mr. Busch. I didn't earn it. I didn't do a thing. I didn't call anybody or look anywhere for him or anything. It was no use. And I didn't mean to upset Mrs. Busch either. But my idea is, look at it this way: think of all the parents whose sons are way around the world slogging through the rice paddies, stepping on mines, getting blown up and maimed. I mean, at least we know he's not over there."

"Do we? Willie, we don't know dog manure! That's the key thing here. May God forgive me for saying it, but I'd rather *know* that Andy was killed by yellow Communists than go on and on, like we are, in the dark, forever."

"Boy, if that's the way you think—that's a terrible way to think, and if that's the way you think, *I* think you're an asshole."

He just sighs and sits in Mrs. Busch's chair.

Still standing, I flinch and step away when he reaches for me.

"C'mere," he says, wagging his hand. "What am I gonna do, bite? I want you to have something. C'mere and sit down a minute." He pulls a wad of chinkling keys from his pocket.

I stay where I am.

"All right, don't sit. You're the most contrary kid I ever met. This hippie age was just made for you, wasn't it? Anytime somebody says do something, you do the opposite. The attraction of that's the mystery of the age, to me. You know, before he ran away, Andy started acting like you. Silent. Stubborn. Lost. Up in his room a lot. The beads, the hair. Burning punks in this brass Buddha statue. Chanting like a stuck record. Got so his mother couldn't function. He wouldn't eat what she cooked—just rice. Wouldn't even wash. She was a wreck. I get home here and there's no houselights on. She's in bed already, she's watching TV in bed. She doesn't want to hear him in there, going, 'Wanh, wanh, woh-woh, wanh, wanh, woh-woh, wanh, wanh, woh-woh.' What I did, I had one empty apartment over on the Bay. Orange County Board of Health wouldn't let me rent the place for a year because last October this poor surfer kid from Michigan, in there one short month, he gets murdered in there. But good. Cut up into pieces and stuffed in his wet suit. It was two weeks before they found him. They found him by *smell*. That smell, too, by Jesus, a week after they got him out you could go stand on the landing and throw up before you opened the door. Had to tear out the carpeting, repaint every wall, and I still had to wait a year before I could let the place out. County law.

"Well, by March this Zen bilge is just poison—it's poisoning our whole life—and I tell Andy he's got to move out, his mother and I have had it. He agrees to it. For free, I tell him, he can stay at three-oh-three East Bay. There's no furniture in there, but it's fresh as a daisy, and he's welcome to it. He agrees to all of it, like I say, he's very agreeable. I'm telling him, you know, try it over there a few days and see, that's all we ask, and he stuffs his navy duffel with sweaters and socks, and I drag a clean mattress and lamps and an easy chair out of storage, and we go over there in the truck. He was so cooperative about it all that maybe I should've known, but I thought good, this is good, this is breathing room, and soon this hippie garbage'll blow over or he'll get drafted, and we're gonna see improvements, you know? Well, I go back in a couple days, and there's a stray cat in there. The place is wide open, doors, windows, and no sign of him. He didn't stay ten minutes by the looks. He ran. We had problems maybe—not maybe . . . OK, we *did*, we had problems, but he ran from everything, not just his problems. He ran. He has everything right here, and whatever it is, we got tongues, we can talk, but he does this to us. It makes no sense.''

"To him it must have made sense," I say, "or he wouldn't have done it."

He glares at me. "Sense! You think it makes sense to drop out of college where you're going to become a history teacher, and sit up there in diapers all day, moaning and groaning like you got a bellyache? And now you, Willie. You're running, too, you say. You're blowin' town, you say. *And* the country. For where, Baja? Tahiti? Willie, Willie, don't run. Don't! Sure you got your problems, who doesn't? You need some time, some peace. You need to figure a few things out, I know that. So here. This is the key to Andy's apartment. Here, I'll give you *both* keys, and you got the only keys, where you won't be disturbed. I swear. Here now, take 'em. *Take* 'em!" He jabs the keys at me like a dagger.

I extend my palm, and he drops the keys into it.

"There," he says. "The power's off, but you just flip the main switch in the breaker box next to the water heater, and you're in business. Three-oh-three East Bay."

I pocket the keys, knowing I'll never set eyes on that apartment. The thought of spending even two seconds inside the place is as repulsive to me as it probably was to Andy. The vibes in there must be horrendous.

"I'm going, Mr. Busch. Thanks for your advice and everything."

"You try it," he says. "Nobody over there to badger you. Anybody asks what you're up to, you just have 'em call me, got it?"

"Mr. Busch, I just want to tell you I truly wish I had some good Father's Day news for you—the way you were hoping I did. But, well, no news is good news—you could look at it that way."

I'm halfway to the front door before he says from the kitchen, "Father's Day is next Sunday."

I stop. "What do you mean? You said yesterday it was today."

"No, I didn't. And if I did, you misunderstood me. It's next Sunday. Don't let your father down, Will, even if it's just a card."

I spin around and hustle out the door, suddenly furious with everything, humanity, and the way the world's arranged. I gouge a chunk out of the lawn with the toe of my workboot. Fucking Father's Day, what the fuck do I care anyway?

I back hard into the street, front end skidding around, but a bunch of kids playing Wiffleball on the pavement slows me right down. The little pricks, they see what a hurry I'm in, so they take their time getting out of the way. But hold it—what hurry *am* I in? Where am I going? This is Now, remember? Christ, if I go on madly trying to hurry out of my continuous Now, I won't be satisfied until I'm dead.

Off to one side the blond kid with the plastic bat flips me the bird as I crawl on by. I wave. "Stay mellow, boys," I say.

I take a deep breath and let it out gradually. The sun's got lower and weaker, a flat brass buckle now in the horizon's belt of haze. Darkness, shit, I think, I don't need darkness. I need courage—that's my missing ingredient, valor, rock-hard resolve. Hell, who's the hero of this unfurling adventure? Me, that's who. Hours ago, the beautiful damsel of my dreams begged me for deliverance—"*soon*"—and here I am still diddling around, waiting for my precious Now to link up with safe circumstances. God*damn, go*, you shithead, she needs you! Go and pull her loose!

A hero is not impetuous. A hero is bold but cunning, the captain of events. A hero is wise. The would-be hero who goes off half-cocked ends up a suicide, a sacrifice to the vanity of his heart. And posthumous decorations are not worth Melvin Laird's spit.

I figure all this out inside Charlie's Chili. I have not sunk teeth into a jumbo chiliburger since last August, I became aware, as I buzzed up the peninsula toward the Coast Highway, also becoming aware that to storm Cici's dungeon in daylight with no good plan of action, but simply trusting to instinct like last time, however courageously, is a wacky reckless notion. So, over that massive, dripping meat pie on a bun and a beer smuggled into the corner booth under my jacket, I devise a scintillating scheme: I will wait till dark (after all), creep into the bushes under Cici's bedroom window, rap softly on the glass, and tell her, *pssst*, Cici, you can make a break for it! I'll be waiting in the car! Actually, this seems very reasonable because, I reason, Cici will have the whole interior scoped out (routes of escape and so on), and she can handle the dog (a big plus), and she's as fleet of foot as any girl I've ever known, on those long, muscled legs. She'll be sitting breathless beside me before the Colonel can wrestle his ass off the sofa.

Later, with a need to spur my digestion, I take a stroll along the boardwalk in the crimson sunset feeling pretty good until I suddenly pitch myself into the fear that the Porsche will run out of gas just idling away back in the parking lot. If it does that, it will suck dirt into the carburetors, and then not idle for me at all, which will be a disaster.

The car is still thrumming loyally, of course, but it's low enough on the gauge so I was right to worry. And what about the oil? I haven't dipped the crankcase since last summer, or checked the brake fluid, or tapped the tires for pressure, and here I am embarked on the trip of my life, about to sling myself to the outer reaches of civilization. This is not like me, I think. I'm smart enough to know how much I'll be depending on this German bathtub. (You don't want to get carried away with this living-in-the-Now stuff. Sure, Now is all you've got to work with, but still it's foolish to take needless chances—you never know what the Now of the future will bring.)

By the time I drive back to the nearest Mobil (my only credit card is Mobil) and whip my machine into fighting shape (it takes some air and a quart of thirty-weight), the sky is nearly dark, or as dark as it gets in this electric playland, and I can think of nothing left between me and Cici's kiss but a fifteen-minute drive and the rescue itself. Though my heart begins racing at the thought, I feel an odd, purposeful calm. It's like feverishly waiting weeks for Christmas when you're a kid, and then when the splendiferous morning comes at last and you have only to walk down the stairs before you can tear into the goodies, you emerge from the fever onto a plateau of savory excitement, and you take the stairs with a restraint you wonder at yourself.

Yes, fine. Except I've been parked here across the street for ten minutes now, and my restraint, if that's what it was, has turned rancid and sticky with doubt. Like, what if she's not in her room? I mean, this place is very bad news. The stunted shrubs around the Bamberger bunker will offer lousy cover for a protracted guerrilla operation—as if they've been gassed with defoliant—and the broad no-man's-land of crushed rock between the street and the walls glimmers forbiddingly in the not-dark Costa Mesa night. What if the dog's outside patrolling the perimeter?

Then Barry's cavalier recommendations of last night come somehow to mind, and I decide he was right, a car aerial would be an excellent and potentially vicious weapon. Also unobtrusive—I could conceal it up my sleeve, in case . . . shit, in case *nothing*—capture is unthinkable. I'll just feel safer with a weapon. It'll multiply my options.

The simplest move, it seems, would be to snap off the aerial from the shark-gray air force Plymouth parked on the more shadowy side of the driveway as I creep between their two automobiles to the wall of the house.

OK. But creep? No, that's pointless. In this light, anybody parting the drapes will see me, whether I'm creeping or not, and the house has no windows in front anyway. Also, if I should catch some neighbor's eye, I'd better not be skulking around like the Cro-Magnon man. Boldness is what's called for. So, fuck it, I'm off. I cross the street, stride right up to the Colonel's set of wheels, and with a crack, wiggle, and twist, I take his aerial— this is very satisfying. This is how the Vikings must have felt lumbering down the alleys in some crummy Celtic village grabbing off whatever they wanted.

Around me all is quiet. I elongate my aerial and continue striding right at the house. Although I'm in full view, there is of course no reason for any Bamberger to be peering out the front door—this drab terrain isn't worth a look even in the daytime.

I duck past the corner of the house and pause there against the wall. Really, this is a cinch so far. What did I expect— barbed wire? More slowly, I proceed along the brick walkway toward the back wing of this big squashed-out abomination of a house, where in her rooms Cici pines for me in secret.

Here, a lamp shining within, is the Colonel's study. The old pecker could well be in there doing bomb research, plotting optimum-kill patterns on graph paper. He's replaced the broken window, but bits of glass still glitter here and there over the barren ground. (My heel twinges as I think about it.) I can hear nothing—nothing except the faint, inevitable jangle of Cici's radio. Ahead and also lit up are Cici's windows with those few scrubby bushes struggling up from a plot beneath them. I'll have to squat there rapping on her plate glass loudly enough for her to notice me over the music and pimple ointment ads and yet softly enough so as not to alert the military. All I can hope is that she's ready for me and waiting with keen senses.

I scuttle quickly to a spot behind the shrubs. Damn it, she's got her tunes *blaring* in there. I listen, and I can't even tell whether she's singing along. *Shit.* What is wrong with her? *Tick-tick-tick* . . . I tap the glass with the tip of my aerial, but it's hopeless. All the Colonel has to do is imagine he's heard something out here—after what went down last time—and he'll just flip on the floodlights and unleash that savage hound. Jesus, *then*, even if I do somehow slash my way out of bright-red mayhem with two or three limbs still attached, Cici and I will be finished for sure. So why doesn't she realize this? Why isn't she crouched by her window with her curtain drawn slightly aside watching eagerly for me? Cici, remember how you sneaked out that night so we could drive to Dana Point and sleep on the beach? And how you took off a whole weekend from work and lied to your mom so we could camp out in San Jacinto, when we made love up in the tree? And how, when she snooped around and found your little hash pipe, you told her to kiss your heinie? What's this shit now about doctors and hospitals and not having boyfriends and missing graduation? Where's your old carefree and innocent abandon?

Suddenly, as if in answer, Cici jacks up her radio to full volume. The Beatles are bellowing "All You Need Is Love." I jump up. It's our song! It's our sweet theme of hope from last summer! She's signaling me, I think stupidly, she's trumpeting me to charge. I pound my knuckles on the glass, just as—

"*Eeeeee!*" Cici shrieks! "Biiiitch!"

"*Shut up!*" yells her mother. "You shut your crazy mouth!"

"*Eeeeeeeeeeee!*"

The radio is silenced. I duck down.

"Get those clothes off the floor and into that suitcase! I'm not asking you anymore, young lady—I'm telling you!"

"You can't make me!" Christ, she's sobbing. "You can't make me do one single thing!"

"Edmund?" calls the mother. "Edmund? We need you in here!"

"You maniac!" yells Cici. "You *bitch*! You're the one that's sick—sick in the head!"

"Edmund!"

"Bitch-ass *bag*!"

The radio noise leaps back into the exchange—a Stevie Wonder song. And next to me the study darkens abruptly. I press my ear to her window.

Off goes the music again, leaving poor Cici's muffled wailing. "I won't! I can run away, and you'll never find me!"

"Go on! Keep it up, little Miss Toothpick! Dr. Sullivan will just lock you in a padded cell! We'll call him and get you in there tonight if this keeps up. We can put you in through emergency if we have to, and strap you down!"

"Eeeeeee!"

"HEY!" barks the Colonel. "Does my girl want slap? Hey? Slappity-slap time?"

"You . . ." I whisper. "You big, fucking. . . ."

"My girl dump these clothes?"

"—had her all packed ten minutes ago," the mother's whining. "Her toilet things and makeup's spread all over the bathroom rug—"

"My girl dump these clothes?"

"Edmund—"

Whack, I hear it! He belted her, the fat prick bastard.

Now she really lets go, helplessly, hysterically.

"What's that number?" he's shouting. "You got that number? What's *wrong* with this damn thing?"

"We disconnected it."

A phone clashes down.

"Get me that number! Hear me? This fight's over! We'll get her a bed up there tonight if they gotta kick somebody else into the street to do it!"

He stomps out.

I listen for the mother, straining for any sound over Cici's choking sobs. I can't tell—she may still be in there repacking the suitcase, but odds are she's gone to get the doctor's phone number. I have to chance it—no telling what's coming next—so I rap on the glass.

Instantly, Cici's hushed.

I rap again.

A corner of the curtain moves, making a triangle of light. I flutter my fingers before it. And there—her tangled hair, and one wide eye. . . .

"Cici, it's me! You OK?"

"*Wait*," she whispers hoarsely.

The curtain closes. In a second her lamp goes out, and her radio resumes its pumping. Then she shows her delicate face, gray and mottled against the dark of her room, her hair a dim cloud around it.

"Hi," she says, forcing a thin smile.

"Long time no see," I say idiotically.

She rolls her eyes. "What're you gonna do?"

"Me? Cici, I just *did* it. I got here! My car's all loaded and everything. You ready to roll?"

She drops the curtain.

Jesus, they back already?

No—she reappears. She looks miserable.

"Cici, let's hustle! C'mon, put on your sneaks and rip out here. I'm right across the street."

"I don't know if I can," she mews against the glass.

"What? Sure you can! Come on! You have to!"

"I can't! They'll catch me!"

"Bullshit! Just go for it, Cici! Run your buns off! They couldn't catch a dead turtle!"

She starts to cry. "But see, maybe—oh, Will, they don't let me run anymore. They took my sneakers. Will, you have to do something!"

I stare at her. Christ, how sick is she? What am I getting into? "Listen—OK, Cici, you just sneak out the back, those sliding doors, and then zip around by the side here—"

She disappears. *Shit.* Except for the radio (". . . another KRLA solid gold weekend . . ."), there's silence.

I'm trembling. I'm nervous as hell and sweating in these denims. I compress my aerial. What kind of scene *is* this anyway?

The mother's voice again . . . but I can't quite—

"It's *my life*!" screams Cici.

"You want to go in that nightie? *Do* you? You want to get dragged out like that for the whole world to see just how you look?"

Cici's answer is swallowed by something—her bed, a bunched pillow.

"Pick up the rest yourself," says the mother. "The bathroom, too—you'll be up there without a toothbrush, if you don't!"

A pause—just the absurdly cheerful radio, and then the curtain moves. I jerk back.

Her face is wild and twisted. "I'm coming—" she coughs. "Out the portico, out the back!"

"OK—run! Don't let the dog out!"

She's gone.

Lights burst on in front of the house. I drop to one knee, crouched ready to fly. Rapid shoe-heels clack on the walkway out front. All I can see down my long side of the house is the curved driveway and the rear quarter of the air force car in silhouette, its taillights now glinting orange with reflection. The shadows of the bush branches zigzag toward me over the ground. The mother, in flapping bell-bottoms, rounds the car, sets down a suitcase, and tries to pop the trunk lid. She can't do it. She straightens. Then she stoops to try again—but she can't do it. She clacks up the walk.

I look toward the back of the house. Now, Cici, *now.* But nothing, just more bushes, and the grainy line of a rail fence. Come *on*! Come *on*! I keep peering, expecting any second to see her flash around the corner, scampering like a kitten. . . .

Stillness. The disc jockey babbles on.

"Cici?" Jesus—the mother again, in her room. "*Cici?* Come out of there now. You know that won't work. You know Daddy! *Cici?*" Bam, bam, bam, bam. "*Cici!* You want Daddy all mad now? Do you? Come out!" Bam, bam, bam, bam.

Pressing again to the window, I listen, but I hear no reply from Cici, no shouts, no whimpers.

"Will!" she calls softly.

There she is, her pale head, thrust around the far corner of the house.

I give her a few hurry-up sweeps with my arm, and out she

comes in a shambling trot, one hand clutching up her nightie at her knees.

"Edmund?" the mother's shouting.

"I'm dizzy," breathes Cici.

I catch her. I tug her against me.

"Ow," she says. "Don't."

I shudder. She feels bony. A gassy fear takes my air, and I pant, staring out over the top of her head. She's wiggling. I let her go. "Cici—are you OK?"

Her face crumples.

"What's wrong with you?"

She starts to cry.

Then the Colonel's hammering command: "Open this bathroom! Open it *now*! Double-quick! I'll bust it down—so help me!"

"Give her a chance," says the mother. "Give her a chance!"

I wrap an arm around Cici's back, and together we dash over the brick to the lit-up driveway. I grab her suitcase as we go by into the street. She's barefoot, letting out soft yips.

I pull open the door, urging her, "Hop in, hop in," she's so slow. I shove the suitcase onto her lap, scurry around into the driver's seat, and ease us away, headlights off, toward the main road.

Once we're in traffic, another nugget in the stream, I allow myself a few sidelong glances at Cici. There she sits in timorous silence, on her haunches like a gargoyle, her knees drawn up to her chin beneath that baby-blue nightie, her dull eyes fixed on the play of lights out in the faraway world.

I can't start pummeling her with questions—it seems too soon for words, even if I could come up with any, so I switch on the radio. Some newscaster is importantly spewing out all the cockeyed facts of the day (President Thieu is not happy with President Nixon's new plan for a phased withdrawal of our half-million crusaders. Governor Reagan *is* happy with the police night raid last week on People's Park, where they smashed swing sets and trampled flower beds.)—and Cici's little hand does not dart out to push the buttons. She used to loathe the news. I drive north through Garden Grove and into Anaheim to pick up big I-5, even though my grand plan for far-flung adventures makes no sense anymore. We pass Disneyland just as Tinkerbell's fireworks are going off, and I say, "Hey, look," sort of surprised myself, but she doesn't look, all she does is twitch her cheek like a sleeping cat and tell me she feels cold. I roll up the window.

I know what's wrong with her, of course. She has cancer. She is obviously dying of some hideous, emaciating form of The Disease, and her brutal, selfish parents are obviously terrified she will expire at home with nobody else around to throw a blanket over her wasted face.

And now, Jesus—like a stricken wild bird you'd find feebly beating one wing in the dead leaves, she is mine to carry home, to nurse tenderly, and to bury in a coffee can under the hibiscus. Oh, God, goes my treasonous brain, maybe I should turn her over to the doctors myself. But now, from the halls of my memory, where she lives more vitally than she does in her languid form beside me, she calls for blind loyalty to the end, she calls for small worship, like the dying bird, and my brain gives in. I can't drop her in the hospital and I can't drag her to the wilderness. So where do I take her? Where else?

303 East Bay is an even less pleasant domicile than I'd anticipated. It's a crackerbox painted white with aqua trim up a flight of rickety stairs and over a garage that's filled with bundled magazines, mostly *Engineering News-Record*. (I checked it out, looking for a place to hide the Porsche.) Together with two shacks built behind it in a square of gray sand, it's called Wind and Sea Apartments, so says the aqua sign over the postboxes. Just like Mr. Busch to own the kind of rental properties that offer month-to-month haven to a parade of transients—musicians, Mormons, runaways, drugged veterans, and smelly poets, all the screws rattling loose in the engine of social progress.

Luckily there are no weirdos hanging out in the alley to watch us move in. We're a strange pair ourselves, me in motorcycle denims tugging my half-naked prize up the dark stairs, fiddling nervously with the keys while she whines, "I don't *like* this place, Will. Will? I don't *like* this place."

"What do you want?" I growl in spite of myself. "Bel Air?"

Which just undoes her again. She sits snuffling on the burnt-orange shag (the apartment's best feature) while I find the breaker box and spring the lights. Merciless overhead fixtures are all we've got, and pale Cici, trapped in the empty glare, against that white wall, is the saddest sight I'll ever see. That's when I let go. I snap off the lights and sink down next to her, push my face against her ribs and really cry.

Poor Cici shuts right up herself. She begins rubbing my neck, saying, "Shh. Shh. Shh. Shh. Shh," into my ear.

I keep on, though. It isn't Cici, it's everything, Lou, Barry, the old man, my worthless future, even Andy's mom and dad.

When I do stop, we lie on the carpet for a long time listening to the traffic and the low *boomp* of the waves on the ocean side—good surf. That is, I listen, Cici sleeps. Our bodies are cupped together, touching, but I don't put my arm over her, or rest my hand on her hip. I'm afraid she'll feel hard, like porcelain. I slip into our closet of a bathroom to rinse my face—in cold water (the gas is off), using my jacket for a towel.

There in the shadows—even as I stand idly recalling some times I wept as a boy—I'm also reconstructing my broken plans, setting fresh goals, as if that makes sense. Then, like falling backward through a doorway, I fall upon this truth: plans and goals have nothing to do with the future. They are just a function of the present moment. Plans and goals provide you with the illusion of control over changes. So, actually, they do make some sense after all, which is a relief. Besides, they're irresistible. My new plans have a face-the-music theme.

Cici needs me. That's number one. She needs me, so I can't blow the country. Escape to the wilderness is out. Without Cici's enthusiasm, it would be no fun anyway. I need *her*, then, too. Why else have I gone through hell to get her? I love her. What's more, I need *me*. Yet hasn't it been me, parts of me, at least (what I've been, what I know, my places, my people), that I've been trying to run away from? I'm supposed to love myself, the way I love Cici, right? Sure. I know that, but it's not easy, because I'm such a blockhead. Well, shit, you work with what you've got, and my work's cut out for me now. That induction physical, for one thing. I'll have to balls it out somehow. Even if I pass, though, the war's still eight thousand miles away. I'll have weeks before some bristle-brain sergeant tries clapping me in a troop transport. So I stay. I stay, and tomorrow morning I tell Lou the book deal's on. I get my money. Lou and Barry take off for London. The old man splits to solve his own mysterious problems—or not. I won't feel guilty about that. What do I owe him for? Nothing! One wiggly goddamn sperm twenty-two years ago—that's it. He can just pull a swift fade over the rim of the globe. Then I'll be on my own, like old times. With Cici. We can have the whole summer on the channel. I'll type Lou's book, and Cici'll . . . what? What's wrong with her? Am I nuts? The cops think she's a kidnap victim. They'll be watching the channel for sure. We'll have to hole up here for now, until . . . until I don't know what.

I'm downstairs by this time spending a few seriously violent minutes throwing magazines around to make room for the car. Finally, I calm down by promising myself a nice, relaxing joint when I get the Porsche pushed into the safety of the garage.

With the flimsy door pulled tight as I can get it, I can't see to find my papers in the glove box, except by lighting matches. And then to roll it neatly I have to go back and stand in the sliding door's crack of faint light coming in from the alley. These minute attentions, I reflect, do as much to subdue rampaging emotions as does the foggy, foggy drug itself.

Some stoop-shouldered drunk in a white Windbreaker shuffles by down the alley, and watching him through the crack, holding my burdened breath, I feel my fears begin to smolder again. The weed will do that, I tell myself. But then, I *have* abducted this delicate teenager, and we *are* ensconced now within these death-splashed walls, and—

"*Death*," I whisper smokily. God, that's almost what she acts like. *Death*. Death herself. An icy current spills through me. My heart flutters. Christ, I am responsible for her. I am all she's got.

I rush upstairs with my backpack and Cici's suitcase. She

isn't where I left her. She's kneeling in the corner before the tall cylindrical space heater, fooling with the knobs underneath, filling the place with gas. Not on purpose—she's just cold. But the pilot is off, and now we have to air the room out before we can light it. Most of the windows are stuck shut, so I open the door and manage to coax her out onto our covered landing, wrapped in my down bag. In the bag, she is soft and embraceable. I hold her. We watch a few spiky stars over the ragged line of rooftops.

After a long while, she sighs, and the way she does it, tilting her head toward me, brushing my cheek, seems like a permission to speak. But I can't. My hand rises up along the bone of her chin to trace her lips with a finger the way I used to. Her lips part, and she says, "What now?"

"Don't ask me," I say.

"Who, then?"

"I'm stoned on my wazoo," I say.

"Oh. Smoke?"

"Sure. You know me."

"When?"

"Just now. Downstairs."

"Beer, too?"

"No. Well, some."

"Shoot," she says after a pause. "Used to be I could smell it. Real easy, 'member? Around your ears and in your hair. My smeller's broke down, I guess."

"Nah, you're—you're under the weather a little bit, for now, but I know you'll get better, Cici. Hey, it's summer! We'll get you out in the old vitamin D sunshine, and build you up with good nutrition and exercise . . . and then watch out! Soon you'll be pink and pretty as ever. OK? Did you quit yoga?"

Her shoulders shake, and she lets out an angry jet of breath, *thhh*.

"I'm not going to try to make you do anything you don't want to do," I go on gently. "And forget the hospital. You know, unless you just *have* to—say if, if you . . . like *some* people, when they get sick, they eventually experience pains, but that's up to you. You're a free person—"

"Don't," says Cici.

224

"Don't talk about it?" I say.

"I don't like you saying I'm sick. I feel *fine*. I'm not coo-coo, or anything. I'm fine."

"But . . . Jesus, Cici. I mean, you're *not* fine. How can you be fine? You're pale. You're—"

"I'm *fine!*"

I say, "Swell."

A helicopter goes over, whapping.

For some strange reason I am suddenly recalling my junior-year dorm room at Syracuse, on the tenth floor, how cozy a cubicle it was. It looked out over a huge cemetery. One winter night I sneaked a cute freshman up there, a Cuban girl from Miami, so she could see my view. That day a dry, fluffy snow had fallen, which had been an exciting new experience for her. She was all chirpy over that and jittery over actually being inside a men's dorm. From my window we could see the rising full moon sweeping through thin clouds, lighting up the stark monuments, the obelisks and ironwork and lacy trees, so that they cast shadows that came and went as the sky changed, and what I really wanted to do then, instead of sitting there slugging back our syrupy yellow wine, was go down and walk in the cemetery. But getting the cute freshman to my room had been a lot of trouble, and I didn't want to spoil the mood—and the opportunity for sex—by suggesting we go tromp around in the snow. Later, after I got her safely out and into her own dorm through a laundry-room window left secretly unlatched after curfew, the moon was lost behind new clouds. The feeling that I'd missed a unique chance to have something valuable happen to me (what, I didn't know) bothered me for weeks, and I would keep trying to imagine how my walk would have gone, thinking up all its little details as if I were remembering them, to prick that blister of regret.

But now on the step with Cici slumped against me, when that odd memory resurfaces, I realize that the valuable thing *did* happen to me after all: it was the event of my choosing to miss the glorious walk, and that was valuable because it makes me see that once you've made your choice, for whatever perfect reasons, it has to be the best choice—because each choice you make is the only choice you could have made—because it's the choice you made. This has a sharp but slippery logic, and I'm trying to back it into a corner of my mind where I can return to it later to see it in the light of day, when Cici speaks up.

"Think we can go turn the heat on now?"

"You that cold?"

"What's wrong with being cold?"

"Nothing. But you could never go live someplace where they have winter."

"Could so. Everybody likes to be warm, even at the South Pole."

Inside, striking a match for the pilot makes me think of my film can of weed over in the map pocket of the backpack. Cici kneels next to me. "Roll up a number for you, if you want," I say.

The gas whooshes on. "Oooo, boy," she whispers, leaning toward the heat vents. The blue flames throw a wavering fan of light on the shag.

Slowly she says, "I don't know. It's weird, 'cause, you know, I ran out of that supersmoke you left me last fall, and then I only did a little after that, at parties and stuff, and it would just like make me paranoid and real dizzed-out. It never was the same as it was . . . before. With you and me."

For a few seconds, I let that *before* just hang there, and then, as I stick two papers together for an extra fat number, brightly as I can, I suggest, "Well, hey, maybe you were beginning to experience tiny symptoms. You consider that?"

She stares into the fire.

I wet down the number and wedge it in one of the vents to dry. "God, Cici, remember the first time I kissed you? Low tide, right? And we walked out under the pier on your lunch break. What an electric connection that was, remember? We hadn't even touched yet, except when you would give me change for a fifty-nine-cent peach kefir. And then like magic, like some guardian angel was twiddling her fingers over our noon hour, here we were alone together, the fulfillment of my summerlong fantasy, me and the beautiful California princess herself *together*, making that dash across the boulevard and laughing—

you filled my eyes. I couldn't see past you. That's when I took your elbow to help you run—because you had on those satin flip-flops—and you switched the sack with our sprouts-and-cheese sandwiches in it to your other hand, so you could grip my arm. I swear, my whole body was one endless erotic zone. And in the sand, when you kicked off your flip-flops your bare feet were almost too much, as if they were your bare breasts. It was like we weren't even talking, remember? I mean, we were talking, but our words were empty sounds, like bubbles underwater. Our *eyes*, that's where it was all happening, and our hands, when we let our hands clasp each other, it was like we were discovering the first purpose of hands, and then when I kissed you, in the shade of the pier, when I finally kissed you I only touched my lips to your cheekbone, to the upper curve of it, but it was the perfect kiss. . . ."

Cici's face twitches briefly.

"Remember how we stepped back to breathe? I was swallowing, trying to get my heart down out of my throat, and I broke out my trusty corncob pipe of dope, because, I don't know, all my words were vaporized, and everything was glowing and silently echoing, and I had to do something, I guess. But what did I do? Remember?"

"You threw it in the water," she whispers.

"Right! And so we just ate our sandwiches standing up because the shore there was weedy and rocky, and we burst out laughing because who would want their picnic among those big slimy pilings, who but us would be standing there having lunch in the low-tide silt and muck while all that warm, sugary beach stretched away on both sides of us? Cici, I just want you to know now that I've never been happier in my whole life than I was at that hour."

She takes a pull of air. "Me neither," she breathes.

"And I doubt if I've ever been sadder in my whole life than I am now."

"Me, too," she gets out.

"So, look, Cici, if that noon was the peak for us, this midnight has got to be the pits, or pretty close. Things can only improve from now on, see? They have to."

I light the joint, sip hard on it, and pass it to Cici. She hesitates, but she takes it. We smoke quietly for some minutes while our anxious blood works. The heater shuts itself down. The room is dark and hot.

"Cici?"

She coughs.

"How do you feel?"

"OK."

"You're not really fine, are you?"

She doesn't answer.

"Cici, please just tell me what it is so I can figure out how I can help. Is it the big C?"

"Is what?"

"What you have. Why you're so pale and sad."

"If I tell you, then you'll go look it up in a book, and you'll think I'm crazy."

"Cici, c'mon. This whole goddamn country is crazy. Look around! Every single person I've talked to or met since I got home is crazier than clamshit. *I'm* crazy. I mean, craziness is quite normal. This day and age you're only truly crazy if you're *not* crazy. Get it?"

She giggles softly.

"So, put me wise, BB eyes. Hunh?"

"Well . . . it's—see, it's something that I don't even know if I have it. Just because he said so—*God*, he doesn't even know me. He doesn't know my life-style or anything."

"Who?"

"Doctor Fuller. Besides, it's only mental, and he isn't even that kind of doctor. And he's a retard anyway, that way he looks at you, all goo-goo, like he's about to crack his brain, he's so concerned. He's so dramatic, with his stupid chin—he goes like this." She makes a face, but I can't see it. "And the thing is, which he didn't believe, is that I'm in control. Like if I want to, I can eat . . . God, I could eat apple pie a la mode if I wanted to. Only I know how many calories are in pie—four hundred—and a hundred and fifty in one scoop of vanilla ice cream . . . ugh. And you said let's meet at House of Pies. You could probably get fat just thinking about the House of Pies. So why should I believe him? He didn't know anything. Like I would give him this test. I would say a food, like *hot dog*, and he would have to say the calories, but he would be sitting there tilting back with his cup of coffee, and he wouldn't even know the calories of *that*, so forget it. He is dumb as dirt, and I bet for sure he has a disgusting wife."

"What did he say you have?"

"Anorexia. But it's not a disease or anything. It's just a disorder. It's when you quit eating. You quit eating all kinds of food, not just what's fattening, and you keep it up until you get so bad your organs could poop out any minute, like your kidneys, and they have to put you in the hospital, or else you could die. And if you did die, you would die basically of suicide, which I would never ever do."

"That's all it is?" I say. "Not eating?"

"Yeah, and he has these pictures, too, these photographs, of other girls with the same thing, and you should see how they look. They couldn't eat no matter how hard they tried. But I *do* eat, whenever I feel like it. Very easily, I just eat, so that's why I don't think I have anorexia, and my organs are very healthy, too."

"Well, if you don't have that, what do you have?"

"Nothing!"

"But then, why were they taking you to the hospital?"

"See, that's it. My mother is just fed up with me. To the teeth. She hates me. You know what she does when I'm in the shower? She calls up the doctor, and they discuss ways to trick me. They pretend they don't, but they do, I'm not kidding. Like about the hospital. We're in his grungy office, and he tells her in some cases, in *bad* cases, when they get real wasted like scarecrows, then they have to go in the hospital. And she goes, 'Oh, I don't like that idea, Doctor,' when it's her idea all along, the old bitch. She wants to get rid of me."

"Well, she's rid of you now, I guess."

Cici gives a startled chuckle, as if she hasn't thought of this, saying, "Yeah. Yeah, but Will, you know what I figured out? Just think, even if I don't have anorexia, what if she *wanted* me to get it? Then I would *have* to go in the hospital, and she would make me die of suicide because I would get anorexia, and no-body would know she did it. Or else she would stick tubes in me and pump me and pump me till I was fat as a hippo, just like her.''

"What about your father?"

"Him, too. When he comes home, he *forces* me to eat stuff—like *eggs*. There's a hundred calories in one scrambled egg, but then if I won't eat it, he says, leave her alone, leave her alone, don't make a big deal over it. Then *she* hides my scale so I can't find out if I'm getting fat. Or thin. I don't want to get too thin, either. Like, I know that's just as bad.''

"Well, shit, Cici. I mean, I might gently point out, from my totally unbiased perspective here, that you *could* afford to put on maybe a pound or two.''

A short silence. "Why did you say that?" she shouts. "*God!* A pound! Do you know how heavy a pound is? It even sounds heavy when you say it!''

I pat her on the sleeping bag. "How about a few dozen ounces, then? They're very light.''

Jokes, I should know, are the wrong approach. She spins away from me and throws her shoulders to the floor.

"Cici, I'm sorry. I don't mean to kid around. But I'm only kidding around because I'm relieved. I thought you had *cancer*, for Christ's sake. I've been through a lot lately, worrying about you. Now what a relief to find out all you have is . . . is some-thing you probably don't really have anyway, right? This an-orexia.''

"Go jump," she says.

I split a burnt match with my thumbnail to use as a roach-holder. Cici mutely declines this delicacy, so I finish it off my-self, then crawl over to dig some beers out of the pack, not remembering whether I put any in there to start with. I haven't. They're down in the car.

When I get back upstairs, she's asleep. With the beer, I brought up some cheese and bread and apples and so on, also some candles—provisions for our great expedition—having de-cided I would just gobble away myself right in front of her and not offer her one morsel, unless she came out and asked for it.

But she is asleep. I get down and kiss her on the mouth.

"Oh," she says. She shivers. "That's nice." She means the candle. I have one burning on the countertop. "Are you going?"

"No, no. Just slapping together a bit of supper. Apple slices, green pepper—nothing fattening!"

"OK, but if you do go, if you have to go somewhere, I'm going, too. I'm not staying in this chicken coop all by myself. Especially at night."

Then I explain to her about my physical, how I have to fly up the coast tomorrow, though I'll be back before dark for sure.

She says, "But Will, like what if you *don't* flunk it? What if you have to go in the army? I don't think you should even go up there at all."

Never fear, I tell her. I won't pass it, if I have to yodel my lungs out and roll my eyes the whole time I'm there, whatever it takes. I do not tell her they can lock me up for three days if they think I am operating under the influence of something that might wear off. (And you thought this country had a Bill of Rights.) Then I decide to stay up the whole night gargling Coors, so I will look my best the next day.

My lip-smacking enthusiasm for my healthful meal has no effect on Cici's appetite. She lies on the carpet, humming. Finally, I can't stand it, and I say, "Cici? How about a bite? You want something?"

She rolls around to face me. "No, but you know what I do want? A radio. It's boring in here."

"Cici. . . . Goddamn it, Cici, I thought you said you could eat."

"So what?"

"So then eat! You have to eat!"

"I hate that word. *Eat.* It's disgusting!"

"Oh, Jesus. How can you get well if you won't eat?"

"There's nothing *wrong* with me!"

I sigh. "Then please eat something. This—here, chew it up and swallow it. Yum-yum, good." I hand her a slice of apple, browned by the air, and she bites into it.

"OK?" she says.

I push another slice at her. "Here."

"I'm not that hungry," she says.

"Cici, look, it's just a harmless little apple."

She takes it. "But that's all."

"Sure," I grumble. "Better look out, or soon you won't fit into your sleeping bag."

"I *said* I'm not that hungry. Just 'cause you don't believe me doesn't mean it isn't true."

"I do believe you. That's the worst part of it."

She snorts.

"And I also believe you probably have that weird disease."

"It's not a disease!"

"It's not the class picnic, either."

"Well, so? Why did you *say* that? You don't know anything!"

"Cici, c'mon. Ease off a minute and try to imagine how I feel. When did I last see you?"

"*Who cares?* All I wanted was a shitty little radio!"

I shake my head. We're both so tired there is no sense struggling on toward some height of reason. The way is looking pretty steep. I shut up and drink beer, sitting on the counter, and Cici falls asleep.

I get fairly drunk fairly fast. After a while, I hop down to light the water heater so I can shower in the morning, forgetting for a minute that such sprucing-up would not square with my other preparations for the day ahead. Well, Cici can shower, anyway.

Mr. Busch has left a good mattress and a chair in the other room. I shake Cici awake and lead her in there, then take off my clothes and get in with her under the sleeping bag. I kiss her shoulders, her neck, her hair. She turns to me whispering, or just breathing. I rub her and feel her everywhere, and she doesn't stop me . . . her firm arms, her shallow stomach, her breasts like birds, her hips, her thighs, all her fruitlike smoothness. . . . I am numb. I'm numb in my hands, those thick wedges, numb enough to love her. She is Cici, she is the same. Stroking her, as my dull fingers slide where they want, I get so bluntly excited that my cock aches to splitting, and she tugs it down between her legs, her knee raised to take me in, and there it is, *love*, it is love, we hook into it dumbly, yet surely as any two goony animals, we press ourselves against it, coupled up on either side of it like the halves of a waffle iron. . . . *"It's OK, it's OK,"* she is harshly whispering—I'm crying again—but then, when I let go, I can't feel more than a gush, a loss, a wind-stealing blow to my lopsided soul, to both our souls, and most of that love breaks loose and goes spraying away to wait on the edge somewhere, the edge of blue life, or whatever it is that keeps going around.

A while later when my eyes come open, the windows are already graying. I disentangle myself without waking her and slip down into the garage, to the car, where I sit, trying to think. Things have gotten serious. First, I am a marked man—or at least my car is a marked car. The Colonel knows for sure Cici and her suitcase would get nowhere by themselves. To him, no doubt, the most likely shape her help would come in is the roly-poly shape of my little sports car—with the dastardly shape of me behind the wheel. So I'll have to play it safe this morning and run along the ocean down to the channel. And I'll have to get there early enough to beat the inquisitive cops who're bound to come calling—though probably they showed up there last night. I wonder what Lou made of that. Of course, if she and Barry were out, the cops would return this morning. Boy, I'm really a clear-thinker under stress. I would make a fabulous outlaw. I *am* an outlaw, for Christ's sake. Today being an outlaw is a necessary condition of the moral life. How tragic. How fucked up. This is such a wonderful country, but it's also so pathetic. This country is like Bad Barry Glines, crude, handsome, self-righteous, simpleminded, greedy, loud, conceited, uncertain, with a solid, well-defended heart and a quick temper, and with almost everything going for it—far more than it realizes, for sure. But what other country is much better? What other society is in touch with its conscience? What other government can see it must serve the whole world's people, not just its own? Sweden? Maybe Sweden, maybe Canada, I don't know. Cici's right, I don't know anything. I'm an American, I know that. Love it or leave it, right? And hell, that's it. I love it, the way Lou loves Barry. I'm an American. What a shame.

This building must be papier-mâché. Even Cici's light foot-

233

steps from bed to bathroom make the floorboards creak overhead.

I bound upstairs and rap on the door just as the shower water comes on.

She turns it off. "Will?"

"Yeah, it's me."

The door opens. She's in the sleeping bag. "You snuck out on me."

"I just figured you could use some sleep. Look, I'm going down to the channel for a while, but I'll come back on my way to the airport, OK? I think you should stay inside, Cici, and not even stick your head out the door, because your parents have probably gone berserk over your disappearance, and they'll have bloodhounds and helicopters and the National Guard out hunting for your blonde body under every blade of grass, OK?"

"I guess so, but . . ."

"What?"

"Well, maybe I should write them, like a postcard. To just say, you know, don't worry, I love you."

"Good idea. Also, say something like you'll telephone from Houston. And *do not* mention me. Mention somebody else—Albert or Lois, somebody they don't know."

"OK. Then would you buy me one?"

"If I have a chance."

"And we have no towels, so could you bring some towels?"

"Towels. OK."

"And a hair dryer?"

"Jesus, Cici, why do you need a hair dryer? You're not going to the prom."

"I just do. I'll catch cold if I don't."

"All right, I'll try. But *I* don't use a hair dryer, and my hair's almost as long as yours now. Did you notice?"

"Yeah. I like it." She smiles at me, her old jewelly smile.

"Cici, you know, you're still beautiful."

"I am?"

"Yes. Hey, if I fixed you some cheese and bread would you eat it for me? Whole wheat bread?"

She winces and sighs. "Well, OK—if you bring me back a radio."

"Fair enough." I touch her on the knob of her collarbone. "You could get a job selling cars."

In no time I have two sandwiches constructed. Cici nibbles hers while I sit on the floor supervising.

"Nothing to drink but beer," I say. "Want me to bring back some milk?"

"Water's good," she says.

"Anything else you can think of?"

She frowns. "Will, I hope you're not getting all jazzed and proud of yourself 'cause I'm eating some of your dumb cheese. I mean, whoopee. Because I could drink a banana shake if I wanted, with a big bowl of creamed spinach."

"Great. Wonderful. No, Cici, I only meant, I don't know, some tampons, say, or a toothbrush. Something in the line of personal needs, or toiletries."

She shakes her head. "My period's gone extinct."

"Really?"

"But yeah, get me some Breck Dry. Shampoo. It has a D on the label."

I say okeydokey, see you later, and I'm out the doorway and clattering down the shaky stairs. I'm tired and I want to run again to perk up. Instead, I make myself stop in our tiny court-yard. I turn on the water spigot by the fence and splash my face over and over. Good. It's good I'm not off running because I have to think. I have to settle my feelings for a minute here. Beyond tired I realize that how I actually feel is pretty good. I do. Because of Cici . . . because, shit, I love her. Sure, she's sallow and drifty and down as the Dead Sea, but she's still Cici. She's there within herself. Her spirit's been trampled, that's all, in a storm of hormones, by a beefy mob of doubts. It'll recover. She only has to want it again, to admit she wants it, and it will come back, drawing her timid beauty out of hiding. First her smile will start to slip into view. Then those young muscles along her legs and shoulders will wake up to their duties. They'll remind her blood of its purpose, and her skin will come to wear that peach glow again. She'll have her health. And we'll have each other all to ourselves, and time. Love, health, and time. What more is there to need? Yeah! No wonder I feel good. Practically considered, though, what I will need right now, if Lou and the black buck have hit the highway, is my key to the house. It's in the car, so I go get it, and while I'm there I grab my Dreadnought Driver, too. It's a stimulating object, like an arrowhead or a fossil. It wants to be in your hand.

I trot down the alley, across the boulevard, out onto the beach. Nobody's up and around but the surfers, lean and inward-looking as stray dogs. I swoop the antique racket as I run. If I had to go to a costume party, it would make a perfect accessory. I would be Bill Tilden. I could dig out the old man's white flannel trousers from his big trunk, his old black shoes with points for grass, an old mothbally sweater, and put my hair up under one of those wool caps with the short bill, and swish around on my toes like a dancer. . . . In fact, *in fact*, why not? That's what I *will* do! I'll go into that dead-ass induction center all full of faggotty bluster like Big Bill himself! Sure! This seems like a great idea, and I trot on a bit faster. Then slower again. I'm running on empty.

One short block from the old homestead, though I'm just ambling along sort of with my nose to the ground thinking up fruity mannerisms with which to bedeck my plain personality when the need arises, a sourceless foreboding somehow comes worming in, and I halt in my tracks. What?

A car, that's what. A beige Ford Galaxie easing around the Channel Road curve ahead. I don't like it. It's too slow. I duck behind a parked Karmann Ghia, and damned if the Ford doesn't pause a few seconds, then glide in behind Barry's Mercedes.

Two official-looking jerk-offs climb out, one in a dark suit, the other in a tan uniform of some kind, settling a wide hat on his crew-cut head. Things are getting *very* serious. Well, wait till they leave, right? Simple. They won't be long learning little Willie's whereabouts are known to God alone. They are industrious, though, I'll say that. It's not eight o'clock yet. Old Colonel Dickbrain must have some pull.

I sit on the curb. I could use a breather anyway. Actually,

some speed is what I could use—a couple No-Doz, anything. Whew—also, I don't smell too good. That's a boon, however, fitting the unusual demands of the crisis ahead. Tilden never smelled too good either. He was shy about showing his dingle, so he didn't shower much on tour.

A muffled but powerful shout of rage, unmistakably Barry's, seizes my attention. What is wrong with *him*? I scuttle along low to the edge of our driveway apron by the mailbox and the corner of the jade hedge, ready to dash around behind the shower enclosure if those jerk-offs from the Galaxie should appear in the doorway. Barry's still yelling. He really sounds fierce, even for him. Lou gets off a few angry bursts, too. I can't tell what the hell's going on.

Then the little window in the front door gleams as it's pulled inward, and I break for the shower.

I peek back through the trellis.

It's only Lou, in her lavender terry bathrobe, rounding the Mercedes, coming this way. She's singing. It's the old song she used to sing to me when I was upset and she wanted me to laugh: "Gonna dance with the dolly with the hole in her stockin', while her knees keep a-knockin' and her toes keep a-rockin', gonna dance with the dolly with the hole in her stockin'...."

I sing, "Gonna dance by the light of the Moon."

"Will?"

"Hi, Mom." I step out.

"Gracious," she says. "You ready for a shower?"

"No, go ahead. What's the story with Bluto back there?"

"Oh, God. They're serving papers on him, the bozos. Say, you didn't let it out we were back down here, did you?"

"Shit, Mom, his car's been in the drive for two days now—with 'Bad B' on the license plate."

"I guess so, yeah. Well, would you believe a paternity suit? Brought by his own dumbbell father? For his own sister's child?"

"What?"

"*Step*sister, really. Yeah, but it's been in the works awhile. Barry swears he's been set up. He swears all this is merely how his dumbbell pater famili-ass is kicking dirt over his own mess."

She deepens her voice: " 'Not my juice, man! Negatory. No fuckin' *way*!' I gotta believe him, Will. Though honestly I don't give two hoots. It's what it's doing to him that's the sorrow of it. The old bastard's trying to sabotage Barry's career."

"Amazing. You think he really did do it?"

"I don't care. But hey, now, you're on the wanted list around here, too, Willie. The local fuzz, right?"

"Oh-oh. When were they here?"

"Last night. *Late* last night. I just hope it's nothing scandalous or expensive."

"No, no. Negatory. What did they say?"

"Nothing. They just want a word with you. You're requested to make contact through the main desk—right pronto."

"I am? Shit. Well, could you forget you saw me?"

"What d'ya mean? You live here."

"I mean now—this morning. I only showed up very briefly to tell you the good news. I decided to do the book. I want to do it. It'll be fun."

"I know, Will, and I'm glad. I got your note. I immediately phoned Grampa Jack back last night to get him going on the transfer of funds, but all I got was his service. I left the message, but don't worry, I'll reach him at the office this morning, and we'll make sure it happens today. But I just hope you're not planning to blow the whole wad on a drug deal or some crap like that, because I'll *never* forgive you, Will, believe you me. These cops aren't connected with this at all, I hope, are they?"

"Oh, Mom, Jesus. You remember Andy Busch?"

"Andy Busch . . . Andy Busch . . . I don't think so."

"Yes, you do. Anyway, it's about him, probably. He disappeared off the face of the planet without a trace."

The front door slams. I duck behind the trellis again before I remember those two men are not after me. Lou watches them get into the Galaxie.

She mutters, "Look at that—they escaped with their lives."

"What's this mean now, Mom, you can't go to Wimbledon?"

"Hell, no. If anything, it means we'll go sooner and stay longer. But don't worry, I'll organize my papers and crap for you before we take off. And better yet, I'll go scrounge up your old man's forgotten manuscript. It must be buried upstairs someplace."

"Don't bother, Mom. If I decide I want it, I know where to find it. For now just let me start fresh on the project myself, OK? I don't want to get contaminated by his broken-down approach."

"For research is what I'm saying. He must have a lot of details gathered together, all the basics anyway. However, all right, I see your point. Well, listen, I'll wire you my address right away, so any questions, you know where to reach me, how's that? We may leave real soon, you know, if I can squeeze him into the Queens Club tourney in London, to tune up. He may have to take another shot, too, beforehand. But, shhh, don't tell him." She leans back against the trellis post, hugging herself. "Man, though, Will, I am truly tickled about this—the book, I mean. Do you realize how stupendous this book can be? I see it not as just a history, which would be deadly, you know— Lord! All those dusty names and dates. . . . It should be more like a rhapsody. This *rhapsody* of the game. It should reflect the way I *feel* about tennis. My love, my devotion! You gotta describe the living, breathing world of tennis, not just a lot of statistics—except when you have to, of course. You can't leave the numbers out, they're significant, too, but you grasp my philosophy, don't you?"

"I grasp it, sure. But this is my book, Mom, not your book. It's about you, but how it comes out is totally up to me, and I have no inkling of where it could go."

"I know, I know, that's why I'm revealing these guidelines." She grimaces. "I'm not gonna dictate it to you word for word, come *on*. It just excites me how much potential the thing has. The thing has potential without end. Listen, let me shower up here, and we'll have coffee over it. We'll hammer it out over coffee and toast."

I tell her I would gladly, if I didn't have another engagement, namely my physical, and as she replies, "Hey, and all this reminds me, did you hear Osuna just got *killed*? In a plane in Mexico?" the ever-awesome Barry Glines plows around the corner, considerate as a bulldozer.

Flashing a hard look at me, he says, "Shake it up, Mama, it's check-out time. You and me gotta be dressed, packed, and gone in twenty minutes."

Lou glares at him with mingled anger and affection. "Barry honey, you just cool your heels a second. Relax. We have a detailed schedule, which we agreed upon last night, and we're sticking to it."

"Yeah, well, I just put that through the shredder. We barely got seats on the ten-ten bird to Boston, OK? Get used to it."

"Boston!"

"That's right! Same as New York, right?"

"Not if— Oh, beans. Look, Barry, you want to fly to Boston, be my goddamn guest. I'll meet you in London tomorrow. But meanwhile there's business here I gotta finish up today."

"I'm *not* going alone!"

"So then what's wrong with our three-o'clock flight? What do you improve by taking off now?"

"This place is a fucking shit-hole, that's what's wrong with it! Balboa! We'll be left in peace here, right? That was your line, right? Hey, *secrecy*, too, right? A secret, fucking sunny summer on the beach. But all along you knew we were gonna have this junior G-man over here on the case—"

"Barry, *lay off*!" Lou shouts. "You wanna leave, *leave*. You're a big boy. You can fly where you want when you want why you want. I'm sticking with what we arranged last night, got it?"

"Lou-*eeze*," whines Barry.

"Scram, both of you, while I proceed with my ablutions."

"So then, this is good-bye," I say.

"Looks that way. 'Course we'll be back in East Hampton toward August probably."

"Well, on this book, then," I start to say, "if I can duck the army and all that, maybe in August you and I can—"

But Barry plants the butt of one hand against my breastbone and propels me into the hedge. "*Fuck off*, Junior! I'm talkin' with her now, and we're talkin' in private! Inside, Mama!" He yanks Lou by her forearm.

"*Barry!*" she screams. "*No!*"

I scramble up and hack the brute across the kidneys with my

Dreadnought Driver. He grunts and whirls, and I wallop his broad gut. He doubles up, saying "*Hooonh*," to his feet.

"*Stop it!*" yells Lou.

—though I'm already churning down the drive into the street. I've got too great a jump for him to chase me, but just in case, I swerve off into the maze of alleyways behind the beachfront houses among all the inner peninsula shacks and bungalows. Light as a panicked gazelle, I take a few quick turns, vault some fences, and then drop in back of somebody's little shingled shed for garbage cans.

Whoa, *baby*. Did I clobber the fucker, or what? Son of a *bitch*. My palms still hold an echo of the blows. The old Dreadnought remains in one piece, too. Running my fingers over the frame, I realize I'm trembling like crazy. I'm really trembling all over, and I also feel like crying again. Shit, I must be pretty screwed up. Because he was asking for it, the big prick, wasn't he? Goddamn right. So I gave it to him, *biff*, *bam*.

That's the trouble. I feel half-sick. I mean, I'm glad I gave it to him, I am. But basically I'm not a biff-bam kind of guy. Violence—I hate violence. It's so drastic and uncool. It's purely bad. Yet, it's natural, you must admit. As natural and grim and spontaneous as, say, puking. You hate to puke, but when puking is the answer, it's the only answer. So you puke.

After a minute more of recovery and scattered reflection (maybe I should puke at my draft physical—the doctor raps my kneecap with his hammer and I blow lunch. Whenever somebody says my name, *wrawk*, I retch. Would that work?), I set off trotting back to the Wind and Sea Apartments. I can't remember when my plane leaves, but suddenly I feel very late.

In the car I find an old sweatshirt Cici can use as a towel. I'll just have to explain I couldn't come up with a radio, so she'll just have to spend a quiet day contemplating calories until I get back. By then I'll be in a much better position to assess our needs anyway, and so should she.

Behind the watery rattle of the shower, when I let myself in, is an odd thumping noise, and the whole apartment is shaking. I put my ear to the bathroom door. Christ, she must be *running* in there.

"Cici?"

She stops. "I'm in the shower."

"No kidding. What are you *doing* in the shower?"

"What? Nothing. God—none of your business!"

"Cici, this place is all balsa wood and glue. I walk in here, and it feels like the great quake of 'sixty-nine."

She laughs. "It did not."

I give her the bad news in one big dose: no postcard, no shampoo, no hair dryer, and no radio. My apologies.

"You dufus! Oh, wow, what am I supposed to do all day, take showers?"

Whatever she wants, I tell her, as long as she stays hidden, because now she is one hot item on the police band for sure. I toss the sweatshirt in on the floor.

"OK," she says blackly.

" 'Bye till later. I'll send a telegram if I get into bad trouble, OK?"

" 'Bye," she says.

"You gonna wish me luck, Cici?"

"Good luck," she grumbles.

I charge into the bathroom, rip back the pastel-green shower curtain, and grab her shoulders. She screams and tries to cover herself.

"*Cici, Cici!* For shit's sake, where's your fighting spirit? You were once a cheerleader, remember? Come on! Rah, rah, *Will!* Rah, rah, *Will!* Bo bo skideeten-doten, rah, rah, *Will!* Itten-bitten widdle-diddle, bo bo skideeten-doten! *Whish*, bodley oten-doten, bo bo skideeten-doten, *fight!*"

"OK, OK." She laughs. "What a wacko. They wouldn't pick you for the army in a million years, don't sweat it."

"If I do get out, listen, tonight we'll have *champagne*. We'll have a feast! T-bone steak, baked potatoes, and fresh asparagus for me, and for you my shredded draft card—only two and a half calories."

"You get out of here," she says, laughing. She tugs the shower curtain around herself.

"OK, but let me kiss you first."

We kiss. She raises her hand gently to my cheek and eyebrow, and she rubs my face. "Will—I love you," she whispers.

"You do?"

She nods.

"Great! That's all I need!" I skip out the door and yell, "*Hoota*," as I plunge down the stairs.

There's enough slope to the alley, in the middle down the storm gutter, so I can jump the Porsche by myself—one small plus for our new domicile. Taking no chances, I depart Balboa by the ferry across the harbor, because the cop headquarters are up at the root of the peninsula overlooking the boulevard. I proceed circumspectly up Jamboree Road to the airport. The flight I catch is to Oakland, which is OK. The induction center was kind enough to staple a few bus tickets to my notice with directions about where to go. I'll be late probably, but not by much.

My flight is without significant event, except for my trip to the can, where I roll up a number and kneel bent over the whooshing toilet for evacuation of the fumes, and then decide, no—no, this is a bad idea, I need to keep all my wits in the old corral. I clip the number back under my ponytail with a bobbypin. Instead, I bum a Winston from the matron in blue sitting across the aisle, which she parts with very reluctantly, not desirous of even the slightest commerce with the sorry likes of me.

The induction center turns out to be a huge hollow barracks in a sprawling navy yard with gray navy vehicles zipping every which way like toys in a kid's fort, and as I figured, I turn out to be late. All the other would-be inductees, a surprising number, maybe fifty, are sitting in folding chairs at big folding tables industriously writing.

The sorry likes of me evoke no sneer of disdain from the uniformed proctor of the ongoing test. He just has me pick a stubby pencil out of a shoebox and says in a low voice that I'm to answer all the questions to the best of my ability and not spend too long on any single one. This seems very reasonable. I take the test papers and find a seat, feeling stupidly grateful that I haven't been chewed out for my tardiness and (especially) for my outlandish hippieness. I've got on several strings of love beads, my black tank top, orange Syracuse University sweatpants, and sneakers. But glancing more carefully around me, I see why. Half the saps in here look more wacked out than I do. Really, these guys are *radical*. They are all in fur and satin, or World War I tunics and Hare Krishna wraparounds, or paisley shirts and ties and cowboy boots. One black dude's wearing a lot of jewelry and an old-time-movie striped convict's suit. Jesus, maybe the army really should snap us all up and ship us out *as is*, in our own fucked-up platoon. We could probably take Hanoi in a week.

For a while, nervous and crazed as I feel, I actually make a thoughtful effort on each ridiculous question. I keep looking for tricks. And all the questions are like: "What is Spain? Spain is: (A) a city; (B) a province; (C) a detergent; (D) a nation." Never before, I now realize, have I taken a test that I didn't want to do as well on as I could, even when I knew I'd flunk anyway. I've always been so *earnest*. Spain, obviously, is a detergent. I put C. I chuckle. I whip through the rest of the test filling in the answers without wrestling with the questions, slim impediments though they are, and I find a grave pleasure in such daring: the enemy has been engaged.

Next we're given medical questionnaires to complete. These are basic. History of illnesses. Name and address of family physician. Allergies. Debilities requiring ongoing treatment, e.g., diabetes, asthma, addictions. "Attach supporting documentation where appropriate." I do not have any treatable ailments, and my addictions are better left undeclared. However, I am allergic to dust. There's probably a lot of dust in the army, so I write this down. The last portion of the form amounts to a list of petty problems—flat feet, weak knees, frequent bruises, bedwetting, psoriasis, hemorrhoids, spastic colon, headaches, high blood pressure, bad teeth—exactly sixty of them. Each problem has beside it a little box that you're supposed to x if it appeals to you. I x away with abandon, skipping only the least likely afflictions, like baldness, until I arrive at box 60, homosexual tendencies. Then fuck it, I x that, too, Tilden outfit or no, who cares? My daring attitude, I know, comes from my general Condition Red Alert, but it also comes from all the Camel smoke I've been sucking down. I bought two packs at the airport, and by now

I'm wired on nicotine. (Everyone else is smoking, too. The army has long extended its approval of this addiction.) Now and then I hold my breath and push, empurpling my face, really putting the screws to the old blood pressure.

We all troop out of the test room and into a big hall like a gymnasium, with dirty windows, a high girdered ceiling, and a honeycomb-work of movable gray partitions, like a maze, breaking the space up into jurisdictions for the various testing procedures. We advance in a sort of mumbling herd, but shyly, though some of us exchange short remarks and let out jokey chuckles to show our self-possession.

We stop in a sizable open area like a dance floor in a college bar.

"Men, face the clock!"

We glance around until we spot the clock. The uniformed coordinator of events is standing beneath it on a metal chair. "All right, men," he shouts, "strip down to your shorts and shoes!"

Easily an objectionable order, it seems to me, but nobody hesitates to comply. Nobody except me. Not out of stubbornness, but because I am wearing no shorts. I gave up on underwear in college when I decided it was too much trouble. With everyone around me now stepping out of his pants, belt buckles jingling, what the hell, I unknot the drawstring and peel off the sweatpants anyway, exposing the old banana for the world.

"You!"

I look toward the clock.

"Where's your shorts?"

I shrug.

He angles his gaze away from me in disgust. "Put your trousers on!"

So I do. I'm the only one in pants.

We have to line up at the window of a big cage for wire baskets in which we must deposit our valuables and clothes. Then in groups of ten we're dispersed to examination areas. My group heads first to the toilet hall, where there's a long piss trough. We're given little bottles for samples and labels to fill out.

Eye exam next. No one in my group looks like he's faking anything, so far as I can tell. Bad eyesight would be a logical routine for somebody, you'd think. You only see what you can see, and who knows what you can see but you? Still, near blindness would be tough to make stick, especially if you had a driver's license. My eyes are perfect.

Bad hearing might be an easier scam. We listen through headphones to a range of beeps, and we record our results on a special form. But again, if anyone in my group is fucking up his qualifications, he must be very subtle because none of the examiners appears peeved. My ears are superb.

We don't converse among ourselves much between tests, and we don't look at each other's eyes. We're uptight. Also, it's humiliating to be clomping around this huge warehouse, like laboratory rats, in your brogans without socks and your stained Fruit of the Looms.

At the blood pressure station, waiting my turn, I keep casually trying to jack up whatever it is they're going to measure by holding my breath and pushing. I do this right up to the last second, as the cuff is wrapped around my arm. *Whoosht, whoosht, whoosht*, the guy pumps it up . . . *whisssss*, he lets it out, slips his stethoscope. . . . "Stay seated here and relax awhile," he says.

"Why?" I ask in a small voice.

"Gotta give you a chance to relax," he says.

All *right*—far out. But immediately I'm worrying something's really wrong with me. I've got palpitations, or a brain tumor. How can a few cigarettes knock a sturdy guy like me so off-kilter? But then again, I've been through some wild shit the past few days, which can't be any help. When the guy reads me a second time, I'm still too high. He says they'll have to hit me once more, after lunch. Great. I feel suddenly very confident and sassy. I'm too smart for these assholes.

Last stop is a cubicle we find our way into one at a time, where the doctor within provides a cursory inspection of our posture, our scalps, our tongues, our genitals, and then sits us down to probe irritably into our medical histories as we've represented them. I'm now the last in my group, because of the BP readings, so I have a long wait. Next to me on the bench is the strangest-looking freak in this whole circus—a real dork-nose, as Barry would say. He's sullen and slow, and until my setback, he's brought up the rear in all of the tests. Why he's here I don't know. If I were running this show, I wouldn't have let him in the front door. I would have looked once at him and told him forget it, you can go. Squirm back under your rock. He would undermine morale even in our platoon, the First California Weirdos. He ought to get out on his complexion alone. He's tall, greasy haired, and very thin, with an amazing spread of black-heads and acne that makes his back look like rye bread with strawberry jam. He has on calf-high lace-up boots, the kind you wear with jodhpurs, and frayed boxer trunks printed in a pattern of snowmen and skiers. He stares at the floor. He plucks hairs one at a time from the inside of his thigh, bites off the root of the hair, and flicks it away. Grim indeed.

When he slouches in for his interview, I'm alone on the bench. Before long I can hear the doctor's control of his indignation coming unclamped. His voice is rising.

"*What* drugs?" he yells finally.

"Drugs, man, drugs. You name it, I done it."

"Show me some tracks, then. You have tracks?"

A moment later the doctor's yelling again because the freak's checked every one of the sixty ailment boxes.

"I got a whole lot more wrong with me than just them. At least a hundred," he declares.

He has a belligerent explanation for every problem on the list. By the time they've worked up into the forties, the doctor's fed up.

"We done?" says the freak.

"For now we're done. Get out of here. Come back after lunch."

"What lunch?"

"Get *out* of here!"

The doctor waits a minute to collect himself before he leans around to beckon me with a jerk of his head. I figure I must appear almost as freaky to him as the guy before, so I should play it low-key and respectful to prove my benign intentions.

247

Everything moves briskly along until we get to the sixty boxes. This is obviously the part he hates. He has to plow through them trying to judge the verisimilitude of every damn one by asking picky questions that he hardly ever gets straight answers to. What a job. I feed him polite replies in a soft, nervous voice with my eyes downcast.

He's wearing a rumpled summer suit, brown. His tie is loosened. He has dandruff along his shoulders.

At the last box, one corner of his mouth twitches out in a mean way. "So. You're a homosexual, hunh?"

"Well—of sorts."

"Don't gimme 'of sorts.' Either you are one or you aren't one."

"Well, I've been trying to stay away from boys for a long time."

He scrutinizes me briefly and then makes a savage scribble across the bottom of my form. "Come back after lunch."

My mess coupon is exchanged for a gray pork chop, a heap of fake mashed potatoes and gravy, peas, runny apple sauce, and a brownie. I'm starved, and I eat it all. I drink three cups of coffee and smoke six cigarettes.

A few of us return from the cafeteria to the induction hall for further testing. The freak's the only one I recognize from the morning. He's now dressed in old leather bell-bottoms with fringe and a vest with a US marshal's badge pinned on it. He doesn't look like he ought to be running loose in society. He looks like a reject from the Mongol Horde. He clumps stuporously along behind us. I wish him luck, poor bastard.

My blood pressure, taken by a new tester this time, in a white tunic, remains untamed, I guess (he doesn't tell me what it is exactly, and I don't ask), because he says, "Come back again after the shrink."

I nod, trying to look chagrined. The shrink! *Dr. Shapiro— 1:30* is all that's scribbled on my paper. It figures, though. They're sticking us hard nuts in with some real heavyweight detective of the mind. The army doesn't give in easy.

Or so you might suppose. But Shapiro, when I'm finally ushered in there by his assistant, turns out to be quite a tenderhearted soul. Right away he perceives my terrible shyness. I don't once meet his eyes. I huddle in my chair, holding the back of one hand up to my mouth, a fold of its skin between my teeth.

He asks me to tell him, if I can, how long I have been consciously aware of my homosexual tendencies.

"I don't know," I manage to say. "Not very long."

Have I been able to mention my problem to anyone else, a member of my family, a minister, or another doctor?

"No."

He writes something down, then clears his throat. "Have these . . . tendencies," he says carefully, "—have they ever culminated in . . . an act?"

I nod into my chest.

"Can you say how often these acts . . . have occurred?"

I don't reply.

He rolls his pen between his palms. "Once a year?"

I bite my hand.

"Once a month?" He watches me. "Once a week?"

"Not once a *week*," I say in a rush. "He hasn't—I haven't been with anyone in a long time now."

"Very good," he says slowly, bobbing down to write some more. "OK. Last question, if I may. Tell me now, uh . . . Muldoon. Would the army be a help to you with your problem—or would it be a hindrance? What do you think?"

I shift in my chair. Very softly, I say, "I don't know what I think. I mean, maybe it could be a help . . . but maybe also it could be a hindrance. I can't tell."

"Yes," says the doctor. He writes on two slips of paper, thumps them with a little stamp, clips one to my form, and pushes it toward me across the desk. "Take this to Classification. Muldoon, think about getting some counseling on the outside, will you?"

I take my papers, shrugging at them and nodding.

"When you're ready, Muldoon. You don't have to bear this thing alone."

I shuffle out. Man, what a performance! I fucking juked 'em, man! It's all over! I'm out! I'm OUT!

At Classification, wham-bang, in two minutes I am officially

IV-F. IV-F! Not even I-Y, which is the usual deferment for wackos and queers and other harmless oddballs the army would actually deign to draft only in a dire emergency. When the Russians *do* come swarming across the Canadian border, they'll be met from Maine to Montana by a raw infantry of fairies. But not by me. America will go totally Commie before they'll put a rifle in my mitts. Fabulous. Outasight.

Busing back to the airport over the Bay Bridge, above the boats and drifting gulls, I am elated. I am a free man. My life is my own. Just like Bad Barry, as Lou said this morning, I can go where I want when I want why I want. What luxury.

The pilot generously dips one wing toward the ocean to give some of us a look back at the lovely city. I'm on the other side of the plane, and all I can see is the stitching of the waves. Years ago, as a kid, I used to daydream of a seagoing craft like a huge Plexiglas bubble. Actually a bubble suspended somehow within a bubble, the inner one counterweighted on gimbals, to stay always upright. I had colorful feather pillows in it, and books, and plenty of food and water. You could float in it where the sea currents playfully took you, with no concern for storms or sharks or ports of call, like a note corked in a bottle, gliding by flickering ships at night, washing up on strange island beaches, and washing away again. HMS *Womb Ball I*. With Cici along it would be a perfect adventure. She'd get well fast in *Womb Ball I*.

I'm so happy that in spite of my disheveled appearance, everybody seems to like me. Stewardesses beam at me deplaning, and an ordinary husband and wife act pleased to help me shove my Porsche into locomotion. Even the thin-lipped checkout lady at El Rancho is patient as I lay out my bills to make the steep price of a bottle of Mumm's French champagne.

Without thinking, I drive right past the Bay Avenue turn, heading toward the channel on homing instinct. Might as well give the old man the good news. Lou and Barry should be evacuated by now, too, so he can stumble down out of the attic into the bright light of day. Hell, he can have the whole house all summer if he wants it.

Sure enough, the Mercedes is gone, and the house is locked. I have to go back to the car for my key. I look up to the attic ventilator and shout, *"Yoo-hoo! Dad!* All clear! All-ie all-ie in-free!" But no doubt he was peeking out to watch Barry hurling luggage into the car trunk.

There's lots of beer in the refrigerator, I'm glad to find. I pop one and grab another for the old man. When I set out to hunt him up, however, an uneasy feeling creeps over me. The house is quiet. Upstairs, the bedrooms and study are empty. Lou's room is cleaned out, but there's no sign of the old man's re-claimed occupancy.

I open the attic door and listen.

"Dad?"

Nothing.

"Dad? You still with us?"

Shit. He's gone, right? He must be gone. Out for some air after his long confinement. Maybe a swim. No, not a swim. He detests the ocean. Just a walk, then, an eyeful of the pastey blue sky. He loves the sky. There's so much he loves: cigars, vodka, highways, whiskey, beef, cauliflower, snoozes, soliloquies, mountain vistas, forests, even tennis (he does, I know he does). He loves having all the answers. He loves hoping for salvation against hopeless odds. Me he loves. He loves all kinds of shit. So he wouldn't really blow his brains out. He just loves saying he would.

But I can't go up the stairs. I'm zapped. I have a little wind whirling around between my ears. All I want to do is sit down.

Out on the patio, Lou has tucked all the chairs up close to the house. The slates are still dark under the geraniums where she's watered them, although they've just about expired of neglect anyway. I try the glass doors. They're locked.

Jesus, it was just a few days ago I stood here obsessively straightening the stupid antimacassar on this chair, and now they've all come and gone, and I don't think anyone's sat in it. How trivial are the uses we give to our keenest moments. I drop into the chair.

This now—isn't this a keen moment? And I'm falling asleep in it. Christ. I pick my airplane joint out of my ponytail and light it. By itself, the joint won't imbue this moment with significance, but it will put a significant kink in my perception of it, which may at least keep me awake.

What if I actually do have high blood pressure? What would that mean? Like, can you die of high blood pressure? I want to live! I want to become an old old *old* geezer, a hundred and twenty, a hundred and thirty, with all my faculties happily intact!

I'm up. I bound the stairs to the second floor, swing around the corner, bound up into the attic heat, out of breath, heart slamming in my throat. I beat back his screen of wardrobes—

Nobody home. Stuff strewn all over, rags, papers, bottles, the trunk lid thrown open against the chimney. Khaki clothing hangs limp over the sides, like prisoners killed escaping. The drop-in tray of compartments stands on one end, leaning on its lid. I find his flashlight and beam it inside. Junk. Spilled blazer buttons, letters, wool underwear. . . . Oh-oh, the manuscript is gone. What a shithead, he really thought I'd milk it. I would have, probably, but why should he give a goddamn? The *gun*, too—Jesus. Jesus Christ.

The lit, orange end of my joint falls off into the trunk, and I lean in to snuff it with my flashlight. I beat it out. So he's gone. So what? With the .45 and the crap-o manuscript. So *what*? I don't care, do I? No. Good riddance to bad rubbish, that's my unleavened sentiment. Except, I hope somehow he wriggles out of the jam he's in, I really do. . . . Shit. Now I feel guilty. The daffy old lush has ducked out, maybe forever, and we never quite connected. His last California engagement, and he bombed. He needed me, he begged my help, my father, for the first and only time in our entwined lives, after all he has given me, all the selfless years of love and guidance, and I, venal ingrate that I am, I rebuffed him. Fuck me. I wish I could have wanted to give him the big bread he was so desperate to have, all of it. "Here, my poor dad, my only dad, sure, *sure* you can take it. *Take* it! What's money to come before our love?" Yeah, shit. What a sap I am. I'll get over it.

I eat my roach and slowly go downstairs. In the bedroom on

my bureau, there it is, my new bankbook, next to a note from Lou.

Dearest Will,

I gave Barry apologies on your behalf, if you'll please accept apologies on his. There. You two dopes. You're lucky I love you.

Here's your inheritance in full. Grampa Jack says, don't waste it all in one place. Ha ha.

Hope you broke Uncle Sam's long skinny finger for him. Whatever, let me know soon what's up. I'll wire. And don't forget, any questions regarding the book, don't hesitate. I'm at your beck and call.

Take care,
Mom

P.S.—Sorry we didn't get to hit again this time. But keep swinging, kiddo. You never know. See you in the fall, I hope.

As I slide the bankbook from its plastic envelope, a folded paper slips out to the floor. The old man's crinkly onionskin, with stripes of single-space typing showing through. I open it.

Dear Will,

Useless as it may be to plead, "Do not hate me," do not hate me. Trust me, trust my judgment, trust my love. Failing that, only respect my determination—and believe this, my promise: you have made an investment, and you'll get it all back. You'll get it all back and *much more*, I swear, upon my none-too-distant demise.

I had planned to leave you my Last Will and Testament, as a token, a soothing prospectus, in fair exchange; however, I don't have the time now to finish it. Anyhow, I fear you might tear it to ribbons in blind rage. Better, I shall mail it to you within the month. You may reach me (by written word only) in care of my

brick of a wife, Vivian, at the old address, 8 Irving
Terrace, Sparks, Nevada.

You are my one and only.

And I,

> In Glory,
> Am forever your loving,
> Dad

I flip the bankbook to the first page. *There*, a huge deposit,
June 9, 1969—$50,000. And a withdrawal, June 9, 1969—
$35,000. Fucking shit! The bastard! The fucking bastard!

I kick the bureau and fly down the stairs. I'll call the bank!
I'll call the goddamn police! I'll call . . . Christ, I'll call Grampa
Jack! We'll catch him. We'll snag him out of his desert nest of
sticks and straw like the sneaky vulture he is.

I dial O. "Get me . . . shit, the *police*!"

"Is this an emergency?"

"Fuck, *yes*!"

"One moment."

I hang up. I open the bankbook again. How did he do it?
William R. Muldoon, says the book. Channel Road, Balboa, California. But look, the first entry is fifty bucks, just above the fifty
thousand. Fifty bucks on June 6. That's Friday. This is *his fucking account*, which he opened himself on Friday! The weaselly
prick. He had the whole con planned from the minute he got
here! Once he was sure I was demanding my inheritance, he
only had to trick Lou into handing it to him. That's what her
remark this morning meant. "I read your note," she said. Jesus,
how *simple*. He opens an account in his name, which is *my*
name, then he types up instructions, telling Lou to make the
transfer. What *balls*. Boy, if I put Lou onto this, she would
explode. She'd get the FBI after him, for bank fraud. She'd have
him drawn and quartered, and picked into pieces by lizards and
dragged underground, and she'd bleach his cranium and use it
for a soapdish.

What's so funny? Here I am making big jokes, and I've been
fucked good. But what can I do? Nothing. Nothing! I go back
upstairs for his note. I stand in the window, staring blankly

down into the street. My little car, looking like a melted Volks-wagen from above, is puffing gray exhaust into the sunlight. So am I.

Why couldn't he come clean with me? He could've explained this wonderful investment, and if it really *was* such a wonder-ful investment, hell, I would've gladly given the fart my money, right? Am I kidding? Not if I had to run to Canada. No, he was better off sticking with the con, and he knew it. The rat bastard.

Well, Jesus, if I just sit here now on this sun-blasted spit of sand, whimpering like a puppy dog, trying to subdue myself, it will eat me up. I can't let the crazed windbag shaft me this way and then skip off free into the sagebrush. I have to get him. I have to chase the weasel into the ground and beat on his nose with a stick until he coughs up every nickel of what's mine. *Then*, if I want to fucking invest, I'll invest. I mean, I am the boss!

Yeah. And Cici will be happy with that, too. A mission. A trip. An adventure. We'll head out after him together, and we'll catch him, too, goddamn it. He would never expect it. What he expects is for me to let him fade with all that money and no slightest explanation. What a hyena he is! But I'll get him. He'll be sitting in some plastic chair smoking by some shitty pool that'll be skinned over with yellow dust and soggy moths, and I'll come flying over the fence like a Zulu warrior, beating apart the air molecules with my Dreadnought. He'll scream, "Spare me! *Spare me!*" Because he won't be sure whether I will or not.

In the kitchen, frantically I fill two shopping bags with canned soup, tuna, some melons, eggs, oranges, carrots, ba-nanas, and other stuff from the refrigerator. Then I gallop out into the hall. Just as I switch one bag to the other arm so I can open the door, through its little window I catch sight of the Newport Beach Police cruiser easing swiftly in behind my Porsche. Oh, *Christ*!

Two cops in khaki. Looking very serious. They climb out and slam their doors. Still with the food, I rip into the living room, unlock the glass doors to the patio and slide them apart about a foot. Then I draw the curtain shut across the opening, and I step through out onto the slate.

The doorbell chimes sweetly.

I wait.

More chimes.

"Come right in!" I yell through the curtain.

"Will Muldoon?" one calls back.

"Yeah! Come right in! But don't let the dog out!"

"Muldoon? We're city police officers. We want to talk with you." They don't come in.

"Be downstairs in a flash!" I yell back. "I'm in the bathroom!"

I wait.

After some seconds, they slip inside and close the door quietly. "We want a few words with you," one calls up the stairs.

I rip around the house, dump my supplies on the passenger's seat, and take off squealing. I send the old car barreling down alleys to the Wind and Sea, listening for a siren, hearing nothing. The garage door's open. I back her in, jump out, and tug the door closed on its rollers tight as I can make it.

I lean in and shut off the engine. Quiet. Still no siren. Hooeee! Close! But now, son of a bitch, are we trapped, or what? Only two ways off this peninsula, by the boulevard up at the narrow neck where it abuts the Coast Highway, or by the little six-car ferry that runs across to Balboa Island, then over the bridge, across the Coast Highway, and up Jamboree Road to the Interstate. And it's probably too late already for either one. They're on their cackling radios sealing up this bottle right now. Jesus, do I have the shakes. Man! I topple back across the hood of the Porsche, spread-eagled like a bayonetted VC, finished.

No, not finished. Just beat bad. Not finished by a long shot. We'll have to rest up and think. We'll rest up until after midnight, and then, simple, we'll swim the channel. Would Cici swim the channel? Or we can take the inner tubes out of the car tires and *paddle* across. Yeah! With our supplies in our laps! Brilliant!

I heave myself up. Carefully, I case out the alley, then dash up our stairway in three leaps. "Cici!" Our door is wide open. *Shit. "Cici?"*

She's not here. She's gone.

Those who first came to this southern coast (naming it California after the heroine of some Spanish gothic novel) settled here for the warm ocean, ripe with fish and kind to ships, and that ocean, subliminally, is what's kept them coming. Yet it's the other water, the fresh, hidden water, stolen from far-off rivers, pumped out of inland valleys, piped hundreds of miles south through the mineral flats and tawny hills right to where we all demand to be that allows us to stay and prosper. Which amounts to another facet of the California discombobulation that my father has long decried. ("Flick that dewy can-handle and you send away five gallons of mountain nectar—*five gallons*—to keep the company of your humble pint of pee.") Not that I much care. . . . Water, the waste of it, poisoned and idle in swimming pools, swished over autos to wash away dulling road film, run untouched down countless drains, sprayed all night onto lawns that live only to be mowed, so what? Evidence of our ruinous, cross-eyed idiocy crops up everywhere. Who can change it? Who can stand to care? No question, my father's got one thing together: we're doomed. But he cares, that's the difference between him and me. Behind his flamboyant raging, hopeless as he sounds, I think he secretly believes there is something to be done for it. There isn't. Let 'er rip, that's my bald attitude, akin to my mother's, I guess—when she falls to such awful thoughts. (The great boom doom is her favorite, the storms of fire, the rains of popping nuclei.) Of course, like the rest of insensible, workaday humanity, she falls to such thoughts very seldom. Which is sensible. Because who would pursue those thoughts? To what unwelcome profit?

Only my fearless old man, that's who, to torture himself. And careless me, to prove I'm invulnerable. Hah. Really, I make me laugh.

Cici's suitcase is still in the bedroom, so I figure at least the hounds haven't sniffed us out here. She's off somewhere on her own. I walk to the pavilion arcade and wander through the game halls for half an hour. It seems the last place she'd be, but it's the nearest place to start looking, and I don't expect to find her anyway. I check both laundromats and the library on my roundabout way back to the Wind and Sea, then the post office, even the doughnut shop, just giving her extra time to get home.

By now, though I hold no deep worry about the cops (they'll never recognize *me*—my car is the telltale item), I am seriously wound down. I'm flirting with delirium. I have to drop to the curb every few minutes to let my slogging heart catch up with my sadistic demands on it. When I look at street signs, the print on them breaks up into angular symbols, mysterious as Hebrew. Even the Wind and Sea plaque, though I know what it says, resembles a slide display of chromosome damage. There are no words on it.

Upstairs there is no Cici, either, that much is clear. Coffee or collapse seems my next choice. The coffee is far, far away, however, down in the car. I open a beer instead and leave for the beach.

It's summer all right. The day has advanced enough into evening so most bathers have gone home, but what's always disgusted me in a peculiar way is seeing how the broad swath of sand at the end of a long hot one is tossed into a kind of arrested commotion, pitted and gouged by all those feet and elbows, it's been a spittoon, an ashtray, a toilet, a mattress. What gets to me is the disheveled, debased look of it, which makes me remember the time a dead gray whale washed up near Corona, and the curious populace found themselves needing to dig at it, to poke sticks in its eye, jam rocks in its blowhole, carve their graffiti in its barnacled back, until the coast guard towed it away. Sometimes I'm ashamed just to be alive.

I slosh into the surf and feel better right away. I ride a small wave, stroke out to wait for a bigger one and ride that. Wonderful. If I were incarnated next as a whale, I would not complain at all.

I spot her a long way off trotting toward me on the hard sand below the berm, then walking, then trotting again. She has on my sweatshirt with the sleeves pushed up on her arms. It falls over her hips, and her legs flow out beneath. There's no mistaking her. Her blonde mane flops up and down.

It takes her longer than I expect to recognize me because the sun's setting behind me, but soon as she does, she spins around and starts loping off the other way.

"Cici! For Christ's sake!"

She keeps going. The jerk, she's going to make me run to catch her. But when she slows and looks back, I'm still walking.

"Wait, Cici, let's talk!"

"I *hate* that place, Will!" she shouts. "That place sucks!"

"I know! We're going to Nevada!"

"What?"

"Wait up!"

But she won't stop.

I heave myself into a gallop.

Glancing back, she squeals. She veers toward the surf.

I dive and take her legs right out of the water. She lands on my back. The wash swirls around us.

"You didn't have to *dump* me, you dufus elephant!"

"Didn't I tell you not to go wandering out of our happy hideaway? The cops are *after* you, Cici—and me, too—in helicopters and jeeps and all kinds of shit, dogs, PT boats, spy satellites. . . . And you are quite a unique-looking example of young womanhood. You couldn't be anybody but who you are, to anybody hunting for you, and you are impossible to ignore. You are too beautiful to ignore."

"Well, I been down here forever, and nobody came after me until you." She scoops up a piece of jellyfish and smacks me with it. "Hey, how did your draft thing come out?"

"Cici, I *beat* it. I was fabulous. I mean, I was *masterful*. You should've been there."

"Really? So you don't have to go in the war?"

"That's right. They'll have to pulverize the heathens without me."

"Wow. Super! It's a stupid war anyway. Even Daddy says it's a stupid war. He says the air force could fix the whole thing in one short afternoon."

"Sure—and if he didn't mind skipping supper, he could probably go right ahead and mop up China and Russia, too—the whole, godless continent."

She laughs. "Really. Hey, so c'mon, what did they say at the draft? What was so fabulous?"

I'll lay out the tale of triumph for her back at the Wind and Sea, I say, over iced French champagne, but at that her sour glare returns. She says I can shove that place, she is not going back there, it's very depressing to be in an empty, nothing apartment with not even a magazine in it and all these geeks playing Frisbee in the alley all day, so she's afraid to even look out the window. The refrigerator makes way too much noise, too, and there's no food in it. *Some* food, OK, but—OK, this'll sound dumb, but when she's hungry, she wants just the right thing, the perfect food, and it is just very scary not having any say in that place, or in what's happening, or in what's supposed to happen, or *anything*.

Broken waves are rushing under us, dragging us sideways for a distance, then rushing away again like a football team back to the huddle. I have hold of Cici's ankle so she won't escape me.

I tell her she can stop fretting, we're moving out. Right away. We're going to my old man's in Reno to pick up my inheritance money, and then we're going to travel wherever we feel like for as long as it pleases us, and she'll have as much say about what will come next as I will, which is more say than anyone else in the world is ever likely to get. (I'm not ready yet to reveal my secret plan for getting us off the peninsula—maybe I'm already losing confidence in it.)

"Will, really?" she says, scrambling to her feet to face me. "You mean we're really finally doing it, what you used to jabber about all the time? Camping by babbling brooks? And pine trees and starlight and all that?"

"I am anyway."

"God. Well, then so am I!"

Back at the Wind and Sea, first we take a shower—together, to save time, only in the heat I'm suddenly too tired to stay on my feet. I sit in the corner, and Cici aims the nozzle better, and she stoops down and wraps all her slight self around me. Last summer we would shower this way at the channel house, but standing. Now, weak as I am and blue as she is, and strange a pass as our two lives have come to in a short year, the love again feels the same, like the changeless scent of a flower, season after season. All we really do is sit, too. We are close as can be, and linked tight at our middle, but we stay still. We fall asleep. We only wake when the hot water runs out.

The ocean has soaked my sweatshirt, so we dry ourselves by turning around and around in front of the gas heater until we stop dripping. Again Cici's upset to have no hair dryer ("You went home *twice*, and you never even thought of me the way you promised!"), because now with her head all wet, how can she sleep on it? That's not an issue anymore, I say. We have no time for sleep. Because—I pin my eyes on hers—we are going to swim the channel by dead of night. As I try to elaborate, she reaches over and grabs my mouth.

"*Swim?*" she says, instantly perceiving my stupidity. "You mean, *swim* the channel?"

"Right," I say. "But with inner tubes to float on. You just kick."

"Inner tubes, *sure*. Will, that's pure wacko. Inner tubes! Then what? We walk to Nevada?"

Defeated already, I make a derisive sort of mumble. It's hopeless. I can't think. I am half-asleep here on the rug.

Cici says, "Anyhow, I don't get why you're so freaked. I'm eighteen. I'm totally legal. I can be any dumb place I feel like, and no hog cops can put their disgusting hands on me. So they're looking for me. Big deal."

"Cops, my dear Cici," I say slowly, with my eyes shut, "can do *anything* to keep modern society in the condition they approve of. Remember Chicago. If they want to take you home to Colonel Daddy, they won't care if you're ninety-three, they'll do it."

She sulks at me. "Maybe," she says. "But no way am I going tubing in the dark with boat propellers cutting by all over. You neither. You'd probably just fall right asleep out there and drift out to sea like a log." She laughs. "Or else we could tube across to Honolulu. They'd never expect that. Right, Will?"

I nod and smile and fall asleep. All I'll keep later of the dreams I'm having is me swimming, swimming hard, alone, against a current, making progress, but not enough progress. What for? Maybe I'm not getting away quickly enough, or else I'm not quite closing in on something ahead that my dreams will not name.

Cici and I are humming through the noonday Mojave Desert on 395 along the course of the great LA Aqueduct, traveling against its flow, as my dreams predicted.

We are pleased with ourselves. We've been on the road since seven o'clock, thanks to Cici's invention of a logical plan of escape, which not only put immediate trouble behind us but gave Cici's limp powers of reason a transfusion of utility.

We've been talking nonsense, playing the radio, and laughing, making the commercials into jokes, singing, hollering, and beeping at other cars, who've been beeping back. We're seeing and feeling each other as we did before we knew each other, when all we knew was that we liked how we looked, and our banter just gave texture to the pure looking. And yet now, for me, the looking part of all this is badly warped. Cici has cut off her hair.

This morning she awoke before I did with her plan full bloom in her head. First she went down to the car to dig out some scissors—my Swiss Army knife was what she came up with— and she determinedly snipped into the sink two feet of that golden treasure she'd spent all her girlhood amassing. Then she crept out down the alley until she found a pickup with Washington plates, one of which she was able to unbolt and take home. (The other one took a wrench. We got it just before first

262

light.) Then she had another shower, to rinse away cut hairs, and then she slid back under our blue bag and tickled me awake. She was beaming.

I pushed my face against the mattress. *"Why?"*

"Disguise!" she exclaimed. "Get it?"

"No!" I shouted. "I don't get *any* of it! You're too *much!* You're flipped right out! You're not you, Cici, and I do not get it. Just what is your goddamn problem?"

"I did it for *you!*" she yelled. She whipped out of bed, ran into the bathroom, and slammed the door. The crackerbox swayed a little.

I got up stiffly and padded over there. I couldn't hear anything. "Hey, I'm sorry, Cici, OK? I love you anyhow. Shit, what's hair, right? Dead stuff hanging off your head. Who cares?"

She was quiet.

"Cici?"

"It grows back, you know," was her sullen comment.

I didn't answer that. It would never grow back, I knew.

She said, "You think you're so brainy. You think I can't figure anything out for myself, don't you? Like I'm so double-dumb you won't even let me—"

"Wait!" I said. Suddenly I was awake enough to realize she had just been *smiling* at me, *really smiling*, like the beautiful, radiant Cici of old. "I'll be right back!"

Her smile had made me remember those photos of us last August. They were packed in the car, I was hoping. It took me a few minutes thrashing around in all the junk I'd found reason to stow behind the seats before I uncovered the box of papers and old letters from my closet, but *great*, here they were, in their envelope, in all their Technicolor splendor. I chose the one of her back-lit and draped across my bed, half that smile on her shadowed face, all the gold hair on her body bright as if the sunbeams were dancing just to touch her.

I slipped it under the door. Then I went back to bed.

Before long she came out. She walked slowly into the bedroom and lowered herself to the mattress. She was wearing her blue nightie. She really looked miserable. The hair was the

clincher, but her brief, thorough smile before and then my sifting through those photographs had brought the Cici I remembered back for me so vividly that I half-expected to see her
transformed when she emerged, as if that eight-by-ten, that flattened splash of long-gone light, could break her sad curse.

She held it in her lap. "You made enlargements," she
whispered.

"Yup."

"How come I never saw them?"

I shrugged. "They came in right before I went east. I mailed
you that one, though, right? Of you and me together?"

"You did? When?"

"Didn't you get it? I printed Armstrong's name on the envelope, so your rotten mother would think it came from
guidance."

"*That's* what that was? Oh, crapola! Will, I hate that
Armstrong. He's a scuz! He felt me once, like with his arm, and
he said, 'Oh, excuse me,' the old crud."

"Well, shit, that means your mom has it. And she would open
it! She wouldn't just send it back to the high school, would
she?"

Cici laughed. "Wow, I hope not."

"Wonderful," I said.

She tapped my leg. "Well, so what? Who cares now, you
know?"

"You were supposed to open it," I said.

She was quiet, letting a fingertip glide over the shiny print.
"It was fun when we took these," she said musingly. "They
came out so artistic, too. This one is . . . it's like one of those
famous paintings they put in museums. I remember that day.
We had that dumb paper Chinese kite that wouldn't stay up. It
would go up partway, then zigzag, and then it would corkscrew
and wipe out in the sand. So you gave it away to this little kid,
remember? He went nuts. We swam a little while after, and we
went home to your house, and we had lunch. We had fish. And
white wine. We went in the shower, you know, the way we
always did. Only this time I felt calmer or something, because

the way you were telling me I was . . . like, beautiful. You kept repeating it. My shoulders, my belly, my hair, not just my regular hair, but like under my arms, and all that, and I believed you. I mean, I believed you *before*, too, sure. You meant it, I always believed you meant it. But then, in the shower, I believed it was *true*. I really *was* . . . really beautiful. It made me . . . it sent these ripples all through me—of happiness. So when you started setting up the camera, I didn't get embarrassed or anything. I felt so good. I didn't even feel bad that you had to go in two weeks, I was just feeling smoothed out and good." She paused, set the print aside, and lay back beside me. "It's in the picture, isn't it?" she said, not looking at me. "That's why the picture's so good, because of how we felt right then, you and me. Right?"

I didn't say anything.

She put her ravaged head on my chest. "Will? If I go get the scissors, could you trim up around my neck? I kinda did a hack job, I guess."

For breakfast, while she excitedly outlined her plan, I got her to eat an egg, one hard-boiled fruit-of-hen, which she peeled, cut in half, then in quarters, then in eighths, arranging the sections in a square. She popped them one by one, moving clockwise around the square. She brushed the yolk crumbs to the floor. She ate half a cucumber, too, but when I slid a piece of pumpernickel next to her spot at the counter, her contumacious spirit came focused in the one arched look she gave me, so I withdrew the bread and munched it myself. Shit, I thought, that's what the Colonel's probably been doing for months: shoving hunks of bread at her slathered over with Blue Bonnet.

The escape was simple. We each took a different rush-hour ferry across to Balboa Island, she in my Donald Duck shades driving the Porsche with the white Washington plates, and I on foot, my hair up under my yellow hard hat, which Cici had packed in her suitcase. Sure enough, there was a pearly cop cruiser parked on the island, a block or so from the dock, but for some reason it was empty. Maybe they didn't care that much about us after all. Anyway, we squeezed ourselves out clean, and we felt terrific. It was better than my great draft con of yesterday, I told Cici.

Once we hit the big highway, I revealed the dirty history behind our mission, which is also the history of my abbreviated homecoming, and Cici quickly became absorbed in the details. She was full of comments and questions and even free-form speculation as to the old man's motives. She liked Lou's guess.

"Gambling for sure," she said. "I mean—Reno! C'mon! OK, say he won a lot of money one day, a *whole* lot of money. How lucky would you feel if you did that? So he bets it all, double or nothing on one roll of the bones, right? But luck is fickle, and so he loses. Suddenly he owes all these mucho dollars that he knows these casinos will kill for. So like there's only one thing he can do. He goes back to—"

"No, no, no, Cici, casinos aren't like that. You just can't—"

"Bull! The mob owns the whole state, and they don't care who knows it!"

"I know, Cici, but you can't go in there and bet thirty-five grand that you don't have. They don't work that way."

"God, how do you know? He could've been like a very big gambler."

"Shit, my father? He's no gambler at all."

"Well, he bet a thousand on your tennis match, right?"

"No, no. He didn't have a thousand. He didn't even have ten bucks."

"Well, that's what I just said! That's why they're after him, these casino gangsters. Because he bet all this money he didn't have. That's why he took the gun out of the trunk, too, right?"

"Sure. Then why did he hand me all that garbage about committing suicide?"

"Because if they catch him, then he won't let them have the satisfaction. That's what I'd do."

The intoxication of the road is part of it: the distances opening up, new scenery slapped across the windshield, the anesthesia of speed. Also, the champagne. We're sipping it from the bottle. Cici joins my toast to the Paris Peace Talks, and she tips the bottle back whenever I pass it to her, though I doubt she's swallowing a teaspoon at a time. She doesn't need it. She's obviously feeling better than she's felt in months, which makes me feel fine as well, naturally. Hospital, horseshit. What she's been needing is adventure, and freedom, and *love*, for Christ's sake—just like me.

The talk moves on to other particulars of our recent turbulent past. Cici wants to know "everything about Bad Barry Glines."

After that, she says, "Do you really truly believe you are burned out as a tennis star? Sure you're old, but you're not *that* old."

So we discuss that, my grasp of the hard realities.

I ask her about her school year, which is my only bad move of the morning.

She sinks into the seat and just says, "Bitchen." She turns on the radio.

I turn it off. "OK, tell me about when I invaded your house. You knew it was me, didn't you?"

She bounces right back. "Yes! Your yellow helmet on the floor was the first thing I saw! But I couldn't think. God, Ruby was going nuts clawing the door. I *knew* you were in there, but I didn't know it was you! Not until my mom came in. You should've seen her. You about gave her a coronary!"

"Not me. That goddamn dog gave her the coronary. Without the dog, I would've slipped into your room like fresh air."

"Ruby's a *baby*. She was just scared of you. But that's when it hits me who's in there, when I pick up the helmet. Mom comes running in from out back all terrified, and all of a sudden, *smash*, you smash Daddy's window. God, was he ever *ticked off*! And I saved your life by—you know what? I put on your helmet. I put it on, and I go, 'It's just some old wino, it's just a wino-junkie,' and my mom goes, 'In *here*? In *this house*?' Then later, about forty-eleven cops come in making this very like minute inspection. They said how we were so lucky to have Ruby, and I had to describe you, which I made up all this stuff about his black mustache and a black shirt. And they found your *blood*, your whole blood-type, from where the guy cut himself on the glass. God, I don't know, like if you didn't invade like that, I never would've called you up at your house to come and get me.

267

I only called because you did it once, and I knew you would come again for sure."

I look over at her. "Cici, I would've plowed in there with a bulldozer if I had to."

She laughs and says, "I bet." Her legs are tucked beneath her on the seat. She swivels quickly around and kisses me on the jawbone. "This is so far out," she says. "Full of thrills and spills almost like it's a movie. With you as the main hero. You know what *I* think? I think if you do write that book, don't make it about your mom. Make it about you! That would be much more interesting, and then for sure I would read it."

Now, as Cici is dialing impatiently for music, I spot a wavering roadside bulge ahead that gradually enlarges into . . . people, it looks like, and the flash of metal.

"What's that?"

"An accident?" says Cici. She turns off the radio.

I'm thinking car trouble, somebody blew a hose and boiled over. I shift down.

"Priests!" says Cici.

No cars behind us. I slow to a crawl.

"Not priests," she says. "You know—those old-time guys. *Monks.*"

There are three of them, hairy men in dirty white robes, shuffling easily along the rough shoulder of the road, one alone in the lead with his scraggly head bowed, the two others yoked to a cart of provisions, a U-Haul.

"Pretty flippy," says Cici.

"Pilgrims," I say.

"Yeah, *pilgrims*," she says. "Weird."

I speed up.

Cici twists backward on her knees. "All this stuff in here, you can't *see* anything."

But I keep them a bit longer in my racing mirror out on the fender.

Cici slides back down into her seat. "What kinda trip was that, I wonder. What if they're walking across the whole country—to the *East Coast*?"

"What if they're walking around the whole world?" I say.

Cici gives a puffy whistle. "Yeah! And they have scuba tanks in their wagon." She laughs.

"Really, you know, I'd do that," I tell her. "If I did that, here's what I'd do. I would walk to Maine, take a fish boat to Iceland, walk across that, sail to England, walk that, walk all across Europe and Asia, then Australia, then New Zealand, then Hawaii, and sail on home. And I'd go alone, too. No buddies, no wagons, just my backpack and an oak staff."

"How come alone?"

I look at her. "Why? Think you'd want to join me?"

She grins. "Could be."

"Well, see, somehow it would have to be kept pure. It would be nothing like, say, hitching to Acapulco. It would be a spiritual ordeal. The ultimate quest. For profound spiritual gains. But usually you only make true spiritual gains alone. That's part of the ordeal."

"Yeah? Better go back and tell those guys," says Cici.

At this, we laugh. We laugh and laugh. Nothing's really that funny, we just feel great. The pilgrims are heartening, I think, in their sublime dedication, their immersion in the ultimate quest. The Realm of Possibilities is broader than you may believe. Exaltation is never out of reach. You can fart around for years doing drugs, devoting senseless hours to something like tennis or waitressing, or just generally pursuing puny excitements like sex and good food, or otherwise debilitating yourself, and still one day the moment can come when you will decide to find release. Whenever you're ready, walk around the world, perch on a mountain, sink yourself to the neck in a peat bog, go on, you can always be saved. As long as you keep the Possibilities in sight, you can always be saved.

"Yeah—if you want to be," Cici replies when I try explaining this to her. "Like for me, even when I knew you were back home for the summer and you cared about me and even loved me, I still didn't care if I was saved or if I got anorexia or what. I was *so bummed*. Nothing I could remember out of my past seemed worth it, you know? Like, God, why even bother? The future was just the same grunge day in day out until death do I part."

"OK, but what made you that way, do you think? I mean, specifically. Anything?"

"No. I was just the victim of this very very bad mood, that I couldn't escape. I don't know."

"So you languished."

"I didn't do a *thing*! I mean, I went to school and stuff, but I wasn't into it at all. *Zombietime.*"

"So what made the big difference finally? What made you want to be saved? Me? Wonderful me?"

She laughs. "Wonderful Will Muldoon. Nah. Not you. I don't know what, but not you, definitely."

"Thanks," I say.

"No, but you know what? Maybe it was. Like, sort of. You on the phone, *contacting* me. They were all saying I was gonzo, but you *knew* me, you used to. Then when they started wanting to lock me up, like some retard, so I would totally disappear from the world, then I got scared and you had to come save me. I don't know. Does that make sense?"

"Sure!" I squeeze her arm. "See, you lost sight of the Possibilities. You entered a fog. Last week if somebody told you—or me either—that today we'd be together racing through the desert toward Reno, drinking champagne out of the bottle, we'd have thought the guy was gonzo. Right? Now look. You never know what's next."

"Yeah," says Cici happily. "I know."

At night, droning across the flats north of Carson City toward Reno's mad glitter, we no longer feel great. The intoxication of the road has produced its hangover. Cici, in tones of dropsical irritation, is saying she's cold, and her back aches, and her rear end is sore. She wants to stop now, here, pitch the tent, and sleep. Naturally, I want to *get there*. We're close. I refuse to stop.

Also, I have been subsiding into a glum and nervous awareness of our plight. Cici is such an innocent—an adolescent addlepate, as the old man would put it. We're far, far from the golden coast and so she thinks we're safe. When, in fact, we're fucked. We are. There is just no way her ferocious warlord of a father is going to let some beach-bum hippie with marijuana tracks up and down his arms skip free into the American desert with his mixed-up sugarplum of a daughter. The state fuzz and other weighty pigs are doubtless combing the sagebrush and grasslands for us from here to the Mississippi. Still, we have some slim advantages: Cici's crew-cut, my unadvertised visage, our Washington plates, and the pure, broad spread of the land of the free. But we cannot stop. We must burn gas. We must use the night.

Since the egg, Cici has eaten nothing but a banana. (A banana that was too ripe when I bought it days ago and so had remained cooking between the seats here until Cici discovered it this afternoon, black and shrunken. "Jeez—give that the heave," I said when she held it up. She said, "No, it's perfect." I laughed, ha-ha. But she nibbled off its nub end and proceeded to squeeze its gluey innards between her pursed lips a little at a time, like a kid eating toothpaste. "They're best this way," she told me. "Really, they are.") I have eaten some cheese, bread, beer, an apple, and a sliced green pepper. I consider myself nourished. But Cici and the world of comestibles are going to need time to reach an understanding. I have to remember that.

My map of the western states shows Sparks lying east of Reno proper, in its shadow, it seems. I've been here once before, when I was about ten. My father talked Lou into a winter weekend in the pines up at Lake Tahoe. We would see snow, put me on skis for the first time, relax by a crackling fire in a cabin miles from the rain-soaked city, in the somnolent peace of the forest. As a family, we hardly ever took trips. When Lou was home from weeks on the road, she wanted to stay home. "I want to rest, R-E-S-T rest," she would say. "I don't want to go ramming around the countryside." So our planned jaunt to a snowbound lodge in the mountains was unique, and it was filled for me with the promise of exotic treats, like showshoeing (I saw myself springing across broad fields of white strapped onto big wooden frames with thongs that gave a lift similar to a pogo stick's), tobogganing, igloo-making, and elk-tracking. (Skiing didn't excite me much, my impression being that it was too organized—I wanted to be off on my own.) We left noontime

Friday in the middle of a hard rainstorm. We drove through continual gusts of water all afternoon. It made a veined sheet across the rear window. Sometimes, it would let up, the cover would break a bit—"Say, won't it be something fine in yonder pristine mountains!" my father would say—but then the rains would close in again along our flanks, swooping out of the hills in foamy gray squadrons. We couldn't shake it. Even up to the lodge, where a foot or so of crusted snow was covering the ground when we arrived, the rains pursued us. Off the folks' room, up two little steps, was my room with a bunk tucked under the log-beamed eaves. The storm gushed and pounded overhead all night. By morning the snow outside had been beaten to a few inches of slush. Other guests in the breakfast hall talked of floods and washed-out bridges. There had been a drowning. My parents talked about moving on to Reno. Which we did, in spite of my strident objections. Reno was flat and low and junky-looking to me; after San Francisco it seemed like a city somebody had knocked together in about a week. But it was sunny. I remember stacks of silver dollars on the shining top of our hotel-room bureau, and how I got to swim in a pool and play the nickel machines with the other kids.

Now, maybe it's the complex jitter and flash of all the surrounding lights, but the city feels a lot bigger than my memory has it—of course, in ten years no doubt it has actually gotten a lot bigger. That thought makes me realize how much older I've grown in ten years. Ten years! Christ, that's not a long piece of time at all. Ten pip-squeak years. You get, what, maybe seven decades in your life, *seven*, if you're lucky, before it's over and out. And two of them you spend sleeping. That's just the way it is—one more incontrovertible aspect of the Big Arrangement. Like all the Possibilities, all these aspects of the Big Arrangement are hard to keep in mind. When they're not in mind, you get morose, like Cici. When they are, you get blithe, like me. Blithe. Then again, *in mind* is not exactly where they're supposed to be, is it? The mind is just rental property (large loft to sublet, lots of light)—some locus of more permanent residence is what they're after, someplace plush and exclusive like the soul. Whatever that is.

The first service station attendant I question directs us down the street to a Texaco where they have a map of Sparks plastered on the wall. There, while Cici goes to pee for the first time all day, I find *Irving Ter.* on a high corner of the map behind some hanging fan belts. The tiny brown letters send a prickling chill through me—the place exists! Goddamn, won't the old man dirty his drawers when he sees me! From YOU ARE HERE to *Irving Ter.* looks about seven miles. I copy our route on a casino brochure ("Take One!") and double-check it. My hands shake. I pop the machine by the register for a bag of cashews, go back to the car, open a beer, sit down on the rocker panel with my legs stretched out over the gravel, and try to think. Do I just drive up there and knock on the front door? It's ten o'clock, a little late to be calling. Late, *shit*, the bastard stole my money! But what do I expect? He's going to open the door, say, "Will! Why, yes, certainly. I have it all right here, I certainly do. There, now—you just count it all up, make sure I'm not short." What he'll do is mollify me with that hummed-out look of penitence and then knock me loose from my wrath with a barrage of prolix excuses and explanations. I know his style. But his style now will avail him nothing! Not as opposed to *my* style, which is a style of rock-hard resolve. Yeah.

"Find the map?" Cici leans toward me over the open door, her dandelion head up against the night sky.

"Yeah, I found it. We're dead on-track."

"Well, you know what?" She's smiling, pleased to be free of the car and in a strange new place.

"No, what?"

"This is far out. I just got my period."

"You did?"

"Really. So if we could find a store open, I gotta buy some things."

"Now? There's no machine in there?"

She gives me a stony frown.

I bow my head. "I'm sorry, Cici. It's just that this drive's got me all primed for the confrontation, and I've been trying to think and think of how to handle it, when I guess I'm really trying to know what I'll do before I do it, which is impossible. I mean, what did Davy Crockett say? 'Be sure you're right, and then go ahead.' "

"But Will, that's dumb. You could fall pretty hard behind that. OK, so you're right. For sure you're right. But it still makes sense to plan a few moves so you're sort of prepared. Like, Davy Crockett was right his whole life, but they still shot him."

"I know. What do you suggest, then?"

"Nothing. But when you invaded my house the first time, if you only spied on it awhile beforehand, maybe you would have detected we had Ruby, and you would have brought along like a pound of hamburger, see?" She sits next to me on the vibrating rocker panel, and we watch the traffic. A pickup glides in over the bell-hose, *ding-ding*, and up to the pumps.

"Well, that's what I figured," I say. "We'll just cruise over and scope it out. I wasn't going to bust in there six-guns a-blazin'." As Lou would say.

She pats my hand. "Good! That's your plan. But first can we find a store?"

On the out-squirts of this boring waffle of a city, Irving Terrace turns out to be, of all things, a trailer park—a long U-shaped dirt street with about forty rectangular lots notched into the middle of the U for giant trailers to be towed in and cemented down never more to roam.

We make one slow pass around the U. Each lot has a six-foot tree staked out in front along the curb, but that's it, no shrubs, no grass, no fences—it looks like a barracks for the French foreign legion. Some lots are unoccupied.

"See any numbers?" I ask.

She shrugs. "I'm just peeking in the windows that have lights. This whole place is very freaky."

Suddenly, a maddening thought takes hold of me, and I hiss, "Shhhhit!"

"What?" breathes Cici.

"You know what I bet the old bastard did? Look at this goddamn place. I bet he gave me the bum address of a vacant lot!"

She sighs. "But, Will, why? I mean, this is a real place, you know? He wouldn't have to pick out a real place. He could've said Two-twenty-two Doo-doo Street and what would you know?"

She's right. Of course it's a real place. Hell, I've *written* to this address many times over the years. I can't even think straight, much less around these little curves I throw for myself. My head's jammed with the accumulated static of the engine, as if the engine's a second brain back there in a marathon race with brain number one and about to grab the lead.

I'm stopped at the juncture of one end of the U and the blacktop state highway, my chin on the steering column. The tach flutters at about fourteen, and the speedometer points to zero. My scruffy beard prickles. My ears hum. My eyes burn. My back throbs. My knees twitch.

"Want a couple more No-Doz?" asks Cici after a while.

I don't answer.

"And another frosty brew?"

I let out a long groan. "Yeah—why not?"

She shakes two pills from the box and digs a beer out of the water in our cooler.

I tell her she's a regular Florence Nightingale.

She laughs. "Yeah, well, I doubt if this is really your boss primo-type of medicine, you know?"

"Medicine's medicine."

She laughs again.

"Cici . . . shit, here it is. We've come all this way, and now I wonder what for? You're right, Eight Irving Terrace is probably back there, but I'm afraid to find out, because when I find out I'll have to do something, and what can I do? Nothing. Say I go up there, I tromp up to his trailer, knock-knock, he lets me in, but no way is he going to return my grubstake in life. He just says no. He has that wan, arrogant fucking look on his face, and 'No,' he says, 'I'm sorry, pal, you can't have it.' So what do I do, slug him? Fall on my knees and beg him? See, it's no good. I'm helpless. I'm beat on this one going in."

"Yeah," she says slowly, considering this. "Well, so, we just gonna split? Find a place to stick your tent and crash?"

"You tell me."

She sighs. "You pop those pills?"

I open my palms. " 'Fraid so."

"Well, God, that's it, then."

"You mean, we do it? Wagons-ho?"

"Well, for sure you'll never sleep. Anyhow, we're here now, so I say, yeah, do it. Like maybe he'll be in there all flaked out in front of the TV, and you can tie him up real fast to his chair and you won't untie him until he gives you back everything he took if it takes a zillion years."

"Yeah, you got a zillion years to kill?"

She laughs. "Wow, Will, you are so zapped. Come on, I think this is fun. If you want, I'll drive this bomb back around, and you look for the numbers, OK?"

I cock my head at her. Without another word we both get out and trade seats.

Cici looks very pleased. She grins and wiggles the gear stick. "Boy," she says, "this is such a neat car."

Now it's late. The first two trailers are dark. They share the same driveway, where two cars are parked. Two tricycles, too, the bigger one with its front wheel propped up on the saddle of the smaller one, as if they're mating.

"See anything?" says Cici.

"Not from here. Keep going, keep going."

We cruise by a few vacant parcels toward two more side-by-side trailers, one dark, the other with a yellow bulb lit under the doorway awning, a Mustang in the driveway between them.

"Slow . . ." I'm saying, "slow. . . . That's *it!*"

"That's *it?*" She brakes and stalls out. "Oh, sugar!"

"Cici!"

"I know, I know," she says. "Pretty swift, right?"

We're smack in front of the old man's address. Above the black numeral 8 under the yellow light bulb is the word *Manager*. I hop out and shove the car backward out of direct line-of-view from the trailer to the side of the road.

Revived by this effort, I figure I'm ready to approach the place, if just to somehow make sure he's in there, look for signs.

"What signs?" says Cici.

"I'll know 'em when I see 'em," I tell her, though this is

ridiculous. I can't snoop around to the back porch to see if there are vodka bottles in the trash.

I give Cici thumbs-up, and she shakes her head. "Rah, rah, Will," she says. I ruffle her fuzzy noggin.

The walkway is a concrete strip through the sand. I go right up to the illuminated shelter of the awning, where I can read what's typed on the mailbox.

#8
Vivian Rolfe, Manager
William R. Muldoon

Emergencies, call:
(Security) 723-1165

Maintenance, #15
(Eustace) 723-2849

There it is, the dusty metal receptacle where all my bright collegiate twaddle, scrawled on postcard after postcard, has ended up. In my imagination, I now remember, I used to see my cards being dealt into a gleaming roadside mailbox protruding from the gatepost of a decorative picket fence, pink oleander swarming along it and up the winding walk to the thick-eaved little cottage with its mullioned windows, scalloped shutters, and red dutch door—8 Irving Terrace. What wish had made me embroider a simple address with such Walt Disney sugar paste? I am suddenly so sorry for my tender self that my Adam's apple bobs in my throat, expanding. I rub my hand down my face and look away from the quiet trailer over the dirt street toward darkness, nothing, the empty bluffs or scrubby plateaus that this excuse for a neighborhood is carved out of. Why would anybody come live here? Even bustling downtown Sparks would be better than this. I tiptoe around behind the trailer. Nothing here but one of those collapsible multiarmed clotheslines on a pole. Some lights still glow across the compound, and high against the sky out in the middle of things looms the black linear strutwork of a diving tower. It's huge. Jesus, that's why you'd stick your trailer in Outer Mongoliaville. There's a supermonstro *pool* out there. Now I can make out chairs, and at one end some folded umbrellas, like steeples.

Behind me a toilet flushes. I jump back close to the wall of the trailer. A gurgling sound lingers somewhere overhead—a vent pipe. Strangely, I don't feel nervous, just sort of dazed. The windows, two of them, the only ones with cracks of light behind their curtains, are too high to look through—so much for scoping the place out. At least there's no giant sack of Gravy Train out here on the concrete patio.

I head back toward the front, thinking, OK, we'll cruise a bit farther out of civilization till the lights thin out around us, and then we'll turn off the road to pitch the tent. Tomorrow, sunup, *before* sunup maybe, then we'll roar back up to this place . . . and we'll. . . . Hell.

I about-face and stalk up under the front door awning, toss a wave toward the Porsche's parking lights, and press my finger to the domino-size doorbell button. I can't hear any chimes, so I press again harder as the door is jerked inward.

A face appears behind the screen door, a big face, belonging to a big woman, deep tan and round, with a lot of wiry hair shooting out all over. "Yes?"

"This the Muldoon residence?"

"Not by a long shot." She's holding a hefty chrome flashlight.

"Well, you *are* Vivian Rolfe, his wife, aren't you?"

"Don't get hasty," she says. "Who are you?"

"Will Muldoon. The Second."

The flashlight comes on in my face. "No kidding. Golly." It goes off. "Well?"

"Well, see, Vivian—I've driven all day from Balboa to see the old buzzard, talk to him—"

"Well, shoot, sonny, he's not *here*. He say he was *here*?"

"He's not? You have his name on the mailbox—right there."

"Well, now, never mind that. I could put Tom Mix on my card, and who tells me no?"

"You're not married to Tom Mix."

She pulls her shoulders back. "What gumption. You're a

Muldoon, all right. Listen, that name on there's for messages. What you can do now, you put in a message. I'll see he gets it."

"Then you know where he is. Just tell me where he is, how's that?"

She shakes her head.

"How can you give him my message if you don't know where he is?"

She gives me a narrow look. "You listen now. In a pinch, I can reach him. There's ways. And if he wanted you to reach him, maybe you could, too. But he didn't. Anyhow, you couldn't find the old coot any more than I could, even if I wanted to, which I don't advise. Getting him a message is the best we can either one of us do now. That straight?"

"This is *extremely* important. Can't you just tell me what town he's in? Vivian, you can't keep it a secret. He's my own father!"

"Secret! You want to know a secret? Every last one of us's got a father. That makes you special?"

"What's wrong with telling me his town, just his general *location*? You're my stepmother, think of that. Also, this is life or death! Please. What if I *pay* you? I can *pay* you."

She flips a latch on the screen door and comes outside. She's wearing a sort of thigh-length wraparound kimono and creased slacks. In the light, she has a plain mannish appearance that's reassuring—she looks like some long-ago president. She plays her flashlight beam out over the driveway and into the street. "You didn't *walk* from LA, I guess. Where's your vehicle? That it?"

I say nothing.

She sighs. "Listen . . . Will, right? Listen, I could tell you a town. I could tell you a hundred towns. He's got PO boxes from here to Saint Louis. . . ." She eyes me a second, lowering herself to the doorstep, setting the flashlight down on its lens. "It's real simple, what happens. Say comes a note, a telegram, and such. I get myself down to the Kopy Kat and make up so many dittoes of 'em, front and back, envelopes, too, postmarks, et cetera, and I draw up so many new envelopes, and I send my dittoes away all over—Storm Lake, Pocatello, Whitefish, Trinidad, Kemmerer, Roseburg . . . that enough general locations for you? How's Lusk? Belle Fourche? Yakima? You wanna run off and try those? Lot's more I could provide if they don't pan out."

"But . . . god*damn* it! *He stole all my money!*" I slam my fist into the mailbox.

"Hey! Look at that. Now you sway-backed my mail chute. You happy?"

"Sorry." I flex my fingers, but it's my wrist aching the most.

"Yeah. You remind me of the cowboy that feeds his last cartwheel into the dollar bandit, who can't get satisfaction till he busts his knuckles into it for good measure. And *that* won't even spin the fruits." She stands up. "You're just about too worn out to blink, aren't you? Come on, you can bunk in on the sofa tonight if you don't mind cats. You like cats? I got three. . . ."

She holds the door for me, and in I go without a glance back toward the car.

Two of the cats are fat cross-eyed Siamese, one with a right-angle kink in its tail. They won't come near where I'm sitting. Vivian says the other one's a gray tomcat who spends his nights out spooning and hunting lizards. Their names are Nugget, Athena, and Larry.

It's more pleasant in here than I would've thought. The slablike furniture (green plaid upholstery over foam rubber), big mirrors, indirect lighting on white walls, low pine bookcases, and potted plants all go comfortably together. I tell Vivian I've never been inside a trailer before.

They're so small, she says, you have to know how to fool the eye so a person won't feel crammed in. Have to keep after the clutter, too.

She does that, all right. Even the *Newsweek*s and *National Geographic*s on the tables are arranged in staggered piles so the top edge of one underlines the logo of the one beneath it.

She plops two blankets on the sofa, telling me which bathroom cupboard has my father's toilet kit in it, if I want to shave or use his dental floss. "He was real big on floss," she says.

"He show up here much?"

"Not so I don't have to look twice to recognize him."

"How did you two ever hook up, if you don't mind me being curious."

"Sure. AA meetings, believe it or not."

"Dad was in AA? Boy, that did him a lot of good."

"Watch it! He met me, didn't he?"

"I mean he's still sort of a lush."

She's shaking a pillow down into a pale-green slip. "I play a fair game of tennis, too, you know. Well, *use* to."

In the bathroom I try moving my bowels. They've been bound up all day, from driving around and speedy drugs. It's spotless in here, done up in green and blue, little white pom-poms fringing the curtains and the vanity closet, a repeating meadow scene with sheep and sheepdogs running through the wallpaper. And here next to the can itself is a cat litter box. Jesus, she lives right in the middle of about two hundred square miles of cat litter, and she makes her cats shit in the house. But now as I look vacantly into it, next to a few buried cat turds I spot a familiar-looking grayish cylinder. I poke it. Fuck! A cigar ash!

The bedroom door's ajar, so I rap on it politely and angle my head in.

"Problems?" says Vivian. She's standing over in front of the open closet. A little eight-inch Sony glows on the nightstand, some guy singing.

"While I'm thinking of it, I just wanted to ask you if he might have mentioned his will when he passed through. Or even left me a copy of it."

"Will? Well, now, that was some while ago, but can't say I recall any talk of a will. . . . *Will*. Why? Look likely to you his time's gettin' ripe? We gotta be bothering with *wills* soon?"

"He's your gloom-and-doom man, Vivian, not me. I didn't bring it up."

She turns to rustle the clothing on the hangers. "Shoot, he's full of more guff than a pie-eyed prospector. Probably outlive the both of us, too, just for spite."

I've been quickly surveying the room, the bed with the frilly skirt around the boxspring (plenty could be hidden under there), the dressing table with its platoon of bottles and oval mirror that has dozens of round bulbs set into its frame like

281

Ping-Pong balls, the writing desk, the doily-covered bureau, a low, black-lacquered Chinese chest with many drawers . . . and stepping into the room now I fix on the only anomalous object in it: a cardboard box behind the door, Del Monte whole tomatoes, it says, and above that in my mother's self-conscious print, *MISC*. That carton was among the ones walling in the old man's pallet in the Channel Road attic just days ago, and I'm positive it's here now because it now contains his manuscript— and who knows what else, it's a big box. Also, that means he's probably got—

"You're not sidling in here to pitch me some woo, I hope."

She's half-right. I want to attack her. Jump her and tie her to the bedstead, tickle her with feathers until she tells me everything. OK, lady, exactly when did he get here—and when did he leave? And *where is he*? No bullshit, now, or I'll pour cream in your armpits and let Nugget and Athena lick it out. And what's under the bed? And what you got in that Chinese chest? And why'd the old pecker steal my money? Hunh? You had enough? Hunh? But shit, she's probably about as ticklish as an armadillo.

"I've just never seen a trailer before," I say lamely. "More room than you would think."

"All done with mirrors," she says. "I'm gonna tell you good night, now, if you got all you need out there."

"Oh, hell, I left my parking lights on!"

"Good night, then," she says.

"Thanks, Vivian, see you in the morning." I gently shut the door.

First glance into the dark car and I think she's *gone* again, just as I see she's not gone, she's asleep across the seats under the sleeping bag.

"Cici, wake up. Cici."

"I was . . . God, where are we?"

"It's all scoped out, Cici, and I have a tricky plan. Can you listen now?"

"Wow, this *dream*. I was . . . see, there were all these little like animals. I don't know, like hairy blobs, and you and me—"

"*Cici*, listen now! This is serious!"

"OK." She pushes up on her arms and looks around. "So was he in there? Your father?"

"No, he's gone. But OK, Cici, now listen. We are not camping. We're going to sleep in the trailer tonight. My father's woman lives there—his wife, whoever she is—and she said I can sleep on the sofa. It's all set up. But she thinks I'm alone, so that makes you my ace in the hole. . . . You listening?"

She nods.

"Here it is, then. My father's papers are in a Del Monte box in her bedroom. And there may be more papers in a black lacquer chest in there, or under the bed, or in the closet, and what you're going to do tomorrow morning is sneak in there and take all the papers you can find and drag them out here to the car—"

"Oh, *sure.*"

"No, now listen, it'll be easy. Right now she's in bed. So I'm smuggling you inside, and you can sleep *under* the sofa. There's plenty of room, and I'll drape the blanket down so it's perfectly safe, don't worry. Then the tricky part comes when I have to somehow get her out of the trailer. But don't worry, I'll do it. I'll get her to give me a tour of the grounds. You'll have maybe ten minutes. So no big rush. Stuff the papers into the sleeping bag, and when you get them here to the car, toot *once* on the horn. I'll be listening. There, how's that?"

"Say it all again."

When she gets it straight, we leave the car and hustle up to the trailer. From the bedroom Vivian wouldn't see us; its window opens onto the driveway. I go in, trying to make some natural-sounding noises. All clear. Cici slinks through the room with the sleeping bag over her shoulders. I plump the sofa while she squirms under it. Perfect fit. I drop to my hands and knees to tuck the bag in around her, and then I crawl in far enough to kiss her. She's grinning. One of the cats sniffs her hand.

After I'm tucked in myself and the lights are off, I can't even shut my eyes for all the nauseating pieces of thoughts still streaming along inside me, a river of thoughts like ball bearings making a sibilant ball-bearing hum. Then I hear something else: *cruncha-crunch, cruncha-crunch.*

I hang down over the edge of the sofa. "Cici?" I whisper.

"What?"

"What was that noise?"

"What noise?"

"What are you doing?"

"Oh. Chewing a carrot."

"What?"

"Never mind."

"Well, stop it, OK?"

"OK."

I'm drifting close to slumber when a strange notion jumps me: What if the old man is in there sleeping secretly under *her* bed just as Cici is under mine? I laugh to myself. Well, we'll sure as hell know tomorrow. That's crazy, though. Vivian would have shooed me off if he were still here. Besides, he snores to beat the band.

I pop awake (not much later, I feel, but sun fills the room) because she's gone. I'm sweating, I'm convinced she's gone. I scramble into my pants, hurry to the front door, open it, craning to see the Porsche, and when I do see it, empty, I realize almost at the same time first that she *is* gone, she's *left* me, and then that she's not gone. She's under the sofa. She's Cici, I realize. The woman who's gone is someone else, some beautiful no one, a phantom. I shut the door, my heart thumping. What a sensation! Very strange.

Cici's sleeping legs have thrust the mountain-sky-blue foot of my bag into view. I dart over and push it back under.

"Morning," Cici whispers.

"Shh!"

I stretch out on the sofa to peruse a *National Geographic* piece about the great Santa Barbara spill, photos of awful gooped-up coastline and the oil-laden sea. Cousteau, it says in italics, gives the oceans twenty-five years. When they die, you can kiss off the whole globe, baby, it's curtains. Christ. I slap shut the magazine.

"Sleep OK?" Vivian calls in from the hallway.

"Yeah, fine. Thanks."

"Bathroom's yours."

Jesus, she's up. She's probably peeked in here already. I sit straight and rearrange my blankets.

Vivian bounds out suddenly in a brown-and-white swimsuit. She strikes a pose and sings, "Ta-daaaa."

"Nice."

"Yeah—fer a rubber-shanked old mule." The cats are meowing and arching against her bare legs. "I know, I know," she says.

"Do you swim?"

She walks by me into the kitchenette. "Well, I paddle my carcass around the pool a few times."

"There's a pool?"

"Ho, we got a pool like you wouldn't believe."

"Where is it?"

"Hah! Got trunks? Let me feed my babies and we'll take a constitutional."

"Great!"

Vivian latches the front door before we leave the trailer, just to keep her friends honest, she says. She locks the back, too. "Oh, no," she tells the cats. "You stay home. Want to get squashed by a truck?"

There's a narrow path worn in the dust from her stoop out to the pool enclosure, worn by bare feet, and as she's telling me how all this was once a lead mine that went bankrupt, I'm following along, watching her horny feet press the dust, imagining minuscule men and women and their villages being crushed by her step, screaming, all their lives ending horribly, their serene civilization snuffed out, their comfy homes, their museums and shopping centers, their great arenas for their football teams and rock bands, everything, the pet parakeets they love, the Christmas-tree ornaments packed away for next year, their feelings, too, the ones they couldn't express, and all their hopes and memories—well, we need dust, we're making dust here, folks, it all goes down behind that.

The pool is a sparkling, repulsive aqua-blue, flat as glass. As a kid, I liked pools, private pools at least, but I don't anymore. When I swim I don't like to have to turn around. I feel silly in a pool, like a fish in an aquarium, there's nothing to do in pools.

The thrill of this pool is obviously getting up the nerve to leap off the high board—or maybe walking out on it is enough. You can probably see Mexico.

A brown old man in a necktie and jacket jerks up in his chair when Vivian swings the gate. "Close it! Close it! Close it!" he says. Then he says, "No hippies!"

"Go back to sleep, Mr. Emery!" shouts Vivian. To me she says, "Ding-dong. Hey—wait, we forgot your trunks."

"They're in the car. I'm basically an ocean person, though, Vivian. Chlorine gets to me."

She squinches her face. "Well, la-la," she says and plunges in.

My end of this number couldn't be easier. Cici shouldn't have any trouble either. I told her to stuff the sleeping bag with whatever looked like his and drag it to the car. Already I'm listening for her *toot.*

Vivian's a strong swimmer, strong all around, actually—a lot like Lou, in fact, though somehow tougher-seeming, yet mellower at the same time. I like Vivian. She's being very good to me. Now I feel guilty for how cruel I'm being to her, plundering her bedroom and then running out on her like a thief, a real rat. If I'd only asked her straight, maybe she would've let me go through the tomato box. . . . No. No, she's been too long maintaining the old man's buffer zone. She'd never cross him for me, not a chance.

"You don't know what you're missing!" she calls out.

"OK, Vivian, I want to watch you dive off that high board!"

She's on her back, kicking. "When it gets a hundred and ten, you don't sit around wishing you had an ocean!"

I laugh. "Yeah, that's when you hitch up your trailer and haul it to Monterey."

Toot.

Shit!

Vivian's hoisting herself up onto the pool's lip. She pushes her hair back. "That was the ticket, all right."

"OK, I'm convinced. Stay here, and I'll go get my suit."

"Place is locked," she says. "Can you change in your car?"

"In no time!" I run at the fence and vault it.

Behind the car in the road, Cici sees me galloping toward her, and she waves.

"What did you get?" I say, out of breath.

The car seems filled with sleeping bag, bunched blue guts across both seats.

She says, "I don't know, *a lot*. There was so *much*, so like I just—"

"You left the door open!"

"Well, God, I—"

"The cats are out!"

Side by side in the shade of the trailer gazing toward us, they look like statues, cast-iron yard art. I start their way in long strides, but they scamper off together as though this is a game they know. I go to shut the trailer door, thinking what am I doing? We have to roll! But I want a quick look inside the bedroom myself. I dart through the hall. Christ, it's a terrible mess, drawers yanked out, clothing and papers and knickknacks strewn all over, the Del Monte carton dumped on the bed. I push some drawers in and set the carton on the floor. I snatch up a piece of paper—an old envelope addressed to Lou in San Francisco—and a pen from the desk. I scribble across it: "Dear V., Very very sorry."—I can't think of anything else—"Many thanks, love, Will." I drop my note on the sofa blankets and race out the door, leaving it open for the cats. Maybe they'll go back in.

"I couldn't help it with those cats," says Cici. "You can't control cats."

"I know. It's OK." I shove the bag out of the way, switch on the key, put the transmission in reverse. "Can you jump this wreck, Cici? Just steer and keep the clutch in until I say *pop it*, then give her the gas, OK?"

"*Backwards?*"

"Yeah! Get in!"

Ten yards of push and she's under power once more. What a reliable little car. I sprint after it. Cici scrambles over to let me in behind the wheel.

After a few hell-bent miles, we hit Route 33. We speed north on that through yellow hills, a few dark trees here and there, white peaks up in the milky eastern haze, not slackening at all for fear she'll set a posse of roughriders after us. But if the old man is into something shady, maybe Vivian would be wise enough to it so she wouldn't go calling in the law. Instead, maybe she'd be so riled at having been juked she'd gun her Mustang down the highway in furious pursuit. That doesn't seem very likely though—she would never guess our whicha-way. No, she'll scream to the sheriff for sure. That Vivian, she's feisty. She won't be crossed as meanly as I've crossed her and just take it. Shit, five minutes after we took off with the goods she'd have the sheriff on the horn, Sheriff Horace Bouldergut, her old pal probably since grade school.

"Horace, goddamn it, I been *robbed*. Robbed in my own stinkin' trailer by my own stinkin' stepson, the hippie varmint."

"Say again, Viv? *Hippie?*"

"Hell, yes! Long blond hair in a ponytail. Sandals on his dirty feet. Like to think he's Jesus Christ himself when he's all lit up on his LSD."

"Well, don't that burn your beans. You just shoot off the par-ticulars now, Viv, and me and the boys'll have the varmint all skinned, dressed-out, and hung up by the toes 'fore dinner, don't you fret."

At least we've got that much still going for us: skimpy par-ticulars. She can't be sure which way we went, what sort of car we're in, or who my accomplice might be. . . . Unless old Horace hooks up somehow with the alarm the Colonel's drummed out—vandalism, kidnapping, and interstate flight. Christ, that would burn *my* beans just about black.

We pull over once for quick morning relief, and then I just keep us on fire for a good hour. We end up in an Indian reserva-tion, Pyramid Lake, where we have to slow down because there are people in the road, souvenir-sellers flapping blankets at us, real Indians, too, wearing feathers and domed hats, braids and scruffy jackets.

"Look what we did to them," I say to Cici, "look where we stuck them, the savages." It's very depressing, rotten shacks, worthless land . . . what's wrong? This is *America*, the country that goes to the moon!

"At least they have a big lake," says Cici, but I won't stop for a closer look. I'm running scared, it's that simple.

We go on through until we get to Nixon, that's actually the name of the burg, where we have to stop to buy gas. Food, too, Cici insists.

"This place isn't so bad," she says. "At least they have a *town*, with stores and everything."

"Yeah," I say, "for when they get bored with the lake." A town named Nixon. Shit.

Cici refuses to cross the threshold of any diner. "I hate those dripping signs they have over the grill of what you can order, the corned beef specials and patty-melts and franks and fries and all that, I'll barf if I see that," she says, so she waits in the car while I venture into a dim market. She doesn't want to consider the awful variety of food at all. I come out with more cheese, more bread, more eggs and apples and mustard, and some sardines in olive oil, pretty much what we've been eating since Sunday. We still have several beers, which is a good thing because the market has none—Injuns and firewater don't mix, as their blighted history has taught us.

I'm just slapping the flap down over the gas cap, considering whether to have Cici shut off the motor so I can get an accurate dipstick reading, which would be prudent, if time consuming, when I swear I sense (before I look up to see behind us) the oily approach of a dusty brown Dodge sedan with big evil yellow stars on the hood and doors. *Washoe County Sheriff*. And in each star a black emblem that looks like crossed swords over a waterfall. What could *that* mean, I am wondering idiotically, telling myself at the same time, *No*, jerk, you can't run. *Think. Think.*

In the car Cici is calmly munching another carrot, trying to find where we are on our new map of Nevada.

The sheriff slides out slowly and looks around as if he's stopped maybe just for a Nehi and a pouch of chew. He's short, chunky, hatless, with slicked-back hair.

I look around, too, feeling suddenly sick. I breathe in deep and sigh. Indians are on the sidewalks, placidly ambling, or squatting dull-eyed, backsides propped against a few buildings as if they can't help behaving how they're supposed to behave, tired, broken, whether they want to or not. A barbershop across the way, The Cut-Cut Place, makes me wish to God I'd got a cut-cut like Cici's. It's the first time in my life I've ever wanted to blend in.

Well, the route out of town's wide open, just occasional cars, that's something, and the Porsche is chugging dependably away as I stand in the sun sweating. That's something, too.

I glance at the sheriff, persuading myself that this is reasonable (you always glance at sheriffs), and I walk easily around to the driver's side to get in.

" 'Scuse me there, boy," he says loudly.

I open the door to give Cici a grotesque, toothy sort of a grin and a wink. Her little smile melts into puzzlement.

"You there—in them pretty bangs."

I look over at him. He has black eyebrows slanting to his nose and deep creases slanting away below it so his face seems to have an X through it.

"What's the matter, Sheriff?" I push out.

He sticks his thumbs behind his belt of bullets and works his jaw sideways. "Ain't sure, rightly," he says. "I never seen nothin' like you my whole life, is all."

"Likewise," I say evenly.

He's stepped forward and now he kicks my rear bumper with the heel of his boot. "Boy, how 'bout you show me the papers on this vehicle? Kin you do that?"

I clear my throat, yank out my wallet, and flash my big chromium badge at him. "Listen closely now, Sheriff. I am US law court clerk Andrew Busch. I am here in the Pyramid Lake Reservation on a tour of evaluation for the United States Government Department of the Interior, Bureau of Indian Affairs, and if I have to report to Washington that you imagine your Washoe County jurisdiction overflows onto federal territory, well, I am more than a little afraid you *and* your senior officer will find yourselves in very hot federal hot water."

"I never heard nothin' like that before," says the sheriff, his bleak eyes shrinking closer together. "We always been responsible for trouble on this reservation since I been in this department. Shit, who drags their damn trucks outa the ditch? Who takes their women in to Reno all knifed-up nights so's they don't bleed to death?"

"That prejudiced attitude is at the heart of the whole problem here in Pyramid! You getting this on tape, Miss Perkins? I want every word of this on tape!"

"Yes, sir," says Cici.

The sheriff's lips curl briefly. "OK now. You just stay glued right here while I call in about this. I'm calling in direct right now."

"We have urgent business, Sheriff. But if you insist on playing the fool and dragging your entire department down along with you, you'll have no difficulty finding us here among the true Americans, I'm sure."

I slip into the car and roll out slowly, watching the scowling mule in the mirror. He's watching us as well, memorizing the plate, I guess. Then he hurries back to his Dodge.

When we round the bend out of town toward a flat stretch of highway, I slam her down in second for all the old crate's worth, then whining up to seventy in third, then in fourth to ninety, ninety-five, hoping she won't shimmy into pieces to leave us shrieking along the road on our tailbones. Cici is speechless.

We turn onto a little road north, off the state route, out of the reservation now, roaring along, both looking for some track, some set of ruts that might lead us out of sight of the road, to a spot where we can hide and eat, and take a breather.

"This is bad now, Cici," I'm telling her, panicked. "Oh, Christ. This is very very bad. When that asshole finds out our plates are stolen, he'll have every reason to grab us. He'll come screaming after us with his beady eyes burning and spittle streaming down his neck. They got computers to put it all together. They know right where we are, and what car we're driving, and what we look like—like *hippies*, in the middle of all these cowboys. We're fucked now, Cici, we really are."

"There!" yells Cici. "Will, you passed it! Back there's a good road into those hills!"

I brake hard, crank us around the other way, and jounce us off the pavement over scraping rocks among stunted bushes and red dirt and weeds out behind a few hills until we can't see any part of the main road, just more hills and some big blue and white mountains not far off. I back the Porsche up onto a bank, shut off the motor, and get out to jam stones under the front tires.

Cici is stretching, rising on her toes, loosening her back. "Man! Was that ever a pisser back there!" She laughs. "Will, you did really great with that dufus, you know? Wow, he just about *believed* you. What did you say you were again? What kind of inspector?"

I sit in the shade of the car, but the ground's hot, and the car is fuming and ticking, so I move off toward some pines farther up the hill, saying, "Cici, forget that. We have to figure out what we do next. Don't you get it? We are criminals now. I mean, Jesus, they can lock me up! They can lock you up, too. But they won't. They'll just send you back to Costa Mesa, so your daddy can lock you up until you come down with anorexia so bad you just shrivel up like a caterpillar in a jar. And *die*."

She sits down next to me and pats my knee. "Will, come *on*. We got away, right? You were so cool, too. 'I am the United States Indian Inspector'—that was so *cool*. And they will never ever find us out here. They probably figured we went the other direction back there, to the freeway, right? Which, instead, we came way out here, where they'll never think of looking. See?"

"I sure as hell hope so."

"Yeah!" she says, about to add something else, but she pauses and now jumps up, startling me. "Hey, *I* know! Let's do up some weed, Will. Let's change our outlook on life! You wanna?"

"OK," I say, laughing at her in spite of myself.

She breaks into a wide smile. "Yeah, and then we can sit around and like inspect my giant bag full of papers of your dad, right? See? *That's* what we do next."

"Cici, you're a girl after me own heart."

She laughs. "Will, I don't care what we do next, I swear.

Even if we never do find your dad, which we probably won't the way that lady made it sound—and now with us being criminals and all that—well, to me that's cool, because this whole adventure is pretty fun no matter what, *really* fun, and . . . like, I just all of a sudden think this is the best my life has been so far, and I still want us to find your dad and all, but to me that's only our faraway goal, see? I don't care if we have to look for him forever!''

I splutter like a horse. I flick pebbles into the air with my thumb, while Cici goes after my film can and rolling papers. Jesus, she's feeling how I should be feeling, I think. Hey—*fun, adventure*! Dig what you're into and fuck the future. Maybe that's how I do feel partly, I don't know. Sometimes it's hard to get a bead on what you're feeling when you're right in the middle of feeling it. There must be a reason for that. Yesterday, before we blasted off the peninsula, all I wanted was to get him, whatever it took. I wanted to wrap my fingers around his gullet and shake his eyebrows off. But now after this maniacal car ride and the incident at Nixon, my grip on my purpose is almost lost.

"Cici," I say in a cloud of our druggy smoke, "Cici, I feel like this trip is like a space-shot, with you and me strapped in our capsule like monkeys leaving the sweet Earth behind, and the only guys who remember the point of our mission are down in ground control sipping Cokes and watching our white blip drift through the grid. And we go along and go along deeper and deeper into no-place, and I have to keep reminding myself that my father did a despicable thing. He came back to Balboa just to get my money. He even *told* me that. One way or another he was going to get it. He gave me the chance to turn it over, but he was ready to screw me out of it all along. Now that is a horrible thing for anybody to do, especially your father, agreed?''

"Yes," says Cici. "Very rude."

"Right. Very rude indeed. See, Cici? That's sort of how I feel. I can't get behind the rottenness of it anymore. Shit, it was never really my money to start with, was it?''

"It isn't *now*, that's for sure."

"Yeah. I would like to find out his high-blown reasons, though. I deserve that much. Right, fuzzy?''

"Really."

We boil two eggs in the melt water out of the cooler, on my Coleman stove. Cici eats one. She tells me she would've liked a yogurt, too, if I could've got one.

"Good luck," I say. "Out here they think a yogurt is a kind of wigwam."

Cici leaves her eggshell next to an anthill. She goes to drag the loaded sleeping bag out of the car. It must be heavy, the way she tugs at it, or else it got wedged in there during the chase. She's grunting.

"Need a hand?"

She wrestles it free. "This thing got ruined," she says. "There's little feathers coming out all over."

It's true. White feathers fly out of rents and whisk themselves away on the wind, like kids on the last day of school.

We zip it open.

"Christ, Cici, look at this crap. What a mess."

"Yeah, serves him right," says Cici. "Anyhow, we can straighten it out. Nothing's more than a little crinkled. You can still read it, that's what counts."

The manuscript pages are easy to pick out. They're all typed and scrawled-on in the same way, and they're numbered—four times, each page having three crossed-out numbers in a repetitive pattern at an upper corner and one clean number to stand for its place in the latest order. We put these in loose heaps under paperweights of crumbly rock. Odd, carefully scissored scraps of typing come slipping out now and then. They're labeled "Insert 187-A," and "1938–9 or ?" and so on, and they make me nervous. We make a separate pile of these. Cici is singing under her breath, her head wagging back and forth. This bothers me, too, I don't know why. What's more, I'm trying to resist reading any of this elaborately niggled-over family history heaped around me, and I'm not having much luck. Words and phrases snake out at me, entangling my brain, drawing it off into thickets of recollection. I can't stand it.

I jump up. "Takin' five! Want anything? Steak sandwich?"

She shakes her head.

Brown clumps of grass and twisted juniper sprout from the

red ground up along a crevice in the bluff, also more piñon pines, and under the pines, I find when I scramble up there, little purplish flowers and even littler white ones, like stars. I sit under a pine hunched against the gusty breezes and roll another number. A swirl of pink dust totters by me and caves in going down the hill. Overhead, black before the ribboned silver-gray clouds, two hawks are high in the air, circling on the thermals.

A few healthy drags and I'm circling, too, looking regally down over the rest of existence. I pull off my shirt and let the sun have me.

"*Will!*"

"I'm up on the hill! I'm relaxing!"

. "Well, get your rosy down here. I got something!"

"What is it?"

"I don't know! Maps!"

"Maps?"

"Come *on!*"

Surveyor's maps is what they are, a thick packet of them, each folded neatly in quarters. I open the first one. In blue ruled lines with numbers to indicate degree orientations and feet, it denotes a crooked triangle of land somewhere in Idaho.

Property of William R. Muldoon (Record Owner), highway 46, Gooding, Idaho, Scale—1″ 100′ September 1965 by Truline, Inc. Boise, Idaho Survey by S. M. Tinker Draft by T. T. Linaugh. *Certification*: I hereby certify that the metes and bounds shown hereon are based on a mathematical closure of an actual ground survey and are correct to the best of my knowledge. This plat is prepared for the exclusive use of William R. Muldoon and no representations are made to, or any reliance justified by, any other individual or entity.

It's signed "Samuel M. Tinker" and stamped with his seal as a registered land surveyor. All over the parcel my father—or someone—has meticulously penciled in clusters or strings of small green circles with *W*s inside them, or *B*s.

"Weird, hunh?" says Cici.

We open another one, then several more. They represent odd plots of land all over the plains and prairies, in Utah and Colorado and Wyoming and Montana and Nebraska and New Mexico, even Iowa back east. Some are only two or three acres, a few more than thirty, and all have these circled symbols drawn in precisely, in sharp green pencil.

I relight my joint. "Smoke?"

She takes it. "What's it all mean?"

"Got me. Sure owns a lot of land, the old weasel, doesn't he?"

"Really. Maybe that's why he took your money, to buy more and more land. Like a collection."

"Yeah."

"No, that's dumb," says Cici. "Why was he in such a rush, then? Unless he was really crazy, you know? Like *really fried*."

"Yeah."

"Was he?"

"No. Hard to tell, though."

She watches me make smoke rings. "So what now, Captain Space-shot?"

"Are we done? There's more in there, isn't there?"

"More stuff, yeah. More maps, I don't know."

"Good. OK, listen, I'm the Captain of— What's the opposite of Industry?"

She shrugs.

"Whatever it is, that's what I'm the captain of. You're my secretary, so you do the work. Buzz me if something comes up."

She laughs. "You're pretty buzzed already."

I bat my eyelashes at her.

"Mostly what's here is just his giant book, Will, and these old letters and junk of your mom's. And I guess I took by accident some stuff of your stepmom back there, the cowgirl."

But in two minutes (luckily before I've disappeared around the bend) she makes the big find: a fat brown envelope containing, stapled into gray folders, the original warranty deeds for the old man's holdings, each one described with exhaustive numerical precision, with all the requisite fuzzy language.

"KNOW ALL MEN BY THESE PRESENTS THAT . . ." and so on. Also the will, a rough draft of it. "Last Will and Testament" typed on yellow paper. It's short, only two dense paragraphs, the second one listing his bequest to me.

"The *land*, Cici! It's mine! He's giving it to me!"

"He *is*? Far *out!*"

"Listen! '. . . do hereby freely give, convey, confirm, and bequeath unto the said William R. Muldoon, Junior, and his heirs and assigns forever, these certain pieces of land in—' *Look* at all these places! Slick Rock, Colorado—where the hell's *that*? Dillon, Montana. Byron, Wyoming. . . . I own all these damn places! Amazing! I've never even been there!"

Cici hugs me, and we jump up and down together. It's like I just won a sweepstakes. Land—what I always wanted. *Acres* and *acres* of land, too, mountains and canyons, woods and streams—*fabulous*.

Cici wonders if it's *good* land, not rocks like this land here, and I say sure it's good land, why would the old man buy crummy land?

"Right," says Cici, "for sure, but it's still a mystery, the reasons behind the marks on the maps and why he bought all the land and all that."

"Yeah, true, but anyway," I tell her, "I *like* this land here."

"God, it's rocks," says Cici. "Pure *rocks*."

She goes to fetch our warm beers from the shade of the car while I count up all our maps and deeds. The strange thing is we turn out to have more deeds than maps, thirty-four deeds and thirty-one maps. Matching our deeds to the available maps, we soon discover we're missing the survey drawings of four acres, "more or less," near Bosler, in Wyoming, twelve acres at Muddy Gap, Wyoming, and twenty acres, "more or less," on the Sweetwater River, near South Pass City, Wyoming.

"I didn't lose them, Will. These envelopes were all in that black chest, together in the same drawer, or else in two drawers, but if they're not here now, then they weren't there then, I know it."

"He has them, Cici. Damn it, I'm positive! Whatever these

green marks mean, he's still working on these Wyoming pieces, and he must need those maps with him. . . . Jesus, Cici, the old buckaroo's in Wyoming!"

"Wow," she whispers. "He's barely a day ahead of us."

An hour winding cautiously north through the desert hills along the looming flank of some ragged mountains and by the shores of dried-up lakes brings us to Route 48, an empty stretch of pavement rippling away in two barren directions.

Cici is saying, "Turn right, turn right. See?" She points to a sign with an arrowhead on it and the name *Lovelock*. She is navigating.

I turn. We've decided to keep clear of the Interstate at least until we cross into Utah, figuring if the law's seriously after us, the big road is where they'll look first and hardest.

The farther we drive along through this ugly spectacular desert with no motorcycles snarling out of the buff distance, and no blue-blinking roadblocks up ahead (no cars at all to speak of), the more confident I become, and also the more resigned to calamity should we be fated to confront it. I'm doing all I can do. Let 'er rip.

On we push all afternoon across more and more desert, more desert than should ever have been necessary. The Creator must have dozed off with his elbow on the desert button.

Logic, we reckon, would put the old man now at the nearest of the three Wyoming pieces, the twenty acres beginning, according to the deed, "at a point in the center of that state highway numbered 28 by the State of Wyoming where it intersects the west bank of the Sweetwater River and running 61°N 45′W for a distance of 602.8 feet along the riverbank." But if whatever he's up to doesn't keep him there until tomorrow morning. . . . Well, at least we'll be able to tell whether he's been there, by charred firewood, tracks, empty cans of soup. Twenty acres can't be too big a plot to explore. I hope. I don't really know how big twenty acres is, except that one acre would be a hell of a lot of real estate on the peninsula. The entire Balboa Club isn't more than three or four acres. "How big is an acre anyway?" I ask Cici.

"An acre?" She shuts her eyes. "Wait. I learned that. An acre, an acre. An acre is the amount of land two oxen can plow in one day."

"Come on."

"Well, it is. It's forty-something-thousand square feet, around there."

"Terrific. OK, how big's an acre compared to a tennis court?"

"God, I'm not the *World Almanac*. Is that what you want to do with your land? Put up tennis courts?"

I give her a sharp look. "Cici! That is a *great* idea. Fabulous! The Muldoon Tennis Ranch! Muldoon's Tennis Acres! Twenty lovingly constructed courts spread under the shade of the cottonwoods, at the foot of the breathtaking Rocky Mountains! On the banks of the pure and peaceful Sweetwater River! Luxuriously appointed cabins, saunas, horseback riding, golf, bird-watching, exquisite cuisine! Top-notch pros, exhibition matches, the time of your sporting life! Hell, I could get Lou to drum up our own tournament—the Muldoon Wild West Open. Sure, because she knows all the big promoters and rich sponsors. And we could carve a spectacular stadium right into the side of some granite mountain. It would be the first great tennis facility in the new age of the game. *Damn*—why not?"

"You mean for real? A real tennis facility out here in nowhere?"

"Cici, as my mother says, the game's growing like milkweed in a cow plop. They can't build these resorts fast enough. And with *Muldoon* in the title . . . we're golden. It's a great idea. You can be the diet plan counselor."

"Ha ha ha," she says, smiling.

Later, there is prairie sliding by our windows, grassy enough now so that black cattle pose in places, stock-still herds of them spread over the flat expanse like plastic tokens you would move at the roll of dice, just doped-up beef, heads down, obliging our appetites with theirs.

The sun drops behind us. We press into Utah, congratulating each other with glances, and on toward darkness, across the vast salt waste where the prehistoric lake once lapped high over our heads.

My odometer has just come up nines, and now all zeros for the third or fourth time in its dumb faithful life. I want it to mean something, but it doesn't, it can't. Long ago, in the Dark Ages, everybody thought the world would end in the year 1000. Now I suppose our hopes are pinned on 2000. My car, however, only begins again: 00001. No change, nothing even flinches. Cici is curled in the sleeping bag against the door. Both my hands grip the wheel, as if to keep the world steady and on course. And true, if I did wrench it, wrench it hard, that would do us. The world would disappear, after one final scarlet event.

By midnight, heading north on 187 out of Rock Springs, Wyoming, I lose radio contact with popular culture. A chorus of proud Americans sings, "Oh beautiful, for spacious skies," and then my last stream of sound dries up. The silence wakes Cici briefly. She looks around sleepily and rearranges herself on the seat. I can't stop driving. I'm groggy. It's cold, too. My calves are cramping. My ankles are weak, and a ticklish, syrupy feeling swishes through me down there so I have to flex my muscles to eliminate it, though in minutes it comes oozing back along my sinews. I keep flexing.

I need rest, but I'm close, too close, closing in, and I can't stop. Angling for three inches through the middle of my map, highway 28, a narrow vein of red, crosses the hairline squiggle of the Sweetwater, over the Great Divide, just beyond the pass (el. 7,550). . . . "It's *here*," yelped Cici back in Salt Lake, jabbing her thumb at the hashwork of colored lines, making the paper crackle, "it's on the map! Will, God, it's right here—the intersection. You can see it!"

So I can't stop. We whine up into the Rockies. Thirty miles, twenty . . . ten . . . shooting the pass in the tunnel of night, and down the other side.

"Cici?"

"Hm?"

"Shake a leg, kid. We have done it."

She stretches and groans.

"Hear the river?"

"The *river*. Are we *here*?"

"Yes, ma'am. Glory to the Fatherland. We're here."

"Man," she whispers, peering out the window. "Man oh man."

There's a wind blowing, but the quiet seems enormous. The river sounds shallow, as if it chuckles over boulders and stones. The night is lit by half a moon behind us low above the peaks, and out ahead a ghostly hint of dawn seeps over the dark mountains far away.

"Wow," says Cici. "I can't believe this is really it. The river and everything. Think your dad's around?"

"One way to find out."

"I know, but . . . now?"

"Yup. Come on, before we lose the moon." I shove open my door.

"God, it's *freezing*," she says, and it is. Frost like whiskers has formed along the stony slope at the shoulder of the road.

I tell her she should stay, because all she has are those thong sandals. She says no, she sat in the car last time, and she hates waiting and not knowing what's happening. What if something happened to me, like a bear or a snake, how would she know? If I would just give her a pair of my socks and my sweatshirt again, that's all she needs. We dig around in the dark for those and then slip out into the cold.

"Wow," breathes Cici. "Stars! There's more stars than not-stars."

We look at them, shivering.

"OK," I whisper, "if you were camping here, where would you camp?"

"I wouldn't. It's freezing."

"Shhh. By the river, right? Close to fresh water. We're going to sneak like Indians along the bank until we see something— the outline of his vehicle or his tent-poles."

"Then you go and—what was it you said? You go and throttle him." She grabs her own throat. "*Argh.*"

We walk along the pavement to the bridge, then backtrack to a spot where the shoulder's less steep, and crab down on our bottoms to keep from stumbling in the loose stones. Off the road the ground is level near the river, but studded in a tricky way with clumps of grass and low wiry bushes. Though the bank is not high (maybe six feet), it pitches hard to the water, which is loud and looks fast enough to be deadly, so we stay well back from the edge, not knowing where it may have been undercut by some deeper flow. With the wind sometimes stiffening behind it, the cold is wicked. We step slowly, holding hands.

"Know what?" says Cici. "Teeth really chatter. I never knew that. I thought it was like just a joke for cartoons."

"After we look around a little I'll build a fire out of the wind, and we'll set up the tent and cuddle up."

She giggles. "You think he's really here? Who would want to? It's like Siberia."

"Shhh."

"It's a crummy place for your tennis thing," she whispers.

The long, faint shadows of the jagged ridge to our right and of the nearby hills creep toward us as the moon descends. To the east, as yet the new day shows no color. It will be darker soon before it's lighter.

In the dimness ahead I pick out what seem like large roundish bushes at a bend in the river. Maybe he's set himself up among those, hidden from the road. But when we get closer, I see they're not bushes at all, but the tops of trees that grow up out of a deep ravine, a narrow canyon that reaches probably all the way back to the ridge. That's the place, all right, for sure.

I stop. "How you doing?"

"Good," she says.

And then I catch it, woven into the cold wind: wood-smoke. "Hey! Smell that?"

"*What?*"

I hurry on, taking careful strides through the tangled growth to the lip of the ravine. I kneel. It's black down there; I can make out only the dense limbs of trees.

Cici scrambles up next to me on her hands and knees, scattering pebbles. She's out of breath. "What is it?"

"Fire."

"Where?"

I point.

She sniffs the air.

"Still with me?"

She nods. "If you go first."

We make our way along the rim of the ravine away from the river searching for the place where I figure there should be a cut at the head of a path to the bottom. We enter the moon-shadow and gaze up toward the peaks. Just the tip of the moon is winking.

Next to me Cici spins slowly around on her toes.

"What are you doing?"

"You have to—for luck," she says. "Or else you could get a spell cast over your next day."

Even in the dark the path is obvious, steep, but wide as a road, curving against the wall of the ravine like a freeway ramp. The wind dies out as we go down, yet the cold feels sharper. I keep my hands in my pockets. Tendrils of mist hang above us, produced by a stream we can hear gurgling to the river.

The treetops ahead are tossing high against the yellowing horizon. As we walk, I'm watching them to try to judge their distance.

"Yikes," Cici whispers. She grabs my arm. "See the fire?"

It's only a glimmer of orange coals to one side of us across the stream bed. I pat her icy hand. We head straight at it.

Suddenly an awful *clinkity-clink* of metal tears the stillness.

Cici screams, "*Aaaaaaaahhh!*"

I grunt and duck into a crouch.

Then—*rrrrr-AARRGH!*—an animal roar from beyond the fire paralyzes me.

Cici screams again.

"*If you move, you're dead!*" a voice bellows madly.

I'm sitting on the ground. Cici whimpers and cries against me.

"*This whole canyon is primed to blow!*"

"*Dad?*"

"I peed," says Cici.

"*Dad?* For Christ's sake, it's ME. *Will Muldoon!*"

A scrabbling sound echoes across the ravine, and a beam of light knifes out, sweeping around us.

"Over here!" I shout.

"Will! Goddamn it! You scared the *bejesus* outa me! Who's with you?"

"Can we come over without getting blown up?"

"I peed all down my pants," says Cici, in tears.

"How in hell did you find me?"

"We're coming over! Don't blow us up!"

The coals blaze into flame as we hop the stream. There he is in the tattered glow, stooped, breaking sticks. It's strange, but all I can get myself to feel now, seeing the vulnerable, knobby hulk of him, huffing vapor, is relief, stupefying relief, the breathless kind you bask in when a nightmare's gone as far as it can and then ejected you into the close air of your room, and those giant feet cracking behind you over the sidewalk are coming from your alarm clock.

He coughs and spits. "You must have followed me. Impossible, but that's what you did. You attached a radio beeper to my truck. Am I warm?"

"Dad, this is my very good friend, Cici Bamberger."

"How do you do, Cici Bamberger?" he says, putting both his hands around hers and nodding.

"Fine," says Cici, shyly, into her chest.

"Fine my elbow! You are numb unto the marrow! Cici *Ice*-berger, that's you." He feels around on a log behind him and comes up with a blanket, which he shakes out and wraps around her shoulders.

"My pants . . ." she whispers to me.

"I know. Slip them off, and I'll rinse them in the stream."

The old man's kicking his log nearer the fire. "There, now," he rumbles.

Cici steps out of her fallen pants and sits. "Thank you."

"You're most welcome. Now see if you can knock back a touch of this." He pours some whiskey into a Sierra cup.

"Hard liquor?"

"Dr. Muldoon's Wonder Water. It'll thaw your middle."

"I hate liquor," says Cici, accepting the cup.

"So do I, my dear. But it's small torment opposed to all the therapy it provides."

He follows me down to the stream. My hands are too cold to put into the water, so he does it. He reaches wordlessly for the pants, underpants, too, and dunks them a few times in the silvery flow.

In a low voice he says, "She is very lovely—but sort of peaked. She all right?"

"She's getting better."

He wrings out the pants. "That shriek of hers, Christ Almighty. What was that about? If I could've seen something out there, I would've shot it."

The noise we heard, it turns out, was his perimeter warning system, collections of cans poised just so and strung together with taut nylon trip-cord. Cici must have hit it.

"So you were expecting me?"

"You? Hell, no. Come on, you gonna reveal your modus operandi for me? Where's the chink in my armor?"

"Who *were* you expecting?"

"Who? Who indeed. The muscle, that's who. Barracudas. Knaves and scoundrels. Eaters of broken meats."

"Is that why you stole my money?"

"Oh-oh." He sighs.

"Dad? You know what I want to do to you?"

He straightens slowly, watching my eyes. "What, kill me?"

"I want to punt your nuts into the ocean." But this isn't true. It's what I want to want to do. My throat is thickening.

"Atlantic? Or Pacific?" He points east, then west.

"You are a selfish skunk of a father."

He winces and swallows. "Will—" He hugs me.

I hug him, his sponge-flesh surrendering against me, Cici's wet pants clasped to my shoulders. . . . I hold him. I stare past his neck at the craggy divide we have crossed, my face as calm as that unfinished, gone-by moon. I have all the power, that's what I feel. I have all the power I need—which is no power at all.

The old man's explanations for himself, given his grandiloquence, proved more moving than even I expected. Of course, Cici, whose father is a braying, medieval lout ("My girl want

305

slap?"), was quickly borne away in admiration of his gusty charm and self-abasing mode of narrative. ("Will," she whispered, "your father's so *nice*.") He always could circle my defenses through the breach of my friends' wonder. Also, I think he felt eased, in a kind of jaunty way, that he could come clean with me at last and keep his nuts where they belonged.

He cooked us a big pot of Irish oatmeal, with raisins and molasses in it, and coffee, which was just the thing to put down while the sun rose behind the cottonwoods right in the middle of the canyon's cut where our stream fell into the river.

Five years ago when he abandoned Balboa to wander, he knew that life, or search, whatever it amounted to, would not last long. His finances were slim, and he stretched them further than he should have (so that he was reduced at the end to eating out of orchards and gardens at night), hoping for the answer around the next corner, or for the revelation to come in the next night's sleep. He finally sold his camper-trailer in Reno, where he found work parking cars for a week. Then, through an ad, he landed something a little better—a counter clerk's job in an Indian and antique jewelry shop.

Bosco's was a small, busy business in the heart of the tourist action. He and Bosco hit it off. In weeks he was opening and closing the place, tuning in what music he wanted on the stereo, dickering freely on the merchandise, meeting crazy people, and saving up some money as well, because Bosco was a generous employer. Bosco was a crook, too. He had a fencing operation, mostly in silver and stones, going out the back, so he could afford to be generous with someone like the old man, who was, on a social level, amoral, yet goodhearted and solidly trustworthy. In fact, the old man felt very responsible, since Bosco was out of town frequently, gone to LA or Denver or Dallas, and he even made a temporarily successful stab at Alcoholics Anonymous, because Bosco wanted no drinking on the job, period.

All was well until the morning the cops closed the place down. They had been smart and professional, and they had the goods on poor Bosco, who took the bust in stride. He knew it was coming, anyhow, he said. The old man got off, but Bosco got five years, two and a half suspended when he helped finger various local thieves for the law. Bosco offered the old man a small commission on the sale of the business if he would negotiate the deal with realtors, or else sell it himself. This he did; however, the hefty profit on the sale, which he was to deposit for Bosco in a trust account, was just too much money to give to a bank. And Bosco wouldn't need it for two and a half years.

"Now mind you, never would I have thought to keep that sum if its precipitation into my hands had not coincided with the sign I had known was coming for so long. It was a newspaper piece, just a two-inch item of interest to fill in where the real news peters out before the end of the column. Its headline read, 'Black Walnut Tree Brings Large Price,' and it said: '(Findlay, Ohio) A live eighty-foot black walnut tree was bought at auction here today by the Springfield Arms Company of Massachusetts for ten thousand dollars. The tree's owner, Mrs. Rosalee Franklin, said she was not surprised at the interest shown in the seventy-year-old tree. Mature specimens are rare and always valuable, she said. The first bid of fifty-five hundred was offered by the Loomis Furniture Company, Inc., of Columbus. From there the bidding accelerated and soon topped out at the Springfield offer. The tree will be used to make rifle stocks.'

"Well, that little story did not seize me right off, I'll admit. It snuck up on me. You know what I first thought of when I put that newsprint down? My Dreadnought Driver. My first adult possession, that stoutly beautiful implement designed for that one purposeless purpose . . . and fashioned, Will, from the black walnut tree. That's how the tiny thing got planted in my fecund brain. It itched there, and my brain waves washed over it, coated it with a shell of absolute value, like an oyster and its bit of sand.

"*Trees*, Will! *Trees*, Cici! Stately, graceful, patient trees! They are the crowning glory of our living planet, the finest single expression of life that all cockeyed Nature has allowed! But what about Man, you ask. *Man?* Man is no invention of Nature. Man is an invention of himself. The sole source of Man's distinction is his *will*—which is also the source of his *extinction*. His fatally ambivalent will. To create. . . . To destroy. . . . Man is a virus. Man is the planet's rampant disease. It is *trees* that are the glory! The most numerous and gentle of great breathing things. They are the minions and the masters. They don't *care*! Yet they wield the scepter!'' The old man's arms were spread wide toward the low sun. He drew a breath and a gulp from his cup. "You know, if some sober deity does preside over our fate, who is to say that deity is not a tree?''

"I never thought of that,'' Cici whispered.

"Serve the trees,'' he said, "and you serve the glory. Serve the glory, and you shall be saved.''

The old man had been serving the trees by planting them, fathering them, thousands and thousands of them, mostly black walnut, but other varieties, too (hickory, cherry, oak, chestnut), to suit different climates.

"And every last goddamn sapling's sunk its roots in *our land*, Will—the Muldoon Arboretum—ours. *Yours* when I'm gone beneath the sod.''

I shook my head. "Mine right now, Dad. I paid for it, didn't I?''

"Not at all,'' he said, smiling. "Bosco paid for it.''

"Sure, but I bought it from Bosco.''

"Grampa Jack bought it from Bosco,'' said the old man. "But, ahhh, we *have* it, you and me—a farm in fragments, but a farm in glory all the same. Want to see some trees?''

"Boy, I bet Bosco was *real mad* when he got out of jail,'' said Cici, and she laughed. She was still eating her oatmeal, or, more exactly, eating the raisins out of it one at a time.

"He sure was,'' said my father.

"But OK, then why's his gang still after you, if you gave him back Will's money?''

"Can't take any chances, Cici. They're a freewheeling little fraternity, and I have too much to live for, at the moment.''

We hiked back up to the head of the canyon, where his pickup was parked, full of fertilizer and tools and rooted little trees, and where yesterday's transplants presented their spindly selves to the sun. They were staked in place, wrapped with tape, protected by burlap screens from the prevailing winds, heaped to their shins with a hay and black vinyl mulch, and all linked to a plastic drip-line irrigation tube that fed each tree, siphoning water from a tiled reservoir he'd sunk in stones higher upstream.

"Sort of a risky little plantation here," the old man was saying. "Bad flash flood could take out the whole stand, but the state highway people assure me all the heavy water's been deflected away to the other side of the highway—otherwise the road would wash out every year, they say. Anyhow, had to risk it—this is too fine a piece, and I just couldn't pass it up. Got it for back taxes. You know, I was famous a few years ago—among the realtors, at least, and the county clerks all over the map. Whenever some odd chunk of property would get chopped away from an old wheat farm by a power corridor or a new road coming through, I'd get the notice, usually first crack at it, too. Still get 'em now and again, but the big money's long since paid out. I can just about support what greenery I got in the ground now, by myself. But now, Will, if *you* were interested—"

"God!" Cici suddenly exclaimed. "*That's* what all those green marks on the maps mean! Will—on your maps!"

My father looked at her through his lowered eyebrows. "Maps? *Maps*, eh? Well, you are crafty little Injuns aren't you? What did you do, slip old Vivian a Mickey Finn?"

"She was loyal to the end," I said.

"Sure. Of course she was. You found my will, then, I presume. The deeds and the rest?"

I nodded.

"So. Very wily. Very cunning." He tugged his spade out of the ground and leaned on it. "So we arrive at our grand epiphany. Not by the route I planned, maybe, but here we stand. Well, how lucky, how auspicious." He looked toward the new sky a moment. "Will, I am *fini*. Not yet writhing in the dust, but I'm a goner. I got glands and pumps and organs giving out on me by the hour. But I'm satisfied. I wish I'd begun all this at twenty-one—even as I know it makes no difference, because one last day in glory would have been enough, just enough. So I'm satisfied. Listen, Will, I'll tell you what. I got a spot east of here, north of Laramie, that beats this all hollow. Good soil. Good weather. Picturesque as a John Ford movie. Towering pines. Fish-filled streams. . . . Listen, with the dough you have left you

309

could put up a cabin there that would be your pride and joy forever. Imagine it! Read there. Write poems. Think, grow, love. And roam out maybe twice, three times a year checking on the trees. I promise you satisfaction! I promise you contentment and saving grace! Can you beat that?"

Could I beat that? How did I know?

Cici was saying, "Yeah! Oh, Will, doesn't that just sound *far out*? I love the whole idea of trees, don't you?"

My father began to dig. "Of course he does, Cici. He has to consider the idea for a time, that's all. Trees ask nothing of us. Why should they? Their destinies are fixed. They embrace their fates with their roots and branches. They connect the Earth to the Sun during one fleeting pinhole instant of miraculous life that strains for *nothing*, changes *nothing*, means *nothing*! For us strutting men, this is a lesson that can push us smack off the edge of comprehension. Into horror. The horror awaits. And who wants that? Stiff price to pay for glory, if I do say so my-self." He had his hole. "There now. Shall we plant a tree?"

"We have to go," I said, taking Cici's hand.

She stared at me. "We do? Where?"

I didn't know where, but I said, "Home."

"Home!" She shook free. "God, *home*—that's very hilarious. Will, it was bummer city back there, remember? Anyhow, we *can't* go home, and you know it. There's a zillion sheriffs and deputies and everything zooming around in jeeps and whirly-birds just itching to throw us in the clink. Right? Hunh, Will?"

I nodded.

My father watched us for a moment. Then he stuck his shovel in the loose diggings and went to the truck for a sack of some-thing. He was humming.

I gazed at his frail trees with their few twitching leaves. Would they really make it? Marooned in this moonscape among these constant winds, would they ever find the wherewithal to grow, to bloom and fruit? Would it matter to the old man if they didn't?

"I don't get you," Cici was saying. "You used to be all thrilled about babbling brooks and deep forests and this totally indepen-dent way of life that you would describe to me in this detailed language for me to picture in wild excitement same as you. Living happily ever after, like a fairy tale, where we would have everything, because we wouldn't need anything more than we could supply by ourselves alone. That was your magical dream!" She pulled my chin around so I would look at her. "And now, when we can finally really do it, you don't want to. You want to go home."

"I don't know where home is," I said.

"Well, I do," she said. "Home is where I get superdepressed."

The old man laughed. "Home is where you hang your head," he declared. Then he said, "Will, listen. I think I can sweeten this deal. If you got the modern constabulary sifting your dust for every small clue, you know you won't last a week back there in paradise. Where else you gonna lay low? You have no idea, do you? No, you're a selfish, stubborn sap, like your old man, and what you have is a half-assed hankering to go a-*roaming*, am I right? Roaming, putting not only *your* freedom and future in jeopardy but this lovely young woman's to boot! And what for? For spite of *me*, no more. Poor, moribund me. Hell, I beat you out of a few thousand lousy bucks. That's my goddamn burden, don't you see? Not yours! You're clean! You're staked for decades, thanks to me. So's your son! Your *daughter*, I don't care. For generations onward, we Muldoons will be tethered to the glory . . . if only you, if only *you*—

"All right, all right, all *right*!" I yelled.

The old man moaned and shuddered.

"God, Will—*listen*," said Cici.

"No, no," he said. "I'll cork my jug here, I'll cork it. No, this's what I'm getting at: you're safe in Wyoming. I got connections in this fine state, believe you me. Hang tight here a day or so, and let me drive in, make some phone calls, gather in a few favors, some assurances, nothing fancy . . . but I know I can keep the simple law off your neck in Wyoming—unless you're a pair of bank robbers, heaven forbid. I'll call off Vivian, too, if that's worrying you. You'll be at peace here, Will, that's the short of it, and by the pitch of your present mood I'm guessing peace should top off your list of necessities. Now am I ahold of this one, Cici, or am I?"

She gave a firm nod. "For sure, Mr. Muldoon."

We helped him plant the tree. Cici unwrapped the root-ball, and she and I steadied it there while he filled in the hole with earth and peat moss and fertilizer and water. We all tamped it in with our feet.

"Hey-hey, what a team!" sang my father.

Cici chanted, "Grow, tree, *grow*."

I chuckled and shook my head. His jollity was catching. My father was feeling better than he had his whole life long. He was satisfied, he truly was. Jesus, *that* was one monumental accomplishment for anybody—especially for him, the old misanthrope. Finally he had divined his purpose, his worldly place. He had assuaged his guilts. He had accommodated his passions. Even if he still could smell his end, he could live with himself now until it took him. He was pretty happy.

The tide of relief this quick understanding called up in me was like lava. I went molten for a moment, hot and without senses, and when I firmed up, coming to, I felt new. Just new. It wasn't overwhelming, but it was resonant. I was pretty happy, too, by God. So we would do it, we would stay on the land the old man had picked for us. We would have all summer to build our cabin, explore our domain, prepare for winter, find our ease.

"You mean you *want* to? You really *do*?" Cici whispered when I owned up to it. She was delighted.

Later, in the evening, after all the trees were in the ground and Cici and I had made our camp farther downstream on the bluff, while we were getting our gear from the car, I tried to explain to her how I was feeling, how I felt newly, grandly free, how I felt able to do anything with my days to come because the paths to my satisfaction were numberless. I could relax, I could take my time.

And she said, "*Anything*? You mean like you could still try to be a tennis pro? A great star?"

"No," I said then, laughing. "Shit, no." But now I realize Cici was right. That was what I meant, exactly.